# LINDA LAEL MILLER

## McKettrick's Choice

**HQN™**

Recycling programs
for this product may
not exist in your area.

ISBN-13: 978-0-373-77492-0

McKETTRICK'S CHOICE

This edition published by arrangement with Harlequin Books S.A.

For questions and comments about the quality of this book please contact us at Customer_eCare@Harlequin.ca.

® and TM are trademarks of the publisher. Trademarks indicated with ® are registered in the United States Patent and Trademark Office, the Canadian Trade Marks Office and in other countries.

www.HQNBooks.com

**Printed in U.S.A.**

Dear Reader,

By the time in which this story is set, the proud Comanche tribe had, for all practical intents and purposes, been confined to various reservations. I am convinced, however, that a few ragged bands of renegades still pursued the lost dream of regaining their land and I have included them here, for the sake of the tale itself.

*Paula Earl Miller*

For Jeshua, Stiller of storms

"That's how the bastards get you—
by making you scared. Don't you ever let
anybody or anything do that."
—Angus McKettrick, patriarch of the
McKettrick family

# CHAPTER 1

*Arizona Territory, August 12, 1888*

HOLT MCKETTRICK hooked a finger under his fancy collar in a vain effort to loosen it a little. Wedding guests milled on the wide, grassy stretch of ground alongside the Triple M ranch house, their finery dappled by shivering patches of shade from the young oaks thriving there. Two fiddlers played a mournful rendition of "Lorena," and there was a whole hog roasting in the pit Holt's three half brothers had dug in the ground and lined with flat rocks from the creek. The wedding cake, baked by Holt's sisters-in-law, was the size of a buckboard, and a long table—an improvised arrangement of planks supported by half a dozen fifty-gallon barrels—wobbled under the weight of a week's worth of fancy grub.

The old man and the rest of the McKettrick outfit had spared no effort or expense to make the gathering memorable. Holt reckoned he might have enjoyed it as much as the next fellow—if he hadn't been the bridegroom.

A hand struck his back in jovial greeting, and Holt nearly spilled his cup of fruit punch, generously laced with whiskey from his brother Rafe's flask, down the front of his dandy suit.

"I reckon that's the preacher, yonder," said Holt's father, Angus McKettrick, nodding toward an approaching rider splashing across the sun-dazzled creek, driving his horse hard. "'Bout time he showed up. I was beginning to think we'd have to send somebody out to the mission to fetch that crippled-up padre."

Holt swallowed, squinted. Heat prickled the back of his neck. Something stirred in him, a sweet, aching feeling like he got on hot summer nights, when a high-country breeze curled around his brain like a voice calling him back to Texas.

"I reckon," he muttered. Holt wondered where Rafe had gotten to with that flask, though he didn't look away from the rider to search the crowd.

The newcomer, his features hidden in the glare of midafternoon light, spurred his horse up the creek bank on the near side, man and mount flinging off diamonds of water as they came.

"Margaret is a fine woman," Angus said. He had a way of cutting a statement loose without laying any groundwork first.

"Who?" Holt asked, distracted. The skin between his shoulder blades itched, and his chest felt wet beneath the starched cotton of his shirtfront.

"Your bride," Angus answered, with a note of exasperation. Out of the corner of his eye, Holt saw his father tug at the knot in his string tie. Like as not, his wife, Concepcion, had cinched it tight as a corset ribbon.

The rider gained the edge of the yard and dismounted with the hasty grace of a seasoned cowpuncher, leaving the reins to dangle. He came straight for Holt.

"That ain't the preacher," Angus remarked unnecessarily, and with concern. Though he had almost no formal education, the old man read till his eyes gave out, and when he let his grammar slip, it meant he was agitated.

Holt glanced toward the house, where Miss Margaret Tarquin, his bride-to-be, was shut away in an upstairs bedroom getting herself gussied up for the wedding, then went to meet the messenger. The fiddle-playing ground to a shrill halt, and a silence settled over the crowd. Even the kids and the dogs were quiet.

"I'm lookin' for Holt Cavanagh," the newly arrived young man announced. His denim trousers were wet with creek water, and he shivered, despite the shimmering heat of that August afternoon. "You'd be him, I reckon?"

Holt nodded in brusque acknowledgment. It didn't occur to him to explain that he'd set aside the name Cavanagh, once he and the old man had made their blustery peace, and went by McKettrick these days.

Angus stuck close, bristly brows lowered, and Rafe, Kade and Jeb, elusive until then, seemed to materialize out of the rippling mirages haunting the grounds like ghosts. Holt and his brothers had had their differences in the three years they'd been acquainted—still did—but blood was blood. If the rider brought good news, they'd celebrate. If it was bad, they'd do what they could to help. And if there was trouble in the offing, they'd wade right into the fray and ask for the particulars later.

Holt's affection for them, though sometimes grudging, was in his marrow.

The visitor handed over a slip of paper. "Frank Corrales told me to give you this. He sent you a telegram, and when you didn't answer, he figured it didn't go through and told me to hit the trail. I carried that there letter all the way from Texas."

A shock of alarm surged through Holt, like venom from an invisible snake. He hesitated slightly, then snatched the soggy sheet of brown paper and unfolded it with a snap of his wrist. He felt his father and brothers move a stride closer.

He took in the words in a glance, absorbed the implications, and read them again to make sure he had the right of the situation.

JOHN CAVANAGH ABOUT TO BE DRIVEN
OFF HIS LAND.
GABE TO HANG FOR A HORSE THIEF AND
A MURDERER ON THE FIRST OF OCTO-
BER. COME QUICK.
FRANK CORRALES

Holt was still digesting the news when a feminine voice jarred him out of his stupor, and a slender hand came to rest on his coat sleeve. "Holt? Is something wrong?"

Holt started slightly, turned his head to look down into the upturned face of his bride-to-be, resplendent in her lacy finery and gossamer veil. She was a pretty woman, with fair hair and expressive blue eyes, a sent-for wife, imported all the way from Boston. Holt never looked at her without a stab of guilt; Margaret deserved a man who loved her, not one who wanted a mother for his young daughter, a bed companion for himself and not much else.

"I've got to go back to Texas," he said. The words had been shambling along the far borders of his mind for a long while, but this was the first time he'd let them come to the fore, let alone find their way out of his mouth.

Angus cleared his throat, and the whole party started

up again, like it was some sort of signal. Reluctantly, Rafe, Kade and Jeb moved off, and Angus handed the rider a five-dollar gold piece, then steered him toward the food table.

One of the ranch hands took care of the exhausted horse.

Margaret's smile faltered a little as she gazed up at Holt, waiting.

"Maybe when I get back…" he began awkwardly, but then his voice just fell away.

She sighed, shook her head. "I don't believe I want to wait, Holt," she said. "If that's what you're asking me to do, I mean."

He touched her face, let his hand fall back to his side. "I'm sorry," he rasped, and he was, truly, though he doubted it would count for much in the grand scheme of things. At his brothers' urging, he'd brought this woman out from the east, and now here she was, all got up in a bridal gown, with half the territory in attendance, and there wasn't going to be a wedding.

"I'll go ahead and marry you anyhow," he said, against his every instinct, because he was Angus McKettrick's son and a deal was a deal. But he couldn't make himself sound like that was what he wanted, and Margaret was no fool. "I've still got to leave, though, either way."

A tear shimmered on her cheek, but Margaret held her chin high, shook her head again. "No," she said, with sad pride. "If you really wanted me for a wife, you'd have gone ahead with the ceremony, put a ring on my finger so everybody would know I was taken, maybe even asked me to come along."

"It'll be a hard trip," Holt said. From a verbal standpoint, he felt like a lame cow, turning in fruitless circles, trying to find its way out of a narrow place in the trail.

Nonetheless, he kept right on struggling. "Hard things to attend to, too, once I get there."

She worked up another smile. "Godspeed, Holt McKettrick," she said. Then, to his profound chagrin, she turned to face the gathering.

All attempts at merriment ceased, and a hush fell.

"There will be no wedding today," Margaret announced, in a clear voice, while everyone stared back at her in bleak sympathy. Her spine, Holt noted, with admiration, was straight as a new fence post. "But there *will* be a party. I'm going upstairs right now and change out of this silly dress, and when I come back down again, I expect to find every last one of you making merry."

With that, Margaret started for the house. Holt's sisters-in-law, Emmeline, Mandy and Chloe, all flung poisonous glances in his direction and hurried after his retreating almost-bride.

Only Lizzie, Holt's twelve-year-old daughter, had the temerity to approach him, and her cheeks glowed pink with indignation.

"Papa," she demanded, coming to a stop directly in front of him, "how *could* you?"

Holt loved his child, though he hadn't known she'd existed until last year, and except for Margaret herself, Lizzie was the hardest person in the crowd to face just then. "I've got business in Texas," he said, because that was the stark truth and he had nothing else to offer. "It can't wait."

Lizzie stiffened, blinked her large hazel eyes, and bit her lower lip. "You're leaving?"

He reached out to lay a hand on her shoulder, but she shrank from him.

"Lizzie," he whispered.

She turned on her heel, fled to her grandfather. Angus

put an arm around the child and glowered at Holt. The old man looked like Zeus himself, shooting thunderbolts from his eyes.

"Hell," Holt muttered, and started for the barn.

His brothers fell in beside him, their faces hard. Holt lengthened his stride, but they stuck to his heels like barn muck. Stubborn cusses, cut from the same itchy cloth as their pa, every one of them.

"What the hell is going on here?" Rafe snarled. The firstborn of Angus's three younger sons, Rafe was a bull of a man, and always the first to demand an accounting. He and Kade and Jeb formed a semicircle in front of Holt, barring his way into the barn, where his horse was stabled, blissfully unaware of the long, arduous ride ahead.

Holt might have shoved his way through, if he hadn't figured that would lead to a fight. He wasn't afraid of tangling, but a brawl would mean a delay, and the need to get where he was going made an urgent clench in the pit of his belly.

He pulled out the crumpled letter, thrust into his vest pocket earlier, and shoved it at Kade, who happened to be the one standing directly in front of him. "See for yourself," he said.

Kade scanned the page, while Jeb and Rafe peered at it from either side.

"I'll saddle your horse," Kade said, handing it back. He was the middle brother, the thoughtful, practical one. "Best pack yourself some of that wedding grub, too, for the trail."

"Have a word with Lizzie before you go, Holt," Rafe interjected. "She doesn't look like she's taking this real well."

"I could ride along," Jeb put in, with typical eagerness.

The youngest of the brood, he was also the fastest gun, and hands-down the best rider. Jeb was handy to have around in a tight place, for those reasons and a few others, but the plain and simple truth was that Holt didn't want to have to look out for him. He wasn't fool enough to say so, though.

He might have grinned, if he hadn't just humiliated a fine woman and learned that two of the best friends he'd ever had were in trouble. Jeb had a wife to look after, and a baby daughter, barely walking. Rafe and Kade were in the same situation, since all three of their brides had managed to come a-crop with babies a year ago last Independence Day.

"This is my fight," Holt said. "I'll handle it."

Rafe looked thoughtful. "John Cavanagh. That's the man who raised you, isn't it?"

Holt nodded, though Rafe's assessment didn't begin to cover what Cavanagh meant to him. "He's got a spread outside San Antonio."

"And this Gabe yahoo…?" Jeb fished. "Who's he?"

"We were Rangers together," Holt explained. Gabe Navarro was a wild man—part Comanche, part Mexican, part devil—but he was neither a murderer nor a horse thief. Holt had known him too long and too well ever to believe either accusation.

Apparently satisfied, Kade headed into the barn to get Holt's horse, Traveler, ready.

Rafe and Jeb went to the feast table and commenced gathering food for the journey. Holt looked for Lizzie and found her still in Angus's arms, her head resting against the old man's broad shoulder.

"Here, now," Angus murmured, giving his eldest son an unfriendly but resigned glance as Holt approached.

"You talk to your papa, Lizzie-beth. It's no good parting without saying what needs to be said."

Lizzie sniffled, raised her head, and met Holt's gaze.

Angus squeezed her upper arm, then favoring Holt with a withering glare, he walked away.

"Are you coming back?" Lizzie wanted to know.

"Yes," Holt said, with certainty. He wasn't through with Texas—he'd left too many things undone there—but in the deepest part of his heart, he knew the Arizona Territory and the Triple M were home. He belonged on this stretch of red, rocky dirt, with his impossible father, his rowdy brothers and his spirited daughter.

She dashed at her face with the back of one hand. "You promise?"

"You have my word."

"What if you *can't* come home? What if somebody shoots you?"

"I *will* come back, Lizzie."

"I guess I have to believe you."

He chuckled, extended an arm. Lizzie hesitated, then curled against his chest, clinging a little. "You be a good girl," he said, resting his chin on top of her dark head, wishing he didn't have to leave her behind. "Mind Concepcion and your grandfather."

She trembled, tugged a cherished blue ribbon from her hair and tucked it into Holt's vest pocket. "A remembrance," she said softly, and Holt's heart ached. Before he could find words to assure his daughter that forgetting her would be impossible, she went on, "Are you going to visit Mama's grave? She's buried in San Antonio, in the cemetery behind Saint Ambrose's."

He nodded, still choked up. Lizzie's mother, Olivia, was part of the unfinished business waiting for him in

Texas. He needed to say a proper goodbye to her, put her to rest in his mind and his heart, even though it was too late for her to hear the words.

"Will you take her flowers—the best you can find—for me?"

Holt's throat still wouldn't open. He nodded again.

Lizzie stared into his face, looking, perhaps, for the half-truths people tell to children, or even a bold-faced lie. Finding only truth, she straightened her shoulders and hoisted her chin.

"All right, then," she said. "I guess you'd better ride while there's still enough daylight to see the trail."

He smiled, cupped her chin in one hand. "Don't eat too much cake," he said.

Her eyes glistened with tears. "Don't get yourself shot," she countered.

And that was their farewell.

Lizzie was a woman-child, with the run of one of the biggest ranches in the Arizona Territory. She could already ride like a pony soldier, and Kade's wife, Mandy, a sharpshooter, had taught her niece to handle a shotgun as well as a side arm. Lizzie had lost her mother to a fever and seen her aunt murdered in cold blood alongside a stagecoach. She knew only too well that life was fragile, the world was a dangerous place and that some partings were permanent.

This one wouldn't be, Holt promised himself as he rode out, Lizzie's ribbon in his pocket.

# CHAPTER 2

THE WEDDING DRESS was a voluminous cloud of silk and tulle, billowing in Lorelei Fellows's arms as she marched into the center of the square and dumped it in a heap next to the fountain.

She did not look at the crowd, gathered on all sides, their silence as still and heavy as the hot, humid afternoon. With a flourish, she took a small metal box from the waistband of her skirt, extracted a match and struck it against the bottom of one high-button shoe.

The acrid smell of sulphur wavered in the thick air, and the flame leaped to life. Lorelei stared at it for a moment, then dropped the match into the folds of the dress.

It went up with a satisfying *whoosh*, and Lorelei stepped back, a fraction of a moment before her skirt would have caught fire.

The crowd was silent, except for the man behind the barred window of the stockade overlooking the square. His grin flashed white in the gloom. He put his brown hands between the bars and applauded—once, twice, a third time.

Bits of flaming lace rose from the pyre of Lorelei's dreams and shriveled into wafting embers. Her throat caught, and she almost put a hand to her mouth.

*I will not cry,* she vowed silently.

She was about to walk away, counting on her pride to hold her up despite her buckling knees, when she heard the click of a horse's hooves on the paving stones.

Beside her, a tall man swung down from the saddle, covered in trail dust and sweating through his clothes, and proceeded to stomp out the conflagration with both feet. Lorelei stared at him, amazed at his interference. Once the fire was out, he had the effrontery to take hold of her arm.

"Are you crazy?" he demanded, and his hazel eyes blazed like the flames he'd just squelched.

The question touched a nerve, though she couldn't have said why. Blood surged up her neck, and she tried to wrench free, but the stranger's grasp only tightened. "Release me immediately," she heard herself say.

Instead, he held on, glaring at her. The anger in his eyes turned to puzzlement, then back to anger.

"Holt?" called the man in the stockade, the one who'd clapped earlier. "Holt Cavanagh? Is that you?"

A grin spread over Cavanagh's beard-stubbled face, and he turned his head, though his grip on Lorelei's arm was as tight as ever.

"Gabe?" he called back.

"You'd best let go of Judge Fellows's daughter, Holt," Gabe replied, still grinning like a jackal. For a man sentenced to hang in a little more than a month, he was certainly cheerful—not to mention bold. "She might just gnaw off your arm if you don't."

Lorelei blushed again.

Holt turned to look down into her face. He tried to

assume a serious expression, but his mouth quirked at one corner. "A judge's daughter," he said. "My, my. That makes you an important personage."

"Let—me—*go*," Lorelei ordered.

He waited a beat, then released her so abruptly that she nearly tripped over her hem and fell.

"You must be an outlaw," she said, brushing ashes from her clothes and wondering why she didn't just walk away, "if you're on friendly terms with a horse thief and a killer."

"And you must be a fool," Holt replied, in acid reciprocation, "if you'd set a fire in the middle of town and then stand there like Joan of Arc bound to the stake."

Gabe Navarro laughed, and then a cautious titter spread through the gathering of spectators.

At last, the starch came back into Lorelei's knees, and she was able to turn and walk away, holding her head high and her shoulders straight. She looked neither left nor right, and the crowd wisely parted for her, though they stared after her, she knew that much. She felt their gazes like a faint tremor along the length of her spine. Felt Holt Cavanagh's, too.

She lengthened her stride and, as soon as she'd turned a corner, leaving the square behind, she hoisted her singed skirts and stepped up her pace, wishing she could just keep on going until she'd left the whole state of Texas behind.

By the time she reached her father's front gate, Lorelei was sure Holt Cavanagh—whoever *he* was—had heard all the salient details of her scandalous story.

Today was to have been her wedding day.

The cake was baked, and gifts had been arriving for weeks.

The honeymoon was planned, the tickets bought.

Every church bell in San Antonio was poised to ring out the glad tidings.

It would have been carried out, too, the whole glorious celebration—if the bride hadn't just found her groom rolling on a featherbed with one of the housemaids.

"WHAT THE HELL HAPPENED?" Holt demanded of his old friend when he'd bribed his way past a reluctant deputy and followed a warren of narrow hallways to find Gabe's cell. The place was hardly bigger than a holding pen for a hog marked for slaughter; a prisoner could stand in the center and put a palm to each of the side walls, and the board floor was so warped that the few furnishings—a cot, a rusted enamel commode and a single chair—tilted at a disconcerting variety of angles. The stench made Holt's eyes water.

"Damned if I rightly understand it." Gabe gripped the bars as if to pry them apart and step through to freedom. The jovial grin he'd displayed during the burning wedding dress spectacle in the square below his one window was gone, replaced by a grim expression. Being locked up like that would be an ordeal of the soul for most men, but Holt reckoned it as a special torture for Gabe; he'd lived all his life in the open. Even as a boy, if the stories could be believed, Navarro wouldn't sleep under a roof if he could help it. "How'd you know I was here?"

"Frank sent a rider up to the Triple M with a message."

Gabe let go of the bars, poised to prowl back and forth like a half-starved wolf on display in a circus wagon, but there wasn't room. His jawline tightened, and his eyes narrowed. "You've seen Frank?"

Holt frowned. "Not yet. I just rode in."

Gabe shook his head like a man bestirring himself from a grim vision. "Maybe he's alive after all, then."

"What do you mean, 'Maybe he's alive'? You been thinking he might be otherwise?"

Gabe's broad shoulders sagged. "Hell if I know," he said. "I haven't seen him since the night I was brought in. A month ago, maybe, just after sundown, a dozen men jumped us in an arroyo, where we'd made camp. Beat the hell out of me with rifle butts and whatever else they had handy, and just before I blacked out, I heard a shot. I figured they'd killed Frank."

Holt cursed. The pit of his belly seized with the force of a greased bear trap springing shut, and his hands knotted into fists. "You know who they were?"

Gabe gave a mirthless laugh. "Way they snuck up on us, I figured they had to be Comanches, or at least Tejanos. I didn't see much, but up close, I reckoned them for white men. My guess is they were hired guns, or maybe drifters."

"Hired by whom?"

At last, the grin was back. It steadied Holt, seeing the old insolence, the old defiance, in his friend's face and bearing. "'Whom'?" Gabe taunted. "Well, now, Holt, it seems you must have fallen in with some fancy folks since you left Texas, if you're using words like 'whom.'"

"Answer the question," Holt retorted. "Which brand were they riding for?"

Gabe let out his breath. His long hair, black as jet, was tangled and probably crawling with lice; his buckskin trousers and flour-sack shirt were stiff with dirt and rancid sweat. Once as robust as a prize bull pastured with a harem of prime heifers, Gabe was gaunt, with deep shadows under his eyes.

"I can't say for sure," he said at last. "But if I was laying a wager, I'd put my chips on the Templeton outfit. They're the ones been devilin' John Cavanagh and some of the other ranchers, too."

"Templeton?" the name was unfamiliar to Holt, even though he'd run cattle around San Antonio himself, once upon a time, and thought he knew everybody.

"Isaac Templeton," Gabe said, gripping the bars again, giving them a futile wrench with both hands. "He bought out T. S. Parker a couple of years ago." Navarro paused, squinting as he studied Holt's face. "I know what you're thinking," he said. "You mean to ride out there and ask a lot of questions. Don't do it, Holt. The place is a snake pit."

"Whatever happened to 'one riot, one Ranger'?" Holt asked.

Gabe looked him over. "You're not a Ranger anymore," he said quietly. "You've been up North, living like a rich man. I can tell by your clothes, and that horse you rode into the square just now." Navarro tried to smile but failed. "Besides, with Frank dead or holed up someplace nursing a bullet wound, you're the only hope I have of getting out of here before Judge Fellows puts a noose around my neck. Can't have you getting yourself gunned down in the meantime."

Gabe's assessment stung a little, but Holt reckoned there might be some truth in it. He worked hard on his corner of the Triple M, but he'd been eating three squares and sleeping in featherbeds for a few years. When he was a Ranger, then an independent cattleman, things had been different.

"Maybe you've gone soft, Navarro," he said, "but I'm still meaner than a scalded bear. If you met my old man, you'd see just what kind of rawhide-tough, nail-chewing son of a bitch I'm cut out to be."

Gabe seemed pleased by this remark, and Holt had the feeling he'd just passed some kind of test. "I'd like to meet your old man," Navarro said. "'Cause that would mean I was a long ways from this hellhole."

Holt reached between the bars, laid a hand on Gabe's shoulder. "If I have to dynamite this place, I'll get you out. And I'll find Frank."

"I believe you," Gabe said simply. "Make it quick, will you? These walls are beginning to feel a lot like the sides of a coffin." A bleak expression filled his eyes. "I can't see but a little patch of sky, and I can hardly recall how it felt to walk on solid ground."

Holt felt a constriction in his throat. Briefly, he tightened his grip on his friend's shoulder. "Remember what the Cap'n used to say. This fight will be won or lost in the territory between your ears."

Gabe chuckled, albeit grimly. "You suppose he's still out there someplace—old Cap'n Jack, I mean?"

"Hell, yes," Holt replied, without hesitation. "He's too damn ornery to die, just like my old man."

A door creaked open at the far end of the winding corridor.

"Time's up," the deputy called.

Holt ignored him. "Anything I can bring you?"

"Yeah," Gabe said. "A chunk of meat the size of Kansas. All I get in here is beans."

"Accounts for the smell," Holt replied.

"You comin'?" the deputy demanded. "I don't want to get into no trouble for lettin' you stay too long."

"I'll see that you get the best dinner in this town," Holt said.

"I'll be right here to eat it," Gabe quipped. Then he

sobered, and a plea took shape in his proud dark eyes. "Thanks for making the ride, Holt."

Holt swallowed, nodded. Gabe reached through the bars, and the two men clasped hands, Indian style.

There was no need to say anything more.

# CHAPTER 3

"LORELEI," JUDGE FELLOWS SAID, leaning forward in the chair behind the desk in his study, "be reasonable. I've spent a fortune on this wedding. There are guests in every hotel room in town. The food can't be sent back. And Creighton is a good man—he can't be blamed for wanting to make the most of his last hours of freedom."

Lorelei flushed with indignation. It was like her father to take Creighton Bannings's part, not to mention bemoaning the money he'd spent to make his daughter's ceremony the grandest spectacle Texas had ever seen. "I will not marry that reprehensible scoundrel," she said flatly. "Not today, not tomorrow, not ever. Not if all the angels in heaven come down and beg me to forgive and forget!"

The judge sighed a martyr's sigh, but his eyes were canny, taking her measure. Creighton Bannings was a lawyer, and a wealthy man in his own right. He had powerful connections in Austin, as well as Washington. He was, in short, the proverbial good catch—and a fish her father would not willingly let off the hook.

"Must I remind you, my dear, that you'll be thirty next month? You're a beautiful woman, and you have a good mind, but you've been on the shelf for a good long while, and with your disposition…"

Lorelei, leaning against the thick door of the study, stiffened. Glancing at her reflection in the glass of the tall gun cabinet behind her father's desk, she took a distracted inventory. Dark hair, upswept. A long neck. Blue eyes, high cheekbones, a slender but womanly figure. Yes, she supposed she could be called beautiful, but the knowledge gave her no satisfaction. It hadn't been enough to keep her fiancé from straying, had it?

"What's wrong with my disposition?" she demanded, after relaxing her clenched jaw by force of will.

The judge arched his bushy white eyebrows, ran a hand over his balding pate. "Please, Lorelei," he said, with a mild note of disdain. "Do you think I haven't heard that you burned your wedding dress—which cost plenty, mind you, coming all the way from that fancy place in Dallas like it did—in front of the whole city of San Antonio? Was that the act of a sensible, gracious, sweet-tempered woman?"

"It was the act," Lorelei said pointedly, "of a woman who just found her intended husband *in bed with a house-maid* on her wedding day!"

"I'm sure Creighton could explain everything to your satisfaction, if you would only give him the chance."

Lorelei rolled her eyes. "What excuse could he possibly give? I *saw* him with another woman!"

The judge tried again, saturating his words with saintly patience. "A man of Creighton's sophistication—"

"To hell with sophistication!" Lorelei burst out. "What about loyalty, Father? What about common decency? How can you expect me to bind myself to a man who would betray me so brazenly on our wedding day—or any other?"

Her father sat back in his chair, tenting his chubby fingers under his chin. She'd seen that expression on his face a hundred times—in a courtroom, it meant a death sentence was about to be handed down. "Do you know what I think, Lorelei? I think you *want* to be a spinster. How many suitors have you rejected in the last ten years?"

Sudden tears throbbed behind Lorelei's eyes, but she would not shed them. Not in her father's presence. She braced herself for what she knew was coming and held her tongue. He wasn't expecting an answer anyway, and wouldn't leave space for one.

"Michael Chandler has been in his grave for almost a decade," he said. "It's time you stopped waiting for him to come back."

One tear escaped and trickled down Lorelei's overheated cheek. Dropped to her bodice. "You hated Michael," she whispered. "You were relieved that he died."

"He was weak," the judge said, quietly relentless. "You would have tired of him within a year and come weeping to me to get you out of the marriage."

"When," Lorelei countered, "have I ever 'come weeping' to you over anything?"

A muscle twitched in the judge's jaw. "Creighton is your chance to have a home of your own, and a family. I know you want those things. If you persist in this—this *tantrum* of yours, you will be alone for the rest of your life."

A chill quivered in the pit of Lorelei's stomach. "Better alone, with my self-respect intact, than alone in a marriage with a man who doesn't love me enough to be faithful."

The judge gave a derisive snort. "Love? Come now,

Lorelei. You aren't a stupid woman. Love is for story-books and road-show melodramas. Marriage is an alliance, and sentiment has no place in it. Pull yourself together. Put on one of your ball gowns and let's get on with this."

Lorelei shook her head, momentarily unable to speak.

"Then I guess I have no choice," the judge said, with a dolorous shake of his own head. "If you persist in this foolishness, I will have to send you away. Perhaps even to an asylum." He frowned, studying her pensively. "I fear you are not quite sane."

Lorelei's knees threatened to give out. Though she'd never heard this particular threat before, she knew it wasn't an idle one. Her father had the power and the means to lock her up in some sanitarium; it would be a matter of signing a few documents. He'd sent Jim Mason's troublesome wife off to one of those places with the air of a man doing a simple favor for a friend, and there had been others, too.

"I see I've gotten your attention," the judge said, a gleam of satisfaction in his eyes. Then, more gently, he added, "Go to Creighton now. Make things right. I shall expect you at the church at six o'clock, as planned, ready to go through with the wedding."

Lorelei pushed away from the door, stiffening her spine once again. "Then you will be disappointed," she said calmly. She turned the knob, pulled the great panel open.

"If you step over that threshold," her father warned, "there will be no turning back. Just remember that."

Lorelei hesitated a moment, then rushed out. She was so intent on packing her things and laying plans to escape before the judge sent her away to some madhouse that she didn't see the man standing in the entryway until she collided with him.

"Lorelei!" her father roared, from inside his study.

"Looks like I came at a bad time," said Holt Cavanagh.

HOLT STEADIED the hellcat by gripping her slender shoulders in his hands. She'd changed clothes since their encounter, as he had, but her ebony hair still smelled faintly of burning wedding dress.

"Holt McKettrick," he said by way of introduction when she looked up at him, blinking cornflower-blue eyes in a vain effort to hide a sheen of tears. Her lashes were thick, even darker than her hair, and her lips…

Well, never mind her lips.

"I thought your name was Cavanagh," she said.

"I didn't say that, Gabe did. I went by it once."

She raised a finely shaped eyebrow. "Neither here nor there," she said crisply. Then, in a demanding tone of voice, "What do *you* want?"

She didn't try to pull away, though. Nor, he reflected, with detached interest, was he particularly interested in releasing her. Curious, he thought.

"Actually," Holt said, reluctantly letting his hands fall to his sides, "I came to see your father."

"God help you," Lorelei said, and, pushing past him, rushed up the broad, curving stairway.

This, Holt thought idly, was some hacienda.

"I don't believe I've made your acquaintance, Mr. McKettrick," observed a masculine voice from somewhere on Holt's right. "Are you a friend of my daughter's? If so, perhaps you can reason with her."

Judge Fellows stood in the doorway of what was probably his office. He was around sixty, with shrewd eyes, mutton-chop whiskers and a well-fitted suit. Somewhere upstairs a door slammed, and Fellows flinched.

Holt didn't bother to put out his hand. "I never met your daughter before today," he said forthrightly. "I'm here about Gabe Navarro."

Fellows's mouth tightened. "The Indian."

Holt did some tightening of his own, but it was all inside, out of the judge's sight. "The Texas Ranger," he said.

The other man shrugged. "I'm afraid Mr. Navarro's past glories, whatever they might be, were rendered meaningless by the murder of a settler and his wife. He butchered them with a Bowie knife and then stole their horses."

"He didn't kill anybody," Holt maintained. "Or steal any horses."

"You're entitled to your opinion, Mr. McKettrick," Fellows said, with false regret. "However, as I said, your friend has determined his own fate. The knife used to cut those poor souls to ribbons was his, and the horses were found penned up outside that lean-to he calls a home."

Holt didn't bother to argue. He knew conviction when he butted heads with it. Evidently, Judge Fellows was as unreasonable and ill-tempered as his daughter. "Who represented him? During the trial, I mean?"

"Creighton Bannings," the judge said, nodding toward the front walk, visible through the long leaded-glass window beside the front door. "Here he is now."

Holt turned, frowning thoughtfully. Bannings. Where had he heard that name before? The answer tugged at the edge of his mind, staying just out of reach.

There was a brief, obligatory knock, then Bannings strolled in, fidgeting with his tie. He was tall, as tall as Holt, but leaner, and his clothes, though expensive, were rumpled. The face, fine-boned and too pretty, was as familiar as the name, but Holt still couldn't place the man.

"Holt McKettrick," Holt said.

"I remember you as Cavanagh," Bannings replied. He put out a hand, hail fellow well met, and Holt hesitated a moment before shaking it.

"I guess I ought to remember you, too," Holt allowed, "but I can't say as I do."

Bannings smiled, showing white but crooked teeth. "We got into a fight once, at a dance, over a girl. I believe we were sixteen or seventeen at the time. John Cavanagh hauled you off me by the scruff of your neck."

It all came back to Holt then, clear as high-country creek water. So did the enmity he'd felt that night, when he'd found Mary Sue Kenton crying behind her pa's buckboard because Bannings, down from Austin to visit his country cousins, had torn her sky-blue party dress.

Holt felt a rush of primitive satisfaction, recalling the punch he'd landed in the middle of Bannings's smug face five minutes after he'd turned Mary Sue over to the care of a rancher's wife. For a reason he couldn't define, he glanced toward the stairs, where he'd last seen Lorelei.

"I understand you defended Gabe Navarro," he said, after wrenching his brain back to the business at hand.

Bannings grimaced, resigned. "I fear I wasn't successful," he admitted.

Holt's gaze strayed to the judge, shot back to Bannings. "You a friend of the family?" he asked.

"I'm about to marry the judge's daughter, Lorelei," Bannings said.

Holt gave him credit for confidence. "Given the fact that she set fire to her wedding dress in a public square this afternoon," he ventured, "it would seem there's been a change in plans."

Bannings looked pained, but the expression in his eyes was watchful. "Lorelei has a temper," he admitted. "But she'll come around."

Having been a witness to the burning of all that lace and silk, Holt had his doubts, but he hadn't come here to discuss what he considered a private matter. "Gabe Navarro," he said, "is an old friend of mine. We were Rangers together. He's innocent, and he's being treated like a dog. Just now, I'm wondering why you didn't file an appeal."

"How do you know I didn't?"

"I read the paperwork over at the courthouse," Holt said. "Along with the clerk's notes. Seems to me, you didn't put up much of an argument."

Bannings glanced questioningly at the judge, which confirmed a few suspicions on Holt's part. Gabe's trial had been a monkey show, as sorry as the case against him.

"I did my best," Bannings said, a little defensively.

"I'm thinking your best is pretty sorry," Holt replied.

Bannings flushed. Holt suspected the lawyer would have liked to land a haymaker, but apparently his memory was better than his ethics. He clearly remembered the set-to over Mary Sue and her torn dress well enough to think better of the idea, which showed he was prudent, as well as spineless.

"Navarro was tried and found guilty," Fellows put in. "He won't be missed around here."

Holt set his back teeth, pulled hard on the reins of his temper. Gabe was behind bars, and if he, Holt, got Fellows's back up, Gabe would suffer for it. He'd sent a wire to the governor after leaving the courthouse, but there was no telling how long it would be before he got an answer.

"I won't take up any more of your time," he said.

The judge nodded.

Holt reclaimed his hat from its hook on the coat tree, where the maid had hung it after admitting him, and opened the door. There were still several hours of daylight left; he could reach the Cavanagh ranch before sunset if he rode hard. In the morning, he would return to San Antonio, look in on Gabe and find a lawyer with some backbone.

Deep in these thoughts, he was taken by surprise when Bannings followed him onto the porch.

"Leave this alone," the lawyer said, in an anxious whisper, after glancing back at the closed door. He must have seen the judge looking out at him through that long window, because he paled a little. "You've got no idea what kind of man you're dealing with."

"Neither have you," Holt said, and kept walking.

# CHAPTER

## 4

GABE FIGURED he must be hallucinating. Roy, the jailer, was standing just on the other side of the cell doors with a covered tray in his hands, and the savory smells coming from under that checkered dish towel made Gabe's mouth water and his belly rumble.

He sat up, blinking, and swung his legs over the edge of the cot.

Grumbling, the jailer set the food down on the floor and fumbled with his keys. Not for the first time, Gabe considered overpowering him—which would be easy—and taking his chances getting past the guards outside—which would *not* be so easy. He'd most likely get himself gut-shot if he tried.

"That friend of yours must have himself quite a bank account," Roy muttered, pushing the door open cautiously and shoving the tray inside with his foot. "That there's a fancy dinner from over the hotel."

Roy slammed the cell door shut and locked it, while Gabe went for the grub. "I'll be damned," he murmured, crouching to toss back the dish towel. It was beef all right, and prime rib to boot. There were potatoes, a mountain of them, swimming in gravy, and green beans cooked up with bacon and onion.

The blood drained from Gabe's head.

Roy tarried. "I wouldn't have figured you *had* a friend," he said.

Gabe sat on the side of the cot, the tray of food in his lap. His hand shook as he took up a fork. "What are you having for supper tonight, Roy?" he asked.

"What I'm having for supper ain't none of your never-mind," Roy said, but he still didn't seem to be in any hurry to go on about his business. Maybe he was sucking in the smell of that feast.

Gabe cut off a chunk of beef with the side of his fork. Tender as stewed cloud. He damn near swooned when he took that first bite.

"Who is that feller, anyhow?" Roy persisted.

"Ain't none of your never-mind," Gabe answered with his mouth full.

"You're pretty cocky for somebody about to be strung up."

Gabe was busy savoring a second forkful of prime rib, so he didn't bite on the gibe. His stomach seized on the food, growled for more.

"Hope you ain't thinkin' he can get you out of here. Nobody could do that, short of the governor."

The mashed potatoes were as good as the beef, and the gravy—well, it was fare fit for angels. "You'd better get yourself ready for some real trouble," Gabe said, chewing. "Holt Cavanagh, he's like a freight train when he sets his mind on something. If I were you, I'd stay off the tracks."

Roy paled, which gave Gabe almost as much satisfaction as the food. "Cavanagh? Same name as that rancher, the one who's been tanglin' with the Templeton bunch?"

Gabe smiled, though the mention of the name

Templeton made all his old injuries take to aching again. "Same name," he said.

"They can't be related," Roy fretted.

Gabe forked up some beans and a big hunk of bacon. "Can't they?"

JOHN CAVANAGH'S old heart nearly stopped when he looked up and saw the rider at the edge of the hayfield, with the last rays of the setting sun framing man and horse. He rubbed his stubbly chin, leaning on the long-handled scythe, and squinted into the glare.

Tillie, working beside him, let her scythe fall into the grass. "That's Holt," she whispered, and began to run, fairly tripping on the hem of her calico skirt. She fell once, got up again and went right on running.

It couldn't be Holt, John thought. He was up in the Arizona Territory, helping to run the family ranch and raising up a daughter.

The rider swung down from the saddle as Tillie barreled toward him, and held his arms out wide. Tillie gave a shout of joy and flung herself into them.

God in heaven. It *was* Holt.

John let his own scythe fall, though he was not a man to be careless with tools, and hurried toward the pair, moving as fast as his rheumatism would allow.

Holt swung Tillie around in a circle and planted a smacking kiss on her forehead. She was laughing and crying, both at once, and hugging Holt's neck as if she'd drown if he let her go.

"Holt," John said, drawing up at the edge of the field and fair choking on the word.

The familiar grin flashed. "Yes, sir. It's me, all right."

John took a step toward him, still disbelieving. His

vision blurred, and his throat closed up so tight he couldn't have swallowed a hayseed, even with good whiskey to wash it down.

Holt stroked Tillie's back; she still hadn't turned loose of his neck. "I see my little sister is all grown-up," he said.

Hope swelled up inside John Cavanagh, hope such as he hadn't felt in a year of Sundays. "You figurin' on stayin'?" he asked, and ran an arm across his mouth.

"Until you run me off," Holt replied, and grinned again.

"Go ahead and hug him, Pa," Tillie said joyously. "It's the only way you'll believe he's real."

John took another step, stumbling a little, and put his arms around the man he still thought of as his son. The two of them clung for a moment, and John felt tears on his old black face.

"Come on inside," he managed when they drew apart again. "With you here, Tillie's like to cook up a storm."

Holt was looking around the place, taking in the sagging barn, the downed fences, the skinny cattle and slat-ribbed horses.

If John hadn't been so damn glad to see the boy, he might have felt shame. Time enough later on to answer all those questions he saw brewing in Holt's face. Tell him how Templeton and the bankers were trying to force him out.

Right now, there were more important things to be said.

"You bring me a picture of that little girl of yours?" John demanded, hobbling along between Holt and Tillie as the three of them made for the house.

Holt took a wallet from his inside pocket and pulled out a daguerreotype.

John snatched it from his hand and paused, right in the middle of the path, to have himself a look. "She's the image of Olivia," he said, just before his throat closed up again.

"Let me see," Tillie pleaded. "Let me see!"

Reluctantly, John handed over the likeness.

Tillie gave a little cry, drinking in the image with her eyes. "You should have brought her," she wailed. "Why didn't you bring her?"

Holt laid a gentle hand on Tillie's shoulder. She was twenty-eight years old, but simple-minded as a child. Something to do with the troubles her mother had bringing her into the world.

"It's too far," Holt said quietly. "And she's going to school." He glanced toward his horse, grazing happily in the good Texas grass. At least they still had the grass. "I brought you something, though. It's in my saddlebags— left-hand side."

Tillie picked up her skirts and ran for the gelding, supper forgotten, for the moment at least.

"Frank Corrales sent me a letter," Holt said, watching as Tillie unbuckled the saddlebag and plunged an eager hand inside. "Said somebody was trying to force you off your land. Looks like he knew what he was talking about."

Tillie pulled out a doll with long dark ringlets and skin the same coffee color as her own.

"Where the devil did you find a colored doll?" John asked.

"Bought it along the way," Holt said, watching fondly as Tillie hugged the doll to her flat chest and danced around in a circle. In the next instant, he looked somber again. "Who's after the land, John? Gabe told me his version, but I want to hear it from you."

John rubbed his chin. Once Holt got his mind around something, there was no getting it loose. "Man named Templeton. His place borders this one, and he wants the grass for his fancy English cattle." Tears welled in John's eyes as he watched Tillie. Where would they go, if they left this ranch?

Four of John's children were buried here, and so was Ella, his angel of a wife. There'd been as much blood and sweat fall on the land as rain, and more than a few tears, too.

"The banker's his friend," John went on, when he could. "They called my loans. Tried to cut off my water supply, too. Even rustled some of my cattle, though I can't prove it."

Holt laid a hand on John's back. He didn't speak, but he didn't need to. John knew his intentions well enough.

"You can't fight them, Holt," John said, because he knew how Holt's mind worked. "There must be three dozen men riding for that ranch, and they're fierce as Comanches on the warpath."

Tillie was on her way back, beaming and hugging that doll for all she was worth.

"Maybe," Holt said. "But I reckon I'm at least twice that ornery."

# CHAPTER 5

LORELEI WAITED until after her father had left the house the next morning before unlocking her bedroom door and making for the back stairs. Angelina, the family's long-time cook and housekeeper, turned from the gleaming cookstove to favor her with an encouraging if somewhat strained smile.

"I was about to bring your breakfast on a tray," Angelina said, in gentle reprimand. "Do you know it's past ten o'clock?"

The mere idea of food made Lorelei shudder, and she was only too aware of the time; she'd been watching the clock on her vanity table since just after sunrise. "Where's Maria?" she asked, and was ashamed that she'd almost whispered the words.

Angelina's generous mouth pursed. *"Puta,"* she muttered. "She is gone—good riddance to her." In case she'd offended heaven by calling the errant housemaid a whore, the woman crossed herself in a hasty, practiced motion.

Lorelei stood behind a chair at the kitchen table, realizing she'd been gripping the back of it with such force that her knuckles stood out, the skin white with stretching. "Father sent her away?"

Angelina made a face and waved a plump, dismissive hand. "Men are no good at sending *las putas* away. I told her to get out, or I'd work a chicken curse and make her sprout feathers full of lice."

In spite of the lingering tension, and a strange and totally irrational disappointment that the judge hadn't been the one to dismiss Creighton's little baggage from under his roof, Lorelei laughed. "You *didn't*."

"I did," Angelina confirmed with satisfaction, motioning for Lorelei to take her customary place at the table. When she complied, the older woman poured a cup of freshly brewed tea and set it in front of her. "Drink. Your breakfast is almost ready. Hotcakes, brown on the edges, just the way you like them."

Lorelei lifted the china tea cup in both hands, fearing she'd spill it if she didn't take a firm hold. "I don't want anything to eat," she said, after a restorative sip.

"I don't care what you want," Angelina replied crisply, and went back to the stove. "Your papa, he is very angry. You will need all your strength to deal with him." She paused in her deft labors, regarding Lorelei as though she were a jigsaw puzzle with one piece missing. "Why did you do it? Why did you burn your wedding dress for all of San Antonio to see?"

"You know why, Angelina," Lorelei said.

"I am not asking why you did not marry Mr. Bannings," Angelina pointed out. "He is a coyote dropping, not a man. What I want to know is, if you had to burn the dress, why do it in front of the whole town? Now, all the women will be gossiping, and all of the men will avoid you."

Lorelei took another sip of tea, then sighed. "The men would do well to avoid me," she said, with a trace of humor, "and the women would gossip, one way or the other."

"It was a foolish thing to do," Angelina maintained, setting the plate of hotcakes and scrambled eggs down in front of Lorelei with an eloquent thump. "People will say you are *loco* in the head."

Lorelei twisted her hands in her lap. Her father's words echoed in her mind. *I fear you are not quite sane.* Would he actually go so far as to commit her to an asylum? Surely not—she'd defied him many times in the past, and he'd never sent her away. On the other hand, he'd never threatened to, either, and there was no question that he had the judicial power to do it. As a female, she had about as many legal rights as the old hound that slept behind the Republic Hotel, waiting for scraps from the kitchen.

"Is that what *you* think, Angelina? That I'm a madwoman?" She held her breath for the answer.

Angelina spat a Spanish expletive. "Of course not," she added, when she'd stopped sputtering. "But I *know* you, Conchita. These others, they do not. They will talk about this for years!"

Lorelei took up her fork, only to push her rapidly cooling eggs apart into little, unappetizing heaps. "I was just so—angry."

"*Sí,*" Angelina agreed, laying a hand on Lorelei's shoulder. "This temper of yours, it will bring you to grief if you do not learn to control it." She gave a gusty sigh. "It is done now, and there is no changing it. We will have to deal with the consequences."

"Father is furious," Lorelei said, with resignation. "He threatened to have me locked away in a madhouse, and I'm fairly certain he wasn't joking."

Angelina blinked, and in that instant her whole

demeanor changed. *"Madre de Dios,"* she muttered, and crossed herself again, and then twice more for good measure. "This is more serious than I thought."

Lorelei's mouth went dry. She'd spent much of the night in frantic speculation, but she'd expected Angelina to soothe her fears, not compound them. "What am I going to do?" she murmured, more to herself than the housekeeper.

"For the time being, you must stay out of your father's way," Angelina counseled gravely. She paused, thinking, then shook her head. "No," she reflected. "I do not think he would actually do this thing. The scandal would be too great. After yesterday, he will not be looking for more of that."

The clatter of horses' hooves and the rattle of carriage wheels rolling up the driveway silenced them both.

Angelina rushed to the bay window overlooking the long crushed-shell driveway. *"Vaya!"* she cried. "Go. It is the judge, and Mr. Bannings is with him!"

Lorelei nearly overturned her chair in her haste to be gone, but then her pride got the better of her good sense, as it so often did.

"No," she said. "I will not run away like some rabbit startled in the carrot patch."

"Lorelei," Angelina whispered, her eyes pleading.

Lorelei planted her feet. *"No,"* she repeated, but her heart was hammering fit to shatter her breastbone, and she felt sick to her stomach.

She heard the carriage doors closing, heard her father and Creighton talking in earnest tones. Oddly, though, another voice supplanted those, an echo rising suddenly in her brain.

It belonged to Holt McKettrick.

*Are you crazy?*

HOLT TOOK PLEASURE in the look of surprise on the banker's face when he looked up and saw him standing there, with John Cavanagh beside him.

A moment too late, the man shoved back his swivel chair and stood, extending a hand in greeting. The fancy name plate on his desk read G. F. Sexton. He was probably no older than Jeb, but already developing jowls and a paunch. That was a banker's life for you, Holt thought. Too easy.

"Mr. Cavanagh!" Sexton cried, fixing his attention on John. "It's good to see you."

John regarded the pale, freckled hand for a long moment, then shook it. "Under the circumstances," he said, "it's good to see you, too." Sexton's gaze shifted to Holt, full of wary curiosity.

Holt didn't offer a handshake, or an explanation. "We're here about those loans you called," he said.

A flush stole up Sexton's neck, if that narrow band of pallid flesh could be called a neck, and pulsed along the edge of his jaw. "You understand, of course, that business is business—"

"I understand perfectly," Holt said.

Sexton tugged at his celluloid collar. A fine sheen of sweat glimmered on his forehead. His gaze kept flitting back and forth between Holt's face and John's, skittish about lighting too long on either one. "I'm afraid the foreclosure is quite legal, if you've a mind to discuss that," the banker said. He consulted the calendar on the wall behind his chair. "In two weeks, the ranch will be sold for outstanding debts."

Holt indulged in a slow smile. "Will it?" he asked softly.

Sexton took a half step back. "Mr. Cavanagh owes—"

"Ten thousand dollars," Holt interrupted, and laid a telegram from his bank in Indian Rock on the desk. "They're sending a draft by wire. You should have it by tomorrow morning."

Sexton got even redder. He fumbled in his breast pocket for spectacles, put them on, read the telegram and blanched. "My God," he said, and sank heavily into his chair.

"There'll be another draft sent to First Cattleman's, up in Austin," John put in. "You see, my son here just bought my place, lock, stock and barrel. I could have deposited the money here, I reckon, but—you'll understand, business being business—that I had some concerns about its safekeeping."

The banker was a few horse-lengths behind. "Your son?" he squeaked.

Holt swallowed a laugh.

"Foster son," John relented, having had his fun. "Holt's taken his real daddy's name—McKettrick—but he went by Cavanagh for a good part of his life." He braced his work-worn hands on the edge of Sexton's desk and leaned in. "You tell Mr. Templeton he'll find Holt a sight harder to deal with than an old black man and a slow-witted girl."

"Mr. Templeton?" Sexton croaked. "What does he have to do with this?"

"A whole lot, I reckon," John said smoothly. "You ever think about punchin' cattle for a livin', Mr. Sexton? Mr. McKettrick, here, he's hirin'. Lookin' for thirty men or so. A season in the saddle might put some *color* in your cheeks."

"My knees are bad," Sexton said fretfully.

"I reckon your conscience smarts some, too," John replied. "If you've got one, that is." He turned to Holt, his eyes gleaming with the old spirit. "Best we be goin'. Tillie'll be through at the general store, and there's Gabe to be looked in on before we head back out to the ranch. Make sure he's getting the meals my son arranged for, over to the Republic Hotel."

Sexton rallied. His train was still back a couple of stations. "Austin's a long ways from here. You might want to reconsider that deposit, Mr. Cavanagh."

"Then again," John answered lightly, "I might not."

Holt chuckled.

"What about you, Mr. McKettrick?" Sexton asked anxiously, standing up again. Even on his feet, he was knee-high to a burro, but he was still steaming along. "You'll need banking services, I'm sure."

Holt, in the process of turning away, paused. John had already gained the door.

"You've got more guts than I would have given you credit for, Mr. Sexton," he said. "Goodbye. And don't forget to give my best regards to Isaac Templeton."

He joined John on the wooden sidewalk.

"Damn," John said jubilantly, "that felt good."

Holt laughed and slapped him on the back. "Let's collect Tillie and pay Gabe a visit. How long do you figure we have before Templeton comes to call?"

John made a show of taking out his watch. He'd fought on the Union side during the war, and the timepiece, a gift from his captain, was the only memento he'd kept from his days as a Buffalo Soldier, except, of course, for that chunk of cannonball lodged deep in his right thigh. "I reckon he'll get word by sundown."

"You think he'll order a raid on the herd?"

Cavanagh shook his head. "Not without sizing you up first," he said. "Mr. Templeton, he likes to have the facts in his possession before he makes a move."

They stepped into the cool dimness of the general store, and the typical mercantile smells of clean sawdust, saddle leather, onions and dust greeted them.

Holt scanned the room for Tillie, found her standing alone at the counter, with a pile of goods stacked in front of her, while the clerk jawed with a cowboy a few feet away. Tillie might as well have been one of the outdated notices pinned to the wall for all the attention she was getting, and her eyes were huge as she watched Holt and her father approach.

"What can I do for you—gentlemen?" the clerk inquired.

"You can wait on the lady, for a start," Holt said, with a nod toward Tillie.

"I don't see no lady," the clerk replied. Scrawny little rooster.

Holt smiled broadly, reached across the counter, took a good, firm hold on the man's shirtfront and thrust him upward, off the floor. "Then there's something wrong with your eyesight, my friend," he drawled, as John stepped between him and the cowhand. "You might want to invest in a pair of those fine spectacles on display in the front window."

"Mac," the clerk choked. "Ain't you gonna do somethin'?"

"No, sir," Mac said cheerfully, and Holt turned his head long enough to take in the cowboy. "I reckon you've got this coming." He turned easily, resting his weight against the counter. "You Holt McKettrick?" he asked. "I heard on the street that you might be looking for ranch hands."

Holt eased the clerk down onto the balls of his feet. "I might be," he said.

The clerk scrambled along the counter to face Tillie with a feverish smile. "Mornin', ma'am," he said. "What can I do for you today?"

# CHAPTER 6

"MAC KAHILL," the cowboy said, as Holt and John loaded Tillie's purchases into the back of the buckboard. "You don't remember me, do you?"

"Can't say as I do," Holt replied, hoisting a fifty-pound bag of pinto beans off the sidewalk.

"We rode together, a time or two," Kahill told him. "I was part of Cap'n Jack Walton's bunch."

Holt stopped, giving Kahill a thoroughly doubtful once-over. "You were a Ranger?"

Kahill flashed a grin. "No. I just fetched and carried. Took care of the horses. I was fourteen at the time."

Holt squinted. "You were that towheaded kid with the freckles, always tripping over his feet and wiping his nose on his shirtsleeve?"

Kahill laughed. "You recollect correctly," he said. He turned to John, then to Tillie, touching the brim of his hat both times. "I apologize for your poor treatment in the general store, folks. I surely don't countenance such deeds."

"It troubles me a little," Holt told Kahill bluntly, "that you didn't step in."

"I didn't have to," Kahill replied good-naturedly. "You did."

"I think we ought to hire him," John said, rubbing his chin.

The kid had tended horses on a few trips into Indian Territory. So what? That had been a long time back. Today, on the other hand, he'd been a party to Tillie's mistreatment, if only indirectly, and it seemed mighty convenient, after the fact, to claim he'd been about to take matters in hand with the clerk. "Why?" Holt asked.

"Because we're desperate," John said simply.

Kahill's grin didn't slip. "I reckon I've had more enthusiastic welcomes in my time," he confessed. "I'm good with a gun, I've herded my share of longhorns and I need a job."

"Thirty a month, a bed in the bunkhouse and grub," Holt said grimly.

"You provide your own horse and gear."

"Done," Kahill said, and put out his hand.

Holt hesitated, then extended his own.

GABE LOOKED MORE like his old self than he had the day before. He was still in need of yellow soap, clean clothes and a week of good meals, but he was coming along.

"That was a damn fine supper you sent over last night," he said. "Thanks." His gaze moved past Holt to John. Tillie was waiting up front, in the marshal's office, the ass-end of a jail being no place for a woman. "How-do, Mr. Cavanagh. You're lookin' spry, for an old soldier."

He and John shook hands through the bars.

"I reckon I'll be returning the compliment," John said, "once you've been out of this cage for a month or two."

"I had another visitor first thing this morning," Gabe said, keeping his voice low. "Judge Alexander Fellows."

That caught Holt's interest. "What did he have to say?"

"That they're moving me to a cell on the other side of the stockade," Gabe answered. "So I can watch my gallows being built."

Holt felt his back teeth grind, and he must have stiffened visibly, because John gave him a sidelong, knowing look. "Easy," he warned. "We've got the better part of a month to straighten this out."

"You'll understand," Gabe intoned, "if that doesn't sound like a real long time to me."

"I ran into your lawyer yesterday before I rode out to John's place," Holt said. "Worthless as tits on a boar, and he's pretty friendly with the judge."

"You've got the right of that," Gabe said. "That wedding dress Miss Lorelei burned in the square yesterday? Bannings was supposed to be the bridegroom."

Somehow, remembering Lorelei calmly watching that bonfire with her chin high and her arms folded cheered Holt up a little. It amazed him that a woman like Miss Fellows—beautiful, spirited, and obviously intelligent, even if she did lack the common sense to know how fast a blaze like that could spread—would even consider hitching herself to a waste of hide and hair like Creighton Bannings.

"He mentioned that when we met," Holt said. "Seemed to believe the lady would come around to his way of thinking, sooner or later."

Gabe gave a snort of laughter. "I'd say later," he replied. "About a week after the Second Coming."

Holt raised an eyebrow, curious. "You seem to know Miss Fellows pretty well," he observed.

"We don't travel in the same social circles," Gabe said, "but, yeah, I know her."

"How?"

"She feeds an old dog behind the Republic Hotel. So did I. Now and then, we ran into each other."

"And you just happened to strike up a conversation?"

"I like to talk to a pretty woman whenever I get the chance—even if she has the disposition of a sow bear guarding a cub."

Before Holt could offer a comment, a door creaked open at the far end of the corridor, where there was light and fresh coffee and freedom. The yearning for all those things was stark in Gabe's face. "She came to the trial every day," he went on pensively. "Sat right in the front row, and favored me with a smile whenever the judge and Bannings weren't looking."

Holt absorbed this, unsure of how he felt about it. On the one hand, the thought stuck under his skin like a burr. On the other, Lorelei Fellows was the judge's daughter, and possibly sympathetic to Gabe's cause. Maybe she knew something that might come in handy when the appeal was filed.

Which had better be soon, if Gabe's gallows was going up on the other side of the stockade.

SURE ENOUGH, she was there, behind the Republic Hotel, with a battered dishpan full of supper scraps. The dog, an old yellow hound with a notch bitten out of one ear and signs of mange, gobbled them up eagerly.

Holt stepped out of the shadows. "Evening, Miss Fellows," he said.

She started, almost dropped the pan, but she recovered quickly enough. "Mr. Cavanagh," she said coolly. "Or is it McKettrick? I've heard both." She wore an old calico dress and a tattered shawl, and the brim of a man's hat hid her face. Evidently, feeding the dog was something she did in secret.

"I go by McKettrick now," he said. "But you can call me Holt."

"If I choose to," Lorelei agreed. "Which I don't."

He laughed. "Fair enough," he said.

She bent, stroked the dog's head as he lapped up the scraps. There was something tender in the lightness of her hand, something that made Holt's breath catch. "What do you want, Mr. McKettrick?" A corner of her fine mouth twitched ever so slightly. "As you can see, there are no fires to put out."

"Gabe told me you went to the courthouse every day during his trial. I guess I'd like to know why, considering that you didn't seem all that kindly disposed to him yesterday. I believe you referred to him as a horse thief and a killer?"

She regarded him steadily. "The people he murdered were decent. Maybe I just wanted to see that justice was done."

"Maybe," Holt agreed. "And maybe you figured a man who made a habit of feeding a starving dog wouldn't be inclined to butcher a rancher and his wife just for something to do of an evening."

Even under the brim of the hat, he saw her eyes shift away from his face, then back again. "He's going to hang," she said flatly. "If you knew my father, you wouldn't waste your time thinking otherwise."

"If you knew me," Holt answered, "you wouldn't be so sure of that."

She took a step toward him, index finger raised for shaking, then stopped. Sighed heavily. Her shoulders sagged a little. "I don't know who you think you are,

Mr. McKettrick, but you don't want to come up against my father and—my father."

"Your father and Isaac Templeton?" Holt prompted. "Is that what you were going to say?"

Color suffused her face. "Just leave. Go back to your wife and children."

"I don't have a wife," Holt said. "My daughter is with people who love her. And I'm not leaving until I've finished my business here."

Lorelei opened her mouth, closed it. Smacked the now-empty dishpan against her thigh in apparent frustration. Turned away.

He whistled to the dog, and she spun about, watching as the hound trotted over to lick his hand.

"Don't tease him," she said anxiously.

"I'm not teasing him. I'm taking him back to my ranch. We could use a good watchdog."

She almost smiled, Holt decided, but damned if she didn't catch herself in time. "His name is Sorrowful," she said, in a soft voice. She was a complicated woman, Holt decided. Setting fire to wedding dresses, watching murder trials and loving an abandoned dog enough to bring him supper scraps.

Holt ruffled the critter's floppy, misshapen ears. "Howdy, Sorrowful. Pleased to make your acquaintance."

"Since when do you have a ranch around here?" she pressed, sounding worried. "I know everybody in this county, and you're a stranger to me."

"Since I bought the Cavanagh place," Holt answered, watching for a reaction.

Her throat worked. "Next to Mr. Templeton's spread," she murmured.

"You friendly with him, too?" Holt asked lightly. "Or maybe your father is."

She bristled. "What are you implying, Mr. McKettrick?"

He shrugged one shoulder. "Nothing, Miss Fellows. Nothing at all. Now, if I were you, I'd get on home. There are lots of unsavory types in San Antonio these days."

She looked him over. "I'm well aware of that," she said. Then she stiffened her spine, and hitched up her chin again. "You'd better be good to my dog," she finished. She turned on one heel and marched away into the gathering twilight.

Sorrowful lived up to his name and gave a forlorn whimper, watching Lorelei go.

Holt felt like doing the same.

"A DOG!" Tillie cried joyously, a couple of minutes later, when Holt hoisted the mutt into the back of the buckboard, where he immediately commenced to sniffing the groceries.

"Sure enough," agreed John, not so joyously. "He the kind to kill chickens?"

Tillie was already unwrapping the leftovers from the fancy supper they'd taken in the dining room of the Republic Hotel and offering them to the hound.

"He's the kind to let us know if anybody's sneaking around outside the house of a night," Holt answered, climbing up to take the reins. He released the brake lever with one foot and urged the team into motion.

He looked up at the stockade as they passed. It gave him a lonely feeling to know Gabe was in there, even if he was feasting on the fried chicken dinner and whole strawberry pie sent over for his supper.

"He can sleep in my room," Tillie said.

"Not unless you scrub him down with lye soap first, he can't," John decreed. Clearly, he had misgivings where the dog was concerned, but Holt was confident he'd come around in time. John was a tenderhearted man, though he liked to pretend otherwise.

Holt pondered how different things were as they headed out of town.

Once, he'd thought of the Cavanagh place as home.

Now, home was the Triple M. He wondered how Lizzie was getting along, and the old man and those three knuckleheaded brothers of his.

Margaret Tarquin never crossed his mind, but Lorelei Fellows sure cut a wide swath through his thoughts.

# CHAPTER 7

THE WEDDING GIFTS, each one labeled for return to its original owner with many wrapped to mail, filled the twelve-foot table in the formal dining room. They teetered on chairs, crowded the long bureau top and took up most of the floor as well.

Lorelei surveyed the loot with relief. "That's the last of them, then," she told Angelina, dusting her hands together. "Raul can start loading them into the wagon."

Angelina, having wended her way in from the kitchen traveling a path between the packages, shook her head at the sight. "Now what?" she asked.

Lorelei consulted the watch pinned to the bodice of her crisply pressed shirtwaist. After the interview with her father and Creighton in the kitchen yesterday morning, her resolution had wavered a little. The judge hadn't mentioned an asylum, thankfully, but he did rant about the shame she'd brought upon the family name and threaten to confine her to the house until she'd come to her senses.

"I'm due at the Ladies' Benevolence Society meeting in half an hour," she said, and patted the tidy chignon at the back of her head. "I'd sooner run the gauntlet in a Comanche camp. Unfortunately, I don't have that option."

Angelina's eyes rounded, then narrowed. "What are you thinking, doing such a thing? Those old biddies will eat you alive!"

"They'll try," Lorelei said, with false good cheer.

"Then why serve yourself to them like a sponge cake?"

"If I avoided them," Lorelei reasoned, "they would call me a coward. And, worse, they'd be right."

Angelina sighed. "I suppose there is no talking you out of this."

Lorelei looked at her watch again. "If I don't hurry, I'll be late," she said. With that, she took herself to the entryway, where her handbag awaited on the table next to the door, and left the freighting of the gifts to Angelina and her husband.

"Be careful," Angelina fretted, hovering at her elbow.

Lorelei kissed the other woman's creased forehead. "I don't know how," she answered, and left the house.

The membership of the Ladies' Malevolence Society, as Lorelei privately referred to them, met once a month, in the spacious parlor of Mrs. Herbert J. Braughm, for tea, social exchange and precious little benevolence. Lorelei attended faithfully, for three reasons. Number one, they didn't want her there. Thus, being a member constituted an exercise in principle. Number two, it was the best way to keep up with the doings in San Antonio. Number three, on admittedly rare occasions, the group actually did something constructive.

It was a ten-minute walk to the Braughm house, and the weather was muggy. Inwardly, Lorelei dragged her feet every step of the way.

Outwardly, she was the very personification of dignified haste.

Mrs. Braughm's maid, Rosita, actually gaped when she opened the door to her.

Lorelei smiled and waited expectantly to be admitted.

Rosita ducked her head and stepped back to clear the way. "The ladies," she said, in accented English, "are in the garden."

"Thank you," Lorelei said, adjusting her spotless gloves and shifting her handbag from her left wrist to her right. Her very bones quavered, but her voice was steady.

Mrs. Braughm's garden was gained through a set of French doors, standing open to the weighted air. Plump roses nodded, almost as colorful as the hats and dresses of the women seated around pretty white tables, sipping tea and nibbling at dainty refreshments. The chatter ceased the moment Lorelei stepped onto the tiled patio.

She straightened her spine and smiled.

"Why, Lorelei," Mrs. Braughm said, too loudly. The legs of her chair scraped shrilly as she stood, small and fluttery, to greet an obviously unexpected guest.

"I hope I'm not late," Lorelei said, meeting the gazes of the other guests, one at a time. Most were cold, but she saw a glimmer of sympathy in some of the younger faces.

"Of course not," Mrs. Braughm chirped. "Come, sit down. Have some tea. We were just about to start."

No one moved, and every extra chair held a handbag, a knitting basket, or a small, watchful dog.

Mrs. Eustacia Malvern, who had held the meetings at her home on Houston Street until the task had become too much for her, reached for her cane and used it to steady herself as she raised her considerable bulk out of her chair. Her Pekinese, Precious, took the opportunity to stand on its hind legs and lick the whipped cream off Mrs. Malvern's dessert.

"What we were just about to do," Mrs. Malvern said, ignoring the dog, "was review our standards of membership."

Murmurings were heard, here and there. No one dared look directly at Lorelei, who stood still and straight, waiting.

"As you know," Eustacia went on, "we have certain criteria." Among other things, Mrs. Malvern was Creighton's second cousin, Lorelei recalled. Raul was probably loading her wedding gift, a silver compote, into the back of the wagon at that very moment.

Lorelei did not speak. Bees buzzed from flower to flower, their drone growing louder with every passing moment.

Mrs. Malvern took in the gathering. The dog finished the whipped cream and went for a tea cake.

"I think we are all agreed, Miss Fellows, that you are not our sort."

NOT OUR SORT.

Standing there in Mrs. Braughm's lush garden, surrounded by the cream of San Antonio society, Lorelei felt a sting of mortification and, conversely, not a little exhilaration. "Do you speak for everyone?" she asked mildly.

No one spoke. No one met Lorelei's gaze, save Mrs. Malvern, who seemed intent on glaring a hole right through her.

With a delicate lapping sound, the Pekinese began

to drink tea from the old woman's cup. Except for that, the hum of a few bees and the nervous tinkle of a cup against a saucer, the silence was absolute.

"Very well, then," Lorelei said. With that, she turned, keeping her shoulders and spine as straight as she could, and took her leave.

She couldn't go home, not yet.

She might have visited her old friend, Sorrowful, behind the Republic Hotel, but now even the dog was gone. He would surely be better off on the Cavanagh place, with regular feeding and room to run, but the knowledge of his absence was a thrumming ache in her heart.

It was sad indeed, she reflected, when a person's truest friend was an old war veteran of a dog.

Pausing in the shade of an oak, Lorelei pulled a lace-trimmed handkerchief from beneath her sleeve and dabbed at her eyes. *Stop feeling sorry for yourself,* she scolded silently. *You still have Angelina.*

She hadn't heard the horse approaching, and by the time she realized she wasn't alone, it was too late.

"Morning, Miss Fellows," said Holt McKettrick, swinging down from the back of a fine-looking Appaloosa gelding. "Maybe I'm mistaken, but you give the appearance of being a damsel in distress."

Lorelei's throat ached. Her eyes felt puffy and red, and the edges of her nostrils burned. It galled her that this man, of all people, had to be the one to catch her weeping. "I'm perfectly fine," she said, with a sniff.

His smile was slow and easy, and it pulled at something deep inside her. "Whatever you say," he allowed. His eyes twinkled with good-natured skepticism.

"How do you expect to make that ranch pay if you

spend all your time in town?" Lorelei challenged, taking in his fine suit.

He chuckled, belatedly removing his hat. The band, made of hammered silver, caught the light and made it dance. "I'll make it pay, all right," he said, with quiet confidence. "And it happens I have business in town."

Lorelei knew she should simply walk away, but she couldn't find it within herself to do that, so she simply stood there, with one gloved hand against the trunk of the oak tree. "How is Sorrowful faring?" she asked. It was a safe topic, as far as she could tell.

Again, that slow, lethal grin. His teeth were good—white and straight. He'd probably never had a cavity in his life. "Sorrowful," he said, "is glad of a bed behind the stove and table scraps twice a day. He's a fair hand at chasing rabbits, too."

Lorelei smiled. "Good," she said.

"You're welcome to visit him anytime, if you're so disposed."

"Thank you," she replied softly.

"I could see you home," Holt ventured, turning the fancy hat in his hands.

She shook her head. "I don't think I'm ready to go there just yet," she said.

He didn't press for a reason. "Well, I guess I'd better get along."

He turned, put a foot in the stirrup and mounted with an ease Lorelei couldn't help admiring. She yearned to ride, just get up on a horse's back and race over the ground, travel as far and as fast as she could, with the wind buffeting her face and playing in her hair. Her father had forbidden her that pleasure, along with many others, claiming it was not a suitable enterprise for a lady.

In reality, it was because her older brother, William,

had been thrown from a pony when he was nine. He'd struck his head on a rock and died three days later. The judge's mourning had been terrible to behold.

Holt tilted his head to one side, watching her face. "Something the matter?"

Lorelei was swamped with memories—her father's utter grief. All the mirrors in the house draped in black crepe. The sound of the rifle shot, ringing through the heavy air of a summer afternoon, as William's pony was put down.

All of this had happened the day she turned six. Raul had led away the little spotted Shetland that was to have been her birthday gift, later admitting that he'd given it to a rancher.

Child that she was, she'd mourned the lost pony more than William, at the time, and the recollection of that caused a sharp pang of guilty sorrow.

She sighed. "No," she lied, catching hold of his question, left dangling in the air for a long moment. "Nothing's wrong."

"I don't believe you," Holt answered quietly.

Then he took the reins in one hand, touched the brim of his hat and went on, toward town.

Lorelei stared after him, wondering when he'd leave San Antonio and go back to wherever he'd come from.

# CHAPTER 8

GUILT, AND A NEED for some errand to quiet her mind and keep her out of the house for a while, sent Lorelei toward St. Ambrose's, an old mission at the edge of town. The walk was long and the heat insufferable, but when she reached the shady plot where her mother and William rested side by side, she found some solace.

Selma Hanson Fellows's marker was a marble angel with a trumpet raised to its stone lips. The angel's eyes gazed with longing into the far reaches of eternity, and the mold and lichen in the crevices of its finely chiseled face and the folds of its flowing gown gave it an eerie dimension.

Lorelei kissed the tips of her fingers and set them against the *S* in her mother's name. A gentle breeze wafted through the cemetery, cooling her scalp.

She searched her mind for even the ghost of a memory of her lost mother and waited, but nothing came.

William's grave was more modest, with a smaller angel to oversee it, but the words carved in the granite base had a poignancy that Selma's lacked.

BELOVED SON OF ALEXANDER FELLOWS
MY SOUL PERISHED WITH HIM.

Lorelei pulled out her handkerchief, for the second time that morning, and touched it to her eyes. The judge had stayed drunk for a solid month after William's funeral, night and day. She remembered his ragged beard, his unkempt hair, standing up in ridges from the repeated thrust of his fingers. The sweat-and-tobacco stench of his clothes, underlaid by the subtler smell of despair.

"You," her father had muttered once, when she'd crept into his study and tried to crawl into his lap. He'd pushed her away with a rough motion of one hand and a surly, "If one of you had to die, why did it have to be him? My only son. My only hope."

Lorelei wrapped both arms tightly around her middle and lowered her head, remembering. That day, in the space of an instant, Alexander Fellows had stopped being "Papa" and become the Judge. They'd been on opposite shores of an invisible river ever since, and if there was a ford or a bridge, Lorelei had yet to find it.

Except for Angelina, and a few school chums and far-away cousins, she'd been alone ever since. Until Michael had come along.

A sob rose in her throat. She swallowed it with a painful intake of breath.

Determinedly, she pulled herself together. There was no profit in weakness, no value in looking back.

Michael was buried in the Chandler plot, among his own people—parents, grandparents, a sister who'd died in infancy, numerous aunts and uncles.

Lorelei made her way to him and sat down on a bench nearby. Michael's final resting place was a simple one, with only a stone cross to commemorate him.

In the depths of her heart, Lorelei thought she heard him speak her name.

CROUCHING, Holt laid Lizzie's flowers within the circle of white stones enclosing Olivia's gravesite. A slab, long-fallen and half-covered by the encroaching grass, bore only her first name and the date of her death.

The flowers were yellow roses, heady with scent. He'd seen them from the street, flourishing in a garden, shortly after leaving Lorelei under the oak tree, and stopped to knock on the front door of the house and ask if he might buy a dozen or so.

The old woman who'd answered had regarded him solemnly. "Are they for a lady?" she'd asked, when she was through sizing him up. He was glad he'd shaved and put on good clothes.

"Yes," Holt had said, without hesitation, for Olivia *had* been a lady, in every sense of the word. And she'd given him Lizzie, the single greatest gift of his life.

"Reckon she must be right pretty, if a fellow like you wants to give her roses."

Holt had smiled, albeit sadly. "She was," he said. "Prettiest woman in San Antonio. Olivia died of a fever a few years back."

Lorelei had slipped into his mind then, out of nowhere, but he'd set her firmly aside.

"I'll cut them for you," the woman said.

Holt had reached for his wallet.

The old lady shook her head. "It's a sorry day when I have to take money for a few flowers," she said. Then she'd slipped back into the cool dimness of the house, returning momentarily wearing a sun bonnet and carrying a pair of shears.

Now, in the graveyard, Holt arranged the flowers with distracted care.

Lorelei was seated on a bench, not twenty yards from

him, her hands clasped in her lap. The breeze danced in the tendrils of dark hair curling at her nape.

If she saw him, she'd think he was following her. Probably go straight to her father, the judge, and lodge a complaint.

He might have smiled at the image if he hadn't been putting flowers on Olivia's grave, and if Lorelei hadn't looked as though she might splinter into tiny shards at any moment, like a vase irretrievably broken, caught in that tenuous place between wholeness and utter disintegration.

He lowered his head, laid a hand on Olivia's stone. *I'm sorry,* he told her, in the privacy of his mind. *I'd have come back for you, if I'd known about Lizzie. Wouldn't have left in the first place, if I'd had any sense.*

His eyes took to burning, and he rubbed them with a thumb and forefinger.

Some sound, or perhaps a scent or a movement, made him look up.

Lorelei stood opposite him, surveying him with a slight frown marring her otherwise perfect forehead.

"You loved her," she surmised.

He nodded. "Not enough," he replied hoarsely.

She bent down, peered at the marker. "Olivia," she mused quietly. "I knew her. She was a fine seamstress." Their gazes met across the narrow circle of stones. Lorelei looked thoughtful. "She had a young daughter. Lindy? Libby?"

Holt got to his feet. He'd left his hat with the horse, perched on the saddle horn, but he reached up as if to touch the brim before remembering that. "Lizzie," he said.

Lorelei absorbed that. "Yours?" she asked, very quietly, and after a very long time.

Holt nodded. He would have told just about anybody else that it was none of their business who had fathered Lizzie, but it seemed a natural question coming from Lorelei, though he couldn't have said why.

"I see," Lorelei said, and Holt feared that she *did* see, all too clearly. Olivia had had to make her own way in the world, and Lizzie's way as well, with only the help of her sister, Geneva. After Olivia's passing, Geneva had managed to track Holt to the Arizona Territory, and she'd been on her way to Indian Rock, the nearest town to the Triple M, to leave Lizzie with him, when Jack Barrett had come upon their stagecoach, broken down alongside the road, and decided on robbery. In the course of that, he'd killed both Geneva and the driver. Holt's brother, Jeb, and the town marshal, Sam Fee, had come upon the stage the next morning, and found Lizzie there, alone and scared.

Holt set his back teeth. It had fallen to Jeb to deal with Barrett, when the time came, but every time he thought of that night, Holt wished he'd been the one to put the bastard out of his misery.

"I won't keep you, Mr. McKettrick," Lorelei said, and by the look on her face, he knew she'd judged him and found him wanting. He'd left his woman and his daughter to fend for themselves, that was the fact of the matter. There wasn't much he could say in his own defense.

He simply nodded, and watched as Lorelei turned and walked away.

He wasn't given to excuses or explanations.

So why did he want to hurry after her and make some kind of case for himself? Say he hadn't known about Lizzie—that he'd always meant to patch things up with Olivia but had never found the time. Never gotten past his stupid pride.

He swore under his breath. If his hat hadn't been with the horse, he'd have wrenched it off his head and slapped it against one thigh in sheer aggravation.

# CHAPTER 9

JOHN CAVANAGH felt a prickle trip down his spine, the same one he'd felt back in '64, just before a rebel cannonball took off a piece of his thigh. He looked around for Tillie—saw her on the other side of the draw, bouncing along on the back of her mule, with that worthless yellow dog bringing up the rear.

She was probably out of rifle range, so he didn't shout a warning, though one sure as hell surged up into the back of his throat, bitter and raw.

Holt was in town, trying, among other things, to hire a lawyer for Gabe and the new man, Kahill, was rounding up strays. The herd, once two hundred head of cattle strong, had dwindled down to less than fifty, by John's reckoning, and they needed every one they could drive out of the brush.

The prickle came again. Somebody was watching him, from someplace nearby, and probably looking down the barrel of a gun.

He drew back on the reins, looked around.

The rider sat at the top of the draw, under a stand of oak trees.

He recognized the man by his shape and bulk. Templeton.

John spat, ran one arm across his mouth and headed straight for the trespassing sum-bitch.

Templeton waited, the barrel of his rifle resting easy across the front of his saddle. He wore a fancy bowler hat and the kind of duds a Texan would get married—or buried—in but never take out of mothballs otherwise. His sandy mustache twitched slightly, and he shouldered away the fly buzzing around his muttonchop whiskers. Something meant to pass as a smile played on his bow-shaped mouth.

"Afternoon, John," he said. His accent was English, and right fancy. Better suited to a tea party in some castle than the Texas range.

John let his gaze travel to the rifle. "You hunting something?" he asked.

"This is rough country," Templeton replied smoothly. "A man can't be too careful."

"That's for sure and certain," John answered, resettling his hat. The band itched, soaked with sweat. "I don't reckon you'd mistake any of my cattle for game. Fine sportsman like you."

Templeton heaved a great sigh. "The poor beasts look pretty scrawny to me," he said, with mock regret. "Hair, hide, hooves and horns, that's about all you've got here. Not worth driving to market, as far as I can see."

"Then I reckon you ain't looked far enough," John replied evenly.

The Englishman spared a thin smile. "I hear you sold out. I'm disappointed, John. I would have given you a good price."

John smiled back and spat again. "I'd sooner deed this place over to the devil," he said. "And you were planning on buying this spread from the bank, pennies on the dollar."

Templeton shifted in the saddle. Cradled the rifle as gently as a babe just drawing its first breath. "That fellow McKettrick. Is he really your son?"

"Good as," John said.

"I've been expecting him to pay me a call."

"He's had better things to do."

With a mocking air, Templeton put a hand to his heart, fingers splayed, as though to cover a fresh wound. The rifle barely moved. The Englishman's smile sent that prickle rolling along John's spine again. "Now that was an unkind thing to say," Templeton drawled. His gaze moved past John, tracking Tillie and the mule in the distance, like a snake about to spring at a field mouse. John's aging heart lurched over a beat. "Looks as if you're pretty hard up for ranch hands."

John sat up straighter in the saddle and fondled the handle of the .45 strapped to his hip just to draw Templeton's eyes back to him and, therefore, off Tillie. "That's the truth," he allowed. "Holt's hiring, though. Like as not, he'll have that bunkhouse filled in no time."

"You tell your...*son* that I'd like a word with him. I'll be receiving whenever he chooses to make a visit." Templeton paused, smiled at John's .45, like it was a toy whittled out of wood instead of a Colt, and sheathed his rifle. "Best if it's soon, though. I'm an impatient man."

"'Receiving,' is it?" John countered lightly. "Sounds pretty fancy."

Templeton was watching Tillie again. "Just tell him what I said."

"Oh, I surely will." John maneuvered his horse to block Templeton's view of the girl. "I doubt Holt'll take kindly to it, though. My guess is, he'll wait for you to come to him."

Templeton reined his fine Irish horse away, toward

home. "He won't like it if I do," he said, and before John could answer, he rode off into the trees.

John gulped back the bile that rose into his throat, then turned and headed down the hillside, toward the draw. "Tillie!" he called. "You get yourself back to the house now, and start supper!"

GABE STOOD with his back to the bars of the new cell, staring out the window. The rasping of a saw rode the air, along with the steady tattoo of hammers. The gallows was well underway.

"I don't suppose you've heard back from the governor," Gabe said, without turning around.

Holt took off his hat, ran a hand through his hair. "No," he admitted. "I stopped by the telegraph office on my way here."

"Most likely that wire never went out, any more than the one Frank sent to you did."

"I'll ride up to Austin if I don't hear by tomorrow," Holt said. He felt every blow of those hammers as if they'd struck his bare bones instead of the new and fragrant lumber of a hangman's platform.

Gabe didn't speak. It was clear he wasn't holding out much hope.

"Is there anything in particular you want me to do?" Holt asked quietly. "Besides get you out of here, I mean?"

At last, Gabe faced him. "I've been worrying about Melina. Somebody ought to tell her that I'm not staying away on purpose." He paused, rubbed his chin with one hand. "She's carrying my baby, Holt."

Holt wanted to avert his eyes, because his friend's pain was a hard thing to look upon, but he didn't. "Where will I find her?"

"Waco," Gabe answered, relaxing a little. "Her last name is Garcia. Last I knew, she was doing laundry for a rich rancher's wife. Parkinson, I think they call themselves."

"Done," Holt said.

Gabe's throat worked. "If anything happens—"

"Nothing," Holt interrupted, "is going to happen. But I'll tell her, Gabe."

"She'll want to come here, to San Antonio. You've got to talk her out of that."

Holt's grin felt more like a grimace. "You don't know much about women if you think I could say anything to change her mind, once it's made up."

Gabe prowled across the space between them, gripped the bars in both hands. The skin of his face was taut, and his eyes glittered with savage conviction. "There's nothing for her here," he said. "They'll make a whore of her."

"And you think I'd stand by and see that happen?"

Gabe let out his breath, nodded toward the other end of the corridor, where the jailer waited. "I had a hundred dollars when they brought me here. They took it, along with my knife and my boots. You get that money and fetch it to Melina."

Holt nodded, wishing there was more he could say, more he could do.

"How's John?" Gabe asked, and the change of subject was welcome.

"He's holding up," Holt answered. "I hired a man yesterday and sent six more out to the place today." He paused, unsettled. "You remember that kid who used to tend the horses back when we rode with the Rangers? Mac Kahill?"

Gabe hesitated, thinking, then said, "Sure. Sneaky

little bastard. I caught him going through my saddlebags one time."

Holt reached back, rubbed the nape of his neck. "He's working for me now."

Gabe narrowed his eyes. "You watch him, Holt. Watch him real close."

Holt didn't reckon he'd have time to watch anybody, real close or otherwise, with all he had to do to get that ranch back on sound footing. There were cattle to buy, which meant he'd have to run a herd up from Mexico, and he needed at least another dozen men for a drive like that. He ought to find Frank, and go to Austin to meet with the governor. And then there was Melina, up in Waco.

All the while, Gabe's life was getting shorter with every tick of the clock in the town square.

In the back of his mind, Holt heard Angus McKettrick's voice. *It's there to do, boy. Best leave off worrying and get on with the business at hand.*

God, what he wouldn't give to have his pa and brothers with him right now.

"It might be a few days before I can get back here to see you," he said aloud. "You getting the meals from the hotel?"

Gabe nodded, managed a semblance of the old grin. "It's a lot of food, Holt. I reckon I can count on that coffin being a real tight fit."

"You won't be needing a coffin," Holt said. "Not for a long while, anyway."

Gabe studied him. "You losing your sense of humor, old friend?"

"That's a peculiar question, coming from you. Talking about coffins, and your woman ending up a whore."

The other man sighed, ran his palms down the legs

of his buckskin trousers. "Old Cap'n Jack, he'd have a thing or two to say about all this, wouldn't he?"

The mention of the seasoned Ranger cheered Holt considerably. "He surely would," he said. "And most of it would take the paint off a wall."

Gabe gave a low guffaw. "Yes, sir. Call us a pair of down-in-the-mouth yellow-bellied tit babies, probably. Give us the sole of his boot."

Holt laughed, heartened. He put a hand through the bars, gripped Gabe's shoulder. "Don't pay too much mind to that gallows out there," he counseled. "One day real soon, we'll burn it for firewood and dance around the flames, whooping like Comanches."

"'Like Comanches'?" Gabe retorted. "I *am* a Comanche, White Eyes."

"Then act like one," Holt said, turning to go.

"Son of a bitch," Gabe called, in cheerful farewell.

Holt laughed.

It took some doing, but he got Gabe's hundred dollars out of the jailer.

He'd stop by the ranch, to look in on John and Tillie and the yellow dog, then ride for Waco. With luck, he'd be there by mid-day tomorrow.

# CHAPTER 10

THERE WAS A THIRD PLACE set at the dining room table, and the sound of masculine laughter came from behind the closed doors of the judge's study. Lorelei marched to the kitchen and pushed the door open with the flat of her hand.

"Angelina!"

The other woman was just setting a pan of biscuits in the oven. She looked back at Lorelei over one plump shoulder. *"Sí?"* she asked innocently.

"I'm having supper in my room tonight. I refuse to sit across the table from Creighton Bannings!"

Angelina smiled as she straightened, wiping her hands on her apron. "How was the Ladies' Benevolence Society meeting?"

The reminder of her summary dismissal made Lorelei flinch, but she recovered almost immediately. "I was asked to leave," she said, setting her shoulders. "I'm thinking of starting my own group, just to spite them."

Angelina drew herself up, indignant. "Hateful old hens," she muttered. "I ought to make them all come down with the grippe."

Despite the unseemly reference, Lorelei took a plate from the cupboard, planning to fill it with whatever

Angelina had made for supper and sneak up the back stairs. "Start with Mrs. Malvern," she said lightly, then lowered her voice to a whisper and cast a glance over one shoulder as the laughter in the study swelled again. "She's Creighton's cousin, you know. She's the one who threw me out of the society."

Angelina checked the kettle of potatoes boiling on the back of the stove, then peered into the warming oven at the platter of fried chicken. The heat in the room was almost palpable.

"Put that plate back where you found it," Angelina said. "It isn't Bannings in there with your father. It's the banker, Mr. Sexton."

Lorelei was both relieved and unsettled. Mr. Sexton was not the jovial sort, and neither was her father. What were they laughing about in there?

"Since when does the judge socialize with clerks?"

Angelina met her gaze. "Since today," she said meaningfully.

Lorelei smoothed her hair, then her skirts. Sexton managed her father's accounts, as well as Lorelei's inheritance from her maternal grandfather. "I guess I'd better greet our guest," she said.

Angelina merely nodded.

A few moments later, after straightening her hair and skirts again, Lorelei tapped circumspectly at the study door.

"Come in," the judge called.

Lorelei took a deep breath, wondering if her father had heard about her ousting from the society, and turned the latch.

Mr. Sexton stood, tugging at his tight collar, and tried to smile. "Miss Fellows," he said, in greeting. Her father regarded her smugly from the chair behind that half-acre desk of his.

Lorelei summoned up a smile. "Good evening, Mr. Sexton."

"Tell her," urged the judge.

Sexton flushed. Whatever he'd been laughing about earlier must have been far from his mind, because he looked miserable, and not just from the cloying heat. "It's about the property you inherited," he said.

"What property?" Lorelei asked.

"Why, the ranch," Sexton replied, after a quick glance at the judge. "The hundred acres downriver." He fiddled with his collar again. "An offer of purchase has been made."

Lorelei was confounded. She looked at her father, but his face gave away nothing, as usual. "It's mine to sell?" she asked.

The judge cleared his throat. "Not precisely. But your signature is required. Just a formality."

"I want to see the place first."

Her father sighed. "There is no point in that, Lorelei," he said. "It's just an old cabin, surrounded by scrub brush and rattlesnakes."

"Mr. Templeton is prepared to be very generous," Sexton put in nervously, and got a quelling glare from the judge for his trouble.

"I'm sure he is," Lorelei said, "but I'm not signing anything until I see that land with my own eyes."

The judge pinched the bridge of his nose. "I should have known you would be difficult about this," he said.

"Yes," Lorelei agreed. "You should have."

He glowered at her. "Will you excuse us for a few moments, Mr. Sexton?"

Sexton fled with such haste that Lorelei half expected to see a little cloud of dust trailing behind him. The study door closed with a crisp catch of the latch.

"Why didn't you tell me about this land?" Lorelei asked.

"You are a woman," the judge replied wearily. "It was of no concern to you."

"Until you decided to sell it," Lorelei pointed out.

"The sale will provide a substantial dowry," the judge reasoned, but with an edge of impatience in his voice. "God knows, you'll need one to get a husband."

"I don't want a husband."

"You have made that quite clear. Nonetheless, my dear, you will have one."

"Tell me about the ranch."

Another sigh, this one long-suffering. "It belonged to your mother's family. If William had lived, the place would have gone to him. Your grandfather's will stated that, should William fail to survive, the land would be yours."

"I'm not surprised that I wasn't consulted," Lorelei said glumly. "After all, I *am* only a woman." The judge would simply have appropriated the estate if he'd been able to do so, which meant there was something he wasn't telling her.

Her father hoisted himself from his chair. His lips had a bluish tinge, and there was a strange pallor to his face. "Please, Lorelei. For once in your life, do not argue with me. Mr. Sexton has brought the documents." He shoved a pile of papers toward her without lifting them from the desktop.

Lorelei took a step toward him. "You don't look well. Perhaps I should ask Angelina to send Raul for the doctor."

"Never mind the damn doctor!" the judge shouted, collapsing back into his chair. *"Sign the papers!"*

Lorelei bit her lower lip. Sometimes, she wished she were more tractable.

"No," she said. "Absolutely not."

HOLT RODE INTO Waco about an hour after sunup. A freight wagon jostled by, and the driver touched his hat brim in greeting. Two prostitutes gossiped in front of the Blue Bullet Saloon, pausing to regard Holt through a haze of tobacco smoke, and a Chinaman trotted along the sidewalk, a broomstick braced across his narrow shoulders, yokelike, with a huge covered basket suspended from either end. A dead man—shot through the chest if the pattern of dried blood was any indication—leaned against the wall beside the undertaker's door, strapped to a board. A crude sign dangled from a nail above his head. The Wages Of Sin Is Death.

Holt had seen worse things, especially while riding with the Rangers, but the sight sent a shiver down his spine just the same. He couldn't help thinking of Gabe.

He spotted a livery stable and headed in that direction. Gabe had said Melina was working for a rancher's wife, which meant he wasn't likely to find her in town, but his horse was played out, in need of water, feed and a few hours' rest. He would see to the Appaloosa first, then scare up some breakfast for himself. With any luck, the folks in the restaurant would steer him in the right direction.

He'd just taken a chair by the window and ordered up a plate of eggs, fried potatoes and sausage when Captain Jack Walton himself ambled in. Grizzled and wiry, the man was deceptively small. Holt had seen him take on

Comanches two at a time and come out of it with his hair still on and his hide unmarked.

Holt blinked, sure he was seeing things, and set down his mug of coffee.

Captain Jack laughed. "Thought I was dead, didn't you?" he drawled, taking off his round-brimmed hat and easing himself into the chair across from Holt's.

"Hell, yes," Holt said, recovering, taking in the Captain's thinning gray hair and hard, watchful eyes. "Fact is, I'm still not sure you're real."

Walton's skin was leathery from the Texas sun, and his hands were age-spotted, the fingers clawlike, yet still, Holt would have bet, as quick to the trigger as ever. "I had the same thought about you, when I saw you ride in. That's a fine-looking Appaloosa you've got there."

Holt nodded. He didn't know how to make small talk, not with the Captain, anyhow. "Thanks," he said, at some length, noting the star pinned to the old man's vest.

Walton signaled the waitress, and she hurried over with a blue enamel coffeepot and an outsized cup. Evidently, the Captain still liked his brew.

"What brings you to Waco?" he asked, after adding half a pound of sugar and taking an appreciative slurp.

"I'm looking for a woman called Melina Garcia," Holt said, wondering if the Captain had been the one to put a bullet in that outlaw over at the undertaker's and then display the corpse as a deterrent to those with criminal inclinations. He was a man to take harsh measures when he deemed them appropriate, which was often.

The Captain arched one eyebrow. "Gabe Navarro's woman?"

Holt's stomach soured, and he regarded his unfinished breakfast with mournful resignation. "Yes."

Walton leaned forward. "You the bearer of bad tidings,

Mr. Cavanagh?" he asked. "Last I heard, you was up in the Arizona Territory someplace, building yourself another ranch."

"Gabe's been tried and sentenced to hang, down in San Antonio," Holt said. The details about Arizona could wait.

The Captain narrowed his eyes. "The hell you say."

"I would have thought you'd have heard about it," Holt said. "Word like that usually spreads fast."

"I've been in Mexico the last little while. Just came up here to collect a bounty or two."

"'The wages of sin is death'?"

The Captain smiled. He still had all his teeth. "You seen him, did you? Name was Jake Green. Robbed a freight wagon between here and Austin, and shot the driver in cold blood."

Holt glanced at the star on Walton's chest. "Bounty hunters wear badges now?"

"They do if the money's right," the Captain answered. He settled back in his chair, took a thoughtful sip of his coffee. "You gonna eat that grub or leave it sit?"

Holt shoved the plate across the table, along with his fork and knife.

The Captain speared a sausage link and ate it in two bites. Still chewing, he said, "Melina's working on the Parkinson place, about five miles west of town. I'd be careful how you broach the subject of Gabe if I was you. She's brewing up a baby, and she's none too happy with him right now."

"I'll take my chances," Holt said.

The Captain grinned and tucked into the eggs. "You always were a reckless sum-bitch," he allowed. "It's good to see you. Brings the good old days to mind."

The waitress returned, refilled the coffee cups and left again.

"The good old days," Holt reminisced with a wry smile. "Sleeping on the ground. Eating jerky and jackrabbit for every meal. Fighting Comanches for every inch of ground we crossed. And all for less money than Melina probably makes washing Mrs. Parkinson's bloomers."

The Captain gave a hoot of laughter. "Made you tough," he said.

"You ever thought of going to San Antonio?" Holt inquired.

Walton speared another link of sausage. "Not until you said Gabe was in the hoosegow. Then the idea got real attractive, all of the sudden. If they're fixing to lynch him, he must have been charged with murder."

"Murder and horse thieving," Holt confirmed.

"Bullshit," the Captain said. "Gabe never killed nobody that didn't need killing. Probably not above helping himself to a horse now and again, though."

He paused to savor more coffee, then grunted with lusty satisfaction as he set the cup down again. "Who's behind this monkey circus, anyhow?"

"I'm not sure," Holt said, "but I'd say it was a rancher named Isaac Templeton."

The name evidently registered with Walton. He sighed and shook his head, but whatever his misgivings, they didn't seem to affect his appetite. "Now there's more bad news," he said. "When do you figure on heading back to San Antone?"

"First thing tomorrow," Holt answered, pulling a dollar from his pocket and laying it on the table for the bill. "In the meantime, I'd better get a horse and head for the Parkinson place."

Walton helped himself to the checkered napkin the

waitress had left for Holt and wiped his mouth, leaving considerable egg yolk in his handlebar mustache. Then he unpinned the badge.

"Damn," he said. "The wages wasn't much, but I'll miss this job."

# CHAPTER 11

THE RANCH certainly wasn't prepossessing in any way, Lorelei decided, taking in the property from the seat of Raul's wagon. The house leaned to one side, and the barn had disintegrated to a pile of weathered board, but there was a well, and plenty of grass.

Raul wiped his sweating face with the bandana around his neck. "Just over that hill," he said, quite unnecessarily, gesturing to the east, "is Mr. Templeton's place."

Lorelei had fixed her gaze on the far bank of a wide, deep stream, where a few cattle grazed. "And that's Mr. Cavanagh's northern boundary," she said.

"*Sí,*" Raul said, seeming to wilt in the heat. "It was—until he sold it to the man from Arizona."

Lorelei gathered her skirts and scrambled down off the wagon. "I'll need a horse," she said, pushing aside the thought that "the man from Arizona" was none other than Holt McKettrick.

"What?" Raul asked, as if he hadn't heard her correctly.

"A *horse,*" Lorelei said, proceeding toward the ranch house. Perhaps Raul could shore up the walls. She could plant a garden, have the barn rebuilt and buy a few head of cattle.

"But you don't know how to ride," Raul pointed out hastily, sounding worried as he left the wagon to follow her. "Watch where you step, *señorita*—there are snakes."

"I can *learn* to ride," she said. "And I'm not afraid of snakes."

She approached the house. Her mother must have lived here. Played just outside the door, skipping rope, perhaps, or making mud-pies.

She inspected the log walls, peered inside. There was only one room, with a rusted stove, warped wooden floors and evidence of mice, but with a little bracing and some sweeping, the place would be habitable.

"Your father will never allow it," Raul pleaded.

"My father can just go whistle," Lorelei replied, running a hand down the framework of the door. Sturdy.

"You cannot live out here alone, *señorita*."

"I won't be alone," Lorelei said. "Angelina will come with me."

Raul crossed himself and muttered a prayer in rapid Spanish. That done, he pointed wildly toward the Templeton property, then across the wide stream, toward Mr. Cavanagh's land. "There is a range war coming," he told her frantically. "And you will be in the middle!"

Lorelei shaded her eyes with one hand. "Mr. Cavanagh is a very nice man," she said. "I'm sure he wouldn't do anything violent."

"But I told you, *señorita*, he is not really the owner anymore."

Lorelei bit her lower lip. John Cavanagh was a man of peace. He worked hard and kept to himself. Holt McKettrick, on the other hand, was an unknown quantity. He might or might not make a good neighbor.

"I will not permit a range war," she said, after due

consideration. "Mr. Templeton, Mr. Cavanagh and Mr. McKettrick will simply have to work things out between themselves."

"But, *señorita*—"

Lorelei proceeded to the well. Tried in vain to hoist the heavy wooden cover.

Raul moved it for her, and she peered down the shaft.

"I see water down there," she said. She squinted, and her stomach turned. "And a dead animal of some sort."

*"Madre de Dios,"* Raul whispered.

"We'll need shovels," Lorelei decided, already making a list in her mind. "Perhaps Mr. Wilkins, at the mercantile, will know of some substance that will purify the water."

"Ay-yi-yi," lamented Raul.

"Can you teach me to shoot a gun?" Lorelei inquired, dusting her hands together. "If you can't, I shall have to learn on my own."

"A *gun, señorita?"*

"Yes, Raul," Lorelei said, waxing impatient. "A gun."

Raul began to pace, waving his arms and ranting in Spanish.

Lorelei consulted her bodice watch. "I guess we'd better get back to town," she said. "I have to meet with Mr. Sexton, at the bank, and we must order supplies." She assessed the sky, which was blue as Angelina's favorite sugar bowl. "What we need is a tent. Just until the house is habitable. You don't think it will rain in the next few days, do you?"

Raul stopped his pacing and raving and let his hands fall to his sides. *"Sí,"* he said hopefully. "There are dark clouds—there in the west."

Lorelei turned. Sure enough, there were.

"All the more reason to invest in a tent," she said.

Raul lapsed into Spanish again. Since she suspected he was cursing, Lorelei did not attempt to translate. She made for the wagon, her strides long and purposeful, and Raul had no choice but to follow.

He helped her back into the wagon box, then climbed up beside her, breathing hard, his thin shoulders stooped with defeat.

"We must have chickens, too, of course," Lorelei said, scrabbling through her bag for a pencil stub and something to write on. "We can probably eat fish from the creek, and a fifty-pound bag of beans would do nicely for provisions. Angelina can do marvelous things with beans."

The wagon jostled into motion.

"Chickens," Raul fretted. "Beans."

Lorelei concentrated on her list. "Coffee," she said. "And sugar. Flour and yeast—"

Somewhere in the distance, thunder rumbled.

Lorelei paid it no mind.

What was a little rain?

THEY FOUND Melina Garcia in back of the Parkinson's rambling log ranch house bent over a tub of hot water, clasping what looked like a shirt in both hands and scrubbing it against a washboard. She was a little bit of a thing, by Holt's measure, anchored to the earth only by the jutting weight of her lower belly. Her dark hair was twisted into a knot at the nape of her neck and coming loose from its pins, and her brown face gleamed with sweat.

She'd watched them approach, and there was no welcome in her eyes.

"A good day to you, Melina," the Captain said, resettling his hat.

She spared him an unfriendly nod and left off the washing to set her hands on her hips and look Holt over good. From her expression, he'd have said she found him somewhat short of spectacular.

Holt dismounted, hung his hat on his saddle horn and took a step toward her.

"I've met this old coyote once or twice," she said, with a terse nod in the Captain's direction, "but who the devil are you?"

Wisely, Holt stopped in his tracks, folded his arms to show he meant no harm and answered her query with his full name.

She mirrored his stance, but there was no promise of peace in her posture or in her face. She was expecting trouble, that was clear. Either she had good instincts where impending misfortune was concerned, or she'd had a lot of experience in that area.

Holt figured it was probably a little of both.

Her dark eyes flashed with wary temper. "What do you want?"

"I'm here to bring you word about Gabe Navarro."

She stiffened, and he glimpsed a shadow of fear behind her facade, but it was quickly displaced by a wintry fury. She spat fiercely into the hard, hot dirt.

"He's alive," Holt felt compelled to say.

"Maybe not for long," the Captain put in. He hadn't bothered to get off his horse.

Melina's eyes widened, and her gaze flickered from Holt to the Captain and back again. "What's happened?" she asked. She was interested, all right, but she didn't seem to want anyone to know it.

Holt reached into his pocket, brought out the five

twenty-dollar bills he'd threatened and cajoled out of Gabe's jailer. Extended them. "He sent you this."

She hesitated, then stepped forward and snatched the bills from his hand. After looking around, she tucked them into the pocket of her apron and patted them, as if to make sure they stayed put. "He's in trouble," she surmised.

Holt nodded, rubbed the back of his neck with one hand. "Yes, indeed," he said. "He's in jail in San Antonio, sentenced to hang on the first of October."

Melina reached out, grasped the handle of the water pump to steady herself. Her other hand flew to her belly, as if to protect the babe she was carrying. "That's impossible."

"I'm afraid it ain't," the Captain said. He took a tin of tobacco and some papers from his shirt pocket and proceeded to roll himself a smoke, still without dismounting. "Holt here tells me the charges are murder and horse thieving. This is serious business, Melina."

A middle-aged woman came out of the house to stand on the porch, watching them, shading her eyes from the relentless Texas sun with one hand. "Melina?" she called. "Is everything all right?"

Melina didn't so much as glance in that direction. "No, ma'am," she answered, raising her voice just far enough to cover the distance.

The woman, probably Mrs. Parkinson, stepped tentatively off the porch and started toward them. Like Melina, she was clad in practical calico, but she looked a sight cooler. "Who are these men?" she wanted to know.

"Holt McKettrick," Holt said, with a slight inclination of his head. "And this is Captain Jack Walton."

The Captain troubled himself to tug at the brim of his dusty hat. "Mrs. Parkinson," he said politely.

"You," she said, looking up at Walton and lining up shoulder to shoulder with Melina. In that moment, Holt decided he liked the woman. She was obviously nervous of strangers, and with good reason given the state of affairs in modern Texas. It seemed there were no men around to protect her if things should take an ugly turn, but she was willing to stand toe-to-toe with whatever came. "If you came here looking to collect some bounty, you can just ride on out right now. All our men are honest."

Captain Jack leaned forward, resting on arm on the pommel of his saddle, and smiled. "I've got no business with any of your men, Mrs. Parkinson. I just came along with my friend, Holt, here, to bring Melina some news."

Mrs. Parkinson looked down at Melina. "What kind of news?"

Melina didn't turn her head. She was still watching Holt, with an occasional glance at the Captain. "I've got to go to San Antonio," she said.

"Gabe doesn't want you to do that," Holt said, though he'd already guessed there was little hope of convincing her.

"I'll get my things," Melina said.

"Melina," Mrs. Parkinson protested. "You can't just leave! How will I get the washing done?"

At last, Gabe's woman faced the boss lady. "I'm sorry about the washing," she said directly, "but I still have to go."

"But the baby—what will you do in San Antonio? How will you live?"

"I'll see that she's taken care of," Holt said, for

Melina's benefit more than Mrs. Parkinson's. "I have friends she can stay with."

Melina studied him, evidently weighing his words for truth, and must have decided in his favor, for she picked up her skirts and made for the house at a good clip.

Mrs. Parkinson watched her go, probably struggling with the realization that she couldn't stop Melina from leaving. Resignation slackened her shoulders as she turned her attention on Holt and the Captain. "I don't like trusting that child to strangers," she said.

"I do not qualify as a stranger, Mrs. Parkinson," the Captain said. He got off his horse at long last, gathered the reins and led the animal to the water trough. Holt's Appaloosa followed along on its own. "And Mr. McKettrick here is a gentleman. I can assure you of that."

Mrs. Parkinson looked as though she'd like to haul off and spit, the way Melina had, but in the end she refrained and made for the house.

"That woman doesn't think very highly of you, Cap'n," Holt observed, worrying that in his mind the way he kept worrying the sight of that corpse strapped to a board on the main street of town. "Why is that?"

The Captain went to the pump, brought up some water and splashed his face and the back of his neck thoroughly. "I reckon it's because we used to be married," he said.

# CHAPTER 12

LORELEI WATCHED from her bedroom window as the judge climbed into the buggy Raul had hitched up for him, the way he did every weekday morning and most Saturdays, took up the reins and set out for the main part of town. He would not return home until late in the day, as he had court cases to hear.

Once he'd rounded the corner onto the road that ran alongside the river curling through town, she sprang into action.

Kneeling, she pulled out the valise she'd packed the night before from under the bed. A rap at her door startled her so that she nearly choked on an indrawn breath, but she recovered quickly.

"Angelina?"

The door opened, and the housekeeper stood on the threshold. Her eyes traveled to the valise, while Lorelei scrambled to her feet.

"You are really going to do this," Angelina marveled.

"Yes," Lorelei said firmly.

"Mr. Sexton, from the bank, will be waiting on the

courthouse steps to tell the judge what you're planning. And he will put a stop to it."

Lorelei hoisted the valise in one hand, reflecting upon her interview with Mr. Sexton the afternoon before. She'd gone directly to the bank, after her visit to the property, and he'd been pleased to see her—until she'd made it clear that she had no intention of signing her inheritance over to Mr. Templeton.

"I would like to see my account," Lorelei had said, standing her ground.

"The judge has strictly forbidden—"

"I don't care what the judge has forbidden," she'd interrupted.

Sexton had sighed, rummaged until he found the proper ledger and licked a fingertip before flipping through the pages.

"You have two thousand, seven-hundred and twenty-two dollars and seventy-eight cents," he'd said, with the utmost reluctance.

Lorelei, peering over his shoulder, had already deduced that. She'd blinked at the sum, then her gaze had shifted to the debit column. Judging by the long list of tidy figures, her father had made regular withdrawals over the past ten years.

"I'm afraid I must insist that Judge Fellows's wishes be respected," Sexton had said, closing the book. His jowls were flushed, his eyes skittish.

Lorelei had insisted that the funds be moved to another account, and when Sexton balked, she threatened to fetch the constable. At last, he'd relented, but with the greatest reluctance.

She'd narrowed her eyes at him as she prepared to leave the bank with a purseful of cash and move on to the mercantile. "If you run to my father," she'd warned,

"I'll move every cent to another bank and have you audited."

Now, facing Angelina as she was about to leave her bedroom and the house as well, perhaps for the very last time, Lorelei, having recounted the conversation to the older woman, shook her head. "He wouldn't dare go to my father," she said.

"Mr. Sexton is afraid of the judge, like almost everyone else in San Antonio," Angelina maintained, a bit frantically, but she stepped aside to let Lorelei pass into the corridor. "If you had any sense at all, you would be, too."

"It's my land, and my money," Lorelei maintained, starting down the rear stairway. "Are you and Raul coming with me or not?"

Angelina crossed herself, but she nodded. "My cousin Rosa is coming to look after the judge," she said. "Still—"

Lorelei opened the back door and peered toward the carriage house. "Where is Raul?" she fretted. "Mr. Wilkins promised to deliver my order by noon. We have to be there to meet the wagons."

Mr. Wilkins, as it happened, was not among the judge's many admirers. He'd been a vocal supporter of the other candidate during the last election and had written several letters to the editor of the local newspaper complaining about the decisions Judge Fellows had handed down. The merchant had been suspicious at first, then pleased to keep quiet about the wagonload of provisions and supplies Lorelei had purchased and paid for on the spot.

Raul came out of the carriage house, driving the buckboard. Even from a distance, his lack of enthusiasm was readily apparent.

Lorelei felt a pang. Her father was a difficult man, but

he was aging and perhaps even ill. He could get along without her just fine, but losing Angelina and Raul would be a blow.

"If you want to stay here and look after Father," she said, "I'll understand."

Angelina dragged a valise of her own from its hiding place in the pantry. "And let you go off alone, to live in the wilderness, with wolves and savages and outlaws and the *Madre* only knows what else? No. Rosa and her Miguel will take our places."

"I promise you will not regret this," Lorelei said, well aware that the statement was a rash one. Once the judge realized she'd not only taken her funds out of his keeping but helped herself to his housekeeper and handyman, he would be enraged.

Angelina looked doubtful but resolved. "I think I already regret it," she said. Raul came to the door, looking woebegone, and claimed both the valises. "By all the saints and angels, when your father learns of this, the ground will shake."

As if to lend credence to Angelina's words, thunder clapped in the near distance. The horses nickered and tossed their heads, and Lorelei looked up at the sky as she descended the back steps. Fast-moving gray clouds were gathering over San Antonio, churning with mayhem.

Angelina looked up as well and opened her mouth to speak, but at the look Lorelei gave her, she held her tongue.

Raul helped his wife onto the wagon seat, then Lorelei, before climbing up to take the reins.

"Cheer up," Lorelei said. "This is a new beginning."

Five minutes later, the rain began.

MELINA STARED mutely at the gallows, a raw wood structure, half-finished, shimmering in the heavy rain. She was soaked to the skin, as was Holt himself, and the Captain, but she seemed oblivious to everything but the mechanism where Gabe was slated to hang.

She'd ridden behind Holt all the way down from Waco and refused to stop at the Cavanagh place to rest, put on dry clothes and wait for the rain to let up. Watching her now, Holt wished he'd taken her there anyway.

She shivered in the downpour, hair dangling in wet strands down the sides of her face, looking bedraggled and small in Holt's coat.

Still mounted, the Captain lifted the collar of his canvas duster. "Warm as bathwater," he said of the rain, his voice pitched low. "Just the same, we'd best get that woman someplace dry."

Holt swung a leg over the Appaloosa's neck and jumped to the ground. He said her name quietly, reached out to lay a hand on her slight shoulder.

She shrugged him off. "I want to see Gabe," she said. "Right now."

"There he is," the Captain said. "That window, yonder."

Both Holt and Melina looked up. Sure enough, Gabe was gazing down at them, his face like chiseled stone, his hands grasping the bars.

Melina took a step toward him, staggered a little.

Reaching out, Holt caught hold of her arm.

"Where is the way in?" Melina wanted to know.

"Tomorrow," Holt reasoned.

She shook her head, and water flew from the thick tendrils of hair. "Now," she said, laying both hands on her belly.

"Might as well show her inside," the Captain said. "If you don't, we'll be at this all day."

The old man was right. Melina was already prowling

back and forth like a caged cat, and she looked as though she'd climb the drain pipe if that was what she had to do to get to Gabe.

Holt took her arm, and this time he didn't let her pull away. Gabe stared down from his cell, looking as if he might chew his way past those bars and jump two stories to the ground. "This way," Holt said.

"I'll tend to the horses and then join you," the Captain said, leaning from the saddle to catch hold of the Appaloosa's reins. "After that, I'd accept a drink if you're offering one."

Holt merely nodded.

The Captain set out on his errand, and Holt squired Melina into the courthouse and up the stairs to the jail.

"No women allowed," announced old Roy, sitting in a corner next to the window, watching the rain and whittling.

Holt ignored him. Took the keys down off the hook next to the inside door.

"Wait just a minute," Roy protested. "Didn't you hear what I said?"

"I heard," Holt replied, working the lock and then putting the keys back in their place. "I just don't give a damn."

Melina streaked through the opening, and Holt followed.

"I could send for the marshal!" Roy called after them. "He's just downstairs, testifying in Judge Fellows's courtroom."

"You do that," Holt replied, quickening his pace to catch up with Melina.

She strode past the other cells as if she knew exactly where Gabe was—and maybe she did.

Gabe was waiting at the front of his cell. "I told

you I wanted her to stay in Waco!" he hissed, glaring at Holt.

"Maybe you should have told *her*," Holt retorted.

"Why didn't you send word, Gabe?" Melina asked, getting as close to the bars as she could with that stomach of hers. Holt could still feel it pressing against his back, during the long ride from Waco.

"I *did* send word," Gabe answered. His voice was harsh, but his eyes consumed Melina, and he reached through the bars to lay a hand to her cheek. "Jesus, Mary and Joseph, Melina, you shouldn't have come here."

"How could I stay away?" she demanded, covering his hand with her own.

"I'll see if the Cap'n's back from the livery stable," Holt said, turning to go.

Gabe drew in a sharp breath. "The Cap'n? He's with you?"

"I ran into him in Waco. He's getting the horses some water and feed. He'll be in for a word once you and Melina are through talking."

Gabe nodded. "Did you ask him about Frank? Has the Cap'n seen him, or heard anything?"

Holt had broached the subject to Walton on the way out to the Parkinson place. Now, he shook his head. "He's got no more idea where Corrales is than we do."

A ruckus started up out in the front office, and Holt figured the Captain had completed the horse business. He backtracked with some haste, for fear Walton would lose patience with old Roy and get them all thrown in jail.

Sure enough, the Captain had the other man by the shirt collar, slammed up against the wall. Roy's eyes were bugging out and he was sputtering, his wind cut off by Captain Jack's grip.

"Let him go," Holt said, without particular urgency. "You left that star behind in Waco, remember?"

With a flourish, the Captain released the jailer and watched with interest as he struggled for breath.

"We got rules around here!" Roy wailed. "And you can't just go around chokin' folks!"

"The hell I can't," the Captain said. "You got any whiskey in this place?"

# CHAPTER 13

THE FREIGHT WAGON had already arrived when Lorelei, Angelina and Raul got to the ranch, and it was stuck up to its axels in mud. Raul drew the buckboard up alongside and leaped down.

"I put the load inside that old house there!" the driver shouted, in an effort to be heard over the torrent. "Help me unhitch this team."

Raul nodded, and Angelina and Lorelei climbed down on their own. Lorelei would have stayed with the men, but Angelina took her arm and dragged her out of the rain.

"It's an omen," the older woman said, with conviction, when they stood under the relative shelter of the leaking roof.

Lorelei bent to open the rusted door of the woodstove, and it creaked on its hinges. "Is that a mouse's nest?" she asked, peering inside.

*"Madre de Dios,"* said Angelina.

Lorelei shut the stove and turned to survey the piles of provisions, mostly in crates stacked helter-skelter around the room. She picked up a shiny new ax and tested its heft, then set it carefully in a corner. "We won't need a fire, anyway. It's hot as the far corner of Hades, even with this rain."

Angelina went to the door, probably watching for Raul.

Lorelei bent over the tent pole, thinking it was the size of a ship's mast, and wondered if the canvas could be unwrapped and draped over the roof. Then she picked through the crates until she found the shiny new coffee-pot. It was good-sized, for she expected to entertain as soon as she was settled. And the ranch hands—once she hired them and bought some cattle—would want their coffee.

"We'll have to have a fire after all," she said, starting for the door.

Angelina turned to look at her. "Where do you think you're going?"

"Why, to set the pot in the rain," Lorelei said, surprised.

Angelina opened her mouth, closed it again, and went out to join Raul and the driver, who were hobbling the horses.

Lorelei centered the pot in the middle of the dooryard, pleased with the prospect of hot coffee, and went back inside. Purposefully, she emptied a crate, splintered it into manageable pieces with the ax and poked uncertainly at the mouse's nest. Nothing scurried or squeaked, so she assumed it was abandoned.

She had a nice blaze going when Angelina returned and let out a little shriek.

"Lorelei," she cried, rushing over and tugging open the stove door. "The chimney!"

Lorelei frowned, assessing the crooked metal pipe disappearing through the roof. Smoke began to billow out through the opening in the stove and seep through heretofore invisible gaps in the pipe.

"For heaven's sake," she marveled.

Angelina stabbed at the fire with the handle of Lorelei's brand-new broom, chattering in Spanish. "Water," she coughed. "Get me some water!"

Lorelei hesitated, confused, then dashed outside to get the coffeepot, already half-full of rain. She handed it to Angelina, who promptly flung the contents into the stove. There was a puny sizzle, and then Angelina straightened, shutting the squeaky little door against the smoke.

"From now on," Angelina said evenly, "*I* will make the coffee."

Lorelei snatched up a blanket and waved it, but the smoke met the veil of rain at the door and rolled back inside.

Thunder shook the roof.

"A bad omen," Angelina reiterated, crossing herself.

"Nonsense," Lorelei said, reclaiming the broom. "With a little straightening up, this house will be cozy."

Raul came inside, followed by the driver. Both of them were drenched, but then so were Lorelei and Angelina.

"I smell smoke," said the driver.

They all sat down on crates and stared at each other.

"I believe I'll ride one of them horses back to town," the freight man said presently. "Plenty of other mounts, if you all want to go along."

Raul looked longingly toward the door.

"I'm staying right here," said Lorelei.

"That's your privilege, ma'am," the fellow answered, rising from his crate. Raul stared down at his hands, and Angelina shook out her skirts.

The driver took his leave, and Lorelei rose to watch

him go. He mounted one of the four horses, abandoning his wagon, and set out for San Antonio. The remaining three followed along, without benefit of a lead rope.

"He would have been much wiser to spend the night," she observed. "He could be struck by lightning along that road, and, anyway, he'll have to come back to get his wagon."

Neither Angelina nor Raul spoke, or even looked in her direction.

It was up to her, Lorelei decided, to set a cheerful tone. "Raul," she said, bending to pick up the coffeepot Angelina had dropped after putting out the flames. "Perhaps you could make a bonfire in that copse of oak trees next to the water. We'll need one for cooking."

Raul looked at her as though she'd just risen from the dead.

"A bonfire?" he echoed.

Angelina sighed. "Just do it," she said forlornly.

Raul went out.

"We'd better get into dry clothes," Lorelei said. "Warm as it is, we could take a chill. I'll brew up a nice pot of tea."

"How do you plan to do that?" Angelina asked reasonably.

"Why, I'll just catch rain water—or get some from the creek—and set it on the fire to boil."

"And how will you go to and from this fire without getting wet all over again?"

"Oh," said Lorelei.

"Yes," said Angelina. "Oh."

Raul was gone for perhaps a quarter of an hour, and when he returned, he looked defeated.

"There is no dry firewood," he said.

Lorelei and Angelina, wearing dry clothes, sat on crates, brushing the rain out of their hair.

"We shall have to do without our tea," Lorelei said bravely.

IN THE DAMP, thin light of dawn, Lorelei gazed up at the cobwebs swathing the ceiling rafters like entangled ghosts. She'd slept in her clothes, on a pallet of blankets, and her skin was peppered with chigger bites. On the other side of the ranch house, which was, she admitted to herself, really just a cabin, Angelina and Raul slumbered on, their soft snores interweaving.

The remnants of last night's rain dripped through holes in the roof, the chimney was still stopped up with birds' nests, dirt and layers of soot and she would have sold her soul for a cup of hot, fresh coffee.

By now, her father knew that she'd not only defected from his household and claimed her property and what remained of her funds, but stolen his servants as well. He was probably livid.

No, no *probably* about it, she thought, squaring herself to face reality.

Judge Alexander Fellows was surely in a fury, and even now taking steps to deal with his rebellious daughter.

Isaac Templeton's vast spread sprawled on one side of her little ranch, and Holt McKettrick's on the other. For all her brave thoughts to the contrary, a range war was a very real possibility, and if it happened, Lorelei would most likely be caught square in the middle.

She didn't know how to ride. She didn't know how to shoot.

She didn't own a single cow, or a horse.

So why, she wondered, smiling, did she feel so exhilarated?

"GOOD GOD," said Holt McKettrick, right out loud, when, riding along the creekbank, with Tillie's dog trotting along behind his horse, he saw Lorelei Fellows kneeling on the other side, splashing her face with water.

She couldn't have heard him; he was still a hundred yards away, at least, but she looked up, just the same, and took him in with a visible lack of enthusiasm.

The dog, spotting her, barked exuberantly and plunged right into the stream, paddling toward her for all he was worth.

Lorelei's sour expression turned sweet as she watched Sorrowful make his way across. He came up onto the bank beside her and shook off the creek water with a mighty effort, making her laugh aloud, the sound ringing like church bells of a Sunday morning.

It did something to Holt, hearing her erupt with joy like that. Caused a soft, subtle shift inside him.

That riled him.

Setting his jaw, he urged Traveler into the water and crossed.

Lorelei paid him no notice; she was busy having a reunion with the dog.

He felt a sting, watching them, and this did not have a positive effect upon his disposition.

"What the devil are you doing out here?" he asked Lorelei, getting down from the Appaloosa and leaving the horse to drink from the stream.

Lorelei was nose to nose with that dog, ruffling his ears and laughing, and she took her time answering. Got to her feet, fussed over Sorrowful a while longer and patted her hair. Her fine breasts rose when she did that, and Holt felt another sharp shift, somewhere in his middle.

"I live here," she said.

Holt scanned the property and found it sorry to behold. The house was on a tilt, and the barn, such as it was, had probably collapsed before Santa Ana massacred one hundred and eighty-five brave men at the Alamo. There were two wagons, one of them stuck axel-deep in drying mud, and the other dripping rainwater through the floorboards. A pair of town horses, pretty but essentially useless, grazed alongside the stream, and there wasn't a cow to be seen.

"Alone?" he asked, amazed.

Her mouth tightened briefly, and she was sparing with her answer. "Angelina and Raul are with me."

"Does your father know about this?"

She laughed, more at his consternation, he suspected, than because she had any case for mirth. "No doubt he does."

"Just what are you planning on doing, way out here?"

"Making a life for myself," she answered, with a confidence Holt found downright annoying. Didn't the woman know there were outlaws on the prowl, not to mention renegade Indians, wolves, wild boars and every other kind of bad luck?

Holt remembered his hat and took it off, shoving his free hand through his hair. "This is no place for a lady."

"Then it's a good thing I'm not much of a lady," Lorelei retorted.

The words struck Holt like a sucker punch, though he was damned if he could think why.

She chuckled at his expression, rocking a little on her heels. "Come now, Mr. McKettrick. Does that really come as such a shock to you? I'm the woman who burned her wedding dress in the town square, after all, and day before yesterday, when we met on the street, I'd just been booted out of the Ladies' Benevolence Society."

"So you moved out here, to the middle of nowhere?" Holt challenged, strangely exasperated. What did he care if the damn fool female wanted to make her home on this godforsaken patch of no-account ground? "Seems a mite extreme, to me."

"I guess it is," she allowed, obviously enjoying his discomfort. "But I'm here to stay."

He fiddled with his hat, looked away, looked back. "Damned if you're not serious," he marveled.

"I certainly am," she confirmed.

Over her shoulder, he saw a Mexican man come out of the cabin, rubbing his eyes. Seeing Holt, he ducked back inside, probably to get his rifle.

"At least you're not alone," Holt said, as she followed his gaze, but it was precious little comfort—to him at least.

Sure enough, here came the Mexican, rifle in hand, followed by a plump little woman moving at a fast clip. Probably his wife.

"Raul, Angelina," Lorelei called to them, smiling. The dog was hunkered down beside her, wagging his stumpy tail and gazing up at her face with pure adoration. "I'd like you to meet Holt McKettrick—one of our neighbors."

# CHAPTER 14

LORELEI'S CHIGGER BITES itched something fierce, but she wasn't about to scratch with Holt McKettrick looking on.

Raul looked the visitor over, then let the rifle dangle at his side. Gave a brief nod of wary greeting.

Holt put his hand out, and Raul hesitated before clasping it briefly.

Angelina smiled. "Welcome," she said, and she sounded as if she meant it. "Have you had breakfast, Mr. McKettrick?"

"Yes, ma'am," McKettrick replied. "But I wouldn't mind some stout coffee."

"Raul," Angelina said, "build a fire."

"The stove isn't working," Lorelei felt compelled to explain, and then blushed, wishing she hadn't said anything.

Holt eyed the crooked chimney, jutting above the roof at an unlikely angle. "I'll have a look," he said, and set off in the direction of the house.

Sorrowful immediately got to his feet and followed.

"Fine-looking man," Angelina commented mildly,

watching Holt walk away. Raul occupied himself searching for dry wood. "Might be a match for you."

Lorelei's face burned. "Don't be silly," she said and, picking up her skirts, hurried over to supervise the chimney project. All she needed was for Mr. McKettrick to fall through her roof and do further damage.

"I don't suppose you have a ladder," Holt mused, standing at the western corner of the house, where the log beams met and crossed each other.

Lorelei hated admitting the oversight. For all her list-making and practical purchases at the mercantile, she hadn't thought of a ladder, nor had Mr. Wilkins suggested one.

"No," she said, pushing a lock of hair back from her face.

Holt headed for the front door, which stood open, and stepped inside without hesitation.

Lorelei hated for him to see the pallets on the floor, the stacked crates and boxes, the dust and cobwebs, but there was no stopping him.

He stood in the middle of the room, taking it all in. "I've seen worse," he said, and made his way past a variety of obstacles to take hold of the rusted chimney. Before Lorelei could say a word, he'd pulled out the section between the stovetop and the ceiling. A shower of cold ash, dust and soot rained down on both of them.

Lorelei was about to protest when he grinned at her, fair taking her breath away, and carried the stove pipe outside. She followed, dusting off debris from her slept-in dress as she went.

Raul had a fire going on the creek bank, and Angelina went inside, smirking a little as she swept past Lorelei. When she came out, she was carrying the coffeepot and a canister.

Holt raised the stove pipe on end and gave it a couple of good thumps on the ground. Dust, twigs, broken egg shells and a couple of dead mice landed in a heap at his feet. Covered in soot and ash, he looked damnably pleased with himself.

Lorelei felt her heart soften and firmed it right up by an act of will.

Whistling, Holt went back into the house, the dog on his heels.

Fickle creature, Lorelei thought. She'd fed that hound every night for two years, and here he was following a stranger around.

Holt came out again, carrying the broom. Without so much as a glance in Lorelei's direction, he climbed to the roof, using the ends of the logs for footholds, tested the shingles with one foot and then proceeded to stand upright and pull the chimney free.

Lorelei realized she was holding her breath and drew in some air.

Taking up the broom again, Holt turned the bristle side up and jammed the handle into the hole.

Dust billowed out the front door.

Sorrowful barked joyously.

Holt replaced the chimney, tossed the broom to the ground, and started down. Sorrowful thought it was a game, took the broom handle in his teeth and ran madly around in a circle with it.

"Fool dog," Holt said affectionately, tousling the animal's misshapen ears as he passed.

Lorelei had to smile, but she told herself it was the dog's antics that made her feel suddenly and inexplicably happy. Nothing whatsoever to do with Holt McKettrick.

She followed him into the cabin, watched as he put the stovepipe back in place.

"That ought to do it, he said, dusting his hands together. He was filthy, covered in grime, and there were little twigs in his hair.

"Look at this mess," Lorelei fretted.

"You're welcome," Holt said.

Sorrowful tried to come inside, but he was still holding the broom handle in his teeth, and it thumped against the door frame, stopping him at the threshold. He looked abashed when several subsequent attempts failed.

Lorelei laughed, and so did Holt.

She went to the door and relieved Sorrowful of the broom. Feeling suddenly shy, she did the obvious thing and began to sweep.

To her surprise, Holt stopped her, gripping the handle.

"Lorelei," he said quietly. "Go home. There's trouble coming at you from two directions."

She looked up into his handsome, earnest face and remembered their conversation at the cemetery behind St. Ambrose's. He'd been putting yellow roses on a grave when she caught sight of him, his head bowed, but for poor Olivia, it was too little, too late. Holt's abandoned mistress had been left to raise a child alone—his child—on a dressmaker's wages.

She'd best not let herself get too taken with this man, Lorelei admonished herself. He might be engaging, and competent, but in the most important sense, he was no better than Creighton.

"Are you threatening me, Mr. McKettrick?"

*"Threatening you?"* he echoed, in furious amazement.

She stiffened. "This is my land. If you and Mr. Templeton can't make peace, you'll have to fight around me."

"COFFEE'S READY," Angelina said, from the doorway. The air was charged inside that cabin, and she supposed she should just back away, but something compelled her to stay.

Mr. McKettrick had been holding on to the broom handle. Now, he let it go with a thrusting motion.

The yellow dog whimpered.

"I can't stay," McKettrick said, glaring into Lorelei's pink and stubborn face. "I've got a cattle ranch to run."

With that, he turned his back on Lorelei and came toward the door with such purpose that Angelina hastened out of his way.

The dog hesitated, looking mournfully up at Lorelei, and then followed Mr. McKettrick.

Lorelei took to a furious spate of sweeping, and looked so forlorn that Angelina nearly wept. The poor child.

"I think he is a good man," Angelina dared, very softly.

Lorelei would not look at her. She just kept swinging that broom, raising more dust than she cleared away. "You are entitled to your opinion, Angelina," she said tightly.

Angelina sighed. She'd practically raised Lorelei, joining the judge's household a few days after his wife went away to that hospital in San Francisco. She and Raul had never been blessed with children of their own, and they'd often pretended, just between themselves, that Lorelei was their daughter.

"Raul and I, we are getting old," she said tentatively.

"You'll need someone to look after you when we're gone."

A tear slipped down Lorelei's cheek, and she rubbed it away with a quick motion of one shoulder. "I can look after myself," she said, concentrating on her fruitless sweeping.

Angelina crossed to her, took the broom gently from her hands, gathered her close. Lorelei resisted at first, then allowed Angelina to hold her. "Don't you want a husband, Chiquita?" the older woman asked softly. "Don't you want babies of your own?"

Lorelei gave a single, raw sob. Angelina remembered her as a little girl, patiently rocking her dolls to sleep, and her heart ached.

"Poor Chiquita," Angelina crooned softly. "You are too stubborn and too proud. You lost your way when Michael died. Now, you must find it again."

Lorelei sniffled and drew back, out of Angelina's embrace. A smile wobbled on her mouth, failed to stick and fell away. "I've tried that," she said, "and look what happened. I found Creighton in bed with someone else, on our wedding day. I'm just no good at this love business."

Angelina shook her head. "I think you knew Creighton Bannings was not meant to be your husband. That's why you chose him. It kept your father quiet for a while, but you knew all along that there would never be a wedding."

Lorelei's lovely blue eyes widened. She started to speak, then swallowed whatever she'd been about to say.

"You buried your heart with Michael Chandler," Angelina went on gently. "You must take it back."

"He was wonderful, Angelina," Lorelei whispered,

and fresh tears gathered along her lower lashes. "He made me laugh. He would never have betrayed me."

"Chiquita," Angelina said, taking one of Lorelei's hands in both of hers, "he is *dead*. Holt McKettrick is alive. How long will you hide in a tiny corner of yourself, refusing to come out and take your chances like the rest of us?"

Lorelei stared at her for a long moment, her throat working. Then she smiled determinedly and looked around at the boxes of goods from the mercantile.

"I can't remember if I bought calamine lotion," she said brightly. "These chigger bites are driving me insane."

# CHAPTER 15

TWO MILES UPSTREAM, Holt got off his horse, hung his hat on the saddle-horn, and started for the creek bank, unbuttoning his shirt as he went. He couldn't go to town and hire Gabe a decent lawyer covered in stove dirt, and there wasn't time to go back home for a bath and fresh clothes.

He'd just have to shake them out as best he could and sluice himself off in the stream.

Sorrowful lay down on the bank to watch, his muzzle resting on his forelegs. If that dog had had eyebrows, he would have raised them.

"Go on home," Holt said, stripping to the skin and wading into the slow-moving water. "I shouldn't have let you follow me."

Sorrowful whimpered, but he didn't move.

Holt realized it was Lorelei he was mad at, and here he was, taking it out on an old hound dog. "All right, you can stay," he grumbled, splashing himself industriously, "but you'll never make it on your own. I'll have to hoist you up into the saddle with me, and won't we be a sight, riding into San Antonio like that. A real pair to draw to."

The dog snapped at a passing fly, then settled into the grass again, waiting. Perking up his sorry ears when Holt spoke again.

"I don't know what you see in that woman," Holt complained, slogging up the bank and wondering how long it would take to dry off so he could put his clothes back on. Hell of a thing if he got caught out here, say by some of Templeton's crew, naked as a whore doing business. "I clean out her chimney—risk my neck climbing on that broken-down roof of hers to do it—and she doesn't even say 'thank you.'"

Sorrowful commiserated with a little whine.

Holt shook out his pants and pulled them on, then did the same with his shirt, fumbling with the buttons. He shook a finger at Sorrowful.

"If I didn't have so damned much to do," he vowed, "I'd get falling-down, piss-assed drunk!"

Sorrowful raised himself on his hind legs and stretched, yawning.

"Am I boring you?" Holt demanded.

The dog stood on all fours now, switching that pitiful tail of his back and forth.

Holt strapped on his gun-belt, and saw a buggy in the distance, careening along the old cattle trail that passed as a road.

"Who's that?" he asked, feeling uneasy.

The dog didn't answer, which was probably for the best.

LORELEI STOOD with her back straight, watching the buggy approach. Angelina flanked her on one side and Raul on the other, but she knew she was going to have to fight this battle on her own. Her stomach was jumping and her heart was thudding in her throat, but she was ready.

Her father's face was the color of raw liver as he wrenched on the reins and set the brake lever with a hard motion of one foot.

He was a bulky man, though not very tall, and Lorelei felt a touch of pity as he climbed awkwardly down to the ground.

"You're as crazy as your mother was!" he bellowed, after a few sputtering attempts at speech.

Lorelei flinched. It wasn't the first time he'd made a statement like that, but this time the words struck her like stones. She drew herself up. Waited.

"I will have you committed!" he thundered, storming toward her, and for one terrifying moment, she thought he might actually strike her. Or drop over from apoplexy, right at her feet.

"I am of sound mind and body," she said evenly. "And I can prove it."

The judge flung his arms out wide. "Oh, you're doing a fine job of that!" he raged. "Look at you—look at this place!" He turned his narrowed gaze on Angelina, and then Raul. "And as for *you* *pe*ople—stabbing me in the back after all I've done for you!"

"Father," Lorelei interceded, "please be calm. There's a vein jumping in your right temple. I fear it might rupture."

The judge pointed toward his buggy. "Enough of this nonsense, Lorelei. Get into that rig this instant. We're going back to town!"

"No," Lorelei said. "I will not."

Her father took a step toward her, and Raul moved to block his way.

Lorelei was touched by Raul's gallantry; he was afraid

of the judge, like most everyone else in San Antonio, and not without reason. Still, he wanted to protect her.

The judge tugged at his tie. He was dressed much too warmly for such a hot day, and he was sweating copiously. The vein in his temple still pulsed visibly. "Hitch up that wagon, Raul," he said in a dangerous tone, so low that Lorelei had to strain to hear it. "Take your wife and get as far from San Antonio as you can, because your hide isn't worth a nickel around here. Not after what you've done."

The muscles in Raul's shoulders quivered, but he stood his ground.

Angelina, meanwhile, took the judge's arm. "Come," she said. "Sit down. We'll discuss the matter calmly—"

He shook her off, and the look in his eyes was so full of hatred that Lorelei, standing beside Raul now, recoiled when her father's gaze sliced to her.

"You've been a trial to me from the day of your birth," he snarled. "Well, I wash my hands of you, do you hear me? *I am through.*"

Inwardly, Lorelei winced, but if Raul could face down a tiger, so could she.

Angelina whispered some sad imprecation in Spanish.

"Your mother," the judge went on ruthlessly, "was a madwoman and a slut. You're no better."

"Why do you keep saying that?" Lorelei asked, feeling as though she'd been lashed.

The judge indulged in an ugly little smile. "Ask Angelina," he said. "She'll tell you about it. Won't you, Angelina?"

Out of the corner of her eye, Lorelei saw Angelina lower her head.

"Angelina?" Lorelei whispered.

But Angelina shook her head. "Not now," she said weakly. "Not now."

The judge came to stand directly in front of Lorelei, leaning in so close that she could feel his breath on her face, hot as the winds of hell itself. "You'll fail, Lorelei," he told her softly. "You'll run through that money you filched from my bank account in no time at all. You'll have Templeton trying to drive you out from one side, and John Cavanagh's 'son' from the other. Do not think for *one blessed moment* that I'll take you in after this."

Lorelei didn't dare speak, or even move. If she broke down and cried, she might never be able to stop.

Her father turned, walked unsteadily back toward the buggy. Once he'd gotten in and taken up the reins, he turned to deliver one last salvo.

"From this day forward," he said, "you are no longer my daughter."

Angelina put an arm around Lorelei, holding her up.

She watched mutely as the judge drove away.

"Come, Chiquita," Angelina said presently. "You must sit down. I'll make you a cup of tea."

Lorelei watched her father out of sight, his words echoing in her head.

*From this day forward, you are no longer my daughter.*

Angelina patted her hand. "Come," she repeated, and when Lorelei looked at her face, she saw that Angelina was weeping.

"Tell me what you know about my mother," Lorelei said, digging in her heels. She would not take another step until she got an answer, and Angelina must have known that, because she exchanged a sorrowful look with

Raul. He touched Lorelei's shoulder, lightly, briefly, and walked away, leaving the two women alone.

"She did not go to a hospital, Chiquita. She went to an asylum. She's not in that grave behind St. Ambrose's."

Lorelei's knees nearly buckled. She'd been visiting an *empty* grave all these years? "That's impossible—all if it is impossible!"

"I knew Selma very well," Angelina said calmly, her face wet with the memories. "I raised her, just as I raised you."

Lorelei reeled. Had her mother been a *madwoman?*

# CHAPTER 16

THERE WAS STILL no word from the governor.

Holt resigned himself to a trip to Austin, even though he couldn't spare the time, and proceeded to hunt down a lawyer. He had bad luck with that, too. None of the three candidates for the job were willing to say so outright, but they were all afraid of Judge Fellows, Isaac Templeton or both.

He went to see Gabe, bringing the dog along with him.

Gabe wouldn't so much as glance his way, let alone talk. He just sat there on his cot, hands clasped, staring at the wall. Playing the stoic savage.

"I told you," Holt said miserably, "that Melina wouldn't stay in Waco, once she knew you were behind bars."

Gabe didn't answer. Didn't move.

"To hell with you, then," Holt said. "Hang if you want to."

He didn't mean it, and Gabe knew that as well as Holt did, but he was wasting his time trying to get that damn Indian to see reason.

He took himself off to the nearest saloon, the dog beside him, and ordered a whiskey. A man stepped up beside him, but Holt didn't trouble himself to see who it was.

"Well, hell," drawled a familiar voice. "Looks like I was right to come. From the looks of you, that mangy hound dog is the only friend you've got."

Holt stiffened, turned his head, full of hope and wild annoyance.

His brother Rafe, trail-worn and dirty, with several days' worth of beard casting a dark shadow over half his face, raised his glass in an easy salute. "Aren't you going to welcome your favorite brother to Texas?" he asked.

Holt felt a corner of his mouth kick upward. "Who says you're my favorite brother?" he countered. Truth was, he was a little choked up, and damned if he wanted Rafe to know it.

Rafe laughed. "I'm the one who rode all the way down here to make sure your sorry ass was all right," he said. "I reckon that entitles me to be the favorite."

Holt frowned as the implications of Rafe's presence started hitting home, one right after another. "You've got a wife and baby at home. You shouldn't have left them."

"And I've got a brother here, even if he *is* a cussed bastard," Rafe said affably, refilling his glass from Holt's bottle. "Emmeline and the baby are fine, and they've got a whole family of other McKettricks looking after them. You, on the other hand, seem to have nobody but this old dog."

Sorrowful gave a little whine. Holt plucked a pickled egg from the crock on the bar and fed it to him.

"How's Lizzie?" Holt asked, fishing for a second egg.

"Fine," Rafe answered, shaking his head as Sorrowful gulped it down. "She misses you, but Pa's buying her a surrey all her own, and Concepcion lets her help with little Katie after school every day, so she's feeling pretty frisky."

Katie was their baby sister, just two years old and already talking back to everybody, including the old man, with the best of them.

"Did Pa put you up to this?"

Rafe grinned. "Nope. Kade and Jeb and I drew lots."

"And you lost?"

Rafe slapped him on the back. "I shouldn't admit it, since you're already bigheaded," he said, "but I won."

Holt swallowed. The dog pawed at his leg, wanting another pickled egg. Holt refused the request with a shake of his head, and Sorrowful lay down with a philosophical sigh.

"I saw the gallows they're building outside the courthouse," Rafe said quietly. "I reckon that means your friend is still behind bars."

Glumly, Holt nodded. "Yeah," he said, discouraged all over again.

Rafe set his glass down on the bar. "What else is going on?"

"I bought John Cavanagh's ranch," Holt answered, after weighing the matter in his mind for a few moments.

Rafe narrowed his eyes. "You bought a ranch? I thought you figured on coming back to the Triple M when you got things squared away down here."

"I haven't changed my mind about that. John's not getting any younger, though, and his back was to the wall. The bank was about to take the whole outfit and hand it over to a rancher named Templeton." The bartender offered another bottle, and Holt shook his head, laid a few coins on the bar. "When the time comes, I'll deed the place back to him and ride for Arizona."

"If you wanted to help Cavanagh," Rafe wondered aloud, "why didn't you just give him the money to pay off the bank?"

Holt sighed. "Templeton was bearing down hard on John. I guess I was looking to draw his fire."

Rafe rubbed the back of his neck. Sighed. "I reckon that makes sense," he said with a slow grin, "in a McKettrick sort of way. You got a bunkhouse on this ranch of yours? I could use a hot bath and about twelve hours' sleep."

"You probably won't get the sleep," Holt allowed, grinning back. He'd never have asked Rafe to come down to Texas, but, at the same time, he was glad of his company. "I'll heat the water for the bath myself, though. Consider it a community service."

Rafe gave a hoot of laughter. "Well, unless you've got some other business in town, we'd better ride. We can reason out some kind of plan on the road."

Sorrowful got to his feet as Rafe and Holt turned to leave the bar.

Rafe's gelding, Chief, was tied to the hitching rail out front, and Holt was irritated with himself for not having noticed the horse earlier. None of the McKettrick horses were branded, but the familiar mark, three *M*'s, interwoven, was tooled into the leather of Rafe's saddle, for anybody to see.

"Aren't you forgetting something?" Rafe asked, untying Chief and mounting up with the ease of a man who'd been riding longer than he'd been walking on his own two feet.

Holt climbed into the saddle and whistled to the dog. Sorrowful jumped up in front of him and perched on the pommel like a bird on a branch. "Like what?" he asked, honestly baffled.

"Like Margaret," Rafe said.

Holt swore under his breath. He ought to be shot for a rounder, the way he treated women. First he'd gone off and left Olivia alone and carrying his baby, then he'd completely forgotten the mail-order bride he'd sent for and courted and finally abandoned.

Rafe's grin flashed white in his unwashed face. "No need to fret about her, Big Brother," he said. "Seth Bates, over on the Southern Cross, asked her to dance right after you rode out. When the preacher finally showed up, Margaret put her fancy gown back on and married old Seth on the spot."

"I'll be damned," Holt said, thinking he was a son of a bitch for being irritated. "Didn't take her long."

Rafe laughed. "I guess she had her mind set on getting married that day. Hell, we had the cake right there handy, and the preacher, and all those people dressed up and primed to celebrate. Seemed like a practical decision to me."

They headed for the outskirts of town, following the river road.

There was a ripping sound. The dog looked up at him with confidence in his charitable nature, and Holt decided the pickled eggs had been a bad idea.

"WHAT WAS SHE LIKE?" Lorelei asked numbly. Seated on a rock down by the stream, she held a cup of Angelina's tea in both hands. "Was my mother really insane?"

Angelina stared out at the water, watching light frolic on the surface. "No," she said, in a tone of remembrance. "It began after William was born. She grew morose. Wouldn't eat and wandered the house at all hours of the night, as if she'd misplaced something and wanted to find it. The judge was patient at first—took her to doctors as far away as Houston. They said it sometimes happened after a woman had a child, and there was nothing they could do. She was better for a while, and then—"

"And then she had me," Lorelei murmured. "Is that what you were going to say?"

Angelina met her gaze. Her eyes were swollen with misery. "Yes," she answered. "She used to push you around in a little carriage, then leave you places and forget where. Once, when I'd gone to do the marketing, she decided to give you a bath, and then got distracted and went off to do something else. You would have drowned if little William hadn't climbed up onto a stool and pulled you out of that basin."

Lorelei closed her eyes.

"The judge sent her away, then—to this ranch. Said her own people would have to look after her. But poor William cried so—sometimes he couldn't catch his breath, he'd get so wrought up. Night and day, he called for her. So, finally, your father brought her back home."

Lorelei waited.

"When you were three, Selma finally broke down completely." Angelina choked, dashed at her cheek with the back of one hand. "William fell out of a tree in the backyard—just a little gash to his head, but there was a lot of blood. Didn't even knock him out. When Selma saw him lying there, stunned and bleeding, she started screaming and didn't stop until Dr. Carson came and gave her medicine. She didn't speak at all then—didn't seem to know any of the rest of us were there. Even seeing that William was all right didn't bring her around. She just sat in that rocking chair in the parlor and stared at the wall, like she saw horrible things happening there."

Lorelei put a hand over her mouth, waiting out a wave of emotion. "How long did Mama live, after she went to the asylum?"

"Six months or so," Angelina said, watching the stream again. "Then one day a letter came, saying she was gone."

Lorelei leaned forward, spilling her tea to the ground, and pressed her face to her knees. She was full of sorrow, fair bursting with it, but no tears would come. Angelina stroked her back.

"There, now," she said.

"Maybe that's why I've never married," Lorelei said, straightening as she drew a deep breath. "Maybe I'd go crazy, too, if I had babies."

"Child," Angelina scolded tenderly. "There is no reason to think such a thing." But when she met Lorelei's gaze, her eyes were worried.

# CHAPTER 17

HOLT TOOK CARE to go around Lorelei's place, lest he run into her again. The decision, though prudent, left him feeling oddly disjointed. He'd seen that buggy racing along the trail earlier, after his bath in the creek, and guessed who was driving it: the judge, mad as a wet cat.

Holt and Rafe crossed the creek more than a mile downstream, the dog still riding with Holt. When they rode into the dooryard at John's place, Tillie appeared on the porch, and her face lit up when she saw Sorrowful. He let out a yelp of delight and loped toward her.

Rafe looked on curiously as Tillie knelt, so she and the hound could wrestle in the tall grass. John came out on the porch and raised a tentative hand to Holt. No doubt he figured Rafe for a cowboy, hired in town.

"Where's Mr. Cavanagh?" Rafe asked.

"That's him," Holt answered.

Old Angus McKettrick had done one thing right; he'd raised his three younger sons to measure a man by what he did, not the color of his skin. Rafe, Kade and Jeb were equally ornery to just about everybody.

"I'll be damned," Rafe said. "You never said he was a black man."

"You never asked," Holt replied, dismounting. By then, Holt's foster father was within earshot. "John, meet my brother, Rafe McKettrick."

Rafe nodded. "Mr. Cavanagh," he said.

A broad smile broke over John's face. He thrust out a hand, and Rafe shook it.

"There's a powerful resemblance," John said.

Rafe's grin was even broader than John's. "Since I don't reckon you really intended to insult me right out of the chute like that," he said, "I will not take that remark to heart."

John laughed, hooked his thumbs under his suspenders. "You come all the way from the Arizona Territory?"

"Yes, sir," Rafe said. "I did."

"I'll show you to the bunkhouse," Holt told him.

"You can't put your own brother in the bunkhouse," John protested. "There's a spare bed in your room. He can sleep there."

Rafe passed Holt a sidelong glance. "Thanks," he said.

John turned to address his daughter. "Tillie, stop messin' with that dog and put on some coffee. Get them peach pies out of the pantry, too."

Tillie scrambled to her feet, rubbing her hands off on her skirts and looking Rafe over. "Who's that man?" she wanted to know.

"Rafe McKettrick, ma'am," Rafe said, taking off his hat and giving a polite nod. "Pleased to meet you."

She took a wary step toward them. "You bring me anything from town, Holt?" she wanted to know.

Holt pulled a penny bag of gumdrops from his shirt pocket and held it out to her. "You save those until after supper," he said, knowing she wouldn't. Ever since

Tillie'd been no taller than the pump handle, she'd had a penchant for gumdrops.

"She's not quite right in the head," John said regretfully, after she dashed into the house to make the coffee and get out the pies.

"If she can bake a peach pie," Rafe reasoned, "she's right enough."

At that, John smiled again. "She's a good girl," he said fondly.

Right about then, Kahill came out of the bunkhouse. Holt wondered why he wasn't out looking for strays with the other six men he'd hired. Hoped Mac hadn't grown up to be a slacker.

"You sick or something?" Holt asked.

Rafe looked on, pulling off his leather gloves. He didn't introduce himself.

Kahill responded with a crooked grin. "No, sir, Mr. McKettrick. I only came back because my horse threw a shoe." He looked up, checking the sky. "It's about quitting time anyhow, so I just stayed."

John spoke up. "I'd appreciate it if you'd put up these horses," he said. "Rafe here's had a long, hard ride."

Mac was chewing on a matchstick, and he rolled it from one side of his mouth to the other. He waited a beat too long to say, "Yes, sir, I'll do that." Hesitated again before he took Chief's reins in one hand and the Appaloosa's in the other.

"Thanks," Holt said, as Kahill started to lead the animals away, toward the barn.

"Anytime," Kahill drawled in response.

John headed for the house, but Holt and Rafe tarried, staring after Kahill and the horses.

Rafe spoke in an undertone. "What rock did he crawl out from under?"

MELINA WAS IN the kitchen, peeling potatoes for supper, and Captain Jack sat at the table, playing solitaire and nursing a glass of John's best whiskey. The Captain had a cot in the bunkhouse, and Melina shared Tillie's room.

By Holt's count, the place was getting a bit too crowded.

He introduced Rafe all over again. Melina nodded, without smiling, and went back to her potato peeling. Holt knew by the way she bit her lower lip that she wanted to ask about Gabe, but for some reason, she held back. He moved toward her, meaning to confide that Navarro was in good health, though in a sour mood.

"I knew your pa," the Captain told Rafe. "Liked old Angus McKettrick, even if he was a bit of a rough customer."

On his way past Tillie, who was coming out of the pantry with a pie tin balanced on each palm, Holt stopped so suddenly that the two of them nearly collided. It was Rafe who saved the pies.

Holt had ridden with Walton the whole time he was in the Rangers, and the Captain had never said a word about knowing the old man. Not one damn word.

"What did you just say?" he snapped.

The Captain grinned, pleased with himself. "Didn't I mention that?"

Rafe put the pies on the table, his glance moving from the Captain to Holt. Curious, and a little amused.

"No," Holt ground out, "you didn't mention it!"

"Knew your ma, too," the Captain said. "Pretty little thing. Not too sturdy, though."

Rafe hung his hat from a peg on the wall, next to the door.

The silence was thick as mud.

"Old Dill, now, that uncle of yours," the Captain went

on, with a little shake of his head. "Not worth a tinker's damn."

Holt's mouth fell open. He closed it again, shot a look in John's direction.

"I didn't tell him any of this," Cavanagh was quick to say.

Rafe pulled back a chair and sat down, admiring Tillie's peach pies.

Holt sank into a chair of his own. "Why didn't you say anything?" he asked the Captain. "All those years on the trail, fighting Comanches, sleeping in the mud, picking weevils out of the damned flour when there was anything to eat besides beans, and you never thought to mention—"

"You didn't ask me," the Captain interrupted.

Rafe chuckled at that. Tillie set a cup of coffee in front of him, along with a plate and fork, then sliced the pie and gave him a piece the size of an anvil.

He thanked her cordially, took up his fork and turned his gaze back to Walton. "How well did you know our pa?" he asked, chewing.

THAT NIGHT, while Rafe was settling his oversized frame in the bed next to Holt's, he turned chatty as a spinster at a tea party.

"How'd you come to live with John Cavanagh?" he asked, after a hearty sigh of contentment. He'd probably slept along the trail all the way down from the Triple M and was glad to stretch out on a real mattress again.

"What the hell do you care?"

Rafe chuckled. "I don't, really," he said. "But since it obviously isn't something you want to talk about, I mean to persist until you tell me."

Holt sighed eloquently. Out of the corner of his eye,

he saw Rafe lying there with his hands behind his head, smiling up at the ceiling. He did have the look of a man who could yammer all night if he felt disposed to do so.

"I ran away from home when I was sixteen. John caught me stealing eggs out of his chicken coop, figured I needed seeing to and took me in. Are you satisfied?"

"Nope," Rafe said. "There's more I want to know. Like how a black man came to own a place like this. On the ride out here, you said this ranch measures a thousand acres. That's a lot of land. Must have cost plenty, even in the old days."

"Before the war," Holt said, letting his mind reach back and take hold of what he remembered, "John was a slave. He joined up with the Buffalo Soldiers, and he and two other men came upon a couple of wounded Rebels one day, in a gully. His friends wanted to bayonet them and be done with it. John wouldn't have it, and when the Yanks rode out, he stayed behind to do what he could for the Rebs. One of them asked him to get word to his folks, out here in Texas, once he died. John stayed with those boys until they'd breathed their last, and then, figuring he'd catch hell from his captain for consorting with the enemy if he went back to camp, he decided to keep his promise in person, instead of writing a letter. Along the way, he met his wife—she was running away from a plantation in Tennessee. When the two of them finally got to San Antonio, the dead Rebel's mother had already passed on from worry and yellow fever, and his father was sickly. Said the news of his boy's death would be the finish of him, and it was, but before he gave up the ghost, he deeded his homestead and a hundred head of cattle over to John." Holt paused. "Is that enough, or would you like to hear something else that's none of your damned business?"

Rafe laughed. "In the three years I've known you," he said, "I don't believe I've ever heard you say that many words all together, let alone at once. I reckon I'll just content myself with that."

"Good." Holt jerked the covers up to his neck and rolled onto his side, turning his back to the other bed.

"There's one more thing, though," Rafe said.

*"What?"*

"I snore."

He sure as hell did.

HOLT, RAFE AND JOHN were on the range the next morning, trying to haul a bawling heifer out of a mud hole with rope and cursing, when the riders appeared. A dozen of them, lining the rim of the nearest hill like a Comanche war party.

"Company," muttered Rafe, brushing the butt of his .45 with the backs of his fingers.

Three of the riders started down the gentle slope—a fat man in a fancy suit, flanked by two cowhands with rifles resting across the pommels of their saddles.

"Isaac Templeton," John said quietly. "He'll be put out that you didn't go over to his place for a visit, Holt."

"Will he, now?" Holt breathed, keeping his eyes on the man in the middle.

Templeton stopped a dozen yards away, pulled out a handkerchief and wiped the sweat off his broad, whiskered face. "Holt McKettrick, unless I miss my guess," he said.

Holt didn't answer.

"It's customary for a newcomer to greet his neighbors with a proper how-do-you-do," Templeton said. His beady gaze drifted to Rafe, who had drawn his pistol. "I'd put that away if I were you. As you can see, my men have the advantage, carrying rifles as they are. You pull that trigger, and you'll be dead before you hit the ground."

"Maybe," Rafe said. "But I'll put a bullet through your heart on the way down."

Holt thought of Emmeline, Rafe's wife, and little Georgia. He stepped between Rafe and Templeton. His brother spat a curse, and Holt knew there would be a row later—if he and Rafe were lucky enough to live that long.

"Your business is with me," he told the Englishman. The cow bawled, still stuck fast and probably wondering why nobody was doing anything about it.

Templeton gave a slight, vicious smile. His gaze flickered briefly to John, lit on Rafe for a moment, then bored into Holt. "We've gotten off to a poor beginning," the big man said. "I want this land. I'm prepared to pay handsomely for it. Neither I nor my men mean you any harm."

"Send them away, then," John said.

Templeton hesitated, then waved the men off.

Reluctantly, they wheeled their horses around and went to join the rest of the bunch, up on top of the hill.

"I'm not selling," Holt told Templeton.

Templeton wiped his brow again and sighed. "I fear I have offended you, bringing these cowpunchers along," he said, with a poor attempt at regret.

"Those aren't cowpunchers," Rafe put in tersely. "They're hired guns."

Again, Templeton sighed. "I'm trying to be reasonable," he said. "Perhaps I should have approached Miss Fellows first. You do know that she's moved onto the old Hanson place?"

Holt's back teeth came down so hard they nearly severed his tongue. "You stay away from her," he said.

Templeton raised a bushy eyebrow, and his mustache, the size of a horse's tail, quivered. He leaned forward to rest his thick arms on the horn of his saddle. "Sweet on her, are you?" he asked smoothly. "Well, well." He ruminated a bit, studying Holt as if he were a hair in his soup. "You're new around here, so I guess it's my neighborly duty to warn you that Miss Lorelei is a known hellcat. Unstable, too."

Holt took a step toward him, felt Rafe's fingers close on his upper arm.

"She's a silly woman," Templeton confided, with gentlemanly resignation. "Probably thinks she can make that place pay, with two Mexicans to help her and no cattle. She'll come around to my way of thinking soon enough." He paused thoughtfully. "Maybe I ought to marry her. Send her off to England to live with my mother." He laughed, savoring some private thought. "Serve them both right."

Holt felt heat surge up his neck to throb along his jawline, and he silently cursed himself. It was one thing for the Englishman to get under his hide, and another to let him know it.

"I'd give Miss Lorelei credit for more sense than to take up with the likes of you," Holt said.

"Would you?" Templeton asked pleasantly. "She took up with Creighton Bannings. That tells me she's not too choosey, and the judge, well—he'd do just about anything to marry her off. Especially if it meant he'd get the twenty-five thousand dollars I'm willing to pay for that land." He lowered his voice. "Financial problems, you know. It's a shame."

Holt consciously relaxed his jaw. "Are you through?

Because if you are, we've got a heifer to drag out of the mud."

"No, Mr. McKettrick," Templeton said, in a mild tone, "I am not through. Not by a long ways. But I'll leave our…negotiations for another day."

"Save yourself the ride," Holt replied.

"Holt," John said, "shut your mouth."

"Good advice," Templeton put in. Then, calm as a nun in a chapel, he turned his horse around and rode off to rejoin his men.

Within a few minutes, they'd all vanished over the hilltop.

Rafe gave Holt a hard shove from behind. "Don't you ever get in my way like that again!" he rasped, when Holt whirled to face him.

"I wouldn't mind a fight, Rafe," he said, clenching his fists. "Right now I really wouldn't mind a fight."

Rafe beckoned with the fingers of both hands, his face hard with fury.

"Come on, then," he answered. "I'd be glad to accommodate you."

John stepped between them, standing sideways with one palm on Rafe's chest and one on Holt's. "Damn it," he growled, "if either one of you throws a punch, I'll personally chuck you into that mud hole headfirst!"

Rafe and Holt glared at each other, both of them seething, their breath coming hard, but neither of them moved.

John waited them out.

"Why don't you just go back to the Triple M?" Holt snapped, heading back toward the cow and picking up the rope.

"Why don't you just go to hell?" Rafe retorted.

"I'll be goddamned," John said.

All of a sudden, Rafe grinned. He was like that. Unpredictable. "Were you really a Buffalo Soldier?"

"I'm *still* a Buffalo Soldier," John answered. "And right now, I'm giving the orders on this place." He glowered at Holt. "Regardless of whose name is on the deed."

Holt felt like he was sixteen again, learning to do as he was told, and he didn't like it one bit. Just the same, he got behind that no-account heifer and pushed.

Rafe put a shoulder to the other flank. "I'd like to meet this Lorelei woman," he said. "I think Templeton was right about one thing. You're sweet on her."

Holt flushed, and he hated that as much as he hated feeling like a kid and pushing on a cow's ass. "The hell I am," he growled, putting all his strength into the task of separating the heifer and the mud hole. "The only thing Templeton got right was that she's a hellion."

Out front, with the rope in both hands, John laughed. "She's a mighty pretty one," he said. "Make you a fine wife."

Holt cursed. The cow came loose with a sucking sound and an infuriated squall, and he and Rafe both tumbled into the mud. They sat there like a couple of fools, staring at each other, and then Rafe threw back his head and gave a shout of laughter.

Holt did his best to stay angry, but it was a wasted effort. He gave a delighted howl of his own.

John stood watching them, his hands on his hips, and shook his head.

"Must be somethin' about that Arizona sun," he said. "Bakes a man's brain."

# CHAPTER 18

LORELEI HAD NEVER had to deal with problems before—not practical ones, at least. Her father had provided food, shelter, clothing and a modicum of education, if little else. She had never had to do physical labor of any sort—Angelina, Raul and a variety of housemaids had done that. She didn't know one end of a cow from the other—much less how to buy, husband and sell the creatures—and she had never once ridden a horse. And now she had to sort through the brutal truth about her mother.

She was daunted, that steaming morning, as she watched the freight man at work. Now that the mud had dried up, he'd come back to reclaim his wagon, leading a team of sturdy-looking mules behind him.

She was also strangely exhilarated, as if she'd just been rehearsing all these years and now her life had truly begun.

*That's what I need,* she thought, with resolution. *A mule.*

Intending to ask Raul to approach the freight man and ask if he would sell one of the animals, she turned and scanned the property. Raul was on top of the roof, nailing the tent tarp in place. Angelina was downstream, trying to catch fish for their supper.

If the mule was to be purchased, it was up to her to initiate the process.

The driver was a surly sort. He smelled, he cursed and he was constantly spitting a stream of disgusting tobacco into the grass.

After drawing a deep breath and holding it for a moment, Lorelei employed her exhalation to thrust her into motion.

"Excuse me, sir," she said.

The driver ignored her, but spat again, narrowly missing the hem of her ready-made calico dress.

Lorelei bristled and held her skirts aside. "Sir," she repeated.

At last, the man stopped, studying her with amused contempt. Then he executed a mocking bow. "Yes, ma'am," he drawled. "What is it?"

"I would like to buy one of these mules, if you have a mind to sell."

He took a round tin from the pocket of his sweat-soaked shirt and grubbed out a pinch of snuff with one filthy fingertip. "That right?"

Lorelei cringed inwardly as he poked the tobacco into his mouth. Because she wanted to retreat, she forced herself to take one step forward. "How much?"

The freight man rubbed his stained and stubbled chin, chewing and spitting again before he answered, "These are fine mules. Hardworking. Stubborn, though. Right stubborn." He ruminated, both on the snuff and his decision. "I reckon I could hand over old Seesaw here for, say, fifty dollars." He laid one hand on the flank of a pitiful-looking beast with patches of his mud-brown coat missing.

"Fifty dollars seems excessive," Lorelei said, peering at the animal.

"Whatever that means," said the driver, with a desultory shrug.

"It means I think it's too much," Lorelei replied, though in truth she had no idea what a mule—stubborn, mangy or otherwise—should cost. For all she knew, she was getting a bargain.

"All right," came the reply, after more rumination and spitting. "Thirty-five dollars, and that's as low as I'm willing to go."

Lorelei approached the mule, reached out a tentative hand to touch his rough, dusty coat. Seesaw turned his head and brayed, causing her to start. "Can he be ridden?" she inquired uncertainly.

"Yes," said the freight man. "But he does have his own set of ideas about some things."

"Then we ought to get along," Lorelei decided.

"Thirty-five dollars," reiterated the driver.

"Does that include a saddle and bridle?"

The freightman sighed. "I've got an old halter I can let you have," he said. "But that's the best I can do for what you're payin' me."

Lorelei considered the proposition again, then nodded. "I'll get your money," she said, and made for the house.

Seesaw was waiting patiently under a nearby oak tree, his halter rope dangling, when she returned with the agreed-upon payment.

The driver counted the money, folded it and tucked it into his shirt pocket, behind the round snoose can. "Thank you kindly," he said, with a little smirk, tossing the shovel he'd used to dig out the wagon into the back and then turning his attention to the task of hitching two of the remaining three mules to the rigging. He tied the third to the tailgate and set out for the road.

Raul, having cast several curious glances in Lorelei's direction over the course of the transaction, made his way down off the roof and came to stand beside her, watching as mules and man trundled up the slope and onto the trail, headed for San Antonio.

"You bought this mule, *señorita?*" Raul asked.

Lorelei, who'd been watching the team and wagon, turned to look at Raul, expecting disapproval. To her surprise, Angelina's husband was grinning broadly.

"Yes," she said. "His name is Seesaw."

Raul left her side to examine the mule, running practiced hands over Seesaw's legs, checking the animal's hooves and teeth. "He will be good for plowing," he said, when his inspection was complete.

"Plowing? I intend to ride him," Lorelei said.

Raul went still, as if he'd just run across a snake or a scorpion in the wood pile. "*Ride* him? But, *señorita,* you have never—"

"I've never done a lot of things, Raul," Lorelei broke in. "That doesn't mean they're impossible."

"But, *señorita,* he—"

Lorelei joined Raul beside the mule. "Help me onto his back," she said. She was afraid, even terrified, but she knew that waiting would not lessen her fear.

Raul's eyes rounded, and he shook his head. "No, *señorita*—I cannot."

"Fine," Lorelei said. "I'll stand on a box, then."

"Señorita, please—"

Lorelei started for the house again. They'd chopped up most of the crates from the mercantile for firewood, but there were still one or two left.

"Wait!" Raul called, with a note of desperation that

made Lorelei stop and turn around to look at him. "I will ride him first."

Raul was an accomplished horseman, so this approach made sense to her. "All right, then," she said, and waited.

Raul threw the halter rope over the mule's neck, then sprang nimbly onto his back.

That was when they learned why the beast was called Seesaw.

He pitched forward, then back, while Raul clung valiantly with both hands and both legs. Seesaw brayed fit to raise the dead from their slumber, and kicked both hind feet straight out.

Raul flew over the animal's head, turning a perfect somersault in midair, then landed on his back in the deep grass. Seesaw returned to his grazing, as casually as if the whole incident had never happened.

Lorelei, momentarily paralyzed with shock, broke free and rushed toward Raul, who was muttering in Spanish between gasps.

"Are you hurt?" Lorelei cried, dropping to her knees beside him. At the periphery of her vision, she saw Angelina drop her catch of shiny trout, pick up her skirts and hurry in their direction.

"No," Raul gasped. "Just let me—catch my breath—"

Angelina, arriving on the scene, helped her husband to sit up.

"Raul!" she cried.

"I think I've been taken," Lorelei lamented, standing up.

"*Madre de Dios,*" Angelina murmured.

DAMNED IF SHE HADN'T found herself a mule, Holt thought, as he and Rafe rode across the creek, with

Melina behind them on a little spotted pony borrowed from John. Lorelei teetered on top of an overturned box, just about to swing one leg over the critter's back.

"You didn't tell me we were going to see a rodeo," Rafe said dryly.

Holt spurred the Appaloosa up the bank onto Lorelei's spread, his gut suddenly wedged up between his collarbones. She met his gaze with what looked, from that distance, like pure defiance, and mounted the mule.

For a moment, all of time seemed to stop.

The bees didn't buzz.

The creek, if it ran at all, ran silently.

Earth and Heaven waited and watched.

And the show wasn't long in coming.

The mule came unwrapped, splintering the box Lorelei had used as a mounting block with one thrust of its hind legs. Lorelei was hurled forward, clinging to the animal's neck with both arms.

Holt cursed and spurred Traveler to hurry.

The mule leaped in circles, moving so fast that Holt and the Appaloosa had a hell of a time drawing Traveler up alongside. When at long last he did, Holt leaned down, hooked an arm around Lorelei's waist and dragged her off the mule and onto the saddle in front of him. The Appaloosa damn near took a kick to the chest getting out of the way.

Once they were at a safe distance from the furious mule, who was still putting on quite an exhibition, Holt let Lorelei down to the ground and dismounted in one motion, planting himself square in front of her.

"What the—?" he rasped, and then found that everything else he wanted to say was log-jammed behind the knot of pure, terrified fury sticking in his throat.

Lorelei reddened, glaring up at him. "How dare you?" she sputtered. "How *dare* you?"

Somewhere nearby, Rafe gave a hoot of laughter.

Holt didn't spare his brother a glance. Couldn't look away from Lorelei. He wanted to shake her, wanted, conversely, to check her for broken bones, the way he would a horse after a bad fall. He jammed his face to within an inch of hers and spoke through his teeth.

*"How dare I?"* he countered. "I probably just saved your life!"

She shook out her skirts, straightened her spine and touched one hand to her hair, which was tumbling in ebony loops around her neck and shoulders. This last was the only sign of hesitation she gave as she stood toe-to-toe with him. "I could have ridden that mule!" she yelled.

"Hallelujah," said Rafe.

"Shut up," Holt growled, without looking away from Lorelei's face.

"Don't you *dare* use rude language with me!" Lorelei raged. Her eyes flashed with temper, her face was flushed and Holt felt the most contrary urge to kiss her.

So he did. He grabbed her by the shoulders, pulled her even closer and covered her mouth with his.

Dazed and breathless, she slapped him, hard. But it was definitely an afterthought.

# CHAPTER 19

"Where are Raul and Angelina?" Holt asked, the first to break the thrumming silence, one hand to his slap-stung cheek.

Lorelei thrust her shoulders back and lifted her chin, putting Holt in mind of some beautiful bird, settling its feathers after a battle. He thought for sure she wouldn't answer, might slap him again or even spit in his face. But then she sagged a little. "Raul is in the house, lying down," she admitted grudgingly. "Angelina is with him."

At last, she took in Melina, watching with a slight smile from her spotted pony, and Rafe, grinning like a fool.

Rafe tugged at his hat brim, always mannerly with the ladies. "Howdy," he said. "I'm Rafe McKettrick. Holt here is my brother, but I hope you won't hold that against me."

Lorelei's struggle to keep a sober countenance was visible, but she finally lost the battle and spared Rafe a tenuous smile. Somehow, that made Holt half again as riled as the slap had.

"I guess you can't be blamed for an accident of birth," she said.

Holt seethed. He'd lost his hat in the tussle, getting Lorelei off the back of that goddamned mule, and he stormed through the deep grass to recover it. He bent at the waist and snatched it up, slamming it onto his head. Serve that fool woman right if he'd let her finish the ride, he thought.

In the meantime, Rafe must have introduced Lorelei to Melina, because the two of them were shaking hands, Melina leaning down as best she could from the pony's back and smiling.

Lorelei was cordial as could be—until she turned to face Holt again. She looked like every storm that had ever broken, all compressed into one lightning-eyed woman. "If my mule has been injured in any way," she said, "I shall expect you to pay for it. I have thirty-five dollars invested in that animal."

Holt was mad enough to spit, and he would have, too, if his mouth hadn't gone dry as a dead seed pod, fallen to parched ground. "Your damned mule," he drawled, measuring out each word, "is the least of my concerns right now!"

"Guess I'd better see if this Raul fella is all right," Rafe said, swinging down from his horse.

Holt whistled to the Appaloosa, which was keeping its distance from the mule, now calmly nibbling grass under the oak tree. He checked the gelding over closely, and was relieved to find it sound. The blood was still roaring in his ears, and his heart was in a sprint, though he couldn't rightly have said whether it was the one-woman rodeo event or the kiss that had put him in this pitiful state.

"If you make friends with that mule," Melina said to

Lorelei, stringing together more words than Holt had heard her say at one time since he'd known her, "he'll let you ride him."

"You're not helping the situation, Melina," Holt told her.

She merely smiled and got down awkwardly from the pony's back to survey the property. "Is this yours?" she asked.

Lorelei looked proud, which went to show how damned little she knew about ranching. It was hard, heartbreaking work, and a good man was as likely to go bust as break even, never mind a town-bred woman who didn't have the good sense to know when she was betting on the wrong hand of cards.

"Yes," she said.

"It's a fine spread," Melina replied. "Lots of grass. Plenty of water."

Lorelei nodded.

Holt muttered something he wouldn't have said in the presence of ladies if he hadn't been pushed to the last heel-digging inch of his patience, and they both ignored him.

"You need any hired help?" Melina asked.

Holt gaped at her.

Lorelei pressed her lips together and shook her head with what looked like genuine regret.

"I know a little about buying cattle," Melina persisted.

About that time, Rafe came out of the house, if that shack could be called a house.

"Raul's in need of a doctor," he told the general company. "I think he's fractured a couple of ribs. Angelina's fit to be tied, she's so worried."

Lorelei reacted as though she'd been struck, hard. The

high color drained out of her face, and for a moment Holt thought she was going to swoon. Hell of a thing if he had to rescue her again, he reflected, even as he braced himself to catch her before she went down.

She pushed past Rafe and headed for the house at a lope.

"Better get that man to town," Rafe said, with a thrust of one thumb to indicate the cabin and Raul. "If one of his ribs comes loose, it could stab right through his lung. I've seen it happen."

Holt had plans for that day, and taking an injured man to town for medical care wasn't on the list, but the situation didn't leave much leeway. He noticed the buckboard under a stand of oak trees and looked around for the team. In the distance, he saw two bay horses, drinking from the creek.

"Hell," he growled, and mounted Traveler to bring them in. "See if the rigging is in the wagon bed," he told Rafe.

Half an hour later, the buckboard was hitched up and ready to roll, and Holt and Rafe had managed to get Raul settled on the floorboards, cushioned by a pile of blankets. No matter what they did, though, the Mexican was in for a long, rough ride to town.

"Go along with him," Lorelei told Angelina, giving her a gentle push toward the wagon.

"I'll stay here and look after the lady," Melina told the older woman quietly in Spanish.

Holt frowned. He'd been planning on taking Lorelei back to her father's place, where she belonged, figuring she'd have seen reason at last and learned her lesson, with Raul getting hurt and all.

"I thought you were dead set on finding work in town so you could be close to Gabe," he said.

Melina lined up alongside Lorelei—an unlikely pair of ranchers if Holt had ever seen one. "This is close enough," she said, switching to English. "I'm staying." She hooked her arm through Lorelei's. "Isn't that right, *señorita?*"

Lorelei, her gaze fixed on the wagon, and Angelina, now being helped into the back by Rafe, nodded. Holt thought he saw a shimmer of tears in her eyes, but he was probably imagining it.

"That's right," Lorelei said.

Rafe tied his gelding to the back of the wagon and climbed up into the box. He tipped his hat to Lorelei and Melina but was not so affable with Holt.

"Get on your horse, Brother," he said. "We're burning daylight."

Holt looked from Melina to Lorelei, then shook his head, stuck one foot in the stirrup and swung up onto the Appaloosa's back.

One of these days, he thought with disgust, something was going to go right, and he'd probably pass out from sheer surprise.

LORELEI WATCHED the wagon go, waving halfheartedly to Angelina, who gazed at her sadly over the tailgate. It was her own fault Raul had been hurt, and no one else's. She should never have allowed him to ride that accursed mule.

"He kissed me," she said, and stunned herself. Holt hadn't entered her mind. She'd been thinking of Raul— hadn't she?

"He surely did," Melina replied gently. "You wouldn't happen to have any tea leaves around, would you? I've got a powerful yearning for a cup of tea."

Turning to look at Melina, Lorelei managed a smile. "Me, too," she said.

They went inside the house, now as tidy as Lorelei and Angelina had been able to make it, and Lorelei took a precious tin of orange pekoe down from the cupboards Raul had fashioned from supply crates. The weather was sweltering, but Lorelei found comfort in the ordinary work of stoking up the fire, and Melina carried the kettle to the stream for water. When she returned, she was carrying Angelina's discarded fish, six of them, lined up on a stick.

"I couldn't see leaving them for the critters," Melina said. "They'll make a fine supper."

Lorelei nodded and put the kettle on the stove to boil. Melina laid the fish in a basin and sat down on one of the upturned crates reserved for chairs.

"That was something," Melina said, resting tender hands on her protruding belly. She was obviously expecting, and Lorelei wondered idly who the father was. "The way you rode that mule. I think you would have gentled him, if Holt hadn't gotten in the way like he did." Wearing a brown homespun skirt and a man's shirt, she nevertheless had a delicate look, with wide, dark eyes and glossy black hair. There was no wedding band on her finger, Lorelei noted, and blushed slightly.

"Thank you," she said, and fixed her gaze on the kettle, willing it to boil.

"I guess you're still thinking about the kiss," Melina deduced, in an offhand tone of voice.

Lorelei felt her face heat up again, and it had nothing to do with the temperature, high as it was. "I shouldn't have let him do that," she confided, almost whispering, and fanned herself ineffectually with one hand.

Melina's soft laugh cheered her mightily. "It didn't

look to me like Holt gave you much of a choice," she said. "And you did slap him."

The tea kettle made a surging sound, and Lorelei got up, measured tea leaves into the plain china pot she'd purchased at the mercantile. The task offered a welcome distraction.

"If Raul is badly hurt, I will never forgive myself," she said.

"Things like that happen on ranches."

Lorelei paused in her fussing and lowered her head. "I know," she said. "But Raul didn't want to come out here in the first place. Angelina didn't, either. Now, thanks to me, they've lost their employment in my father's house."

Melina surprised her by laying a small, light hand on her shoulder. "What will you do, then? Go back to town?"

Lorelei turned, wondering how much Holt had guessed about her life in San Antonio and how much he'd told Melina. "I've thought of it once or twice," she admitted. "But there would be nothing left of my self-respect if I did. Besides, my father wouldn't let me step over his threshold. He made that very clear."

"Then I guess you have to make this place pay," Melina said. "Or marry somebody."

The kettle came to a boil, much like Lorelei's feelings, spilling water from the spout onto the hot surface of the stove, making it sizzle. "I have no intention of marrying Holt McKettrick," she blurted.

There was a brief and eloquent silence.

"I didn't say it had to be him," Melina pointed out, with a touch of satisfaction.

Lorelei reached for Angelina's discarded apron and

used it for a pot holder. Poured hot water over the fragrant tea leaves. "No," she said weakly. "You didn't."

"Let's sit in the doorway to have our tea," Melina suggested, carefully taking the kettle of boiling water from Lorelei's unsteady hands and setting it on the back of the stove. "Maybe there will be a breeze coming up off the creek."

There was no breeze. The air was dense, like a blanket of steam. Still, the two women sat side by side on the step, holding their sensible crockery mugs gingerly and waiting for their tea to cool.

"Tell me about yourself, Melina," Lorelei said presently. She truly wanted to listen, although they both knew the change of the subject had another purpose: Lorelei wished to distance herself from talk of Holt McKettrick, the mule ride and the kiss.

Melina sighed, staring sadly at the sparkling water as it tumbled past. "There isn't much to say," she said, in her own good time. "My father and mother died of yellow fever when I was ten, and I lived at a mission outside of Laredo until I was old enough to be on my own. I got a job on one of the ranches, cooking and doing wash. Then…" She paused, looked down at her rounded stomach. "Then I met Gabe Navarro."

Lorelei rested her teacup on one knee and laid her free hand to her heart. "The man my—the man they're going to hang…?"

"Yes," Melina said. "The man your father sentenced to hang."

So, Holt had told her about that. Lorelei's throat ached. She remembered watching Navarro in the courtroom, during the trial. He'd been stoic the whole time, and when he testified on his own behalf, he didn't waste a single word. When the judge pronounced sentence, he hadn't looked surprised, nor had he flinched.

"Do you think he's…?"

"Innocent?" Melina finished for her. "Yes."

"What will you do if—if he hangs?"

"Same thing I would do if he didn't," Melina answered quietly, after considering the question at length. "Cry myself to sleep a lot of nights and keep working, so my baby and I won't go hungry."

"And if he's set free?" That, Lorelei knew, would be a miracle. Men her father sentenced to death were never set free. They went to the gallows, were hanged and then buried.

Melina sighed. "I would still cry myself to sleep and work," she said.

"You wouldn't marry Mr. Navarro?"

"No," Melina said, and shook her head slightly for emphasis.

"Do you love him?" It was a bold question, but Lorelei had to ask it.

"More than my life," Melina confided. "But Gabe is— Well, he's one to roam. Not from woman to woman—he loves me as much as I love him. But from place to place. Me, I just want to settle down in one spot, raise my baby and not be beholden to anyone."

An unspeakable sadness swept over Lorelei. "You can stay here as long as you like," she said, though it would be crowded quarters if Angelina and Raul came back.

*If.*

For the first time since Mr. Rafe McKettrick had driven Angelina and Raul away in that wagon, Lorelei let herself face the possibility that they might not return. Raul couldn't convalesce on a pallet on the floor of a ranch house, especially one as rustic as hers, and

Angelina, devoted to Lorelei as she was, would naturally put her husband's welfare first.

"I can teach you to ride that mule," Melina said, with some pride.

Lorelei looked at her new friend in horror. "Of course you can't!" she protested. "Look at you! You're—well, expecting."

Melina smiled, blew on her tea, and took a sip. "I didn't say I would ride the brute myself. I said I would teach *you* to ride him."

"I'm not certain I have the nerve to try again," Lorelei confessed. Holt McKettrick's interference notwithstanding, she'd been terrified when that mule started to buck.

"Sure you do," Melina said confidently. "What's his name?"

"Seesaw," Lorelei answered, remembering the way that freight man had smirked when she'd handed over the thirty-five precious dollars.

Melina laughed. "That suits him, all right," she said, and sought the creature with thoughtful eyes. "He's been beaten some. Probably starved, too. Any creature, whether it has two legs or four, will balk when scared. We just have to show him we don't mean him any harm, and he'll come around."

"I wish I had some grain," Lorelei said. As a child, she used to watch Raul tending her father's carriage horses; sometimes, he'd allowed her to feed them oats and grain from the palm of her hand.

"You have sugar," Melina said practically. "You put some in our tea."

Lorelei brightened from the inside out. Sugar cost the earth, but if it would make a friend of the demon Seesaw, she could spare a little.

Both women set aside their tea and got to their feet at the same time.

Lorelei went inside, poured the coarse brown crystals into her palm and headed for the mule.

"Here, Seesaw," she said sweetly.

The mule, still grazing under the oak tree, eyed her suspiciously.

"I have sugar," Lorelei cajoled.

His ears twitched. He bent his head to the ground and cropped off a mouthful of grass.

"Don't move too quickly," Melina counseled.

Lorelei took a cautious step forward, holding out the handful of sugar. "I have something for you," she called.

Seesaw raised his head again, snuffled.

"Careful," Melina said, leaning against another tree to watch.

Lorelei advanced slowly.

Seesaw brayed, but companionably, and came to meet her.

# CHAPTER

20

RAUL WAS GRAY around the gills by the time Rafe and Holt unloaded him at the office of Dr. Elias Brown, on a shady side street in San Antonio. His head lolled to one side as they eased him out of the wagon bed and set him on his feet, supporting his slight weight between them. In truth, he was light enough to carry, but they understood that half out of his head with pain, a man wanted to preserve his dignity.

The doctor burst from the house just as they were reaching the front gate, a picket affair with a faulty catch, and at first sight of him, Holt thought he was a tow-headed boy. Brown probably wasn't four feet tall, even wearing boots, and his head was damn near the size of a watermelon.

As the doctor sprinted down the walk, Holt took note of the gray hair and beard and the stethoscope dangling almost to his knees.

"I'll be damned," Rafe muttered, from the other side of Raul, and Holt would have nudged him silent with an elbow if he could have.

"I'm a dwarf," the doctor said straight out, apparently

dispensing with the obvious so that they could all get down to the case at hand. "What's happened to Raul?"

Angelina, silent the whole way in, let fly with a burst of Spanish.

Dr. Brown shook his head, but his eyes were gentle. "Now, Angelina," he said, "you know anything other than *hola* and *adios* is beyond my ken." He turned his attention to Holt and Rafe. "Bring him inside."

"He was thrown from a mule," Rafe said belatedly. Clearly it had taken him a while to get past the shock of meeting a doctor who barely reached his waist. "I figure he's cracked some ribs. Maybe even broken a few."

"What were you doing on a mule?" Brown demanded of Raul, looking back over one shoulder as he led the way up the walk and onto the spacious front porch. "You're not getting any younger, you know."

Raul gave a strangled laugh, and blood trickled out of his mouth. His knees buckled and he almost went down, even with Rafe on one side and Holt on the other, each with one of his arms around their neck.

Angelina gasped and crossed herself, her lips moving in some silent petition. Holt hoped the appropriate saint was on duty; like Rafe, he'd seen plenty of injuries like Raul's, and the bleeding wasn't a good sign. Could be something had come unstuck in there.

The interior of the house was blessedly cool, and shadowy because most of the shutters were closed. The entryway had been turned into a waiting room of sorts, with chairs lining two walls.

"This way," Dr. Brown said, and stepped through an archway on the left, into what would have been a parlor in another house of that considerable size. The examining table was built low to the ground; in fact, Holt knocked a shin against it as he and Rafe laid Raul down.

Angelina began to weep, a small, mewling sound that was hurtful to hear.

"Go on back to the kitchen," Brown told her, kindly but with a firmness that was not to be disregarded. "Jane will make you some tea." He was running his hands, not the small ones you'd expect of such a little man but big mitts, out of proportion to the rest of his body. He paused and murmured something. "Oh, hell, I forgot. My sister is away, taking care of Aunt Tootie. You'll have to brew the stuff yourself."

Angelina sniffled. "I don't want to leave Raul," she said.

"*Vaya,*" Raul told her. *Go.*

After another few moments of hesitation, Angelina shuffled off.

Holt and Rafe glanced at each other and tacitly decided they ought to make themselves scarce, too. Having no yen for tea, they returned to the shady front porch. Rafe lit a cheroot, drew deeply on the smoke.

"I thought you gave that up when little Georgia was born," Holt said, feeling testy and needing to take it out on somebody.

"I did," Rafe said. "Emmeline won't allow tobacco within fifty feet of the house." He paused, his brow creased. "I don't know how you get a damn thing done around here. If somebody isn't trying to intimidate us with a dozen gunmen, they're getting themselves thrown from mules."

Holt sighed, took off his hat, shoved a hand through his hair. It was gritty with trail dust and damp with sweat, and moreover needed cutting. "Thirty-one days until Gabe hangs," he said, "and not a word from the governor. No sign of Frank Corrales. And if we don't hire some cowboys and buy some cattle to restock John's herd, the ranch will go under anyway. I'd have to be three men, instead of one, to get it all done."

"Two McKettricks," Rafe said, "are enough to do just about anything. I say we ride north, see the governor, then head down to that place you know in Mexico, buy some cattle and hire some men to ramrod them back across the border. Along the way, we can ask after this Corrales fella."

"That means leaving Tillie and John alone and pretty much defenseless."

"We could bring them along."

"Good idea," Holt scoffed. "That way, Templeton and his men can just ride in and raze the place to the ground as soon as we disappear over the hill. You got any other brilliant suggestions?"

Rafe was confident as a peacock with its tail feathers spread. "No," he said, "and you haven't got any other choice, as far as I can see."

"I hate it when you're right," Holt said, and he was dead serious.

"I know," Rafe replied smoothly. "Best you get over it."

Holt gave a low, bitter laugh, and even that much was against his will. "You know what I think? I think you and Jeb and Kade got together up there on the Triple M and decided I might just have it a little too easy down here. Figured one of you better hightail it to Texas and complicate matters as much as possible."

Rafe grinned. "You've got it all wrong, Big Brother. What we decided was, you'd be too damned proud and stubborn to ask for help even if you were naked, slathered in honey and up to your hind-end in red ants. I'm here, and I'm not leaving until it's finished, one way or the other. Besides, I gave Lizzie my word that I'd bring your sorry hide back home before the snow flies."

Holt touched his shirt pocket, where he kept the hair ribbon his daughter had given him just before he left, and felt a painful yearning to see her again. Hell, he even wanted to lay his sore eyes on his brothers, and that crotchety old man of theirs.

Rafe laid a hand on his shoulder. "I think the doc will be a while with Raul. Let's go see if we can rustle up a couple of out-of-work cowhands. They could hold down the Cavanagh place while we're on the trail."

Holt thrust out a sigh, resettled his hat. It wasn't much of an idea, but it was better than standing there on the porch, jawing and fretting.

"Maybe Cap'n Walton would agree to stay behind, keep an eye on things."

Holt was the first to the gate. "Hell will sprout petunias first," he said. He untied Traveler from the side of the wagon and climbed into the saddle. Rafe went around and did the same with Chief.

Rafe laughed. "Except for his size, he reminds me of Pa."

"Yeah," Holt agreed. "Damn the luck." He shifted in the saddle, glad for a break from that wagon seat. "Let's stop at the telegraph office first," he said, just as if the subject were open to negotiation, which it wasn't. "Maybe there'll be some word from Austin about Gabe's new trial."

As it turned out, there was a telegram waiting for Holt. And it was from the governor's office.

Trouble was, the news was all bad.

The governor was back East in Washington, hobnobbing with that unruly bunch in Congress.

In the meantime, Holt concluded, Texas was on its

own, and Gabe Navarro was up shit creek, good and proper.

Disheartened, Holt and Rafe headed for the jail.

Gabe was still in a surly mood, but now he was vocal about it. Holt couldn't rightly decide whether that was an improvement or a setback.

"I told you not to let Melina come here!" he raged, never troubling himself with a howdy-do. "She should have stayed in Waco!"

"Melina is fine where she is," Holt said, hoping it was true. He'd left her with Lorelei, and God only knew what the pair of them were up to by now.

Gabe had been clenching the bars of his cell in both hands; now, he thrust himself away and began to prowl back and forth. At least he had the room to do that, since they'd moved him from the other hole in the wall, but with the gallows clearly visible through the one window, Holt didn't reckon it as an advantage.

"You been getting regular meals?" he asked.

"Yes," Gabe spat. Ungrateful, that's what he was. And purely cussed. He jabbed a thumb in Rafe's direction. "Who's this yahoo?"

Holt explained. At least Gabe could still spot a yahoo when he saw one.

Rafe didn't put out a hand, and neither did Gabe. They just stood there, each one sizing up the other and, from the looks on their faces, finding him just shy of suitable. Gabe finally turned his head and spat.

"I came to tell you we'll be on the trail a while," Holt said into the uncomfortable silence. "We'll scare up a decent lawyer along the way and get you out of here."

Gabe's expression was bleak, and not, Holt suspected, because he thought he was being left high and dry, with his death just a month away. He thrived on fresh air, open spaces and the feel of the sun on his face as much as any man Holt had ever known, and it must have half killed him, knowing he couldn't go along with Holt and Rafe.

"You find Frank," Gabe said. "Maybe there's a chance for him, if you get to him in time. See that Melina and the baby are taken care of, and don't let these bastards bury me in a churchyard."

Holt was taken aback and couldn't think what to say.

Rafe had no such problem. "You sound like a man who's fixing to give up," he told Navarro. "You've got a nasty disposition, but I didn't figure you for a chickenshit."

Gabe hurled himself at the bars, would have come through them if he could, just to get Rafe by the throat.

Rafe grinned. "Maybe there's hope for you after all," he said.

# CHAPTER 21

LORELEI BIT HER LOWER LIP, closed her eyes for a moment, and climbed up onto the crate. Melina held Seesaw by his halter and nodded encouragement. They'd spent most of the afternoon making friends with the beast, leading him around and around in ever-widening circles and rewarding him with sugar every time he showed the slightest inclination toward obedience.

Hiking up her skirts and muttering a prayer, Lorelei swung her right leg over the mule and landed as gently as possible on his back.

A great shudder ran through his obstinate body, and Lorelei held her breath. She might meet Raul's fate, or even William's, in the next heartbeat, but she might also succeed.

The decision was Seesaw's.

Melina gripped the halter rope, her eyes big.

Seesaw made a whinnying sound, curling his lips back.

Lorelei gripped his coarse mane in both hands and waited.

Melina tugged at the rope and made a soft clicking sound with her tongue.

Seesaw took a tentative step, then another. He paused, quivering again, perhaps considering his choices.

"Nice donkey," Lorelei said hopefully.

"Don't make any sudden moves," Melina counseled.

Lorelei relaxed a little. "Hand me the rope," she said in a pleasant tone, calculated to be soothing to the undecided animal. "Then walk away. If he starts bucking, there's no point in both of us getting hurt."

Melina stood on tiptoe to give Lorelei the rope. It prickled against her palm.

"Easy," Melina whispered, backing slowly out of Seesaw's range. "Touch your heels to his sides, but not hard. You don't want to startle him."

Lorelei held her breath and then did as she was told.

Seesaw ambled toward the creek.

Lorelei was overjoyed. She was riding! But then she tried to turn the creature to one side, pulling cautiously on the rope, and he plodded on.

"Stop, please," Lorelei said brightly, afraid to raise her voice.

Seesaw plodded on, down the rocky bank and right into the water.

Frcsh panic assailcd Lorclci. Shc didn't know how to swim.

The mule began to paddle in ever-widening circles, moving a little closer to the middle each time.

"Lorelei!" Melina cried, from the shore behind her. "Stop!"

"I'm trying!" Lorelei shouted back, as exasperated as she was afraid.

Seesaw paddled around in a circle, and that was when Lorelei saw the McKettrick brothers riding full-speed toward the bank. Melina had to rush out of their way as they passed, and still they came, splashing up a glittering spray as they gained the water.

The mule brayed gleefully, and must have planted all four feet on the streambed, for he gave a great leap, and Lorelei plunged into the water. The weight of her skirts pulled her under, and she came up gasping for breath.

Holt leaned down from the saddle, extending his hand.

Lorelei clasped at it with both her own and held on for dear life, sputtering and choking as he dragged her up and set her down hard in front of him. She blinked, nearly blind with creek water, and saw Rafe catch hold of Seesaw's halter rope and turn his horse toward shore.

Lorelei would have sworn the man was grinning, but she decided she must be imagining things. Surely the near drowning of a human being was not a source of amusement, even for ruffians like these.

Holt's arm felt like a barrel hoop around her, and she took an improper pleasure in the hard wall of his chest, pressed against her back. Once they'd reached the bank, he set her on her feet and glared down at her, his hair and clothes dripping, his eyelashes spiked with water. His horse shook itself, and Lorelei's vision blurred again, briefly, from the spray.

"Are you all right?" Holt demanded. His voice was low-pitched, with a raspy edge.

Lorelei tried to wring out her skirts. "Yes, thank you," she said, not quite daring to look at him again, now that she'd averted her eyes. "Did you notice? I rode the mule."

Rafe laughed, somewhere nearby.

"Oh, I noticed, all right," Holt said dangerously. He got down off the back of that enormous horse and stood facing her.

"I'm sure once he's over his tendency to head for the creek," Lorelei babbled on, "Seesaw will make a fine mule."

"He'd have to go some to be a better one than you," Holt retorted.

Lorelei lifted her chin. "There is no need to be rude," she pointed out.

"Apparently, there is," Holt said, and took an ominous step toward her. "You don't seem to understand anything else."

"When have you tried any other approach?" Lorelei countered.

"I'll be goddamned!" He took another step, and Lorelei didn't back up, but not because she wasn't alarmed. She wasn't sure how close she was to the water, that was all.

"There is a very good chance of that," she said huffily, and tried to go around him.

He stepped into her path.

"Don't you dare kiss me again!" Lorelei cried.

"Believe me, I wouldn't think of it!"

"The hell you wouldn't," Rafe put in.

Holt flailed at his brother with his hat but didn't take his eyes off Lorelei's face. "You stay out of this!" he roared.

"What do you want?" Lorelei sputtered furiously. "An apology? All right, then—I'm sorry you had to get wet!"

"Is there any coffee?" Rafe wanted to know.

"Are you *trying* to kill yourself?" Holt ranted on, sparing his brother another halfhearted wave of the hat, as though he were a pesky fly.

"Lorelei and I will make some," Melina said eagerly,

rushing in to grasp Lorelei's hand and drag her toward the house. "Right now."

"Why does he always show up at the worst possible time?" Lorelei hissed, once they were inside. She'd ducked behind a blanket suspended from one of the roof beams and began peeling off her sodden clothes.

"I'd say it was the *best* possible time," Melina answered, busy at the stove. "If they hadn't come along when they did, you probably would have drowned."

A lump rose in Lorelei's throat and, for a moment, she was stricken to utter stillness at the thought of her own untimely demise. Would anyone mourn her? she wondered. Not her father, surely. Not Creighton Bannings.

Suddenly cold, standing there in her soaked bloomers and camisole, she began to shiver. Her teeth chattered so that she feared she might be suffering some sort of convulsion—next, she'd bite off her tongue.

Raul and Angelina would have wept at her funeral, she consoled herself, snatching dry clothes from one of the everlasting boxes.

*Raul and Angelina.*

How could she have forgotten?

She peered around the edge of the blanket, careful of her modesty. Holt and Rafe were standing outside the door, both of them gesturing, arguing about something in hoarse undertones.

"How is Raul?" Lorelei called, struggling into her spare calico.

Both Holt and Rafe turned toward her, as though surprised to find her there. Holt's expression darkened.

"It's kind of you to ask," he drawled. "I wondered when you'd finally get around to it."

Rafe shook his head, plainly exasperated with his brother. "We stopped by Doc Brown's before we left town," he said, quite kindly. "Raul's going to be laid up a while. Angelina plans to keep house for the doc in return for their room and board. She says there's room for you, too."

Lorelei put a hand to her throat, silently thanking God and all his angels that she hadn't killed or crippled Raul by buying that accursed mule.

Holt stepped into the doorway, leaned against the frame. His wet clothes hugged his body, stirring things inside Lorelei that were better left to lie fallow. "Not that you'd have the good sense to take her up on the offer," he said.

Lorelei stiffened. "I have a perfectly good home right here," she replied.

"Yes," Holt shot back, but quietly, "and tomorrow is a bright new day. Maybe you can find still another way to break your damn fool neck."

"Holt," Rafe protested.

"You can't stay here by yourself," Holt persisted, ignoring him.

"I'm not by myself," Lorelei reasoned, making sure she was properly buttoned up before stepping from behind the blanket. "Melina is here. Not that it's any of your business anyway."

Holt gave a derisive snort. "Oh, *well*," he said. "That decides it. Two women, one of them pregnant, and the other with no more sense than God gave a fence post, against Templeton and whatever other outlaws might be running the roads."

Lorelei reddened. *A fence post?*

"Better take them with us," Rafe said, edging past Holt to stand near Melina. "You got any whiskey to put in that coffee?"

"I wouldn't dream of going anywhere with either of you," Lorelei said.

Rafe arched a dark eyebrow and accepted the mug of coffee Melina offered. She added a generous dollop of Raul's whiskey, standing on tiptoe to do it. "Not even if it meant a chance to buy cattle and hire cowpunchers, so you could turn this place into a real ranch?"

Lorelei's heartbeat quickened. She didn't dare look at Holt, though she felt his temper like another presence in the room.

"That would be different," she said guardedly.

"Oh, no, it wouldn't," Holt argued.

Lorelei looked at Melina. "Could you manage it—a cattle drive, I mean? In your condition?"

Melina's smile was luminous. "Sure I could," she said.

"No," Holt maintained, "you couldn't."

"Would you rather leave them here?" Rafe asked, after a noisy sip from his mug.

"What if she has that baby on the trail?" Holt wanted to know. A muscle leaped in his jaw.

"What if she has it here?" Rafe countered. "All alone except for the lively Miss Fellows?" He toasted Lorelei affably with his coffee mug, as if to say there was no offense intended. "I figure the two of them could get into all kinds of trouble on their own. Who knows what they might take it into their heads to do?"

Lorelei flushed with indignation and a strange, dizzying hope. She *wanted* to go on the trail drive, wanted it with a staggering intensity—even if it did mean being in close proximity with Holt McKettrick for an indeterminate length of time. It was her chance—maybe her *only* chance—to buy the cattle and hire the men she needed.

She waited, staring at Holt.

"You don't know how to ride," he said.

"I can learn," she replied.

He sighed. "Give me some of that whiskey," he said. "Hold the coffee."

Was he weakening? Lorelei couldn't tell. She held her breath while Melina poured more of Raul's liquor into a cup and held it out to Holt.

He downed it all in a single gulp, shuddered with a curious mixture of satisfaction and shock.

"There will be Indians," he told her, wiping his mouth with the back of one hand.

"I'm not afraid," Lorelei insisted. It was a lie, of course, but if people never did anything frightening, how could they expect to get anywhere? She'd spent her life marking time, waiting for something, *anything,* to change. Now, she was through waiting. She was prepared to take risks and make mistakes and deal with the consequences.

"You should be," Holt said reasonably. "Do you have any idea how many things can go wrong on a cattle drive?"

She didn't, actually, which was probably a mercy, in her opinion.

"You might be carried off by Comanches. You might be bitten by a snake, or thrown from a horse. You might be trampled to death in a stampede, or drowned crossing a river. Only I might not be there to pull you out."

Lorelei drew a deep breath—it felt as if it went clear to her toes—and let it out slowly. "If those things don't stop you," she said, "why should they stop me?"

Rafe grinned.

Melina folded her arms, her head tilted to one side, watching Holt expectantly.

Holt rubbed the back of his neck.

"Oh, the hell with it," he said. "Get your things together. We'll pass the night at John's, and leave at dawn."

"Which one of us is going to break that mule to ride?" Rafe asked, half an hour later, nodding toward Seesaw, who was nibbling grass a few yards away. He'd saddled Melina's pony, and tied her pitiful bundle of belongings behind the cantle. Holt had already sent Lorelei back to the house twice, to lighten her pack, and he was purely exasperated—with her, for wanting to take a party dress and dancing slippers on a trail drive, with himself, for agreeing to take her along, and with Rafe for bringing up the whole lame-brained idea in the first place.

"I thought we'd leave him here," Holt said. He figured it would be better if he didn't look at Rafe for a while, because looking at him would make him want to take a few strips out of his miserable hide. "Lorelei can ride with Tillie."

"Miss Fellows will never agree to that," Rafe replied, cocksure as usual. "That's her mule, and if she's said it once, she's said it half a dozen times…she paid thirty-five dollars for him and she wants her money's worth."

Lorelei came out of the ranch house with her rigging, hopefully minus the frilly getup and the collected works of Mr. William Shakespeare she'd tried to sneak past him on the first round.

Holt bit the proverbial bullet. "We won't need the mule," he told her.

"He's mine, and he's going," Lorelei replied.

Rafe chuckled. He loved to be right, the bastard.

"God*damn* it," Holt bit out. "Last time I looked, I was still running this outfit, and you'll do what I tell you, *Miss* Fellows."

"Within reason," Lorelei allowed, with stiff grace. "I paid—"

"I know, I know," Holt broke in, wholly disgusted. "You paid thirty-five dollars for that mule and—"

"He's going," Lorelei finished.

Holt flung out his hands, startling the Appaloosa, who would have shied if he hadn't taken a firm hold on the bridle strap. "Fine," he snapped. "Never mind that he threw Raul and almost got you drowned. Never mind that he isn't worth *ten* dollars, let alone thirty-five. Just don't come crying to me if you break your fool neck in the middle of nowhere!"

Lorelei stood straight as a broom handle. "I wouldn't *dream* of crying to you over anything on this earth, Mr. McKettrick."

Out of the corner of his eye, Holt saw Rafe fold his arms and rock back on his heels, mighty pleased with himself. "You or me, Big Brother?" he asked, circling around to his original question about breaking the mule to ride.

"You," Holt bit out. "And I hope he throws you clean over the barn roof."

Rafe merely laughed again, as if the horse—or mule—he couldn't ride had never drawn breath. He helped Melina up onto the pony's back, then mounted Chief and leaned on the pommel of his saddle, waiting. Watching. Grinning that grin that made Holt's back teeth clamp together.

Holt suppressed an urge to drag his brother down off that fancy gelding, with its fine Mexican saddle, and knock out a few of his perfect McKettrick teeth. He held out a hand, and Lorelei hesitated, then gave him her pack. It still weighed half again too much, but he was all argued out, for the moment at least. He tied it behind his saddle and got on the horse.

Lorelei stood looking up at him, proud and puzzled. Damned if she wasn't a contrary woman, cussed one moment and vulnerable the next.

He bent, with a creaking of saddle leather, and offered his hand.

Lorelei hesitated, then gripped it, gamely placed a foot in the stirrup, and allowed him to pull her up behind him. She fussed with her skirts a little, and the only indication that she felt any trepidation at all was the way she wrapped her arms around his middle, with a sort of tenuous desperation.

He spurred Traveler lightly with the heels of his boots, and headed for the stream. Melina followed, on her pony, and Rafe brought up the rear, leading that demon mule, Seesaw.

The purple, gold and crimson of a first-class Texas sunset rippled on the water as they made the crossing, and it was full dark when they reached John's ranch house.

Tillie and the dog came out to meet them, and he'd have sworn that mutt was smiling as broadly as Tillie was.

Holt reined in the Appaloosa and swung a leg over its neck, leaping to the ground. The dog bounded toward them, barking with delight, as he lifted Lorelei down. Her skirts were wet from the creek, and she shivered under her thin shawl, but she'd probably have eaten weevil stew before she complained.

Something in the way she greeted that dog, laughing and ruffling his floppy ears, got to a place in Holt that he usually kept under guard.

"Who are you?" Tillie asked Lorelei, straight out,

frowning a little as she watched the reunion between Sorrowful and the stubbornest woman on the face of God's earth. Maybe she was afraid of losing the critter. Maybe she was just curious. With Tillie, it was hard to tell.

Lorelei smiled warmly and introduced herself.

"That's my dog," Tillie said.

"I know," Lorelei replied.

Tillie considered that. "You can be his friend, if you want to."

"I would like that very much," Lorelei said. "Thank you."

At last, Tillie smiled. "He likes to have his belly scratched."

Lorelei simply nodded. She looked bone-tired, as well as cold, and watching her with Tillie had taken the edge off Holt's irritation.

"I hope supper's on," he said.

"Fried chicken," Tillie told him proudly. Then she turned thoughtful. "Pa said you'd come back with cowboys. I don't see any, except for Rafe."

"We'll have to make do," Holt said. "See the women inside, Tillie. Rafe and I will put away the horses."

She nodded, and three females and a hound dog disappeared into the house.

Tomorrow, Holt told himself, by way of consolation, as he turned the Appaloosa toward the barn, was a brand-new day.

He sure hoped it would go better than this one had.

# CHAPTER 22

IF THERE WAS ONE THING Holt McKettrick knew about himself, for sure and for certain, it was that he hated losing. Gunfight, wager, flip of the coin—it didn't matter. But in the case of Seesaw the mule, he made an exception.

The critter wanted gentling, if Lorelei was to ride him to Mexico and back, and since she insisted upon doing so, it was up to either Rafe or Holt to get that mangy devil reconciled to a saddle. When the toss of Rafe's nickel came up heads, Holt was secretly glad he'd called tails.

Rubbing his hands together in the blessedly cool dawn of the last day of August, Rafe approached the mule, who stood untethered out in front of John's barn. Kahill and the six other questionable types Holt had managed to scrape up looked on, their own horses saddled, their gear packed. The Captain and John took an interest, too, though Lorelei, Tillie, Melina and the dog had yet to come out of the house.

Rafe carried a bridle over one shoulder, and the mule accepted that easily enough. Holt himself fetched the saddle and blanket, and when he stepped up to Rafe, he took the opportunity to offer a quiet, "Be careful."

Rafe just smiled, and his apparent confidence both nettled Holt and made him feel a twinge of guilt. He was the eldest brother, and this was his outfit, for all practical intents and purposes. *He* ought to be the one taking the risks.

With a practiced motion, Rafe put the blanket on the mule's back.

Seesaw quivered and swung his head around, tried to take a nip out of Rafe's upper arm.

The door of the house creaked open, and Holt didn't have to look to know the spectator list had just grown by three women and a slat-ribbed hound. He felt Lorelei's presence as sure as if she'd planted herself square in front of him, and that was troubling. He'd think about it more, once Rafe had either subdued the mule or eaten a few mouthfuls of barnyard dirt.

The mule gave a long shudder when the saddle came to rest on top of the blanket.

"Easy," Rafe told the animal.

"Easy," Holt told Rafe at the same moment.

Rafe hooked the stirrup over the horn and reached under Seesaw's belly for the cinch. The mule sidestepped and tried again for a chunk of Rafe's hide. Rafe gave Seesaw's upper lip a firm tug, to let him know who was in charge.

Holt wasn't so sure it was Rafe. He stepped back, to give his brother and the mule all the room they needed, which was likely to be about a square acre.

Rafe slipped the cinch strap through the buckle and pulled it tight.

The mule huffed ominously, all four feet planted to put up a fight, and swelled his belly. Rafe elbowed him, made him let out his breath, and gave the cinch strap another pull. He tested it by slipping his fingers underneath the leather, and nodded to himself. Then he brought down the stirrup, put a foot in it and mounted. He was a big man, Rafe was, but he was all grace as he settled himself on the back of that contrary mule.

Holt held his breath.

The mule pondered his predicament, lowered his head and propelled himself straight up in the air, just as if he had springs in those dinner-plate hooves of his.

Rafe let out a whoop and spurred the bastard hard with his heels.

The mule pitched forward, then back, living up to his name.

Rafe sat him like a rocking horse. "You can do better than that, you flea-bitten bag of sorry misery!" he yelled.

Seesaw set out to prove him right. He spun to the left, kicking all the way, and then to the right.

Rafe laughed, and that was his undoing. Seesaw took another plunge, dropping to his knees, and sent Rafe sailing over his head.

Rafe landed rolling, Triple M style, and came up laughing even harder. The mule raised a storm of dust, but when it cleared, Rafe was back in the saddle and kicking hard.

The cowboys cheered.

Holt tried to swallow his heart, which had surged up into his throat when Rafe went flying. He felt a tug at his sleeve and knew it was Lorelei, even before he spared her a furious glance.

"There's your thirty-five dollar mule, Miss Lorelei," he growled. "You'd better hope he doesn't kill my brother, because if he does, I'll drop him in his worthless tracks."

Lorelei put a hand to her throat. "Maybe I *should* ride behind Tillie," she said.

"It's a little late to make that concession," Holt retorted, keeping his eyes on Rafe and the mule. Between them, they were plowing up a whole new field. Dirt flew in every direction, and Rafe cut loose with another whoop, loving every minute of that ride, damn fool that he was.

"You wouldn't really shoot him," Lorelei ventured, watching the fracas.

"That's what you think," Holt answered. As proof, his right hand rested on the handle of his .45.

After a good fifteen minutes, Seesaw began to tire. Fifteen minutes after that, he came to see the situation Rafe's way and settled down with a halfhearted bray and a quiver of powerful muscles.

Rafe rode the mule around in a circle, spurred him to a trot, and finally dismounted, directly in front of Holt and Lorelei. He, like the mule, was coated from head to foot in good Texas dust, and his grin was as wide as the Rio Grande.

He executed a bow and handed the reins to Lorelei.

She stared at them, then at Rafe. Holt noticed she didn't look at *him,* and it was a good thing, too. He wouldn't have wanted her to see what was probably plain in his face—cold fury, and a conflicting desire to keep her off that mule at all costs.

Gamely, she stepped in close to Seesaw. Rafe steadied him while she gripped the saddle horn, stepped into the stirrup and swung herself up. She was wearing a pair of Tillie's trousers, a cotton shirt and a floppy hat, and as she sat there waiting for the mule to explode, the way he'd done with Rafe, she almost looked like a cowpuncher.

Holt breathed his way through the tension, and a rush

of admiration that boiled up out of nowhere like a flash flood.

The mule nickered. Rafe stroked his nose, then let him go, stepping away easily but obviously ready to leap back in if old Seesaw decided to unwind.

"Give him a tap with your heels," Rafe told her. Holt wished he'd been the one to say it, but the fact was, he couldn't have gotten a word out if it meant his life.

Lorelei did as she was told, and the mule took a few tentative steps, swung his head to take Rafe's measure, and decided to listen to his better angels. Next thing Holt knew, Lorelei had Seesaw up to a canter. She bounced a bit in the saddle, but with some practice, she'd get in stride with the animal's gait.

Rafe stood beside Holt, watching, arms folded, dirty face split by a wide grin. Sunlight spilled, golden, over the eastern hills, flooding the landscape with a heated glow.

"She's something, isn't she?" Rafe said with frank admiration. "If I weren't a happily married man, I believe I'd court Miss Lorelei in earnest."

"But you *are* a happily married man," Holt pointed out. He'd meant to speak the words lightly, but they came out sounding fierce.

Rafe chuckled, whistled to Chief and mounted up.

John drove up alongside Holt in the supply wagon, with the dog on the seat beside him. Tillie was on her mule, Melina close behind on her pony. The Captain, too, was ready to hit the trail.

"Are you going to stand there all day?" John demanded, gazing down at Holt with a look of knowing amusement in his eyes.

Against his will, Holt sought Lorelei, sitting atop Seesaw's back as if she'd been born there. Rafe was next to her, on Chief, still grinning.

Holt muttered a curse, waded through the horse flesh to find Traveler and climbed into the saddle.

They hadn't even left the dooryard, and already he felt as though he'd been dragged across three states and a territory behind a freight train.

WHEN SHE THOUGHT no one was looking, Lorelei consulted her watch, which was pinned to the pocket of the cotton shirt she'd borrowed from Tillie, along with her trousers, boots and hat. Ten o'clock.

Only ten o'clock? By the ache in her thighs and lower back and the oppressive glare of the sun, it should have been at least four-thirty in the afternoon.

With every jostling step Seesaw took, Lorelei questioned her decision to undertake this journey, but she would have bitten off her tongue and swallowed it before admitting as much to Holt McKettrick.

He rode at the front of the party, with Rafe alongside, back straight and head high, like a king about to conquer a rebellious country.

"You doin' all right, Miss Lorelei?" John Cavanagh called kindly from the seat of his wagon. Sorrowful rode with him, tongue lolling contentedly as he surveyed the countryside.

Lorelei managed a taut smile—it still took all her concentration to ride, since she was so new at the enterprise—and nodded. It wouldn't do to let Mr. Cavanagh know she envied the dog, and would have traded places if it were feasible.

He seemed to read her mind. "We've still got a long way to go before this day is done, if I know Holt. Maybe you ought to ride with me a while. I could stop and tie the mule behind."

Lorelei looked ahead, to Holt. He thought she was unfit for a cattle drive, he'd made that plain enough; her riding with Mr. Cavanagh, blissful respite though it would surely be, would only prove him right. "I'll be fine," she said. "But thank you kindly."

They'd traveled miles when a stream appeared, shimmering like a river of silver in the near distance, and Holt raised a hand to signal that they'd be stopping there. Lorelei suffered no illusions that he was giving mere humans a chance to rest—most likely, he was concerned about the livestock.

The banks of the stream were grassy, and probably softened by the recent rains. Lorelei slid from Seesaw's back and felt a jolt of pain as the balls of her feet made contact with the ground. She rested her forehead against the side of the saddle and closed her eyes until the worst of it passed.

Something bumped her arm, and she turned to see Rafe standing beside her, offering a canteen and an understanding smile.

She took it with a murmur of thanks, and drank deeply of the clean, cool water.

"You ought to ride in the wagon for a while," he said quietly.

Lorelei betrayed her thoughts by glancing in Holt's direction. He was crouched beside the water, conferring with one of the cowboys. "No," she said, feeling a surge of heat rise into her cheeks.

"Might be better for your pride to smart a little," Rafe ventured, "than your legs and…other parts. It's going to be a long time until we make camp for the night. You're bound to be sore as all get out, this being your first real ride."

Tears of fatigue and frustration burned behind Lorelei's eyes, but she'd be damned if she'd let them show. She took another long draught from the canteen and then wiped her mouth with the back of one hand, the way she'd seen the cowboys do. "Don't worry about me, Mr. McKettrick," she said, "I can keep up just fine."

"Rafe," he said. A grin quirked at one corner of his mouth. "I figure you and I ought to be friends, since I'm the one who ironed out the kinks in your mule."

Lorelei laughed, despite the numbness in her limbs and the ferocious ache in the lower part of her back. She felt as though her spine would crumble into powder at any moment, and the big predawn breakfast Tillie and Melina had served up back at the ranch had long since worn off. Her stomach seemed as empty as a windswept canyon.

"I can't argue with that...Rafe," she said. "You might as well call me Lorelei."

He turned to glance at Holt, and Holt looked up at the same moment.

His expression was unreadable, but something unsettling passed between the two men before Holt's gaze shifted to Lorelei. He stood, then started toward them.

"I reckon I'll check Chief's hooves and make sure he hasn't picked up a stone along the way," Rafe said, but, curiously, he didn't move from Lorelei's side.

Facing them, Holt took off his hat with one hand and pushed the fingers of the other through his hair. "Change your mind yet, Miss Fellows?" he drawled.

Lorelei planted her feet, much the way Seesaw had, just before Rafe took the saddle that morning. "About what?"

Holt's smile didn't reach those watchful hazel eyes of his. "It's a long way to Mexico," he said. "Time we get there, you might just be bowlegged."

Anger rushed through Lorelei's system like heat through a teakettle ready to boil. "Don't you worry about my legs," she said tersely, and Rafe's low whistle made her regret her choice of words. She watched, her face hot, as he walked away, leaving her alone with Holt. A raw ache took shape in her most private place, and her face grew even warmer.

Something flickered in his eyes—humor, perhaps— and Lorelei yearned to slap him again, with even more force than she had after he kissed her. He gave an insolent, barely perceptible shrug. "Suit yourself," he said, and turned away.

At his orders, the cowboys mounted up.

John Cavanagh hoisted Sorrowful into the back of the wagon, and the dog lay down to sleep. Lucky creature.

Lorelei's thigh muscles screamed in protest as she hauled herself back into the saddle. Once again, she wanted to weep, but she didn't. She *wouldn't*.

Rafe rode alongside her as they crossed the stream, holding Seesaw's bridle with a firm hand. Lorelei's boots filled with water, and she was wet to her hips. She was terrified, remembering her near-drowning the day before, and bit down hard on the inside of her lip to keep from crying out.

Once they'd gained the other side, Rafe left her on her own and spurred his horse to catch up with Holt. The younger man said something, gesturing angrily, and Holt shook his head.

Lorelei's body hurt so badly that she retreated into a corner of her mind, wondering how Raul and Angelina were faring at Dr. Brown's, and if her father's temper might have cooled a little, now that he'd had some time to think.

"Lorelei?"

The voice startled her. She turned her head, and Melina's face came into focus.

"Here," Melina said gently, holding out something wrapped in a piece of cloth. "It's bread and cheese. Mr. Cavanagh said to give it to you."

Lorelei's hand trembled a little as she accepted the food. Her stomach clenched, then churned. "Thank you," she said, and tried not to shove it all into her mouth at once.

"You don't have to prove anything to Holt, you know," Melina persisted, in a quiet voice. "Why don't you ride with Mr. Cavanagh?"

Lorelei looked with longing at the wagon, but she shook her head. "You're the one who ought to take a rest," she said, thinking of Melina's pregnancy.

"I've been riding all my life. You're pale, Lorelei," Melina said, clearly worried. "You look as if you might pitch off that mule headfirst."

Lorelei forced herself to nibble at the cheese, bit by bit. Never, in the whole of her life, had she ever been so ravenously hungry. "If I'm going to run a ranch," she reasoned, feeling a frisson of oddly delicious alarm as Holt suddenly reined his horse around and started back toward the main party at a lope, "I've got to be strong."

As Holt's Appaloosa fell into an impatient stride beside her plodding mule, Melina drew back to ride with Tillie.

"You win," Holt said, through his teeth. Rafe watched them from up the trail, glaring over one shoulder. "Whatever it is you're trying to prove, you've proved it. Get into the wagon with John."

Lorelei took a huge bite of bread, chewed it assiduously and swallowed before troubling herself to answer. "I'm quite all right," she said, when she damn well felt like talking. "Thank you for your kind concern, however."

Holt swept off his hat and whacked it once against his thigh. Dust flew. He jammed the Stetson back onto his head. "You are a trial to my patience," he said, after a few moments of tight-jawed silence.

She smiled, though she wanted more than anything to lean forward and sob into Seesaw's mane. "There's always a bright side to every situation," she observed.

"If I have to drag you off that mule and *throw* you into the wagon, Miss Fellows, I will."

"I assure you, Mr. McKettrick, I will put up a fight if you make the attempt."

"And I assure *you,* you little hellion, that if I make the attempt, I will succeed."

"It appears we have reached an impasse," Lorelei said, after finishing off the bread.

"It may appear that way from your end," Holt retorted rigidly. "From mine, it looks like an easy win."

"I despise you," Lorelei informed him crisply.

"Good," he replied. "I would not want my own sentiments to go unreciprocated." He signaled to John Cavanagh, who drew back on the reins of the team and brought the wagon to a noisy, jostling halt in the middle of the trail. Sorrowful peered curiously over the side, yawning.

The cowboys and Captain Walton tried to look as though they weren't watching. Rafe made no such effort.

"What'll it be, Miss Fellows?" Holt asked, in a slow drawl. "Will you get into that wagon peaceably, or do we put on a show for the whole outfit?"

Lorelei imagined the delight the drovers would take in such an undignified scene and was forced to relent. She brought Seesaw to a stop, braced herself and dismounted. This time, there was no flash of pain, but her legs were numb, and her knees buckled. If she hadn't grasped hold of the saddle, she would have fallen into a heap on the ground.

She looked up at Holt, rimmed with sunlight like Apollo in his chariot, and hated him with a dizzying intensity. As he bent to snatch up Seesaw's reins in one hand, she saw the self-satisfied smirk on his face and would have flung herself at him, clawing like a scalded cat, if she'd had the strength.

She waited until she could trust herself to walk as far as the waiting wagon, then did so. Mr. Cavanagh got down from the box, gave Holt a withering look and took charge of Seesaw.

Lorelei looked up at the wagon box in pure despair. She couldn't climb that far, and she couldn't ask for help, either.

It was Captain Walton who came to her rescue. He got down off his horse, made a stirrup of his hands and nodded to Lorelei. "I can see that you're about to cry," he told her with quiet good humor, "and I would strongly advise you not to do so. If ever there was a time for a poker face, this is it."

Lorelei put one foot in his cupped palms, grabbed for the edge of the wagon and hauled herself, with the very last of her strength, up into the box.

"Thank you," she told the Captain.

He smiled up at her. "You done real good, Miss Lorelei," he said. "I'd say you won that hand."

Lorelei felt Holt's gaze on her, but she refused to meet

his eyes. If she did, her poker face might slip. "Would you?"

"Yes, ma'am." The Captain chuckled and got back on his horse.

The sun was on a distinctly westward path when they stopped again, at a water hole, to rest the stock. This time, Holt didn't come near Lorelei, and she told herself she was glad of it, despite a pang of disappointment.

"You ought to get down and walk around a bit," Mr. Cavanagh suggested. "Stretch your legs." The dog had already leaped over the tailgate to squat, then chase merrily around in the grass.

Melina and Tillie dismounted easily and waited for Lorelei.

"I'm not sure I can stand," Lorelei confessed.

Mr. Cavanagh patted her hand. "Sure you can. You've got more grit than any five women."

Buoyed by this unexpected and, to her mind, unearned praise, Lorelei steeled herself, then climbed down off the wagon.

Melina and Tillie gestured, and the three of them made a necessary visit to the bushes.

Half an hour later, at Holt's command, they were rolling again. It was almost six o'clock when they reached the abandoned mission.

The tireless and wholly obnoxious Holt McKettrick once again raised an officious hand, and the party came to a merciful halt.

"We'll be making camp this time," Mr. Cavanagh assured Lorelei. "I reckon we'll all sleep like logs tonight." He got down, walked around the back of the wagon and reached up a hand to her.

She took it gratefully, and nearly collapsed against him before she could make her legs work.

She and Mr. Cavanagh had ridden in companionable silence all afternoon. Now, watching Holt riding amid the travelers, probably giving orders, Lorelei asked, "What makes him so ornery?"

Mr. Cavanagh laughed. "Holt can be a hard man when he's trying to get something done," he conceded, unhitching the weary team from the wagon. "But I've never known anybody finer."

Lorelei made a huffy sound, resting her hands on her hips. "I think he's insufferable," she said.

If Mr. Cavanagh heard her, he didn't let on. But he grinned as he turned the horses loose to graze on the plenteous grass and drink thirstily from the little spring next to the mission chapel. A hundred yards beyond, a stream flowed, invitingly cool.

Lorelei shifted her attention to Melina and Tillie, who were chatting as they gathered bits of wood and dried cow dung for the supper fire. She joined them, for she would not have it said that she expected special treatment. She might be a greenhorn, but she meant to keep going until she collapsed, if that was what she had to do.

Using rope, which he wrapped around tree trunks at appropriate junctures, one of the cowboys constructed a makeshift corral for the horses and mules. Two other men took buckets from the back of the wagon and filled them at the spring so the animals could drink, and when that was done, all of them except Rafe, Mr. Cavanagh, the Captain and Holt went scrambling for the stream, hooting with exuberant laughter and pulling off their boots as they went.

Lorelei decided to explore the mission, partly because she knew it would be cool inside the adobe structure, and partly because she wanted to avoid Holt McKettrick for as long as possible.

The moment she stepped over the threshold, a sweet sense of reverence washed over her. The floor was stone, worn smooth by time and the passage of sandaled feet. The pale outline of a large cross marked one wall. The altar, if there had ever been one, was long gone, but one pew remained.

Lorelei took off her borrowed hat and drank in the silence. The sounds of men and horses were distant, and the light pouring in through the crude stained-glass windows was soft.

She sat down in the pew, lowered her head and wept.

It wasn't just that every muscle in her body thrummed with pain. It wasn't even that she'd set out on a journey and couldn't let herself turn back, even though she didn't know the first thing about running a ranch, with or without cattle.

It was poor Raul, badly injured and in pain, perhaps even crippled.

It was the fact that her mother had died in an asylum.

It was William, taking a fatal fall before he'd lived out his childhood.

It was the sound of that rifle shot, still echoing in her mind all these years later, and knowing the pony had paid a terrible price for stumbling with all of Judge Alexander Fellows's hopes riding on his back.

"Lorelei?"

She stiffened. Of all the people who might have wandered into that dusty, forgotten little sanctuary and caught her with her face in her hands and her shoulders trembling, why did it have to be Holt McKettrick?

"Go away," she said, and drew in a deep, shuddering breath, desperate to compose herself.

She might have known he'd do precisely the opposite of what she'd asked. He swung one leg over the pew bench and sat astraddle it, facing her, turning his hat in his hands.

"I was pretty rough on you today," Holt said quietly. "I'm sorry."

She knew he didn't use those words often, both by his behavior and the awkward way he said them, but it was little or no consolation. "You flatter yourself if you think you've broken me," she said.

"Lorelei, I'm not *trying* to break you."

She met his gaze, defiant, swiping away the traces of her tears with the back of one hand. "Oh, no? Kindly do not insult my intelligence with lies, Mr. McKettrick. You'd like nothing better than to see me run back to San Antonio, leaving my ranch for you and Mr. Templeton to fight over."

He lowered his head for a moment, perhaps searching his thoughts, and when he looked at her again, his eyes held an unsettling blend of laughter and chagrin. "If you weren't crying about a hard day on the trail," he began, "what was it?"

"It's personal."

He pulled a surprisingly clean handkerchief from his shirt pocket and handed it to her, but not before a thin blue ribbon, the kind a young girl might wear in her hair, wafted to the stone floor.

He bent to retrieve it, smiled as he ran a callused thumb along its length.

In the meantime, Lorelei employed the handkerchief to good effect, first swabbing her wet face, then, as delicately as possible, blowing her nose. The linen cloth was streaked with trail dirt when she'd finished.

"Does that belong to your daughter?" she heard herself ask, referring to the little strip of blue silk.

Holt nodded, closed his fingers around the ribbon for a moment, then slipped it back into his pocket. "Lizzie gave it to me before I left the Triple M." He smiled wistfully. "I guess she was afraid I'd forget her."

Lorelei could have made a pointed comment, given that he'd apparently forgotten Lizzie's mother easily enough, but somehow, she didn't have the heart to do it. The way he'd held that ribbon, clasped it in his palm, said a great deal about his affection for the child.

Moreover, she'd been presumptuous, assuming that he'd followed her into the mission just to bedevil her. Perhaps he hadn't even known she was there. He could have come in for reasons of his own, ones that had nothing whatsoever to do with her.

"Why were you crying?" he asked.

"I'm not going to tell you," she said, "so please stop asking."

He chuckled. Shook his head.

"Did you come in here expecting to be alone?"

He studied her face with an exaggerated, mocking sort of interest, his eyes dancing. He was probably thinking about repeating her own words back to her. "No," he said, at such length that Lorelei nearly perished from the waiting. "I saw you come in. And I wanted to apologize." He paused, considering. "Maybe *wanted* is the wrong word. Both John and the Cap'n threatened to horsewhip me if I didn't."

The smiled reached her lips before she had a fair chance to catch it.

"Apology accepted?" he asked.

"Yes," she said, after much thought. "But it's probably a wasted effort, because we're bound to lock horns again tomorrow."

He laughed. "Most likely, you're right."

"I'm nearly always right," she said boldly.

He pretended to glower. "Or maybe it won't take until tomorrow," he said.

Then he stood, stepped over the bench, and put out his hand to her. "Truce?"

She hesitated, then allowed him to help her to her feet. "For the time being," she said.

He laughed. "Fair enough," he agreed.

# CHAPTER 23

A TRAILSIDE SUPPER, Lorelei soon discovered, left a lot to be desired. It consisted of cold biscuits and the huge pot of pinto beans Tillie had cooked up the night before, at the ranch. Nevertheless, the food filled the empty places, and the coffee was hot, strong and plentiful.

The sky was pierced with stars, from one horizon to the other, and even though Lorelei hurt in places she hadn't thought it was possible to feel pain, she felt strangely content, sitting beside that campfire, with Tillie perched on one side of her and Melina on the other.

"Look at that moon," Melina marveled, tipping her head back to admire the huge silvery orb.

Tillie was admiring her doll, which rested in her lap, stroking its frilly little dress with one hand, but Lorelei followed Melina's gaze.

That moon had looked down on all manner of things in its time, Lorelei reflected. And when they were all dead and gone, it would still be there, following its path, while new generations of people lived out their stories. "What do you suppose it was like out here, when the mission was still open?" she mused.

"Lonely," Melina said, with a small sigh. Sorrowful

had come to rest his muzzle on her thigh, and she stroked his head idly, still sky-gazing. "I wonder if Gabe can see that moon."

Tentatively, Lorelei touched Melina's hand. "Whatever happens to Gabe," she said, "you'll be all right."

"Will I?" Melina asked softly. And when she turned her head, Lorelei saw that there were tears standing in her eyes. "Gabe and I, we've been apart more than we've been together, but I always knew he was out there someplace. That he'd turn up when I least expected, bringing me presents, saying pretty words, making me laugh and cry and everything in between. He gets me mad enough to pull the nails out of a horseshoe with my teeth, but when he's around, well, even the most ordinary things seem special."

Tillie held up her doll for their inspection. "Doesn't she look pretty in her store-bought dress?"

"She surely does," Lorelei said.

"Her name is Pearl," Tillie announced. "I wish *my* name was Pearl."

Melina leaned forward to catch the other woman's eye. "What's wrong with Tillie?"

Tillie shrugged. "It's plain," she said. She sighed, stood up. "I guess I'd better put Pearl to bed. She's had a real long day."

"Haven't we all?" Lorelei replied. She would have sold her soul for a hot bath, but there was no sense in wanting what she couldn't have. "Where *are* we sleeping tonight?"

Melina, too, got to her feet, gently dislodging the dog in the process. "Holt said we ought to put our bedrolls in the mission."

Despite the truce they'd agreed upon earlier, Lorelei tightened her mouth a little. Holt said this, Holt said that. It made her want to rebel, with or without a valid reason.

"I think I'll stay up a while longer," she said.

"Don't be too long," Melina counseled, stretching. "We'll be rolling again before you know it." With that, she departed, as Tillie had, with the feckless Sorrowful trotting at her heels.

Lorelei sighed, watching the fire. The wood was beginning to crumble into embers, and the sparks rose like lightning bugs, bursting toward the sky as though trying to reach the moon.

Most of the cowboys had already spread their blankets on the ground and stretched out for the night, but Holt, Rafe, Captain Walton and Mr. Cavanagh crouched nearby, in a tight circle. Holt drew in the dirt with a stick, and the others nodded and made comments.

Presently, the conference ended, and the four men stood wearily and went their separate ways.

Holt nodded to Lorelei as he passed, headed in the direction of the stream, but he didn't speak. She was at once relieved and disappointed by that, and, being embroiled in this small paradox, she failed to notice that she wasn't alone until the Captain sat right down beside her.

"You ever played poker?" he asked.

Lorelei laughed. "No," she said.

"A person can learn a lot from a good game of five-card stud," he told her, his eyes twinkling. "When to hold and when to fold, for instance."

"I have no earthly idea what those terms mean," Lorelei said, tossing the dregs of her coffee into the fire. "Holding and folding, I mean."

"That's plain to see, Miss Fellows," the Captain told her good-naturedly. "When you hold, it means you've got good cards, or a chance to bluff your way through if they aren't what you'd hoped for. It's knowing when to fold that's tricky. If you've drawn a losing hand, you'd best throw in your cards."

Lorelei frowned. "Are you trying to tell me that I ought to give up?" she asked. Even mustering up some indignation would be too much work after the day she'd put in, but she felt the stirrings of it, just the same.

"No, ma'am," the Captain said. "I'm just saying that some battles are worth fighting and others are a pure waste of time and effort."

"If you're not talking about my ranch—"

The Captain patted her hand. "You think about it," he said. With that, he stood up again, tugged at the brim of his hat in mannerly farewell and disappeared into the darkness, going from substance to shadow to nothing at all.

Lorelei felt a peculiar tightening in her throat, along with a twinge of confusion. *You think about it,* the Captain had said.

Think about what?

She was too weary and sore to wrestle with a mystery, but she knew she'd worry at it until she went to sleep. She carried her cup to the spring, rinsed it thoroughly and returned it to the supply wagon, as she had seen the others do.

Mr. Cavanagh handed her a roll of blankets. "Tillie and Melina have already bedded down," he said. "You'd best do the same, Miss Lorelei."

She nodded and yawned. If she'd had the strength, she'd have asked him about the Captain's cryptic remark, but she would be lucky to get inside the mission before she collapsed from exhaustion, so her questions would have to wait.

She crossed the grassy camp, the bedroll in both arms, and resigned herself to a stone floor and a short night.

Tillie was already asleep, cradling her doll under her chin. Sorrowful lay curled at her feet, Melina a few feet away, eyes closed, her fingers entangled in a rosary. Lorelei spread out her blankets, took off her shoes and lay down.

Having so much on her mind, she had expected to toss and turn a while; instead, she plunged into sleep like someone hurled headfirst down a well.

A stirring awakened her, somewhere in the depths of the night.

Crickets chirped outside the mission, and a coyote howled in the distance. Except for those things, the silence was vast, a dark cloak spread over the sprawling landscape. What, then, had brought her out of that fathomless, dreamless slumber?

Lorelei raised herself onto her elbows and squinted, waiting for her eyes to adjust to the dim light. If it hadn't been for the moon, strained by the colored windows and pouring through the open doorway, she wouldn't have been able to see at all.

Melina lay sleeping, moonlight illuminating the soft contours of her face. She was still clutching her rosary.

Tillie and Sorrowful were gone.

Lorelei put a hand to her throat as a sense of alarm surged up from her insides. There was no clear reason to be afraid, but she was.

She flung back her blankets, pulled on her high-button shoes and scrambled to her feet. Outside the door, she paused, listening hard, trying to get some idea which way they might have gone. If she shouted Tillie's name, she'd awaken the whole camp. She choked, swallowing her own voice.

They'd probably gone to the supply wagon, she decided, calming down a little. Yes, that was it. Tillie must have gotten hungry, or perhaps she'd had a bad dream and wanted to be near her father. Physically, she was a woman, but in every other way Tillie was a child.

Lorelei rushed for the wagon, peered under it.

John Cavanagh slept in the grass, snoring lightly. There was no sign of Tillie.

A touch at her elbow made Lorelei jump, and she whirled to see Holt standing behind her, hair and clothes rumpled, yawning.

"What's the matter?"

Before she could think of an answer, for she was still half-asleep herself, Sorrowful began to bark, somewhere in the endless dark that surrounded them.

Lorelei drew a mental bead on the sound. "It's Tillie," she explained, hurrying over the rough ground, Holt taking long strides beside her. "She's wandered off someplace."

Sorrowful's barking intensified, and there was a frantic note to it that made both Lorelei and Holt break into a full run. Lorelei couldn't hope to match his pace; her feet kept catching on roots and sinking into unseen holes. Still, she raced on. Once, she caught the flash of moonlight on the barrel of Holt's .45 as he drew it, and a chill spun its way up her spine.

When she came to the stream bank, Lorelei was breathless with exertion and fear. There was Tillie, on her knees on the ground, her face buried in both hands. One of the cowboys stood over her, his hands out in a conciliatory gesture, and Sorrowful bounded around them in a circle.

Holt shoved his pistol back into his holster, grabbed

the cowboy by the back of his collar and flung him away from Tillie.

"What happened here?" he demanded.

Tillie raised her head, and the moonlight glimmered in the tears on her face. "He broke Pearl," she said, with plaintive sorrow. "He broke Pearl. She's dead."

Holt whirled on the cowboy.

"I didn't do nothin', boss," the young man said, backing away.

Lorelei regained her breath and hurried to Tillie, kneeling beside her, gathering her close. Tillie clung to her with both arms, sobbing into her shoulder, and Sorrowful ceased his barking to lie down nearby, with a sympathetic whimper.

"Tillie," Lorelei whispered, holding the girl tightly and watching Holt and the drover over her head. "Tillie, did he hurt you?"

"All I wanted was a little kiss," the cowboy complained.

"What am I going to do without Pearl?" Tillie wailed.

Holt drew back his fist and struck the other man, first in the face, then in the belly. The cowboy knelt in the grass, vomiting. "I think you done knocked out one of my teeth!" he cried, when he'd stopped gagging.

Holt got him by the shirt and hauled him back to his feet.

Lorelei held her breath.

"Get your gear," Holt said, "and ride out. If I ever so much as lay eyes on you again, I'll kill you where you stand."

Lorelei had no doubt that he meant what he said, and neither, apparently, did the cowboy. He snatched his hat

off the ground, slapped it onto his head and staggered
back toward the camp, one hand to his jaw.

Holt watched him go for a long moment, then turned
and walked over to crouch beside the two women.

"Tillie," he said, with a gentleness so at variance with
what Lorelei had just seen that she almost couldn't believe he was the same man. "It's all right."

Tillie pulled free of Lorelei to scrabble about in the
grass. Finally, she found the doll, and held it up as evidence. The beautiful china head was shattered, dangling
by a bit of thread and cloth. The tiny dress, the one Tillie
had been so proud of by the campfire earlier that night,
was torn and soiled.

She gave a despairing cry. "It's *not* all right, Holt," she
said, stumbling between one word and the next. "Look
at her. She's kilt!"

"I'll get you another one," Holt told her.

"Another one won't be Pearl," Tillie said with such
sorrow that Lorelei's own eyes filled with tears. "We've
got to bury her proper, Holt. I got to know she's buried
proper!"

"We'll do it," Holt said, and at last his eyes met
Lorelei's.

She nodded silently and stood up. Holt raised Tillie
from the ground, gripping her shoulders.

"She was my baby," Tillie wept.

Holt put his arms around the young woman, his chin
resting on top of her head. "I know, sweetheart," he said.
"I know." Then he lifted Tillie up into his arms, as easily
as if she were a child, and started for the camp.

Sorrowful and Lorelei followed.

John Cavanagh was up, and so was Rafe. The cowboy
had saddled his horse by then, and he rode off at a
gallop.

John's face contorted when he saw Tillie being carried, her cheeks slick with tears. "My God in heaven," he rasped.

"She's all right, Mr. Cavanagh," Lorelei said quickly.

"I need a shovel," Holt said, setting Tillie on her feet.

"A shovel?" Rafe asked, thrusting a hand through his hair. He turned and looked in the direction the cowboy had taken. "Did that son of a bitch kill somebody?" He made a move toward the corral, as if to mount his horse and give chase.

"He murdered Pearl," Tillie said.

Rafe looked confounded. "Pearl?"

"Just get the damned shovel!" Holt snapped.

Rafe did as he was asked.

Holt dug a grave over by the mission, and Tillie knelt to lay her baby in it with shaking hands. She whispered some private prayer, then looked up at Holt and nodded, just once.

Lorelei put a hand over her mouth as he covered the doll with dirt. The sun was creeping up over the eastern horizon, spilling light ahead of itself, while the moon still stood bright in the west.

Rafe had bound two sticks together with a piece of rawhide to make a cross, and he gave it to Tillie, who stuck it into the ground to mark the place.

The men lingered a few moments, none of them knowing what to say, and finally walked away.

Tillie, still kneeling beside Pearl's grave, looked up at Lorelei with a plea in her eyes.

"Do you think dolls go to heaven?" she asked.

BREAKFAST WAS a solemn and necessarily hasty affair. With the help of a subdued and thoughtful Mr. Kahill,

John brewed coffee, reheated last night's beans and fried up slabs of salt pork for everybody who wanted one.

Lorelei's appetite was gone; she shook her head when Holt offered her a plate.

"Eat," he said impatiently. "We might run across a lot worse than a dead doll along the trail, and you won't be any good if you're hungry."

She accepted the plate. Another time, she might have argued, but at that moment she felt as broken as poor Tillie's little Pearl.

Holt started to walk away, then stopped, in the grip of some afterthought, and turned back. "Thanks," he said.

Lorelei was puzzled, and her face must have shown it.

"For looking after Tillie," he explained.

She swallowed, tried to smile and failed. A strange thought shouldered its way into her mind. If she felt this undone over burying a doll, what must her father have felt seeing William laid in his grave?

"I thought you were going to kill that cowboy," she said, without thinking.

"I might have, if you and Tillie hadn't been there."

She believed him.

"Eat your breakfast," he repeated. "We don't have all day."

When the meal was over, the cowboys broke camp, exchanging glances but not quite daring to ask about the man who was missing.

Lorelei was trying to work out how to connect saddle and mule when Rafe approached and took over the task.

"I ought to do that myself," Lorelei said, but without much conviction.

"Watch me," he said, "and you'll get the idea."

She watched, and when it was over, she didn't know any more about saddling a mule than she had before.

"What happened out there, with Tillie and that cowboy?" Rafe asked, as he helped Lorelei mount up.

She settled herself astride the animal, took a light grip on the reins and immediately discovered that her palms were sore from holding onto them for dear life the morning before. "From what I could gather, he tried to kiss her. That's what he claimed, anyway. She must have struggled and dropped the doll." Lorelei's eyes burned at the memory of Tillie's grief; even now, the young woman was stricken, kneeling in the back of her father's wagon and gripping the tailgate, her gaze fixed on Pearl's grave.

Rafe watched as Holt climbed into the saddle and calmed Traveler with a pat to its glistening neck. The animal was skittish, yearning to run. Strength and violence seemed to course through the gelding's very veins.

"That explains the scrapes on my brother's knuckles," Rafe mused.

Lorelei remembered the cold conviction in Holt's face when he'd said he would have killed the cowboy if it hadn't been for her and Tillie, and shivered.

Holt gave the order, and the party mounted up. Rafe sighed philosophically and mounted his gelding. John Cavanagh released the brake lever on the wagon and whistled to the team, Sorrowful riding beside him on the seat and casting the occasional look back at Tillie as the rig and horses rolled forward.

Melina drew her pony up beside Lorelei. A floppy straw hat shielded her face from the sun, casting a netted shadow.

"Poor Tillie," she said, biting her lip.

Lorelei could only nod.

They rode past the place where she and Holt had found Tillie the night before. To Lorelei's secret relief, they followed the stream instead of crossing it. The pace was slower than the day before, but just as grueling, because the farther south they traveled, the rougher the terrain became.

Trees gave way to scrub brush and cacti, and the glare of the sun beat down on Lorelei's head, even through her hat, until her skull began to pound from the inside. Off in the distance, a cloud of smoke bloomed against the sky.

"Indians?" Lorelei asked, trying to hide her dread, when Captain Walton joined her and Melina. They were bringing up the rear, not even keeping pace with the wagon, and she suspected he'd been sent back to hurry them along.

"Not likely," the Captain said. "Mostly Comanches around here, and they don't generally give themselves away like that. They favor an ambush. Scream like demons escaping from hell when they're on you, though."

Lorelei swallowed and straightened her spine.

"They won't bother with us," Melina said. No doubt she'd noticed Lorelei's reaction and wanted to reassure her. "We don't have anything worth stealing. When we come back through with the cattle, that's when we'll have to be careful."

Oh, Lord, Lorelei thought.

The smoke plume billowed and grew.

"Maybe it's a wildfire," she fretted.

"More likely it's a homestead," the Captain suggested, relentlessly realistic.

Lorelei shuddered.

"You ladies had best hurry it up," urged the Captain, and even he was beginning to look worried now. He rode through the cluster of cowboys to join Holt and Rafe, who were in the lead.

Lorelei peered through the dust, stirred by the hooves of so many horses, trying to guess, by the motions of their hands and heads, what the three men were talking about.

Finally, Holt reined the Appaloosa around and came back to speak to the cowboys. They immediately fanned out, three on either side of the wagon.

Holt drew up alongside the wagon and spoke to John.

"See that little ravine down there?" he said, pointing at a large gash in the earth, gouged out by some ancient upheaval.

The smell of smoke mingled with the dust, and Lorelei swore she could feel the heat of that fire, even though she couldn't see the flames.

"I see it," John confirmed.

"I want you to hole up in there while Rafe, the Cap'n and I do some scouting up ahead," Holt said. His gaze shifted to Lorelei. "I don't suppose you know piss-all about guns."

"I can learn," Lorelei said, swelling with indignation. It was true that she'd never handled a firearm, but he didn't have to be rude about it.

Holt shook his head and turned his attention back to John. "Keep the women close to the wagon," he went on. "Give them each a rifle and show them how to load it. And make sure they don't shoot each other."

Lorelei flushed with a mixture of stark fear and righteous offense.

Holt chuckled grimly, resettled his hat and rode off to join Rafe and the Captain.

John sent the team high-stepping down a steep incline, bumping toward the ravine, while Holt, Rafe and the Captain rode hard for the fire. The cowboys stayed back, their rifles drawn and resting across the pommels of their saddles, forming a broad circle around the wagon.

When they'd reached the bottom of that great hole in the ground, John jumped down from the wagon and lowered the tailgate. Tillie and the dog wedged themselves back into a corner.

Mr. Cavanagh, meanwhile, dragged a long wooden crate within reach, raised the lid and lifted out one rifle, then another. Lorelei dismounted after Melina, and rubbed her sweating palms down the legs of her trousers just before John thrust a rifle into them.

The thing was heavy, and Lorelei had to stiffen her knees to keep from stumbling.

"Tillie, get over here," John snapped. "You've got to show these ladies how to handle a gun!"

"I thought you were going to—" Lorelei began.

"No time," John said, rounding the wagon to climb into the box and reclaim his own rifle from under the seat. Most likely, it was already loaded. "Tillie-girl, you stop that mopin' and do as you're told!"

With that, Mr. Cavanagh made his way up the ravine, rifle in hand.

Tillie blinked, crawled to the tailgate, and got down.

"You do it like this here," she told Lorelei, taking a gun from the crate and expertly popping it open to shove in a shell with one motion of her thumb.

Melina apparently didn't need instruction; she helped herself to a rifle of her own, loaded it and sighted in on a pile of rocks on the other side of the ravine. Without a moment's hesitation, she pulled the trigger.

The shot boomed like thunder, the sound bouncing off the walls of the ravine. Sorrowful howled piteously, and John and a couple of the cowboys rushed to peer down at the three women.

Melina smiled and lowered the rifle. "Just making sure the bullets are good," she called up to them.

"I don't know if I can do this," Lorelei said.

"You will if there's a Comanche coming at you," Melina replied.

"Here," Tillie urged, and handed Lorelei the rifle she'd just loaded. "You try it."

Lorelei recoiled instinctively, then thought about Comanches and took a firm hold.

"There's another shot coming!" Melina called to the men above. "Everybody stay back!" She should have been afraid, by rights, but her eyes glittered with excitement.

Lorelei's arms shook as she raised the gun, the way she'd seen Melina do, and fired at random. Sorrowful yowled and shinnied under the wagon. The rifle kicked, almost knocking Lorelei to the ground, and she knew she'd have a bruise where the stock struck her shoulder.

"You took off a hunk of the buckboard," Tillie said, impressed.

"You're not supposed to just haul off and shoot," Melina put in, less genially. "We're lucky that bullet didn't ricochet off the wall of the ravine and kill one of us."

"*You* shot at the rocks," Lorelei pointed out defensively. She was dizzy with contained fear and something else, too—a sense of power. She could protect herself if she had to, and the knowledge of that was heady.

"*I* know what I'm doing," Melina fired back.

Sorrowful belly-crawled his way out from under the wagon, looked around carefully. Tillie laughed, and the sound was beautiful to Lorelei, even with all their lives in danger.

John leaned over the edge of the ravine. "Are you women through shootin'?" he asked, glowering.

"Yes, sir," Melina called back, shading her eyes with one hand. She'd lost her hat somewhere along the way, and her dark hair was coming down from its pins, tumbling around her shoulders.

"Well, good," John said. "Let's hope the Comanches didn't hear it!"

"Oh, my Lord," Lorelei whispered.

"Holt's gonna be good and mad," Tillie confided, grinning.

Lorelei found a flat rock and sat down. She'd rather deal with an angry Holt McKettrick than a Comanche raiding party, but not by much.

THEY FOUND the rancher first, lying on his back next to the horse trough, with an arrow jutting from his chest. He'd been scalped, and the flies were already gathering.

"Christ," Rafe said.

Holt got down off Traveler and crouched to lay the backs of his fingers to the man's throat, though he knew he wouldn't find a pulse. The pit of his stomach quivered, and he swallowed the bile that rushed into the back of his throat. Riding with the Rangers, he'd seen a hundred of these raids if he'd seen one. But it wasn't the sort of thing a man ever got used to.

Kahill, the Captain and one of the other men approached the blazing house, and Kahill peered through the open doorway, his bandana pressed to his face. They all reeled away, coughing from the smoke.

"There's a woman in there, and two little girls," Kahill said, then retched in the dirt. The Captain looked haunted.

Holt rushed for the door and was met with a wall of heat. Before the flames forced him back, he saw the bodies. The woman still gripped a pistol in one charred hand; he knew she'd shot the children and then herself. Given what Holt knew about Comanches, he didn't blame her.

"Sweet Jesus," he said, as Rafe met him in the middle of the yard and handed him a canteen.

Kahill staggered to the trough and splashed his face with water. Then he looked at the dead rancher and took to retching again.

"What do we do now?" Rafe asked quietly, watching Holt drink. "Go after them?"

"Not with three women and a wagon slowing us down," Holt said, wiping his mouth. "And we sure as hell can't leave them in that ravine."

Rafe scanned the small homestead. If there'd been horses or a milk cow, the Comanches had helped themselves to them. The shed was still standing, though.

"Better have a look in there," Holt said.

"Might be a shovel," Rafe agreed, frowning. "We have to bury these folks."

Holt wanted to say there wasn't time, because there wasn't, but he knew they couldn't leave the bodies. He turned to Kahill, who was gray around the mouth.

"Take a couple of men and go back for the others," he said. "We'll spend the night here."

Kahill nodded and mounted up. Rafe pushed open the creaky shed door as the three men rode out at a gallop. He and Holt both peered inside. Holt blinked, unable to see anything at first.

Moment by moment, he made out a barrel, then a stack of wood and tools hanging on the far wall. There was a wheelbarrow, too, and a flash of movement inside it.

"What the hell?" Rafe whispered.

Holt stepped over the high threshold, walked over to the wheelbarrow and looked inside.

"I'll be damned," he said, and broke into a grin.

# CHAPTER 24

THE BABY WAS NAKED, except for a diaper fashioned from a piece of scrap calico. It gurgled, kicking both feet and clutching at the air with plump little fists, and its head bristled with a thatch of fine, wheat-colored hair, curly and moist with sweat.

"It's a kid," Rafe said, sounding confounded.

"I gathered that much," Holt replied. "You pick it up. You've been around babies."

Rafe hesitated, just the same. Then he rubbed his big hands together, as though the task required friction, and leaned down to lift the child from its bed of straw. "It's wet," he said. Evidently, matters such as that fell to his wife, Emmeline, at home; he did not seem to know what to do. "Maybe hungry, too."

"Damn," Holt marveled. "She must have hid it here— the woman, I mean."

Gingerly, Rafe tucked a finger under the front of the sodden diaper and peered inside. "We can stop calling him 'it,'" he said. "This here is a little boy."

Finding that baby alive made up for a lot, in Holt's mind. There were still bodies to bury, and the task would be a grim one, but here was the proof that life will always find a way to push through. Reminded him of a wild-flower he'd seen once, in the high-country of Arizona, growing right up through a flat rock, with no apparent regard for impossibility.

"What are we going to do with him?" Rafe asked. It was a reasonable question, once you got past the obvious fact that they'd have to take the infant as far as the next town. In the meantime, he'd need feeding, and diapers.

"We ought to reach Laredo in a day or two," Holt said. "Maybe he's got folks there."

"And maybe he doesn't," Rafe replied gravely. He nodded toward the house. "Everything's burned up. We don't even know this family's last name."

"There ought to be some property records in Laredo. A deed or a homestead claim, maybe. Our part is to get him there. The law will do the rest."

Rafe laid the baby back down in the straw, pulled off his bandana and set about unpinning the scrap of calico. The effort was an awkward one, but he managed the diaper change, and Holt was impressed.

"Maybe she left a letter or something," Holt said, chagrined because he hadn't been of any practical help. "The boy's mother, I mean."

Rafe looked skeptical, holding the baby against one broad shoulder. "I don't reckon she had time for that," he said. "I'm trying not to think about how things might have turned out different if we'd gotten here sooner."

Holt nodded. "Me, too," he said quietly. Then he frowned. "Why do you figure she didn't hide the little girls out here, too?"

Rafe shook his head. "Most likely, they were real scared, and raising a fuss. If they carried on, the raiders would have heard them and come right for this shed."

Holt was still perplexed. "The missus must have been

expecting somebody to come along later. He'd have died of starvation or exposure, left alone like that."

"Maybe she didn't think that far," Rafe answered sadly. "It's not like those red devils gave notice that they'd be stopping by to massacre everybody they ran across. Christ, I wish we'd been just an hour or two faster on the trail."

Holt laid a hand on his brother's shoulder. "We weren't. That's the fact of the matter. Even if we had been, there's no guarantee we could have held them off. From the number of tracks out there, I'd say there were at least three dozen of them."

"Comanches?" Rafe asked. Sometimes, raids like this were blamed on the Indians, when the real culprits were white men, with an ax of their own to grind. Arrows were easy enough to come by—even a schoolboy could make one—and any cold-hearted son of a bitch with a knife could scalp somebody.

"Probably," Holt said. "The horses were unshod."

They stepped out into the brutal sunshine, Holt having gathered what shovels and spades were available, Rafe bringing up the rear with the baby. The fire was dying down now, burning itself out. Just the same, it would be hours before they could safely remove the burned bodies and give them proper burial.

John's wagon was rolling toward them, maybe a quarter of a mile distant, and raising plenty of dust. Captain Jack approached, squinting at the child.

"Well," he said. "Look what you found. Poor little cuss."

Holt nodded glumly and looked around for a good place to dig four graves. "We'd best get the holes ready," he said.

The Captain cocked a thumb toward the cabin, just as

the roof caved in. Sparks flew heavenward, the way Holt hoped the spirits of that woman and those two innocent little girls had done. "Smart lady," the old man said. "She managed to hide one of them, anyhow, God rest her."

Holt watched the wagon approaching. When the women arrived, they could look after the baby while the men dug. "Somebody cover that body," he said, with a nod at the dead rancher. "I don't want Lorelei or any of the others to see what those bastards did."

"Not much we can do to hide it," the Captain said. "I'll go out to meet them. Get a blanket and tell them to hold up a few minutes before they come in."

Holt merely nodded again, took a grip on one of the shovels and headed for a copse of oak trees nearly. The little clearing at the center would do for a plot as well as any other.

Rafe sat down nearby, on a rock, holding the baby. "He must have put up a fuss when he heard all that ruckus," he mused thoughtfully. "Guess it was just good luck or the grace of God those Indians didn't hear him."

"They might not have killed a baby boy," Holt answered, jamming the shovel into hard ground. "The girls on the other hand—that doesn't bear thinking about."

"Makes me want to go home," Rafe admitted. "See that Emmeline and little Georgia are all right."

"I feel the same about Lizzie," Holt said. "But we're in this thing now, and we've got to see it through. Anyway, if there's one thing we can be sure of, it's that Pa and Kade and Jeb will look after our womenfolk like they were their own."

Rafe spared a slight grin. "Hell," he said. "Far as those three are concerned, a McKettrick is a McKettrick, born that way or married in. I pity the poor fool who thinks otherwise."

Holt felt a slackening in the muscles between his shoulders as he shoveled up more dirt. There weren't many things he was sure of in this life, but he knew Rafe was right. If anybody came after a McKettrick, he had best be prepared to deal with the whole outfit, and win or lose, it would be a fight to remember.

The Captain rode out to meet the wagon, as he'd said he would, and came back with an armload of blankets. He covered the rancher with a gentleness that belied his many years of doing hard battle with every enemy he came across, and then fired his six-gun into the air as a signal to John to bring the wagon in.

"Did you see that?" Rafe asked.

For a moment, Holt was confused. "See what?" he asked, with some irritation, as some of the other men took up shovels and spades and joined in the digging.

"This baby didn't bat an eye when that gun went off," Rafe said, studying the child. "I don't reckon he can hear."

LORELEI'S GAZE went right to the baby nestled against Rafe's shoulder, but before she could even get down off Seesaw's back, Tillie was on the ground and running, Sorrowful bounding along behind her.

Lorelei and Melina exchanged glances and rode to the edge of the copse.

Tillie stood staring at the child with her eyes wide and her mouth open. She seemed struck with wonder, like a shepherd coming upon the Nativity.

Rafe smiled at her. "Do you want to hold him?" he asked quietly, while Holt paused to rest on the handle of his shovel and watch. He was up to his knees in the dirt, and Lorelei reckoned the digging for a bad sign. She looked around uneasily.

"What's his name?" Tillie demanded, as though that were a factor in her decision to touch him or not.

"Don't know," Rafe said.

The child tugged at a lock of Rafe's dark, sweat-matted hair.

Lorelei's gaze connected with Holt's. It required an effort, but she broke away and took in the scene she'd been trying to ignore. She saw the shape of a man beneath one of the blankets the Captain had requested, and knew by the graves being dug, and the way some of the men were staring at the burned cabin and shaking their heads, that something truly horrible had happened here.

Bile surged into the back of her throat, scalding like acid, and she swallowed, willing herself not to throw up.

"He's got to have a name," Tillie insisted, her voice rising a little. The baby began to cry, an odd, thwarted sound. "Everybody needs a name."

"You pick one, then," Rafe said.

"Pearl," Tillie replied resolutely.

Nobody argued.

Melina stepped up to Rafe and held out her arms. "He wants feeding," she said. "I'll give him some sugar water. Find something to cover him up, too, so the sun doesn't fry him like a trout in a skillet."

Rafe hesitated, then surrendered the baby. He stood, stretched and reached for Holt's shovel. Holt's fingers locked around the handle, but then he let go.

He approached Lorelei, holding his hat in both hands.

"It's a far cry from the life you're used to, isn't it?" he asked. There was no disdain in his tone or manner; he was simply pointing out a lamentable fact.

"Yes," she said bleakly, thinking of the tea parties she'd attended in San Antonio prior to her ignoble expulsion from the Ladies' Benevolence Society, of the smooth, crisp sheets on her bed in the judge's house. She'd spent the majority of her days reading or sewing or playing the spinet. The hardest decision she'd been called upon to make was whether to wear a bonnet when she went out to the shops, or what Angelina ought to fix for supper. "There—there was a massacre?"

Holt might have made something of the fact that the answer to her question was patently obvious, but he didn't. He rubbed the back of his neck with one hand and thrust out a sigh.

"Four people are dead," he told her, straight out. "A woman and two little girls in the cabin, and that's the man of the family under that blanket."

Lorelei closed her eyes. The heat of that place was intense, as though a crack had opened in the earth and hell itself had broken through. The smells were enough to turn her stomach, and the sounds of those shovels, striking stone…

She shuddered, and felt Holt's hands close on her shoulders. When she opened her eyes, his face was inches from her own. His skin was brown from years in the sun, she noticed, and his features had hardened in the brief time since she'd seen him leave camp that morning.

"We'll be in Laredo in a day or so," he told her. "Maybe you've seen enough now to convince you that life in San Antonio wasn't so bad, even with your father calling all the shots."

She blinked. "I can't go back," she said.

"I know you had words with him," Holt reasoned, "but he's your father. He'll take you in."

"I don't want to be 'taken in'!" Lorelei burst

out in a fierce whisper. "I was safe in that house—I had everything I needed and most of what I wanted. But I wasn't *alive!* I was just marking time, waiting for things to change. Waiting for something—anything—to happen. I won't go back to that!"

A muscle bunched in Holt's jaw, and his grip on her shoulders tightened.

"Maybe if you looked under that blanket over there, you'd change your mind," he growled. "This isn't a game, *Miss* Fellows. This is what it's really like out here!"

Lorelei pulled away and half-stumbled toward the body on the ground. "Oh, God," she whispered.

"Come away," Holt said, in a tone that might have been gentle if it hadn't been for the fierce urgency underlying the words.

She nodded miserably.

"What—what can I do to help?"

"Stay out—" *Stay out of the way,* he'd been about to say. But he stopped himself. "See if Melina needs help with the baby," he said. "And keep Tillie occupied. She'll get underfoot if you don't."

Lorelei bit her lower lip. "It doesn't seem like much," she said, after a quick nod.

"It's what there is," he replied, and turned away from her, striding back toward the trees, where the graves were being dug.

For a long moment, she stood staring down at that blanket-covered body. Then, after straightening her shoulders, Lorelei headed for the wagon.

The tailgate was lowered, and Melina sat in the wagon bed, legs dangling, attempting to interest the baby in a twisted bit of cloth, soaked in sugar water. Tillie hovered, and Lorelei could see restraint quivering in every line of her lithe body—she wanted to reach out and take the child into her own arms.

"He needs milk," Lorelei said.

"You see a cow around here anyplace?" Melina countered, though not unkindly.

If there had been a cow, the Indians had taken it, along with whatever other livestock the homesteaders had possessed. There wasn't even a chicken in sight.

"Sugar will not provide proper nourishment," Lorelei said. With that, she lifted the lid off the pot of cold beans left over from that morning and, in turn, from the night before. She found a clean cup and plunged it into the pot, then located a spoon, and used that to mash the stuff into a pulp.

Melina smiled, wiped her forehead with one hand, and surrendered the child to Tillie, after instructing her to sit down on a small keg. Lorelei crouched and offered the child a taste of the beans.

He made a face, widened his ice-blue eyes, and then, waving both hands, sampled the fare.

Lorelei beamed at him. "Good boy," she said.

Tillie looked enormously pleased. "Pearl is a *very* good boy."

HOLT, HAVING COME TO the water barrel fixed to the side of the wagon and found the ladle missing, rounded the tailgate to search for it. Seeing Lorelei on her lovely haunches, smiling and spooning something into the boy's mouth, stopped him with the efficacy of a blow to the stomach.

She was still clad in trail clothes, and covered with half the dirt that lay between San Antonio and this God-forsaken homestead. Her hair was tumbling down from beneath her hat in untidy loops. The sight should not have been profound—but it was.

The moment, there in the midst of some of the worst carnage he'd ever seen, was a holy one.

He caught his breath.

She sensed his presence then, and looked away from the child's face to meet his eyes.

He cleared his throat. "Where's the ladle?" he asked, because that was all that came to mind.

Her mouth twitched slightly. "About six inches from your right hand, Mr. McKettrick," she said mildly, and went back to what she was doing.

Holt felt himself color up, and he was glad as hell that she wasn't looking at him anymore, even though he'd felt the shift of her gaze like a tearing-away of flesh. "Thanks," he grumbled, snatching up the ladle, which rested in plain sight on the floorboards of the wagon and would have bitten him if it had been a snake, and headed back to the water barrel. He drank his fill, then sluiced a couple of ladles' full down the back of his neck.

"Pearl likes beans a whole lot," Tillie called.

*Pearl,* Holt thought. Wasn't it bad enough that the kid had lost his whole family in an Indian raid? Did he have to be saddled with a female name into the bargain?

Rafe wandered over, appropriated the ladle, and wet his own whistle. "We've got the graves dug, and the Cap'n and I brought the woman and the little girls out of the embers. That's a job I'll see again in my nightmares." He took more water and, as Holt had done, poured it down the back of his neck. "Seems like somebody ought to say a few words."

"I'll do it," said John, wiping his sweating, sooty face with his bandana as he approached. He hadn't done much digging, but he'd gathered piles of stones to cover the graves, in the hope that the wild animals wouldn't get to them. "I can't say as I have much to say on God's behalf just now, though."

"Just ask the Lord if maybe He'd trouble Himself to let four souls pass through the pearly gates," Rafe said. "Though from the looks of things around here, I'd say He was away from home, or maybe laid up with the gout."

If the subject hadn't been so serious, Holt might have laughed. Rafe was a believer, but not an agreeable one, for the most part, and he had a contentious theology all his own. Holt, on the other hand, was undecided. Sometimes, when he looked out over a broad, green valley, he figured there had to be a God of some kind. On days like that one, his thoughts tended to come down on one of two possibilities: either there was no God at all, or He was a hardhearted old coot who didn't really give a damn about much of anything.

IT WAS SUNSET by the time the graves were covered. The men stood with their hats off, and John Cavanagh said a brief prayer. "Lord, we don't know what these folks' names were. We hope to find out, once we get to Laredo. We thank You that this little boy—Pearl—was spared. Receive these innocent souls unto Your bosom. Amen."

"Amen," Lorelei murmured, holding Pearl, now freshly diapered in a section of her favorite petticoat, with one of the Captain's none-too-clean shirts over that. He was a sturdy little fellow, perhaps six months old, and over the course of the afternoon, Lorelei had come to accept Rafe's theory—the child was not only an orphan, he was deaf.

They made camp about a hundred yards from the house, on the other side of the trees, but the smell of death followed them, clinging to their clothes, their hair, their very skin.

"I would give ten years of my life for a bath," Lorelei said, when supper—more beans, supplemented with jackrabbit—was over.

"There's a little pond down yonder," Tillie said, nodding her head toward a stand of trees, well on the other side of the homestead. "I saw it when I was hunting rabbits."

Melina, rocking the sleeping baby in her arms, widened her eyes. "What would Holt say if he knew you went so far? Land sakes, Tillie, there are Indians around here!"

"They're a long ways off by now," Tillie said. Slow-witted and childlike though she was, she had moments when she almost sounded normal. "And I don't do everything Holt tells me no-how." She sniffed. "I'm not a cowboy, so it doesn't matter that he's trail boss."

"We couldn't," Lorelei said hesitantly, imagining that pond and what it would be like to be clean. "Could we?"

"Reckon we could if we brought a rifle," Melina said.

Lorelei frowned. "If the Indians are gone—"

"You want to bet your life on it?" Melina asked. "I'm not tossing mine into the ante."

"All right," Lorelei said. "Maybe we should just tell Holt—"

"And have a couple of cowboys watching the whole show, on the pretense of standing guard?" Melina shook her head. "Not me."

"You two go on," Tillie said. "I'll look after Pearl. If anybody asks about you, I'll just say you're in the bushes."

Lorelei hesitated to leave Tillie alone with the baby, but there was plenty of help around if she needed it.

"It's the only way we're going to get a bath, I guess," Melina whispered, with a combination of reluctance and urgency.

Lorelei looked around the camp. Holt, the Captain and Mr. Cavanagh were conferring again, over by the wagon. Rafe was probably there, too, but she couldn't make him out, what with all the shadows.

The rest of the men were either standing watch or playing a subdued game of poker in a shaft of moonlight underneath a lone oak tree.

"All right," she said. "But how do we get our things, and a rifle? I've got soap in my bedroll."

"Just walk right over to the pile of gear and get both our bundles," Melina told her, nodding toward the heap that had formed when all the horses and mules were relieved of their saddles and bridles. "Kahill left his rifle leaning against the rear wheel of the buckboard when he went to join the poker game. I'll fetch it while Tillie and Pearl are bedding down underneath the wagon. Tillie, I know you don't want to wake the baby, but you need to make a little stir getting situated. That way, if anybody attracts attention, it will be you."

Tillie nodded. It was probably all a game to her, and if anyone asked her directly, she'd most likely tell them without compunction that Lorelei and Melina had sneaked off to the pond to take a bath.

It was a chance they would have to take, in the name of personal hygiene.

"HOLT?" RAFE SAID QUIETLY, when the jawing fest was over and the Captain and Mr. Cavanagh went about their business. "Could I have a word with you?"

Holt shoved a hand through his hair. "I thought you were playing poker," he said wearily.

"I like to size up the situation a while before I go betting on the other man's game," Rafe replied. "I've just been walking around the camp, thinking. Wishing I could lie down beside Emmeline tonight. I miss her something fierce."

Holt sighed. "I know," he said, feeling long on sympathy but a little short on patience. "Is that what you wanted to tell me?"

Rafe's grin gleamed in the moonlight. Damned if he didn't know something Holt didn't. "It's about the women," he said. "Lorelei and Melina, I mean. They just stole Kahill's rifle and lit out for the pond, down over that little hill on the other side of the homestead. They mean to take a bath."

*"What?"* Holt rasped, and started in that direction.

Rafe reached out and grasped his arm. "Wait. They haven't been gone more than a couple of minutes."

Holt stared at his brother, baffled and furious. "God-*damn*," he growled. "Just when I'm thinking Lorelei might have sense enough to pound sand into a gopher hole after all, she goes wandering off in the dark, to lather herself up in some pond!" He wrenched free of Rafe's grasp, pulled his .45 from the holster and spun the cylinder to make sure it was loaded.

"Hold on, Holt," Rafe reiterated. "They've had a hell of a day, just like we have. And women need to fuss with such things."

"This isn't a fancy hotel in some big city," Holt retorted. "It's the goddamn middle of Comanche territory!"

"You know those bastards are off celebrating somewhere, Holt. Most likely roasting up whatever cattle they managed to scavenge from this pitiful place. I say we let the women have their baths. We'll just follow along and make sure nothing happens. We don't have to let them know we're there."

Holt peered at Rafe, even angrier than before. "If you think you're going to watch Lorelei take off her clothes—"

Rafe laughed. "As enjoyable as that would be, I'm a married man, and a happy one. I'd like to stay that way. What I'm suggesting is that we just hang around, within shouting distance. If they need help, we'll be right there handy."

Holt considered. Lorelei, naked in the moonlight.

His groin ached, and he was glad as hell that it was dark.

"All right," he said.

They started toward the pond.

"Why don't you just admit you're sweet on her?" Rafe taunted, as they walked.

"I'm not sweet on anybody," Holt growled.

Rafe laughed, real low. "Bullshit," he said. "If looking at a woman was the same as bedding her, you'd be in jail."

The word *jail* made Holt think of Gabe, which would have been a welcome distraction if his old friend wasn't a step closer to the gallows with every day that passed. "You're full of sheep-dip," he snapped. "I don't even *like* that woman."

"You don't have to like a woman to take her to bed," Rafe reasoned, and given his colorful history, pre-Emmeline, he could claim a certain authority. "You don't have to like her to love her, either."

"Now you're just running off at the mouth," Holt accused, exasperated. "I might expect crazy talk like that from our little brother Jeb, but you're supposed to have more sense."

Rafe chuckled. "Just answer one question, and I'll let the matter drop."

"That depends on the *question*."

"If that rider hadn't shown up when he did and prevented the wedding, would you have made love to your bride?"

"Hell, yes," Holt admitted, because he knew Rafe wouldn't buy it if he said no. "But I don't see what that has to do with anything. I *liked* Margaret."

"Exactly. You liked her. But she didn't get under your hide the way Lorelei does. She didn't piss you off. And I never once saw you kiss her the way you kissed Lorelei that day after you jerked her off that bucking mule, back there on her so-called ranch."

Holt lengthened his strides. He could hear Lorelei and Melina up ahead, talking. Did they think they were being quiet? Hell, every Indian within fifty miles could probably hear them.

"I'm glad you didn't decide to be a lawyer," he bit out, "because you don't have the knack for it. What does kissing Lorelei have to do with liking or loving or any of that other bull crap?"

"I'm saying," Rafe answered, with exaggerated patience, "that you may not like Lorelei, but it seems to me that there's a pretty good chance that you love her."

"You," Holt said, wishing he had the time to stop and beat the hell out of Rafe, right there on the spot, "are three kinds of an idiot, and blind on top of it. The sooner I get shut of that woman, the happier I'm going to be!"

Rafe didn't say anything more, but he was smirking.

Holt jerked off his hat and struck his brother in the belly with it.

Rafe laughed, under his breath.

Up ahead, the women rustled through the trees and underbrush surrounding the pond. Holt stopped, still as a statue, trying not to let his imagination run away with him.

Lorelei.

Bathing.

Oh, God.

# CHAPTER 25

THE POND WAS TEPID, a black expanse splashed with dancing fragments of moonlight. Having taken off her shoes and rolled the legs of her trousers almost to her knees, Lorelei waded back to shore to shed her clothes. She had never undressed in the open air that way, and there was a glorious freedom in the very recklessness of such an act. After pulling a bar of soap from her bundle, she splashed back into the water.

Melina soon joined her, though she still wore her bloomers and camisole.

Belatedly, Lorelei remembered the pins in her hair. She'd already lost most of them, but a few still held. Once she'd tossed them ashore, she ducked under the surface and came up with a sigh of purest pleasure.

Using the soap, she lathered her hair, rinsed it, and went through the whole process again. She scoured every inch of her body, and was floating peacefully on her back, soaking cool evening air and moonlight into her flesh, when Melina suddenly cried out.

Lorelei scrambled to her feet, shook her wet hair back from her face. "What is it?"

Melina gave a squeal and splashed for the bank. "Leeches!" she shrieked. "They're all over me!"

Lorelei stood absolutely still, too stunned to react.

"Lorelei!" Melina shouted. "Get out of the water!" She was sitting on the bank now, kicking her feet and clawing at her bare arms. Dark, liver-colored blotches clung to her flesh.

The sight spurred Lorelei out of her stupor. She rose out of the pond just as Rafe and Holt came crashing through the brush.

Lorelei ducked behind a scanty bush, as conscious of her nakedness as Eve after the Fall.

"What the devil?" Rafe demanded.

"Leeches!" Melina shrieked. "Do something! Do something!"

Lorelei looked down at herself, and her stomach lurched. The dreadful creatures clung to her thighs, her stomach, her bosom. She gave a little cry of despondent horror and nearly swooned.

Holt caught her by the arms before she got to her knees. "Take it easy," he said. "They're not poisonous—they're just ugly."

Lorelei was too distraught to weep, or to worry that she was naked. It seemed a bothersome detail, in comparison to those disgusting *things* attached to her, drinking her very blood.

"Help me," she pleaded.

"Stand still," Holt said. He pulled off one leech, and then another, tossing them into the brush. Just down the bank, Rafe was squatting beside Melina, who was prone and squirming, performing the same task.

"Turn around," Holt urged. "They're all over your back and your—well, they're all over you."

"Oh, God," Lorelei whimpered.

"I think I've just found religion," Holt remarked.

"Don't you *dare* tease me!"

He merely chuckled and went on plucking away the leeches. Each one clung tenaciously, and the pulling hurt, but Lorelei didn't care. She just wanted the beastly globs *gone*.

"If Emmeline hears about this," Rafe called merrily, "I'll be sleeping in the bunkhouse until I'm older than Pa is now."

Holt laughed. "I reckon it qualifies as an emergency." Lorelei felt a leech let go of her left buttock, and wished the ground would open up and swallow her.

"Please hurry!" Melina wailed.

"Stop that squirming," Rafe counseled.

At last, at last, the humiliating ordeal was over. Holt gave Lorelei a cursory inspection. "Good as new," he said. "Where are your clothes?"

Lorelei's face flamed. "There—that bundle beside the rock," she said desperately. It seemed to her that Holt McKettrick took his sweet time fetching her nightgown, and he indulged himself in a long, brazen look at her before he handed it over.

"You were watching us bathe!" she accused, as soon as she'd pulled the garment over her head.

Melina, apparently free of leeches, sat shivering in the blanket from her bedroll.

"I swear we weren't," Rafe declared. "We were just up the trail a ways."

"Lucky thing, too," Holt said. He was trying not to grin, and he was a miserable failure at it. "If you'd had to depend on each other, you'd still be jumping around, screaming."

Lorelei drew herself up on a swell of pure exasperated

embarrassment. "You might have warned us that there were leeches in this pond," she said.

"You didn't ask and, anyway, we wouldn't have known for sure. One thing about Texas—there can be some real nasty critters in the water. Snakes, for one, and flesh-eating fish."

Lorelei suddenly felt dizzy. "Flesh-eating…?"

"They've been known to eat a whole cow in five minutes," Holt said.

"Holt," Rafe protested. "I believe that's more than the lady really needs to be apprised of right now."

Holt leaned in, his nose an inch from Lorelei's. "Be glad it was leeches," he whispered.

Lorelei trembled with rage, and a good bit of residual fear. "If you say one single thing about this, to *anyone*—"

Holt raised his eyebrows. His arms were folded, each of his hands tucked beneath the opposite elbow, as though to keep himself from touching her. "Oh, I won't tell," he said. "I like to keep my encounters with naked ladies to myself." A corner of his mouth quirked with infuriating delight.

Lorelei longed to slap him, yearned for the release of her palm making contact with his smug face, but she restrained herself. For one thing, she feared she'd use up the last of her strength if she did, and for another, he *had* rescued her, woefully arrogant creature that he was.

She plopped down on a rock and picked up one of her shoes.

"I'd shake that out first, if I were you," Holt said mildly.

A thrill of terror went through Lorelei.

"Could be a scorpion in there, or a tarantula."

Lorelei peered into her shoe and then turned it upside

down and shook it with all her might. Nothing fell out, but that wasn't good enough. She banged the heel against the rock she was sitting on, which relieved some of her tension, and wrenched it onto her foot. While she went through the whole process again with the other shoe, Holt watched her with a sort of quizzical good humor.

"In two days we'll be in Laredo," he said. "Maybe you'd like to think some more about this whole ranching idea."

Lorelei shot to her feet, wavered and slapped Holt's hand away when he tried to steady her.

"Don't *touch* me!" she snarled.

He grinned. "Too late," he said. "Like it or not, there's been some touching done here tonight."

Rafe hefted a dazed and speechless Melina to her feet. "That'll do, Holt," he said quietly. "Best we get back to camp before we run into some Comanches. They won't be as easy to deal with as leeches."

Holt ignored his brother and gestured for Lorelei to pass ahead of him. Rafe led, with Melina and Lorelei following.

"Sometimes leeches get such a good grip on a person's hide that they have to be burned off with matches," Holt said cordially. "One time, on the Brazos River—"

Rafe turned to catch Holt's eye, glaring. He carried Melina's borrowed rifle in one hand.

Holt shrugged affably. "Folks ought to know what they're getting themselves into, in country like this," he said. "Especially *women*folks."

AN HOUR LATER, Lorelei lay under the wagon, cosseted in her bedroll. Tillie was sound asleep beside her, the little boy cuddled in her arms, and Melina rested on the other side of them, curled into a little ball and making a soft sniffling sound. The rest of the camp was quiet; except for the men keeping the first watch, everyone had apparently gone to sleep.

"Melina?" Lorelei whispered. "Are you all right?"

"I can still feel them on me," Melina answered.

"Me, too," Lorelei admitted. "Does it make you want to go back?"

"Go back where?" Melina murmured despairingly. "I don't have a judge for a father, or a big house in San Antonio."

Lorelei swallowed. "I don't, either," she said.

Melina sat up, taking care not to bump her head on the bottom of the wagon. "I'm sorry," she told Lorelei, wiping her eyes. "I shouldn't have said that. I was just feeling sorry for myself, that's all."

Lorelei was in a forgiving mood, except when it came to Holt. Sure, he'd helped her with the leeches, but he'd been insufferable about it. If it hadn't been for Rafe, he would have joshed her all the way back to camp.

"It was like acting in a play," she reflected. "Living in my father's house, I mean."

Melina frowned, looking puzzled, and reached out absently to pat the sleeping baby when he stirred against Tillie's chest. "I don't reckon I understand what you mean," she said.

"My dresses were really costumes," Lorelei went on. "I played the judge's spinster daughter. He wrote the lines, and I said them right on cue—most of the time anyway. But none of it was real."

"A play," Melina muttered thoughtfully, working her way through the metaphor. She was bright and found her way quickly. "I'm not so sure I'd choose Indian raids and dusty trails and leeches over a nice clean life like that, though."

Lorelei sighed. "It was easy enough, I guess. There was a bathtub, and plenty of hot water. We never ate beans, or slept on the ground or had to worry about leeches. But I never really *felt* anything. It was as though I was walking in my sleep."

Melina shook her head, smiling a little in the diffused moonlight, which fell through the floorboards of the wagon bed in silvery streaks. "You are an odd woman, Lorelei Fellows," she said. "I never knew anybody who took to hardship the way you do. It's as if you *like* trouble."

"I don't," Lorelei said quietly. "But I do like feeling alive."

"You must like fighting with Holt, too, because you sure do a lot of it."

Lorelei considered that. Creighton had largely ignored her, underscoring the sense of invisibility that had plagued her from childhood. Michael, sweet, affable Michael, had always agreed with her, as though he thought she'd shatter if he didn't. Holt, on the other hand, seemed to relish a challenge as much as she did. And every time he pushed her, she grew a little, just by taking her own part.

"He is the most obnoxious man I have ever met," she said.

"Then how come you're smiling?"

"Hush up, Melina, and go to sleep."

Melina giggled.

Lorelei stifled a giggle of her own. *"Go to sleep,"* she repeated.

"One of these days, Lorelei, Holt's going to want to make love to you. And I bet you'll let him."

The idea caused an expansive, melting sensation in the most private part of Lorelei's body. "Melina!"

Melina yawned and lay down again. "Good night, Lorelei," she said, with laughter in her voice. "Sweet dreams."

Lorelei's dreams that night were anything but sweet. They were urgent. They were fiery. She was naked again, and lying in the grass with Holt, not just letting him touch her, but thrilling to every pass of his hands, every brush of his lips. Crying out in hoarse welcome when he thrust himself inside her.

She awakened in a fever of delicious heat, almost expecting to find him lying on top of her, joined with her.

It was both a relief and a disappointment to realize she was alone, tangled in her bedroll and the hem of her nightgown.

Tillie sat up, blinking. "Are you taking sick, Lorelei?"

The baby stirred, whimpering, but didn't awaken.

"I'm fine," Lorelei said, but it wasn't true.

She wasn't fine.

She wanted the wrong man.

After that, there was no going back to sleep.

When the first birds began to sing just before dawn, she gave up the effort, crawled out from beneath the wagon, gathered up her clothes and found a place to dress in private. Wearing the second of the two pairs of trousers she'd borrowed from Tillie, along with a clean shirt, she brushed the wild tangles out of her hair, braided it into a heavy plait and left it to fall down her back.

She already had the fire going and the coffee started when Mr. Cavanagh joined her, yawning and stretching his arms. His smile was pleasant, but there was nothing *knowing* about it. Apparently, neither Rafe nor Holt had told him the story of last night, but of course that didn't mean they wouldn't, despite Holt's promise to the contrary. Rafe could probably be trusted to be discreet—he was a gentleman, if a rustic one—but Holt was another matter. He would do whatever served his purposes, and make no apologies for it.

Lorelei flushed, remembering her dreams the night before. The ache of her arousal was still with her, clamoring for a satisfaction she didn't fully understand.

As luck would have it, Holt was the next person to come to the campfire. He'd slept in his clothes, like all the other men, but he still managed to look good, damn him.

He gave her a slanted grin, helped himself to one of the row of metal coffee mugs John had set out and filled it from the pot sitting at the edge of the fire. Leather gloves protected his hands from the heat.

"Morning, Miss Fellows," he said.

Lorelei couldn't answer. She just stood there, burning up on the inside.

"You look real nice," he allowed, after looking her over from head to foot. "I like your hair that way."

She blushed even harder. Dreams were supposed to fade with the coming of day, weren't they? Well, hers hadn't. And she felt as if he could see right through her clothes, to her pinkened, leech-bitten flesh.

"Thank you," she said, but the words were hard-won.

"I think there'll be a mutiny if I serve these cowboys beans again," John said, busily slicing salt pork into a skillet. "We'll need to get us some perishables in Laredo. Eggs and the like."

Holt sipped his coffee, tilted his head back to assess the sky. "You're getting soft in your old age, John," he said.

Mr. Cavanagh laughed. Cowboys began to stir from their bedrolls, muttering, shoving their hands through their hair, getting a fix on the coffeepot and coming straight for it.

Lorelei's anxious plea was out before she could catch it. "Please don't say anything," she whispered.

Holt gave her a sidelong glance and took another sip of coffee. Spared her a nod. "Like I said last night," he whispered back, meeting her eyes, "when I run across a woman in the altogether, I like to savor the experience. Keep it private, for my own entertainment."

Her cheeks throbbed. "When are you going to let this drop?" she hissed.

"Oh, Miss Lorelei," he beamed, "when I've been in heaven ten thousand years, I'll still be thinking what a fine thing leeches are."

Lorelei clamped her back teeth together, nearly bit off her tongue. "I wouldn't count on going to heaven if I were you," she said.

He raised his coffee mug in a toast. "Even hell would be bearable," he said, "with an image like that in my head."

"I truly despise you."

"So you've said," Holt replied, and walked away.

After breakfast, the cowboys saddled the horses and mules, and John hitched the team to the wagon. Holt put the fire out with a bucket of water, carried from the homesteaders well, and mounted up, bold as Hannibal about to cross the Alps.

Lorelei led Seesaw over to the copse of trees where the four fresh graves were. "We'll take care of your little boy," she said, very softly. When she turned to mount the mule, she saw Holt nearby, on his Appaloosa gelding, watching her from under the brim of his hat.

She braced herself, expecting him to reprimand her for holding up the rest of the party. Instead, he simply reined the gelding away and galloped off.

The men seemed especially watchful as they rode, Lorelei noticed uneasily. They traveled more slowly than the day before, staying close by the wagon. She knew they were on the lookout for Indians, mainly, and probably a few other deadly perils she had yet to think about.

All morning long, the women of the party took turns riding in the wagon with John, Sorrowful and the baby. The child was an amazingly durable little creature; except for a happy gurgling, he didn't make a sound.

Lorelei was sorry when it was time to give him up to an eager Tillie and get back on the mule.

AROUND NOON, they came upon another homestead. This one, blessedly, was still standing, and there were welcome signs of life everywhere.

Chickens, pecking at the dirt.

A black and white milk cow, grazing on lush green grass.

A man came out of the shed that probably served as a barn, carrying a rifle and looking earnest. He gestured at the house with a stay-back motion of his hand—a warning, no doubt, to his wife.

"Howdy," he said cautiously, looking the party over with measuring eyes.

Holt swung down off Traveler's back and pushed his hat to the back of his head. "Holt McKettrick," he said, though he didn't put out his hand. "We're on our way to pick up some cattle, by way of Laredo."

The man nodded, lowered the rifle and introduced himself, cautiously friendly. "My name's Bill Davis," he said. "You can water your horses if you like. Let them graze a while."

"Thanks," Holt said, and turned to signal the riders to dismount.

When he faced Mr. Davis again, he cleared his throat. "You know your neighbors, over on the other side of that valley?" he asked.

Mr. Davis smiled. "Good people. Don't know them too well, though. Proving up on a homestead doesn't leave much time for socializing."

Lorelei stayed close, trying to pretend she wasn't listening as she let Seesaw slurp from the Davis's water trough.

Holt looked down at his boots, then met the other man's gaze again. "They're all dead, except for the baby," he said. "Comanches."

Davis paled. Turned toward the house, where a slender woman in a calico dress, washed so often it had no discernible color, hovered in the doorway, looking on. A little boy, no older than two, clung to her skirts, his thumb jammed into his mouth.

"Mary," he called hoarsely. "Those folks that settled over yonder, last spring? They've been kilt by Comanches."

Mary put a hand to her mouth.

"Like I said," Holt went on quietly, "we found the baby alive. We don't know what to call him."

Davis frowned. "I reckon their name was…Johnson, or Jefferson, something like that." He looked back at his wife. "Mary?"

The woman hefted her little boy into her arms, scanned the horizon, probably for Comanche war parties, and came out to stand next to her husband. "Jackson," she said, pale behind a spattering of delicate freckles. "Horace and Callie Jackson." She blinked. "The children…?"

"These folks found the baby," Davis explained, putting a hand on her shoulder. "You happen to know his name?"

"It's Pearl," Tillie put in fiercely, from behind the wagon seat. She was holding onto the baby with both arms, like she thought someone would try to wrench him from her.

Mary glanced at Tillie, obviously confounded, then shook her head. "I only met them a couple of times— the first time was when they came over in the wagon to ask to buy some milk. Their cow went dry. Callie was still carrying the boy then." Tears filled her faded blue eyes, and she held her son a bit more tightly. "Those little girls were such good children. Polite as could be. I'd baked molasses cookies the morning they came, and when I offered them some, you'd have thought it was Christmas."

"You know if they had family around here anyplace?" Holt asked.

Again, Davis looked to his wife for the answer.

She shook her head. "Callie told me they hailed from someplace in Illinois. She was right homesick. Broke down and cried when she ate that cookie—said her mama used to make them, once upon a time. They didn't say for sure, but I figured they couldn't afford to buy sugar and cinnamon and the like." Mary's gaze wandered back to the boy Tillie called Pearl and stuck there. "We could take him in," she said. "We've just got little Gideon, here."

"No, Mary," Davis said gently. "It's all we can do to feed ourselves. Anyways, he can't hear proper."

Lorelei was startled, and a bit unsettled, by the degree

of relief she felt. It was selfish of her, she knew, but she was already dreading the inevitable parting from the baby. Of all of them, though, Tillie would take it hardest. She simply wouldn't understand.

"We've got a cow," Mary said, not looking at him. "Plenty of chickens and eggs, too. He's just a baby, Bill."

"He's my baby," Tillie said, jutting out her chin.

John, still sitting in the wagon seat, reached back to touch her arm. "No, girl," he told her gruffly. "We've just borrowed him for a little bit."

An uncomfortable silence fell. A tear slipped down Mary's cheek, but she held her head high and proud. "Bill and me, we don't get much company," she said. "We'd be grateful if you'd stay for a meal. Pass the night, if you want to."

Holt tried for a smile, but fell short. "Best we move on, while there's still plenty of daylight," he said, with a shake of his head. "We'd be grateful if you'd sell us some milk, though, and whatever eggs and butter you might be able to spare."

"Glad to do it," Bill replied. "I'd just give you those things outright, but winter's coming on and the money will run low, like it always does. Mary, you put Gideon in the house and bring out what the hens laid this morning." He turned back to Holt. "I reckon we could let you have half a dozen chickens if you want them."

Mary hesitated, then turned to do her husband's bidding. Lorelei felt the other woman's disappointment as though it were her own; Mrs. Davis longed for company. Leaving Seesaw's reins to dangle while he continued to monopolize the water trough, she followed as far as the doorway.

The inside of the house was plain but tidy. The walls

were lined with shelves of preserves, and the fifty-gallon barrels supporting the worktable next to the stove were probably filled with flour, beans or cornmeal. There was no stove, but the fireplace served for cooking. The bed was of carved wood, covered with a quilt—probably a relic of another life, in a more civilized place. Gideon lay in the center of the mattress, sound asleep.

"Did you see those Indians with your own two eyes?" Mary asked. Until that moment, Lorelei hadn't realized the other woman knew she was there.

"No," Lorelei said.

"I lie awake some nights, worrying that they'll come and scalp us all." As Mary spoke, she was busily taking eggs from a crock filled with water glass, setting each one carefully in a bowl. "Times like this, I wish we'd stayed in Iowa."

"You must get pretty lonesome out here," Lorelei observed, stepping over the high threshold.

Mary dashed at one cheek with the back of her hand and went right on counting out eggs. "Sometimes I think I'll die of it," she said, very softly.

Lorelei didn't know how to respond to that stark admission. She wondered, in fact, what Mary would say if she knew about the safe and easy life Lorelei had left behind in San Antonio. She'd probably think her a fool to throw it all away.

"What's your name?" Mary asked.

"Lorelei Fellows."

"That good-looking man, the one who did all the talking—he must be your husband?"

Lorelei felt that odd heat rise in her again, and shook her head. Holt McKettrick, her husband? Now there was a disturbing thought. "I'm not married," she said.

Mary stopped, stared at her. "Not married?" she asked

practically. Then she blushed. "I'm sorry. I've got no right asking questions like that."

Lorelei summoned up a smile, though the mention of Holt and the word *husband* in the same sentence had shaken her. "It's all right, Mary. I'm on my way to Mexico, to buy cattle for my ranch. Mr. McKettrick was headed that way, too, so—"

"Where are my manners?" Mary spouted, smiling, when Lorelei's words fell away like so many pebbles rolling downhill. "Sit yourself down. I'll make you a cup of tea."

Lorelei would have given just about anything for tea, but there had been no mention of including Tillie and Melina inside, so she was reluctant. She averted her eyes and caught sight of a large pan of cinnamon buns, cooling on the table. Her mouth watered.

"I don't think there's time," she said at last. "Mr. Mc-Kettrick wants to keep moving." When she looked back at Mary, she saw that the other woman had followed her gaze.

"Nonsense. Men are always in a hurry. You go out there and get your lady friends, and we'll all four have a chat, whether any of *them* like it or not."

Lorelei's throat tightened. She turned and hurried outside to collect Tillie and Melina. Melina came eagerly, if a little shyly, while Tillie looked wary. Maybe she thought it was a trap, that they were all going to gang up on her and take away the baby.

"Please join us, Tillie," Lorelei urged gently. "It won't be a tea party without you."

"I've never been to a tea party," Tillie said, wavering. "And I'll bet Pearl ain't, either."

Mary was tidying her hair in front of a small cracked mirror when they came in. She'd set out four pretty, if mismatched, plates and some cracked china cups. "There's hot water in that kettle on the hearth," she said cheerfully, "and the basin's over there, on the washstand." She smiled at Tillie. "Put the baby down on the bed, with my boy. He'll be tuckered from riding in that wagon."

Tillie hesitated, then did as Mary asked.

They all washed up at the basin, in their turn, and sat down at Mary's table for tea and cinnamon buns.

Lorelei couldn't remember when she'd eaten anything better.

"Will you be passing by this way again? On your way back to San Antonio, I mean?" Mary asked, when they'd chatted about weather, eastern fashions and the obscene price of sugar. Time was running out; any minute, one of the men, probably Holt, would come to the doorway and tell them it was time to get back on the trail.

"I don't know," Lorelei said.

"Probably," Melina put in. She'd been careful of her manners throughout the visit, saying little.

"If you could bring me back a bolt of checked ging-ham," Mary said, her cheeks pink with the difficulty of asking a favor of strangers, "I'd be mighty grateful. I haven't had the material to make a new dress since I don't know when." She got up from her short-legged stool, probably built by her husband, and opened a can-ister on the worktable. "I've got five dollars saved," she confided, lowering her voice. "That ought to be plenty."

"We'll bring the gingham if we can," Lorelei said, touched by Mary's childlike eagerness. "You can pay us then."

Mary withdrew her hand from the canister, looking baffled and shy. "I do hope you can come back. And not just because of the gingham, either."

Rafe loomed in the doorway. "Time to go," he said. "Holt's chomping at the bit."

On impulse, Lorelei went to Mary, hugged her. "What color?" she asked.

Tillie gathered up the baby, and Melina said a muffled "thank you." They both left the house.

"What color?" Mary echoed, confused.

"The gingham," Lorelei said, thinking of all the grand dresses stuffed into her wardrobe in the San Antonio house. She wished she could fetch them, somehow, and give them all to Mary Davis.

Mary's eyes twinkled with hope. "Blue," she said. "I do dearly love blue."

"Blue," Lorelei confirmed, and took her leave.

# CHAPTER 26

MOUNTED ON SEESAW, but reluctant to leave the Davis place, Lorelei watched from beneath the brim of her hat, tugged down low over her face, as Mary went from one rider to another, platter upraised in both hands, making sure every member of the party got one of her cinnamon buns. That this represented a significant personal sacrifice, Lorelei did not doubt. Sugar, flour, yeast and spices were all hard to come by, especially on a hardscrabble ranch in the middle of nowhere.

She swallowed painfully. When, in all her sheltered life, had she ever made a genuine sacrifice? She couldn't think of a single instance, and that shamed her.

"You look mighty pensive," Rafe commented, riding up beside her. He'd pulled off his leather trail gloves to accept one of Mary's rolls, and he was just finishing it off.

Lorelei swallowed again. "I was just thinking about what a hard life it is, way out here," she said. "Lonely and dangerous." That wasn't all of it, of course, and maybe he'd guessed that, but the regrets she felt were too personal to share.

Rafe adjusted his hat, rested one forearm on the horn

of his saddle. "Folks like the Davises here, and the Jacksons, they're a special breed. They aren't satisfied with getting by in some safe, settled town. There's something in them that makes them grit their teeth and step over any line in the dirt, if only to see what's on the other side."

"I admire that," Lorelei said. Holt gave the customary signal, raising an arm and spurring his own horse forward, and the party began its lumbering movement back onto the trail.

"So do I," Rafe answered. "I'd venture to say you're a lot like them, Miss Lorelei. Real brave, and real stubborn. You know the truth—that anything is better than living a half life. Even dying."

Lorelei kept her mule alongside Rafe's magnificent black gelding. She wanted to look back, but she knew it wouldn't serve any purpose except to make her sorrowful. "You're not afraid of that? Dying, I mean?"

Rafe sighed. "I don't want to leave this party any sooner than I have to," he said. "But just about the first thing our pa taught us was that a man *decides* whether he's going to be scared or not. That decision determines whatever he does after that. Same goes for a woman, naturally."

Being fairly certain that her eyes were in shadow, thanks to her hat brim, Lorelei let her gaze stray to Holt, riding ahead. His back was straight, and she knew every one of his senses was in full play. Wondered what it was like to be so sure of oneself, trusting in an innate ability to handle whatever presented itself, be it expected or unexpected.

"So that's why your brother is like he is," she mused.

Rafe shifted in the saddle. They'd gained the trail now, and the whole party was picking up speed. Chief traveled at a trot, and Seesaw kept pace. "Holt didn't grow up with the rest of the family," he said. "Pa left him behind with his first wife's people, here in Texas, after she gave up the ghost. I know Pa thought it was for the best, at the time, since Holt was about the size of Pearl there, and needed a mother and a roof over his head. I'm not sure Holt would agree, though. He went through some hard times, until Mr. Cavanagh took him in. He and Pa have had their go-rounds about the matter right along, that's for sure."

Lorelei was intrigued, and there was a long, hard and perilous ride ahead. A conversation would serve as a welcome distraction, and fill in some gaps between wondering and knowing, too. "Do you come from a large family?" she ventured, keeping her tone carefully light. She still missed William, and wished there had been other brothers and sisters to grow up with.

"We've got two younger brothers—Kade and Jeb. The three of us were born and raised on the Triple M Ranch, up in the Arizona Territory. Our ma died when we were boys—took a fever after a horse spilled her off in the creek—but we were lucky, just the same. We had Concepcion, the housekeeper, and she mothered us from there." He paused, smiled. "Pa married up with Concepcion a while back, and now we've got a sister, too. Her name is Katie and she's something. Then there's Lizzie, that's Holt's girl. My wife and I, we've got a daughter, Georgia, and Kade and Jeb are both married, too, with little girls of their own."

"That's wonderful," Lorelei said, and she meant it, but something inside her cracked, saying the words. Opened up a bleak and lonely place, yawning square in the middle of who she was.

"I guess I'm talking your leg off," Rafe said.

"I'm enjoying it," she answered.

"What about you, Lorelei? How'd you grow up?"

Lorelei supposed turn-about was fair play. "My brother and mother both died when I was pretty young. Angelina and Raul took care of me."

"The judge never remarried, then?"

"No," Lorelei said, and for the first time in her life, she realized she was sorry about that. A stepmother might have changed everything—maybe for the worse, but more likely, for the better.

Rafe stood in the stirrups, stretching his long, powerful legs. "I'd better ride up ahead and keep Holt company for a while," he said, with some resignation. "Don't want him thinking I'm a slacker."

Lorelei smiled at that, though she was sorry to see Rafe go. She liked him, and wanted to know more about the McKettrick tribe, though she couldn't have said what any of their doings had to do with her. "Go ahead," she said.

They stopped at midday, to rest and water the horses at a stream, and made a meal of what was left of the beans and biscuits. Mr. Cavanagh washed out the big kettle he carried in the back of the wagon, filled it with water, and poured in hard pinto beans to soak until supper.

Lorelei stayed clear of Holt during the stop, and he stayed clear of her. She wasn't sure how she felt about that, but it seemed prudent, so she just let things be.

When it was time to move on again, she took her turn in the back of the wagon with Sorrowful and baby Pearl.

Once or twice, they spotted figures on the distant hills. Indians, most likely, watching the party pass from the backs of their war ponies. Lorelei remembered what Rafe had said his pa had taught him and his brothers, and decided not to be afraid. It wasn't as easy as he'd made it sound, but just the effort helped, because it kept her mind off all the things that could happen if the Comanches descended upon them.

She fixed her mind on purchasing blue gingham for Mary Davis, once she got to Laredo, and finding a way to get the material back to Mary. She thought about the cattle she'd buy, when they got to Mexico, and prayed that Raul and Angelina were all right.

She considered the prisoner, Gabe Navarro, jailed in San Antonio and sentenced, by her father, to hang by the neck until dead. If Holt believed in Navarro enough to come all the way to Texas to take his part, maybe he really was innocent. Melina certainly thought so. And his care for Sorrowful spoke in his favor.

Just before sunset, they stopped for the night at another mission. This one wasn't abandoned, though. It had walls and a couple of small houses, with garden plots, recently harvested, and an apple orchard. The padre, a rotund man in a rope-belted robe and sandals, came out to welcome them.

His bald head gleamed in the fading sunlight, and his smile was broad. "Travelers!" he exulted joyously, gesturing to the open gate behind him. "God has blessed us with travelers! Come in, come in. You must be weary of the road."

Holt tipped his hat in acknowledgment of the invitation and led the way through the rustic portal into a large courtyard. The horses and mules gravitated to the spring-fed fountain, tumbling clear water into a wide brick pool.

"You all alone here, Father?" Mr. Cavanagh asked, glancing around from his perch on the wagon seat. Lorelei had been about to ask pretty much the same question, confused that the priest had used the word *us* when there didn't seem to be another soul around.

"Of course not," the padre said happily. "All my brothers are here."

Lorelei looked around again, in case she'd missed them, but if there were other friars at the mission, they were inside the various buildings, or up in the branches of some of the apple trees. Her mouth watered, just from thinking of those apples.

"Make yourselves at home," the padre boomed, moving from man to man and horse to horse. "That's the stable, over there. And Brother Lawrence's kitchen is that way. I dare say the ladies will appreciate their own quarters—just past the fountain, there, on the right."

Lorelei dismounted and took Seesaw's reins to lead him toward the big stone barn. Lord, it would be a pleasure to sleep in "quarters," maybe on a real bed. And there might be a bathtub, too.

She was only a little surprised when Holt came up alongside her, leading his own horse. He looked thoughtful.

"Is it just me," he asked, "or is there something strange about this place?"

Lorelei felt a small dust-devil of delight spin up from her center, and she would have quelled it if she could have. It galled her that a simple question from this man could excite her that way. "It does seem a little—quiet," she said, without looking directly at him. There was a danger that he'd see something in her face if she did.

"Where is everybody?" Holt asked, though whether he was putting the question to her or to himself she didn't know.

Lorelei answered with a question of her own. "Have you ever been here before?"

Holt shook his head. "I've seen the place from a distance," he said. They'd reached the doorway of the barn, and he stopped to let her and Seesaw go in first. "Always thought it was deserted."

There were stalls on either side of the long stable, every one of them empty. The place was immaculate, and when Lorelei peered inside one of the large wooden bins just inside the door, she found it full of grain. The next one held oats.

Holt left his gelding in the aisle and took Seesaw by the reins, leading him into a stall, relieving him of his saddle and bridle. Lorelei walked the length of the barn, peering into the other stalls. Every one boasted its own water trough, and a thick bed of clean straw on the floor.

"You'd think he'd have a donkey, at least," she called back to Holt, bemused.

He'd left Seesaw by then to take care of his own horse. "I'd like to see those 'brothers' he mentioned," he replied.

About then, the other cowboys began wandering in, putting away their mounts, filling the water troughs with buckets from the neat stack out by the fountain.

Lorelei went back outside, looking for Melina, Tillie and the baby. The padre was still standing in the middle of the courtyard, glowing with pleasure, but the other monks remained out of sight.

A chill shivered up Lorelei's spine. She smiled at the padre and headed for the quarters he'd mentioned earlier, where she and the other women would pass the night.

Sure enough, there were cots, four of them, complete with pillows and blankets.

Tillie sat stiffly in a straight-backed chair, watching while Melina settled the baby on one of the narrow beds.

Lorelei touched Tillie's shoulder, and the other woman flinched as though she'd been startled out of a sound sleep. Her eyes were huge as she looked up at Lorelei.

"They're all dead," she said.

Lorelei went still, and so did Melina.

"Who?" Melina asked, when a few moments had passed.

Lorelei laid her hand to Tillie's forehead, in case of fever.

"The other padres," Tillie said, and trembled.

"What on earth are you talking about?" Melina wanted to know. Her hands rested on her hips now, and she looked peevish.

Tillie gulped. "They're out there, walking around. But I can see through them."

Melina crossed herself.

Lorelei crouched in front of Tillie's chair, gripping her hands. They were trembling, and as cold as if she'd just dipped them in a mountain spring. "Tillie," she said softly. "You're tired. You lie down, and I'll bring you some water and something to eat—"

Tillie wrenched her hands back. "I'm not hungry or thirsty, and I'm not *tired,* neither," she said adamantly.

"Tillie, of course you are. We're all—"

"I wish we'd camped on the trail," Tillie broke in. "I don't cotton to dead people."

Lorelei and Melina exchanged a look.

"Maybe I'd better go get Mr. Cavanagh," Melina said.

"So many of them," Tillie whispered. Then she lowered her head and began to cry.

Lorelei stood, laid a hand on Tillie's shoulder. Nodded at Melina.

Melina hurried out, and soon returned with Mr. Cavanagh.

The baby slept soundly on the cot, sucking his thumb.

Mr. Cavanagh dragged up another chair, facing his daughter. "Look at me, girl," he said gently, as Lorelei stepped through the doorway, followed by Melina.

The courtyard was empty now, and for a moment, Lorelei was frightened—until she looked toward the orchard and saw Holt and the others sitting around under the trees, eating apples. She was hungry, and headed off in that direction.

Melina hurried to keep up. "Do you think it's all been—well—too much for Tillie? Our running across those dead homesteaders and all?"

"I don't know," Lorelei said. She wondered if she should fetch Tillie food and drink, in spite of her refusal, and decided it would be best to wait.

"She's slow," Melina mused, "but I didn't think she was crazy."

The word *crazy* lodged in Lorelei's middle like a Comanche arrow. "Tillie's as sane as anybody," she said, and instantly regretted her terseness.

As they approached, Rafe tossed Lorelei an apple, and she caught it handily. He smiled.

She polished the morsel on her shirtsleeve and bit into it. "Thanks," she said. Out of the corner of her eye, she saw Holt watching her. He wasn't smiling like his brother.

Lorelei was mildly pleased by that, though she didn't know why.

The Captain, sitting cross-legged in the grass, was

shuffling a deck of well-worn playing cards. "Anybody want into this game?" he asked, looking directly at Lorelei.

Recalling his cryptic remarks about holding and folding, Lorelei approached. "Sure," she said, sitting down to the Captain's left, Indian style. She removed her hat and set it aside. Took another bite of her apple.

Mr. Kahill and another cowboy joined the circle. "Deal us in," the second man said.

Rafe ambled over, his thumbs hooked under his gunbelt. "Watch out, Lorelei," he said cheerfully. "Don't let these rascals relieve you of your money."

"I reckon she can count on beginner's luck," the Captain observed, glancing at Holt.

Lorelei couldn't resist doing the same. Holt sat with his back to the trunk of a tree, glowering. He tossed aside the apple he'd been eating and got to his feet with a disturbing grace that made Lorelei remember her scandalous dreams and catch fire all over again.

The Captain shuffled and reshuffled the cards and let Lorelei cut them before he dealt.

"No tricks," Holt said ominously, looming over them. His back was to the west, so he cast an impressive shadow.

The Captain smiled, though he didn't look up from his business. "What makes you think I'd trick anybody?" he asked.

"Experience," Holt answered. He moved to stand behind Lorelei, squatted.

She felt the strength and substance of him along the surface of her flesh, and her breathing quickened a little. *Please, God,* she prayed silently, *don't let him notice.*

She watched the other players pick up their cards and did the same with her own, fanning them out in her hand.

Holt reached over her shoulder and rearranged two of them, forming a trio of jacks.

"Everybody ante up," the Captain said. "Dimes to start."

Lorelei's money was in her bedroll. She was about to excuse herself, to fetch some change when Holt tossed a dime into the center of the circle.

"Hold," he said, close to her ear. The heat of his breath made the skin on her nape tingle and, for some reason, she imagined what it would feel like if he kissed her there.

The thought was a mistake. It sent a spike of heat shooting down through Lorelei, clear into the ground. Her three jacks, two of diamonds and four of spades felt slippery in her hand, and her heart galloped like a runaway horse.

Mr. Kahill tossed in his cards. "Fold," he said.

The Captain and the other cowboy ruminated.

"Hit me," the cowboy said.

Lorelei braced herself. She hadn't expected the game to be violent.

"How many?" the Captain asked.

"Two," the cowboy answered. Discarding a pair of cards, face-down.

Lorelei's hand tightened.

"Easy," Holt said. "Raise 'em."

It was probably good advice. The problem was that Lorelei didn't know what it meant.

Holt threw four nickels into the little cluster of dimes.

Mr. Kahill had shifted to one side, and he leaned back on his elbows, chewing on a blade of grass and staring at Lorelei's face.

"Hell," said the other cowboy, and threw down his cards.

"See it and raise you two," the Captain said, flipping two shiny dimes into the pile.

Lorelei was mystified.

Holt shifted behind her, but he didn't prompt her.

She turned her head to look at his face.

He grinned and came up with another forty cents. "See your two, raise you two more," he said.

Lorelei began to sweat, and not just because the stakes were mounting. Poker had a language all its own, it seemed, and she didn't speak a word of it.

"Call," the Captain said.

"Lay down your cards," Holt told Lorelei, when she just sat there.

With a little flourish, all bravado, Lorelei showed her hand.

"Three of a kind," Holt said.

The Captain grimaced. "A pair of aces," he replied. "Like I said, beginner's luck."

"Not to mention a little help from the boss here," Kahill observed languidly.

"Take the pot, Lorelei," Holt said evenly. "It's yours."

She hesitated, then gathered up the money. "It's really yours," she said.

"Damn straight," Kahill remarked.

"I'd shut up if I were you," Rafe put in, from the sidelines.

Kahill looked up at him, his expression bland, and then shrugged.

Lorelei started to get up, but Holt put a hand on her shoulder.

"Here," the Captain said, after gathering up the deck

and shuffling it again. "Let me show you how this works, Miss Lorelei." He demonstrated various groupings of cards—three of a kind, two pairs, something called a royal flush.

"Who's in?" he asked, when he'd finished.

"I am," Lorelei said.

"Not me," said the cowboy.

"Me, either," added Mr. Kahill, but he didn't move.

Rafe sat down in the cowboy's place, and Holt joined the circle, too.

Everybody anted up another dime.

The cards were dealt, and with each one she picked up, Lorelei sat a little straighter.

"Aces high, jacks wild," the Captain announced.

Lorelei didn't know what that meant, but she knew that the ten, jack, queen, king and ace, all in the same suit, were good.

"Hold," she said, pressing them to her chest.

"You look a little too confident for my tastes," Rafe said. "I fold."

"She could be bluffing," the Captain surmised, studying Lorelei with an intensity that would have been disturbing under any other circumstances. He added three dimes to the pot.

Holt followed suit, without comment, and so did Lorelei. She hoped she was right; there was over a dollar in the pot, and that was a lot of money.

Rafe had moved around behind Lorelei to study her cards.

"Don't help me," she said, with a so-there glance at Mr. Kahill, who only grinned and plucked himself another blade of grass to chew on.

"Raise you," said the Captain, and added a dollar bill.

Lorelei's eyes widened, and she held her breath.

"See it," Holt said, and did the same.

Lorelei bit her lip, looked back at Rafe. He didn't bat an eyelash.

Kahill watched her. They all did.

She threw in all her winnings from the first game.

"Call," the Captain said.

Lorelei showed her cards.

Holt gave a hoot of laughter, and the Captain swore under his breath.

"Did I win?" Lorelei asked.

"Yes," Rafe said. "You sure did."

Lorelei scooped up her winnings, then paid Holt back what he'd advanced her at the beginning.

"I reckon that's enough poker for now," the Captain said, reaching for his hat.

"You would reckon that," Holt told him. He got to his feet and offered Lorelei a hand. After a moment's hesitation, she took it. It was as if she'd gripped a lightning bolt.

She blushed and looked away, but she felt his grin on her face, warm as the noonday sun.

"I'd better look in on Tillie," she said, and walked away. To her mingled dismay and pleasure, Holt matched his strides to hers.

"What's the matter with Tillie?" he asked.

Lorelei sighed. "She's just a little overwrought, that's all."

"Why?"

Lorelei stopped, faced him. "Why?" she echoed. "Because she's been through a lot in the last few days. We all have."

"Tillie's tougher than most of the men I know. If she's sick, Lorelei, you'd better tell me."

Lorelei wished she hadn't mentioned Tillie at all. It felt like a betrayal, just talking about her, but Holt had obviously dug in his heels. He wasn't going to settle for less than the truth.

"She's frightened," Lorelei admitted quietly, not wanting anyone else to overhear. It was bad enough that she was telling Holt. "This place bothers her. She said she could see the other monks, and they were all dead."

Holt let out his breath. "Christ," he said.

"Is she given to—well—seeing things?"

"Yes," Holt replied, but he was already heading for the sleeping quarters the padre had set aside for the women.

Lorelei hurried after him, suddenly anxious. "Don't question her now, Holt—please." It cost her plenty, adding that "please." "She's upset."

"That's exactly why I want to see her," he answered, without slowing down. He would have gone right in and confronted Tillie, Lorelei was sure, if he hadn't seen Mr. Cavanagh over by the wagon, plucking the chickens they'd bought from the Davises earlier that day.

Holt changed course abruptly.

Lorelei paused, then dashed in to check on Tillie herself.

She was curled up on the middle cot, with the baby, both of them sleeping soundly. Sorrowful lay on the floor beside them, keeping a mournful watch. Seeing Lorelei, he let out a whimper.

"Shhh," she said, and bent to pat his head.

Tillie stirred, made a soft sobbing sound in her throat.

Lorelei unfolded a blanket and covered her gently before leaving.

Sorrowful followed, his toenails clicking on the spotless stone floor.

The padre had joined Holt and Mr. Cavanagh, watching benignly as the chickens were made ready for the skillet. "Brother Lawrence will be sorely disappointed," he said. "He was planning on venison stew for supper."

Lorelei glanced toward the building where the kitchen was housed. There was no smoke coming from the chimney, and the windows were shuttered. She took a faltering step in that direction.

"We don't want to impose on your good will," Mr. Cavanagh said, smiling. "It would be a favor if you'd join us for fried chicken, here in a little bit. We're gonna have spuds, too. Soon as Holt builds me a fire, I'll put it all on to cook."

Holt looked exasperated, as well as worried, and Lorelei wondered how much Mr. Cavanagh had told him about Tillie's troubling state of mind. "Where do you want this fire?" he ground out.

"Maybe Brother Lawrence wouldn't mind if we used his cookstove," Mr. Cavanagh speculated companionably, looking at the padre.

"Why, he'd be honored, I'm sure," the padre said. "You go right ahead into the kitchen. Tell him I sent you."

Holt grabbed Lorelei's arm as he passed. "You can help," he said, dragging her along.

She stumbled to keep up, baffled. "What are you—"

He propelled her along, but when they reached the door of the kitchen, he stepped in front of her and entered first.

She took a deep breath on the threshold, then stepped in after him.

No Brother Lawrence. No venison stew.

Holt strode over to the stove, touched it. "Stone-cold," he said, and wrenched open the door, started stuffing kindling inside. At least there was a supply of that.

Lorelei put a hand to her throat. "What's going on around here?" she asked, in a voice that was smaller than she would have liked.

"Hell if I know," Holt answered. He took a match from the metal box fixed to the adobe wall next to the stove and struck it against the floor before putting it to the kindling. "If I had to hazard a guess, though, I'd say that old friar is crazier than a tick."

"You think he's here alone?"

In her mind, Lorelei heard Tillie's voice. *They're all dead...I can see through them...I don't like dead people.*

"Have you seen anybody else?" Holt asked, rather snappishly.

"Well, no, but—"

"Or maybe you think there are ghosts everywhere, like Tillie does?"

Lorelei frowned and put her hands on her hips. "Now just a minute—"

He stood and faced her, and his shoulders, usually so straight, slackened a little. "There aren't many things that spook me," he said, "but this does."

Lorelei was taken aback. "You're afraid?"

"I didn't say that." He looked away, then met her gaze again, with some effort, it seemed to her.

"If the padre is cr—insane," Lorelei said, "it doesn't necessarily follow that he's dangerous. He seems kindly to me. And pretty lonely, too."

"We oughtn't to leave him here," Holt told her, or maybe he was telling himself, because he sounded distracted. "He wouldn't have a chance against a pack of Comanches."

Lorelei's throat ached. She wanted to weep, thinking of the padre wandering around the compound alone after they'd gone, talking to a lot of invisible monks. "You're right," she said. "About leaving him behind, I mean. But I don't think he'd go willingly, and it wouldn't be right to force him."

Holt opened the stove door again and threw in a few chunks of wood. "No," he admitted, but grudgingly, "it wouldn't."

Mr. Cavanagh came in, carrying four plucked chickens in one hand, with the padre right behind him.

"Brother Lawrence must have stepped out," the latter said.

"I reckon he's with the others," Mr. Cavanagh replied easily.

# CHAPTER 27

Holt took the midnight watch, climbing the ladder into the bell tower above the chapel to survey the moonlit landscape. Rafe, claiming he couldn't sleep, soon joined him. Below, all was quiet—John slumbered under the wagon, the women took their rest in the small adobe chamber the friar had set aside for the purpose and the rest of the crew had bedded down in the orchard, spreading their bedrolls under the fruit-laden trees.

"You ever see another monk? Besides the padre, I mean?" Rafe asked.

"I don't reckon there are any," Holt said. "The old codger's short a few rosary beads, for a fact."

Like a bear, Rafe scratched his back against the corner of one of the four open archways surrounding the gleaming chapel bell. "I wouldn't say this to anybody but you," he confided, "but there are moments when I'm not sure the friar's any more real than his Christian brothers."

"Now that's just plain ridiculous," Holt answered, though down deep he wasn't so sure. He'd seen some strange things in his travels, things he couldn't explain, and therefore chose not to think about. Most of the time, anyhow. He straightened, glad of a distraction, as something in the distance caught his eye.

"What?" Rafe asked, coming to attention.

"Indians," Holt said. There were six of them, mounted on nimble ponies, taking shape out of the shadows. One by one, they drew up, maybe two hundred yards from the gate.

Rafe moved to ring the bell, the agreed-upon signal that would rouse the other men for a fight.

Holt held up one hand to stay him. "Wait," he rasped.

The braves seemed poised at the outside perimeter of an invisible circle—their horses fidgeted, as if unwilling to come closer.

"What the hell?" Rafe murmured.

"Look at them," Holt answered, never taking his eyes off the riders. "They're scared."

"Scared? I never heard of a Comanche being scared of anything. They've been watching us—they know we'd be no threat to them in a fight, with the women and that wagon slowing us down."

He couldn't have made a case for what he was thinking. It was instinct, and guesswork, but it rang true, so he said it. "It's not us they're worried about. It's this place."

Rafe frowned, peered out at the visitors. "I don't like this," he said. "Most likely, they mean to jump us as soon as we pull out of here tomorrow morning."

"I'm not so sure of that," Holt mused. "They're superstitious as hell. There's a good chance they think we're bad medicine, if we'd spend the night inside this mission."

Rafe frowned. "Seems to me you're assuming a lot," he said. Unconsciously, he shoved a hand through his hair—perhaps remembering poor Horace Jackson's fate and reflecting that he'd prefer to keep it.

Holt started down the ladder, gripping the rungs with one hand, carrying his rifle in the other.

"Where the devil do you think you're going?" Rafe growled, starting down after him.

"Out there," Holt answered, reaching the bottom and striding for the gates, which loomed on the other side of the courtyard.

"The hell you are!" Rafe protested. "Unless you're looking to get an arrow in your gizzard—"

"If I'm right," Holt said, raising the heavy latch, "it means we have a clear trail to Laredo."

"And if you're wrong," Rafe countered, in an outraged whisper, "it means you'll be dead!"

Not bothering with a reply, Holt swung the gate open and stepped through. Rafe followed, but he wasn't happy about it, and he had his rifle at the ready.

The Indians didn't move, except to control their nervous ponies. Devils that they were, the Comanches were the best horsemen Holt had ever seen. It was as if they became part of the animal the moment they mounted, took over its mind and heart, made its four legs their own.

"Jesus, Holt," Rafe ground out, when Holt kept walking toward the little band of Indians. "You're as loco as the padre!"

"Maybe," Holt said. He kept an eye on the Comanches the whole time, especially the obvious leader, but none of them moved to pull an arrow from the full quivers on their backs, or reach for a knife.

Rafe stuck with him, though he clearly didn't appreciate being called upon to do it. Given his druthers, Holt would have preferred his brother to stay inside the gates, where it was reasonably safe, but he knew it would be a waste of time and breath to ask. Disgruntled as he was, it probably never occurred to Rafe to back down.

Since Holt didn't know just what constituted the edge of that imaginary circle, he came to an easy stop about twenty yards from the Indians.

The leader spat to one side, but he didn't ride in, and he didn't raise his bow. His attention sliced back and forth from the rifle Holt carried to his face, his painted features stiff with angry confusion.

Holt grinned. "Why don't you come inside?" he asked, in his rusty dialect. "Plenty of good scalps in there just going to waste."

The brave looked him over with contempt—most likely for his faulty command of the Comanche language—but his manner was sending another message, too. Fear.

"Of course, there are ghosts, too," Holt went on. He took one more step, well aware that he was risking a hell of a lot more than his own hide. All these Comanches had to do, if they took a mind, was ride him and Rafe down. They'd get off a couple of shots, bring down as many as half of them before they bit the dirt, but the battle would be lost just the same, and the people inside might be slaughtered. On top of that, there were probably a hundred more renegades waiting out there in the darkness.

The Indians hesitated, then backed up their ponies.

Holt felt a rush of triumph. "For all you know," he went on, "the two of us are ghosts, too. Bad medicine. Very bad medicine."

Rafe didn't say anything, but Holt could feel the tension coiling him up like a spring. Chances were, if the

Comanches didn't kill him and do some barbering, Rafe
would, once this was over.

All of the sudden, the head warrior let out a blood-
curdling whoop and thrust one fist toward the sky.

"I'd say it's been nice knowing you," Rafe breathed,
"if it didn't mean I'd go straight to hell for lying."

The moment itself seemed to shiver with a variety
of unsettling possibilities. Then, yapping like a pack of
coyotes after a rabbit, the Indians reined their ponies
around and scattered into the night. As the chilling cries
and the hoofbeats receded, a stirring rose from inside
the mission walls.

"We won't see them again this side of Laredo," Holt
said.

Rafe gave him a hard shove to the shoulder. "God-
*damn* it," he snarled. "If we weren't standing out here
in the open like the pair of fools we are, I swear I'd kick
your ass on the spot!"

"You're welcome to try," Holt said, listening for
the sleek whistle of arrows before turning his back on
the vanished war party. When he was satisfied that he
wouldn't catch a shaft of supple wood between the shoulder blades, he started back for the gates.

Lorelei and Melina were waiting inside, both in night-
gowns, with blankets around them. John and the Captain were handy, too, suspenders dangling, armed with
rifles.

"Injuns?" the Captain asked, facing Holt while Rafe
latched the gates again.

"Crazy," Rafe muttered.

Holt nodded. "Yes, sir," he said, out of habit. He'd
ridden with the Captain for a long time, after all, and
taken orders from him. "Six of them. More out in the
countryside waiting for a signal to attack, I figure."

Lorelei stood close enough that he could have reached out and pulled her into his arms, and the desire to do just that shook him the way a half-dozen Comanches could never do. "Attack?" she whispered. "I didn't think they would make war at night."

"They'll 'make war' anytime it's convenient," he told her. "I don't think they'll bother us again, at least not until we're on the other side of Laredo. By then, they'll have figured out that we're bluffing."

She frowned, one hand clenching the blanket closed at her throat.

Holt felt an unholy need ripple through him. He'd wanted plenty of women in his life, and he'd had most of them, but there was something different about the way he wanted this one. There was an element of need about it, more than physical, and that scared the bejesus out of him.

"You damn fool," John rasped, lowering his brow at Holt. "I ought to horsewhip you for going out there like that!"

The Captain grinned. "Now, John," he soothed. "It was a stupid trick, no saying it wasn't, but it worked. That's what matters."

John stood face-to-face with Holt, with the back of his hand raised, like he meant to use it.

Holt stood his ground. There were two men in all the world who could strike him and get away with it. Angus McKettrick was one, and John Cavanagh was the other.

Cavanagh's eyes flashed, but he slowly lowered his hand. "Them cowboys back there," he grumbled, by way of diffusing his temper. "Not a one of them could find his hind-end with his hat. Lucky we didn't have to depend on them in a fight."

Holt risked a crooked grin. "Tell 'em to bed down again," he said, addressing Rafe, who was still fuming a little himself. "It'll be dawn in a few hours, and it's still a full day's pull to Laredo."

"Tell 'em yourself," Rafe snapped, but he headed for the orchard. Like as not, the conversation would turn in the direction Holt wanted.

John waved a dismissive hand at Holt and turned to leave, bound, no doubt, for the soft, sweet grass under the wagon. Melina, too, slipped away.

The Captain and Lorelei lingered.

"I'll take the next watch," the Captain said, studying Holt. "You'd best get some sleep yourself." With that, he took himself off to the bell tower. Holt heard the old man's boot heels thumping up the rungs of the ladder.

Lorelei stood still as a pillar in one of those Greek temples Holt had seen etchings of, in books. She might have been made of alabaster, the way the moonlight glowed on her skin, but, thanks to those leeches, Holt knew only too well that she was flesh and blood.

She swallowed visibly, and Holt watched her throat work. Imagined what it would be like to kiss that place at the base of her neck where her pulse jumped.

"You could have gotten yourself killed," she said.

"But I didn't."

She moved slightly, as if to approach him. Then, damn the luck, she stopped herself. "What's going to happen to the padre, after we leave here tomorrow?"

Holt drew a deep breath, let it out. Suddenly, he felt weary to the bone, as if he could sleep as long as Rip Van Winkle and still need another day in his bedroll. "My guess is, he'll disappear into thin air," he answered, and he was only half-kidding.

"I asked him to go with us," Lorelei confided bleakly. "He said he couldn't leave the brothers."

"We can't force him, Lorelei," Holt said, sort of herding her back toward the place where she and the others were bunking. He didn't dare take her arm. If he touched her, he figured their flesh would fuse from the heat. "He's got a right to decide for himself."

They'd reached the doorway of the women's quarters. Holt didn't allow his mind to travel over the threshold.

Crickets, silent the last little while, suddenly chattered.

Lorelei bit her lower lip, then suddenly stepped in close and slipped both her arms around Holt's neck. He went rigid, like a wild bronco in a chute, about to be ridden for the first time.

She planted a kiss on his mouth, too quick and too light, and then, before he could think what to do or say, she pulled back and dashed inside.

He stood where she'd left him, waiting to come to his senses.

It was a long time happening.

THE SUN WAS already blazing in the sky, though it wasn't yet seven o'clock by Lorelei's bodice watch, when two of the cowboys swung the mission gates open wide for the party to pass through.

Mounted on Seesaw, her hastily consumed breakfast weighing heavily in her stomach, Lorelei looked back at the padre, stationed by the fountain, smiling with benign sadness and waving farewell.

She drew up just inside the gates, letting the wagon and the last riders go by. A flash of sunlight hit the frolicking water in the fountain, and just for the merest fraction of a moment, Lorelei would have sworn she saw another robed figure beside the padre.

She blinked, and when she looked again, only the priest was there, standing alone.

The Texas sun was fierce, she reminded herself, and pulled her hat brim down to better shade her eyes. Once she'd ridden through the gate, the tall doors swung shut, and she heard the latch fall into place.

A shiver moved through her, and she nudged Seesaw into a trot, catching up with Melina. Tillie and the baby were in the back of the wagon, and Tillie stared back at the mission as though she expected it to dissolve before her eyes.

The morning was uneventful, hot and seemingly endless.

Lorelei watched the hillsides for Indians, and every time her thoughts wandered to the brazen way she'd kissed Holt the night before, she drove them back, like so many sheep about to stumble into a tar pit.

In the early afternoon, they came to another stream and stopped long enough to rest and water the livestock. They ate the cold fried chicken left from last night's supper, and then went on.

Lorelei longed for the sight of Laredo the way a pilgrim might long for the New Jerusalem. It was nearly sundown when the place finally took shape in the distance, and for a few moments she feared it must be a mirage.

Holt called the party to a halt on the outskirts of town, before the dirt trail gave way to a cobble-stoned street. Bringing a wagon and all those horses and mules to a stop was a noisy affair, but finally, it was done.

"We'll meet right here, the day after tomorrow, at sunrise," Holt said clearly, while Traveler danced impatiently.

The cowboys gave a communal yelp of exuberance and rode off in all directions, spurring their horses.

The Captain and Rafe sat silently on their mounts, waiting.

John leaned forward in the wagon box, watching Holt.

Out of the corner of her eye, Lorelei saw Tillie kneeling behind the tailgate, clutching the baby to her with one arm and absently petting the dog with the other. Melina sat on her pony beside Lorelei, shading her eyes from the last wicked rays of the sun.

Holt, Rafe and the Captain rode up alongside the wagon, and conferred with John in low voices. Lorelei felt a flash of resentment at being excluded, but she was too trail weary to sustain it.

Presently, Holt approached her and Melina.

"John and the Cap'n will see you to an inn two streets over from here," he told them. "It's nothing fancy, but it's comfortable. Get as much rest as you can, because the hardest part of the trip is still ahead." With that, he started to rein the Appaloosa away.

"Wait," Lorelei heard herself say. Even though she was mortified, she went on. "Where are you and Rafe going?"

Holt grinned, resettled his hat. "We've got some business to take care of," he said. "Stay out of trouble."

Lorelei watched him ride away.

Ten minutes later, they arrived at the inn. The structure was of adobe and timber, with a well in the dooryard and a big barn to one side. Lantern-light glowed at the windows.

"I'll see to the mule," the Captain said quietly, as Lorelei dismounted. "You'd better see that Melina and Tillie will fit in around here, if you know what I mean."

Lorelei, about to hand over the reins, went absolutely still as his meaning sank in. Melina was Mexican, and Tillie was black. They wouldn't be allowed to set foot in a lot of places, except in the capacity of a servant.

The Captain chuckled at her expression. "Now don't go in there with your feathers all puffed out," he counseled. "Give these folks the benefit of the doubt—at least until they show they don't deserve it."

"Holt sent us here," Lorelei reflected, watching as a rugged-looking woman, probably a mulatto, came out of the inn, wiping her hands on her apron. "Surely—"

"Holt hasn't been in Laredo in a while. Could be the place has changed hands. You need me, you just call my name." With that, the Captain led Seesaw toward the barn. Tillie went along, in the back of the wagon, and Melina followed on her pony, casting one anxious look back at Lorelei.

Summoning up a smile and wishing she were wearing one of her tea-party dresses instead of trousers and boots and a man's shirt, Lorelei approached the innkeeper. Up close, the woman looked even more intimidating—her masses of iron-gray hair looked as though they'd been commandeered into place, instead of just pinned. Her sandalwood skin was pockmarked, from an old case of smallpox, most likely, and her steely eyes narrowed as she looked Lorelei over.

"You traveling with those men?" the woman asked.

"Yes," Lorelei said, and stiffened her spine. "We're part of Holt McKettrick's party. On our way to Mexico to buy cattle."

"I knew a Holt Cavanagh once," came the unsmiling response. "Never heard the name McKettrick before, as I recollect."

"It's the same man," Lorelei said. "He sent us here."

Instantly, the woman's countenance brightened, and the transformation was startling. "Why'd Holt go and change his name?" she asked. "He in some kind of trouble with the law? Don't seem likely, since he was a Ranger when I knew him, but then, there's a few of them go bad." She paused, beaming. "Oh, never mind. I'll ask him myself when I see him."

Lorelei smiled, put out her hand, grimy though it was, and introduced herself.

"I'm Heddy Flett," was the response. "You bunkin' in with Holt, or will you be requirin' a room of your own?"

Lorelei flushed. "I'll be sharing with my friends, Tillie and Melina." She gestured toward the barn. The two women stood outside the barn door, with Sorrowful and the baby, and although neither of them glanced in her direction, Lorelei saw by the way they held themselves that they were waiting for a verdict.

"Well, tell 'em to come on in," Heddy boomed. "I've got a nice room with two big beds in it. The men will have to bunk on the sun porch, with the dog, 'course. You ladies can wash up and rest yourselves a while, while I get supper on."

"Thank you," Lorelei said.

"I'm in the business of hirin' out beds," Heddy stated, in happy dismissal, and turned to trundle back up the dirt path to the porch. There, she paused to call to Tillie and Melina, "You ladies get that baby inside, pronto. Don't want the poor little snippet to take a chill, now do we?"

Tillie and Melina smiled as they hurried over with the baby, and Lorelei felt a pang at their obvious relief. Sorrowful stayed behind, sniffing the grass, and John and the Captain went on tending the stock.

Heddy showed them to the big front bedroom—said she was saving the quiet one at the back for Holt, since she had a soft spot for him—and Lorelei almost wept at the sight of real beds, with sheets and plump pillows and quilts. There were lace curtains at the windows, clean towels hanging over the washstand.

"Settle in, and I'll get you some hot water," Heddy told them.

"Pearl's wet," Tillie said. "And we're down to our last bandana."

"Don't you fret," Heddy replied, with brisk good cheer, from the doorway. "I've got plenty of clean rags downstairs. I'll bring them up when I come back with the water." She tilted her head to one side, almost co-quettishly. "That's a right pretty little girl," she added.

"Pearl's a boy," Tillie pointed out.

Heddy puzzled that one through, and finally dismissed the whole question with a shrug. "I'll be back before you can say 'flapjack,'" she promised.

Melina tested one of the mattresses with her right hand, rubbing the small of her back with the left. "Feath-erbeds," she said softly. "If I didn't want supper so bad, I declare I'd lay myself down right now and sleep until noon tomorrow."

"I could bring up your supper," Lorelei volunteered. Melina did look exhausted; her face was drawn, and there was a fitful look in her eyes.

"You'd do that?" Melina asked, almost in a whisper.

"Of course I would," Lorelei said.

Melina sat down cautiously on the edge of the bed, as though she expected to be expelled at any moment. "Wouldn't that be something?" she murmured. "An Anglo woman waiting on me."

Before Lorelei could think what to say to that, Heddy

returned with a stack of neatly folded flannels and a steaming bucket of hot water.

"Found these in the back of the storeroom," she said, indicating the cloth. "Used to be a nightgown. Knew I'd want them for somethin' one day."

Tillie laid Pearl down on the nearest bed and took them from Heddy's grasp. "I thank you, ma'am," she said.

"I don't answer to ma'am," the older woman replied. "Name's Heddy."

Tillie smiled shyly. "You sure are bein' nice to us."

"Any friend of Holt Cavanagh's—or whatever name he's going by now—is welcome in this house. There's a commode through that door there. Just empty the basin into that." While Tillie changed Pearl into a fresh diaper, Heddy poured hot water into the large china bowl on the washstand, then into the matching pitcher. "Step lively, now," she said, bustling back to the door. "Supper's cookin'."

Lorelei's stomach rumbled with anticipation.

Tillie washed up first, then Melina. Pearl was fidgety with fatigue and hunger.

"I ought to help with the baby," Melina fretted, having just emptied the basin. Her gaze strayed covetously to the featherbed. "Instead of just laying around like I was the lady of the house."

Lorelei gave her a look of mock sternness.

"It would be something to be the lady of a house like this," Tillie said, bouncing Pearl against her shoulder.

"Supper's on!" Heddy bellowed, from somewhere down below.

"I'll be back with a tray," Lorelei told Melina.

She and Tillie descended to the kitchen, a place of bright colors and delicious aromas.

"Where's that pregnant girl?" Heddy asked immediately. "She's got to eat."

"I thought I'd take her a plate," Lorelei said.

Heddy's smile broadened. "I'll do that. You sit down and have yourself some of this chicken-n-dumplin's."

Lorelei sagged gratefully into a chair at the long table, almost overwhelmed with hunger.

Heddy lifted the lid off a massive crock in the center of the table and ladled a generous portion of the steaming delicacy within onto a chipped china plate. She nodded to Tillie.

"You sit down, too, girl. I got some milk heatin' on the stove for the sprout, there. When I get back, I'll take him in hand." She shook her head. "Pearl," she muttered to herself, as she headed for the stairs.

The back door opened just then, and John stepped in, followed by the Captain.

"I gather this is a good place," the Captain said, favoring Lorelei with a little smile.

"Indeed it is," Lorelei replied, having dished up her own serving of chicken and dumplings. In San Antonio, she'd had meals like this one every evening of her life. It might have been years ago, instead of mere days.

"There aren't any ghosts here," Tillie announced, shifting Pearl on her lap and filling a plate for herself. She scooped up a spoonful and blew on it before offering the baby a taste.

Heddy returned, greeted the men with a blustery laugh. "Don't just stand there wearin' out my good rug," she said. "Wash your hands and have some supper." She nodded toward the ceiling. "It will be a wonder if that girl gets three bites down her gullet before she drops off to sleep."

"What about Sorrowful?" Tillie asked.

"That the dog?" Heddy countered.

Tillie swallowed, nodded.

Heddy patted Tillie's shoulder. "Got a pan of scraps for him, don't you worry," she said, and pried the baby out of Tillie's arms. "All of you get to eatin', or I'm going to be insulted. Think you don't like my food."

"Can we stay here, Pa?" Tillie asked. Heddy was seated in a big rocking chair over by the stove, spooning warm milk into the baby's mouth and crooning to him in her rough, comforting way. "Me and Pearl, I mean? I like this place."

John cleared his throat. "Tillie—"

"You know how to work, girl?" Heddy broke in, studying Tillie closely. "You don't look afraid of turnin' a hand to what needs doin'. Fact is, I could use some help around here."

John's eyes widened. Lorelei was as surprised as he appeared to be.

"Please, Pa?" Tillie cajoled. "Maybe just till you come back through with the cattle?"

"I believe this good woman is being polite, Tillie," John said.

Heddy gave a delighted cackle. "First time I ever been called 'polite,'" she said. "I'm offerin' room and board and two dollars a week. Take it or leave it."

"Please?" Tillie whispered.

John shifted on his chair. "I reckon you'd be all right here," he said, with a note of relief in his voice. "You've got to be sure, though, Tillie. What if you get lonesome when we're gone?"

"I won't get lonesome," Tillie said, spearing a hunk of dumpling and lifting it to her mouth.

"I promise I'll look after them," Heddy said, and the note of hopefulness in her voice brought a sting to

Lorelei's eyes. "A cattle drive ain't no place for a young girl and a baby, anyhow."

"You are right about that, ma'am," John conceded. "I thank you for your generosity."

"Heddy," she said firmly.

"Heddy it is," John agreed.

After consuming two helpings of chicken and dumplings, Lorelei decided she'd best stop, even though she could have eaten her way to the bottom of that crock. "I'll tend to the dishes," she said.

"No, you won't," Heddy declared. Pearl had fallen asleep against her enormous bosom, and she rocked him with a gentleness that belied her loud voice and straightforward manner. "You go on upstairs and get yourself into bed. You look about to drop."

Lorelei realized she'd been hoping Holt would arrive, but there was no sign of him or Rafe. John and the Captain had finished their meals and were enjoying coffee. Tillie had gone outside to give Sorrowful the promised scraps.

"Well, good night, then," Lorelei said. "And thank you, Heddy."

Heddy merely nodded.

Lorelei half dragged herself up the stairway to the second floor.

She wasn't going to think about Holt, she decided. It was none of her concern if he missed supper and stayed out half the night. For all she knew, he'd never planned to stay at Heddy's in the first place.

She slipped quietly into the front bedroom, saw that Melina had set her half-finished food aside on the nightstand and fallen into a deep sleep.

Lorelei sighed and sat down in a straight-backed chair to pull of her shoes. No, she told herself, she absolutely did not care what Holt McKettrick did with his free time. He could drink and carouse. He could face down Comanches. He could pass the night with a loose woman.

Well, she didn't care about most of that.

# CHAPTER 28

R.S. BEAUREGARD was, if his professional reputation could be trusted, the best lawyer in the state of Texas. Given that Holt had to trail the man through three saloons and a brothel before finally running him down in a private dining room at the Republic of Texas Hotel—where he was sharing a meal with two half-dressed women—the veracity of Beauregard's legal talents was a matter of some concern.

"Gentlemen," he said, with an affable smile, lifting a wineglass in blithe salute, "I don't believe you were announced."

Holt felt Rafe stiffen beside him, decided his brother was on the verge of saying something better kept to himself and gave him a subtle nudge with his right elbow. If there was one thing Holt didn't suffer from, it was a lack of confidence, but standing on the threshold of that room, with its Oriental carpet, velvet draperies and gas lighting, he was conscious of his trail-worn clothes and dirty boots in a way he normally wouldn't have been.

The women looked him and Rafe over with sultry, kohl-lined eyes. One good pull on their bodices, and they'd leave nothing much to the imagination. Both of them smiled, as if they'd read his thoughts and found them pleasing.

"We apologize for interrupting your supper," Holt said, though it seemed a curious thing to him to have that meal at eleven o'clock at night. Hell, in a few more hours, it would be time to roll out of the hay and get to work. "My name is Holt McKettrick. This is my brother Rafe." He paused. "We've got some business to discuss with you."

Beauregard couldn't have been over thirty-five, and Holt supposed most women would consider him handsome, in a rakish sort of way, but his eyes belonged in the face of a much older man. His beard was growing in, his clothes, though of good quality, were rumpled and stained and his hair could have used barbering.

"It would seem this is a matter of some urgency," he remarked, patting his mouth with his napkin and pushing back his chair. He tried to stand, wavered and sat back down again, with a sheepish grin. "As you would know if you visited my office on Travis Street, I keep regular office hours. Ten in the morning until five in the afternoon. When I'm not in court, of course."

Rafe shifted irritably, fixing to butt in for certain, and Holt elbowed him again.

"Like you said," Holt told Beauregard evenly, "it's urgent."

The lawyer ran a shrewd look over both Holt and Rafe. He seemed to notice Rafe's restrained annoyance and find it mildly amusing. "I'm expensive," Beauregard warned.

"I'm rich," Holt answered, and felt his boot heels press harder into the floor.

"Well, then," Beauregard said, still sporting that infuriating little smile, "perhaps I have time to talk after all."

"Why don't you cowboys join us?" one of the women trilled, gazing at Holt and Rafe like they were water on a dry trail. Her face was painted, and she looked as if she'd been rode hard and put up wet one too many times. Holt didn't reply.

Lorelei's image flickered briefly in his mind, bright as a candle flame on a dark night, and he squelched it.

Beauregard's mouth tightened. He gripped the edge of the table, which was burdened with food and drink, served up on fine china plates and in crystal glasses, and tried once more to stand. This time, he made it, though just barely.

"Cora," he said, wobbling a mite, "Maybeline—if you'll excuse us."

Cora and Maybeline looked pouty, and their cheeks flushed behind thick circles of rouge, giving them a tubercular aspect that Holt found unsettling. Beauregard drew back each of their chairs, in turn, and they grabbed up their beaded handbags and sashayed toward the door.

They way they looked at Holt made him feel as if he'd been gobbled up whole, and he was glad when they went on past.

"Sit down," Beauregard said, with a grand gesture. "We've laid the roast duck to waste, I fear, but I'll have another bottle of wine brought in."

"Looks to me like you've had enough of that already," Rafe said.

Holt gave him a sidelong glance.

"Ah," Beauregard replied easily, "but I have an almost boundless capacity." As if to give the lie to his words, his knees gave out, and he sank into his cushioned seat. "Usually," he added, with good-tempered chagrin.

Scowling, Rafe dragged back the chair Cora had occupied, turned it around and sat astraddle, his forearms resting across the back. Holt sat more circumspectly, in Maybeline's place.

With an unsteady hand, Beauregard drained the dregs of the women's wine into his own glass and took a steadying gulp. After a lusty sigh of satisfaction, he turned his gaze on Holt.

"You're not from around here," he surmised.

"No," Holt said. With Gabe's life getting shorter by the minute, he was disinclined to clarify his connection with Texas. That could wait.

"You're in some kind of trouble with the law?"

Holt shook his head. "I'm here about my friend, Gabe Navarro. He's in jail up in San Antonio, sentenced to hang on the first of October."

Something quickened in Beauregard's hooded eyes. "I read about that case in the newspapers," he said thoughtfully. "First-degree murder, as I recollect. Navarro was a Ranger once, wasn't he?"

Holt nodded grimly. "Gabe and I rode together, under Cap'n Jack Walton. He didn't kill those people."

"He didn't have to kill anybody," Beauregard reflected, staring morosely into his empty wineglass. "All he had to do was get on Judge Fellows's bad side for some reason. It wouldn't take much."

"You're acquainted with the judge, then," Holt said.

"Only by reputation," the lawyer answered. "Navarro's a Mexican, right?"

Holt felt his backbone roll out straight. "Part," he agreed tersely. "His mother was half Comanche."

Beauregard picked a piece of duck meat off a ravaged

bone and nibbled at it. "Well, then," he said, "I imagine that was crime enough, from the judge's point of view." He trained weary eyes on Holt's face. "Your friend is in a peck of trouble, Mr. McKettrick. What is it you'd like me to do?"

"Get him a new trial. Here, or maybe in Austin or Houston. Anywhere but San Antonio."

"You seem to be a very direct man. I trust you've already approached the governor," Beauregard ventured, and though his voice was casual, his face indicated that his interest had gone up a notch.

"He's in Washington, politicking," Holt answered. "He won't be back in time to save Gabe."

"He could order a stay of execution by wire," Beauregard answered.

Rafe moved uneasily on his chair. Either he was hungry—they'd missed supper, tracking down the lawyer—or he wanted to say something.

"Certain telegrams don't seem to get through these days," Holt responded. "Whether they're coming into San Antonio or going out."

Beauregard nodded knowingly. "They get lost, I imagine," he said, "if the message is of some concern to the judge." He smiled. "I wouldn't mind pinning back that old codger's ears, if I got the chance."

Something tight slackened in Holt. "You'll do it, then?"

"Depends on the money," Beauregard said. "Like I said, I'm expensive."

"Name your price," Holt replied, without looking at Rafe.

"Five thousand dollars, win or lose. Half of it up front, along with the usual expenses."

"Five thousand if you win," Holt said. "Half of it when

you file the petition for a new trial, and half when Gabe walks out of that cell a free man. As for the travel expenses, you can go north with us after we pick up a herd south of the border."

Beauregard rested his forearms on the table and leaned forward. "Suppose I refuse?"

"I don't think you will," Holt answered. "I expect something for that money."

"I can name a high price, Mr. McKettrick, because I win my cases."

"I wouldn't have come to you if you didn't." Holt looked around the fancy dining room, then at the remains of the feast. "But I'd guess that you spend what you earn, and then some."

The lawyer gave a hoarse chuckle. "What if your guess is wrong? Are you willing to bet your friend Mr. Navarro's life on it?"

Inwardly, Holt shuddered. The truth was, he'd have sooner faced that Comanche war party outside the mission again than risk Gabe's neck, but he'd learned from long experience to follow up on his hunches, and this one slammed against his gut like a mule's hind foot. So he waited.

Beauregard waited, too.

Rafe helped himself to the last yeast roll in the silver basket at the center of the table.

"All right," Beauregard said at long last, putting out a hand to Holt to seal the bargain. "I've got a few things to do around town before I leave anyhow. When do you figure on coming back through here with that herd you mentioned?"

"Maybe a week from now," Holt said. *If we're lucky,* he thought.

"I'll be ready," the lawyer replied.

"You might want to clean up a little," Rafe offered, chewing.

Beauregard laughed. "I might at that," he said. "I've got a few...obligations, though. If you could give me, say, a hundred dollars, I'd be able to leave Laredo in good conscience. Even get up to San Antonio ahead of you, and get this thing started. First thing I need to do is contact a federal judge or two."

Holt reached for his wallet. God knew, he felt every delay like the lash of a whip, but a man traveling alone could run into a lot of grief between Laredo and San Antonio. Beauregard wouldn't be any good to Gabe with his hair tied to some Comanche's belt.

"I'd just as soon you went with us," he said. "In the meantime, you ought to be able to petition for that new trial from here as well as there."

Beauregard scooped up the five twenty dollar bills Holt had laid on the table, folded them neatly and tucked them into his vest pocket. "Which would mean you owed me twenty-five hundred more," he said.

Holt pushed back his chair and stood. Reluctantly, for he'd been eyeing what was left of a raspberry pie, Rafe did the same.

"I'll be in town all day tomorrow, hiring cowpunchers to drive back that herd. I'll stop by your office—between ten and five, of course."

"I might not be in," Beauregard replied smoothly. "Is there somewhere I can leave word, if I need to?"

Holt nodded. "Heddy Flett's putting us up."

Beauregard smiled. "I know the place," he said.

Rafe reached for the raspberry pie, and Holt stopped him with a look.

"Good night, Mr. Beauregard," he said, heading for the door.

"Hell of a lawyer he is," Rafe grumbled, when they were out in the corridor. "He can't even stand up."

# CHAPTER 29

THE CROW OF A ROOSTER pulled Lorelei from the dark maze of her dreams, and she awakened with a gasp of relief. Slumber fell away from her mind in layers, like a series of loose garments, and she sat up, blinking. In the nightmare world, she'd been taken captive by a band of Comanches and tied to a stake to be burned, while ghostly monks danced around and around, laughing as the flames kindled at her feet.

She sat up, pressed both hands to her face, waiting while the images receded, tidelike.

Outside the window, chickadees twittered.

Voices rose through the floorboards, from the kitchen below, along with the aroma of strong coffee.

Lorelei threw back the covers and scrambled off the bed, hastily donning yesterday's clothes, which she'd shaken out the night before. As the first light of dawn crept into the room, she made out Melina's shape in the next bed, but there was no sign of Tillie or the baby.

She did what she could with her hair and rooted through her valise for tooth-powder, a brush and her bar of yellow soap. She would use the outhouse, a facility only marginally better than the chamber pot under the bed, then perform her ablutions at the pump in the backyard. After a night of horrendous dreams, her head felt clouded, and she needed fresh air and cold well water to dispel the last of the shadows.

Holt was in the kitchen, seated at the table, with a steaming cup of hot coffee in front of him. He wore clean clothes, and there was a scrubbed look about him, too. His hair was still damp, and Lorelei felt an entirely unseemly urge to run her fingers through it.

She shifted her attention firmly to Tillie, who was stirring something at the stove. Pearl played at a safe distance, seated on a blanket on the floor.

"Good morning, Tillie," she said, as merrily as she could, after escaping a horrible death at the hands of Comanches who had seemed all too real. She pretended Holt wasn't in the room. "Where's Heddy?"

"She's out gathering eggs," Tillie answered. "I hope she hurries up, because this cornmeal mush is almost ready."

Lorelei headed for the back door. Had her hand on the knob, ready to turn it, when Holt spoke.

"Did you sleep well, Miss Fellows?" he asked, lending a wry note to the words. He knew she wanted to get by without speaking to him, she thought, and he enjoyed thwarting her.

"Yes," she said, without turning around. Drat it, the doorknob might as well have been greased; she couldn't seem to get a grip. "Did you?"

"Well enough," he allowed.

She hadn't heard him come in the night before. Not that she'd been listening. "Good," she answered, and wrenched on the door again.

His chair made a scraping sound as he pushed it back, and then he was behind her, reaching over her arm, turning the knob with her hand still on it. He chuckled when she bolted through the opening.

It was embarrassing to walk down the path to the privy when she knew he was standing on the threshold, watching her, but she had no choice. She set her soap, toothbrush and powder on a block of wood near the outhouse door and dashed inside.

When she came out, Holt was still there, in the kitchen doorway, one shoulder braced against the frame while he sipped his coffee. She was careful not to look directly at him, but when she'd finished washing her hands and face and scrubbing her teeth at the pump, he hadn't moved.

"No privies on the trail," he said, when she got to the bottom step.

Did he think that would send her scuttling back to San Antonio?

"Thank you, Mr. McKettrick," she replied, "for pointing out a perfectly obvious fact."

He chuckled again, stepped aside to let her through.

"What are you planning to do today?" he asked, as if they were on the best of terms and he had every right to know her comings and goings.

Lorelei helped herself to a mug and filled it from the coffeepot on the back of the stove. "I thought I'd visit some of the shops," she said.

"In need of a flowered bonnet? Dancing shoes, maybe?"

Tillie slopped a scoop of cornmeal mush into a bowl and handed it to her. Lorelei nearly dropped it.

"My purchases are none of your business," she told him, sitting down at the table with her breakfast. If she hadn't been half-starved, she'd have walked right out of that kitchen without a moment's hesitation.

"I reckon that would be true, if you weren't horning

in on my cattle drive," Holt said. "Since you are, I feel called upon to remind you that the trail is no place for a lot of fripperies and geegaws from the mercantile."

"I had deduced that on my own," she said, drawing each word taut, and without looking up from her mush. It was delicious, swimming in fresh cream and generously laced with brown sugar. Before she was halfway through that serving, she wanted seconds, but she was damned if she would indulge the desire with Holt McKettrick watching every bite go into her mouth.

"Here's them eggs," Heddy thundered happily, from the doorway, nearly startling Lorelei out of her skin. "Everybody better eat up. You look peaky, the whole lot of you."

Mercifully, Heddy's arrival shifted Holt's attention away from Lorelei. She wondered at the bereft feeling that gave her, right along with the relief of a worm let off a hook.

"You're the best cook in Texas, Heddy," Holt said. The feckless charmer.

"And you're the biggest liar," Heddy responded fondly. "That mush won't be enough to hold you. Sit tight, and I'll fry up some ham to go with these eggs."

Lorelei's greedy stomach rumbled, even as she filled it.

"No biscuits?" Holt teased.

Lorelei felt her ears heat up.

"If you want biscuits, I'll make you up a batch," Heddy offered, bustling cheerfully around the kitchen. "Did Tillie tell you she's stayin' on here? Her and little Pearl."

"I think it's a good idea," Holt said, with a nod in his voice. "Melina and Miss Fellows ought to do the same, it seems to me."

Lorelei stood, carried her spoon and empty bowl briskly to the sink. If Holt decided to leave her behind, there wouldn't be much she could do about it, so she didn't say what she was thinking, though she had to bite her lower lip to keep the words back. She did meet his gaze, however, and she might have been glaring a little.

He started to say something, but John and the Captain came in from the barn just then, causing a stir. Through the open doorway, Lorelei saw Sorrowful lie down dejectedly at the foot of the steps.

When Heddy brought the aforementioned ham out of the pantry and set it on the table next to the stove, Lorelei snatched a scrap of fat from the side and took it out to the dog.

He ate it gratefully, and trotted after her when she made for the barn. She needed something to do while she waited for the shops to open, something that would keep her out of Holt's path, and giving Seesaw a good brushing was all she could think of on short notice.

She'd been at the task for perhaps twenty minutes when Mr. McKettrick showed up in the barn, where his gelding was stabled. Rafe came with him, gnawing on a huge ham and egg sandwich as he walked.

She tried to ignore them both, but Rafe was in a friendly mood, as usual, and he further softened her heart by giving Sorrowful a generous piece of ham.

"Morning, Miss Lorelei," Rafe said.

Holt banged into his horse's stall without a word and reached for the saddle blanket draped over the top rail.

"Good morning, Rafe," Lorelei said warmly, putting her brush aside and wiping her dusty hands down the legs of her trousers. She intended to change into the only dress she'd dared to bring along, given Holt's mandate about the weight of the belongings she could carry—a practical calico—and pin up her hair before walking to the main part of town. She wasn't out to impress Rafe McKettrick *or* his brother, but she wished she'd taken a little more care with her appearance just the same.

Rafe gave Sorrowful a piece of bread crust. "Holt says you're going to the store," he said, using his free hand to dig in one pants pocket. "I wonder if you'd mind choosing something for my wife and little girl. I don't believe I'm going to get the time." He gave his brother a grudging look at this, and handed Lorelei a five-dollar gold piece. "Emmeline likes combs for her hair, and Georgia would probably favor a nice doll." He frowned, perhaps remembering the burial of Tillie's china baby. "Better make it small, and all cloth."

"I'd be happy to," Lorelei said truthfully, and accepted his money.

"Get your horse saddled, Rafe," Holt commanded gruffly. "We've got things to do."

Rafe smiled and shook his head. "He's a contrary cuss, isn't he?" he asked, in a tone meant to carry across to the other stall.

"You won't get an argument from me," Lorelei said sweetly.

"Not unless you say something sensible," Holt threw in, leading his horse out of the barn into the heavy sunlight of another hot Texas day.

"I hope you don't think we're all like him," Rafe said, with a grin. "Us McKettricks, I mean."

"Rafe!" Holt yelled, from outside.

Rafe rolled his eyes, but he headed for Chief's stall and saddled him up.

Lorelei waited until they'd ridden out of Heddy's dooryard before she left Seesaw to nibble contently on his hay and stepped outside his stall. Rafe's gold piece felt heavy in the pocket of her trousers; she wondered what the other McKettricks were like. Surely not as stubborn and stiff-necked as Holt.

Leaving the barn, she nearly collided with the Captain.

He smiled as he gripped her shoulders to steady her. "There's another poker game tonight," he said. "Right after supper. You care to give me a chance to win back some of that money I lost at the mission?"

The reminder of the mission sent a chill trembling down Lorelei's spine—she didn't know which had been more unnerving, the Comanche visitors or the invisible monks—but she soon shook off the feeling. Best not to think about Comanches, with so much time on the trail still ahead, though she rather enjoyed puzzling over the padres.

She laughed. "I might be willing to put some of my winnings at risk," she said. "Provided Heddy allows gambling in her establishment."

"Heddy," the Captain said pleasantly, "allows most everything, I suspect."

Lorelei was distracted as Heddy came out of the kitchen door and set a pan of scraps on the step for Sorrowful. The dog shot across the yard like a streak of wildfire. "When I first met her," Lorelei mused, "I thought she must be the meanest woman on earth."

"Can't always count on a first impression," the Captain replied, and now his voice was quiet.

Lorelei met the older man's eyes. "That's the second time I've felt as if there was a lot more behind what you say than just the words themselves. Is it my imagination, or are you trying to tell me something?"

The old Ranger sighed. "I reckon it would be better if I

waited for you to figure it out on your own," he said, with some reluctance. "Now, I'd better get my horse saddled and ride. Holt gave me a list of errands as long as the barrel of a Colt .45." With that, he walked on into the barn and left Lorelei standing there, wondering again.

Tillie, the baby and Heddy were in the kitchen when she went inside, but there was no sign of Melina. On the trail, she'd always risen with the rest of the party, and Lorelei was worried.

"That girl needs to rest," Heddy said. Apparently, she'd read Lorelei's thoughts in her face. "It's a trial to a body, keeping up with a bunch of wranglers traveling through Indian country."

Again, Lorelei felt a whisper of dread, and it had nothing to do with Melina's failure to come downstairs for breakfast. "I'd better take her something to eat," she said.

"I've already done that," Heddy told her. "Tillie-girl, knead that bread dough like you mean it. It won't rise any higher'n a flapjack if you don't."

Tillie was a fine cook, but she didn't take offense at Heddy's instruction. In fact, she seemed to like it. "Yes, ma'am," she said.

Upstairs, Lorelei opened the bedroom door quietly, in case Melina was sleeping, and was relieved to find her friend sitting in a rocking chair by the window, fully dressed. Her dark hair gleamed, freshly brushed, and she'd pinned it into a loose knot at the back of her neck.

She smiled at Lorelei's expression. "Don't fret about me," she said. "I'm just being a lazybones while I can."

Lorelei found her calico dress rolled up inside her valise, and shook it out. "Tillie and the baby are going to stay here," she said easily, "at least until we get back from Mexico. Maybe you should, too."

"And leave you the only woman with all those men?" Melina asked, with a dismissive wave of one hand. "I couldn't do that."

Lorelei studied her. "When is your baby due?"

"In a month, maybe two," Melina replied, rocking placidly. She looked toward the window and sighed. "I do like being in a real house, with curtains on the windows and quilts on the beds. If I lived in a place like this, I don't believe I'd ever step outside the front door."

Lorelei forgot her dress and sat down on the edge of one of the beds, both of which had been neatly made. She couldn't help thinking of her father's fine home in San Antonio, and all the luxuries she'd taken for granted. She didn't regret leaving, but she wished she'd been more grateful, if not to the judge, then to a kindly fate for favoring her with things other women only dreamed about.

"You'll have a place someday, Melina," she said softly. Her throat tightened, and her eyes burned, but she took her emotions firmly in hand. "You and Gabe and the baby." The moment she'd spoken, Lorelei could have swallowed her tongue. Gabe was going to hang in less than a month, and Melina and the child would be alone in the world. It was a bleak thought.

Melina looked at her sadly. "Women like you live in houses like this one, Lorelei. Tillie and me, we're cut out to be cooks and maids."

"It isn't right," Lorelei protested, but her voice was small, and she twisted her hands together in her lap.

"A lot of things aren't right," Melina said.

A brief, difficult silence fell.

"You can stay with me, on my ranch, as long as you

need to," Lorelei said, when she couldn't stand it anymore. "You and the baby."

Melina smiled. "You won't live on that ranch for
long, Lorelei," she replied, with as much certainty as if
she could look into the future and read it like a book.
"You'll marry Holt and go back to Arizona Territory
with him."

"I wouldn't marry that man if he were—"

"The last man on earth?" Melina finished, with gentle
humor. "Don't be so sure he isn't, at least as far as you're
concerned."

Lorelei felt a twinge of indignation. "I'd be in a sorry
state indeed if I needed a husband to survive—especially
one like him. Anyway, he wouldn't marry me. He thinks
I'm stubborn and self-centered and heaven only knows
what else."

Melina went right on rocking, but now her smile had
a smug air about it. "You drive him crazy, and that's
exactly why he *would* marry you. A woman could do a
lot worse than Holt McKettrick, you know."

"I don't see how," Lorelei retorted, disgruntled. She
stood and snatched up her calico dress. "I'm going out
to make some purchases," she said. "Would you like to
come along?"

"No, thanks," Melina answered serenely. "I mean to
sit here and pretend that this is my house, and Gabe's
going to come walking through that door any moment
and ask me what's for supper."

Lorelei's throat cinched itself shut again, and tears
filled her eyes. She was careful to keep her back to
Melina while she changed into her calico dress.

Half an hour later, in the second shop she visited, she

made her first and most important purchase—a bolt of blue-and-white gingham for Mary Jackson.

She liked to keep her promises, even when she had no earthly idea how she'd go about it.

# CHAPTER 30

"WE'RE SCRAPING the bottom of the barrel with this bunch," Rafe remarked none too quietly, surveying the motley gathering of down-on-their-luck cowpunchers lined up on the sidewalk in front of the Rusty Buckle Saloon. "I think I've seen a couple of those mugs on Wanted posters."

There were twelve in the crew, all told. A more unlikely bunch of disciples Holt had never seen. But, then, he was no messiah. "We've got a herd to drive north, and we can't afford to be choosey," he told Rafe. "These poor excuses for cowpunchers will have to do."

Rafe sighed, resigned. "Now what?"

"Get them outfitted with saddles and the best horses you can find," Holt replied. "The gear they've got is pitiful." He tugged at his leather gloves and ran a glance from one scraggly end of the assembly to the other. Raised his voice. "My brother Rafe is the ramrod on this drive. You'll do as he says or answer to me. We ride out at daybreak tomorrow morning—Rafe will tell you the place—and anybody who shows up drunk will be fired on the spot. You've all been paid a week's salary in advance, to take care of any obligations you have here in

Laredo. You'll earn every cent I pay you. The drive will be long, it will be hard and it will be dangerous. If you feel inclined to change your mind, now's the time to say so, because once we hit the trail, there'll be no turning back. I reckon you comprehend well enough, without my telling you, that a man on his own wouldn't stand much of a chance in the country we'll be passing through. I feel obligated to make that clear, nonetheless." He paused, took a breath. "Does anybody have a question?"

An old codger belched. A young fella with bad skin hitched up his gun-belt. But nobody said anything.

Holt slapped Rafe on the shoulder. "Have at it," he said. "I'll meet you back at Heddy's in time for supper."

Rafe resettled his hat. "What are you figuring on doing in the meantime?" he asked, with a touch of suspicion.

Holt's first instinct was to bristle, but he got past it soon enough. Rafe didn't have to be there; he could have stayed on the Triple M, in the bosom of the family, and tended to his own business. Instead, he'd ridden all the way to Texas and offered his help. "I told you about Frank Corrales," he said. "He was the one who sent that rider up to the ranch to let me know Gabe was in jail in San Antonio. Frank hasn't been seen or heard from since. I mean to ask around, see if I can track him down."

"You told me about him, all right," Rafe said, keeping one eye on the wranglers, who were getting fidgety, standing in a row like that. "Gabe seems to think he's dead. I gather you don't agree?"

"Frank Corrales saved my life half a dozen times. I did the same for him once or twice. Even in the middle of an Indian fight, with our backs to the wall, we could practically read each other's minds. If he was dead, I'd know it."

Rafe considered the reply. "Good enough for me," he decided.

"Get these sorry specimens off the street before they get arrested for loitering," Holt said, and walked away.

THE CAPTAIN AND JOHN had set up camp out behind Heddy's barn. Either they didn't like the beds they'd been given, on the side-porch, or they didn't want to get too used to fleshly comforts, knowing the trail ahead would be a rough one. Holt didn't know which, and he didn't give a damn, since they were both old enough to decide such things for themselves. The sun was low on the western horizon as he approached their fire.

John saw him coming and poured a mug of coffee without being asked. "Rafe was by a while ago," he said, as Holt took the cup. "Told us you'd hired on a sad collection of barflies and drifters."

Holt smiled grimly. The coffee was hot and strong, and it burned his tongue. "The pickings were slim," he admitted. "By now, the best wranglers are driving the last of the summer herds up to Abilene and Kansas City."

The Captain, hunkered down by the fire, poured a dose of whiskey into his own cup and looked up at Holt, squinting in the last blaze of daylight. "You find out anything about Frank Corrales's whereabouts?"

A sinking feeling quivered in the pit of Holt's stomach, and he shook his head. "No," he admitted, at some length. "Plenty of folks know who he is, but if he's been through Laredo in the last few months, nobody saw him." He blew on his coffee, then ventured another sip. "Did you two sit around here on your hind-ends all day, or did you stock up on supplies for the trail like I told you?"

John smiled benignly. "Wagon's full," he said. "Good

thing Tillie and the baby are staying here, 'cause there wouldn't be room for them in the back."

The reminder of the baby made Holt uneasy. "I spoke to the marshal today," he said. "If the boy's got folks anywhere, he'll find them. It might take some time, but eventually Tillie's most likely going to have to give Pearl up."

John closed his eyes for a moment. "Yes," he agreed. "I know. I can't say I'm not dreading it. She's powerful fond of that little fellow, and if somebody claims him, I don't know as she'll be able to stand it."

"Might never come to that," the Captain said quietly. "Meantime, they'll both be safe. Heddy'll see to that."

"She's a character, Miss Heddy is," John reflected. "How'd you come to know her, Holt?"

Holt crouched, tossed the dregs of his coffee onto the fire and listened to the sizzle. "Heddy and me, we go way back," he said, in his own good time. "She ran a… business in Abilene."

The Captain arched one busy eyebrow. "Would this be the kind of 'business' I'm guessing it was?"

"Probably," Holt said.

"I'll be damned." The Captain grinned. "I wouldn't have figured you for the type to be taken with an older woman."

"I said she *ran* the place," Holt replied. "There's a big difference between that and looking after customers."

John muttered something—no telling what.

Just then, Heddy herself trundled around the corner.

"Come on in and get your supper," she ordered. "Bad enough you'd rather sleep on the ground than in my good beds. If you think you're going to turn your noses up at my cookin', too, you're sadly mistaken!"

Holt laughed and got to his feet. John and the Captain followed suit.

"I would never turn down one of your fine suppers, Miss Heddy," John said.

Heddy beamed at him, blushed like a schoolgirl and even patted her hair.

Holt and the Captain exchanged glances.

The Captain shrugged. "You just never know," he said, and grinned to himself.

MELINA RAN a reverent hand over the bolt of blue-and-white checked gingham when Lorelei pushed back the brown wrapping paper to reveal it.

They were in Heddy's modest front parlor, with the lamps lit, and the sounds and scents of supper preparation drifted in through the open doorway.

"It's very fine," Melina said, and swallowed. When she looked at Lorelei, her eyes were wide with yearning. "I guess Mary will sew this right up into a dress as soon as she lays eyes on it," she added.

Lorelei's heart pinched. She'd almost purchased a length of crimson taffeta for Melina—it would have suited her so well—but she knew her friend's pride would make it hard to accept such a gift. "Yes," she agreed. "I suppose she will."

Tillie stepped over the threshold, dandling Pearl on one slender hip. "Miss Heddy says come to supper before it gets cold," she said.

Lorelei was starved—she hadn't eaten since breakfast, having been out most of the day—but she knew Holt was already in the kitchen. She'd sensed his presence in the house even before she heard his voice.

"We're coming, Tillie," Melina answered. "Hold your horses."

"I'll just put this away," Lorelei said, refolding the brown paper. It was her own business what she bought, but if Holt saw that gingham, he was bound to say there was no room in the wagon for a bolt of cloth, and she didn't want to butt heads with him.

Melina nodded, and Lorelei headed for the front staircase.

Upstairs, in the corridor, she hurried along with her head down—and collided hard with Rafe. Mary Davis's blue-and-white checked gingham toppled to the floor.

Rafe chuckled and put out a hand to stop her when she would have bent to retrieve the package. "I'll get it," he said.

Lorelei's heart was pounding. She pressed a hand to her chest and concentrated on catching her breath.

Rafe straightened, holding the parcel and grinning. "Thought I was Holt for a moment, did you?"

There was no sense in prevaricating. "Yes," she admitted.

"He doesn't bite, you know," Rafe teased. "Not real often, anyhow."

She smiled, perhaps a little wanly, and took the bolt of gingham back. The wrapping crackled. "I'm not so sure of that," she said. "I bought the comb you wanted for your wife, and the doll for your little girl, too. It's cloth, with button eyes and yarn hair."

A distant expression drifted into Rafe's blue eyes. "I sure do miss them," he said. "Especially around this time of day, when it's time to have supper. Emmeline's always got a lot to tell me when I come in off the range."

Lorelei wanted to touch Rafe's arm, reassure him somehow, but it wouldn't be seemly. He was another woman's husband, after all, and a stranger besides. "I wish Holt were more like you," she said, without meaning to say anything of the kind.

Rafe looked both amused and puzzled, but he let the statement go by without remarking on it. "I reckon you'd best hurry," he told her. "Heddy's got quite a spread laid out down there in the kitchen."

Lorelei nodded gratefully, regretting that she'd mentioned Holt at all, and made for the room she shared with Tillie, Pearl and Melina.

This would be her last night of comfort, she thought, as she laid the bundle of cloth down on the foot of her bed, and probably her last night of safety as well. And for all of that, she couldn't wait for morning.

Hastily, she smoothed her hair and washed her hands and face at the basin. Then, after drawing a deep breath on the landing, she descended into the kitchen by the back stairs.

Heddy's table was indeed laden with all sorts of good things—a roast, mashed potatoes and gravy, biscuits, three kinds of vegetables and two kinds of pie.

John and the Captain had already filled their plates, and they sat on the back step, eating and tossing the occasional morsel to the dog. Rafe and Holt stood when Lorelei came into view, Rafe easily, Holt as an apparent afterthought, and with a nettling air of reluctance.

"Sit yourself down," Heddy ordered good-naturedly, from the rocking chair near the stove. "Have to dig right in around here. My food don't last for long." She held Pearl on her lap, feeding him small bites of creamy potatoes, while Tillie sat at one end of the table, eating hastily, but with good appetite. Melina, seated to Holt's right, smiled as Lorelei took the empty chair to his left.

Holt and Rafe sat down again, and took up their forks.

"I told you there wouldn't be any word of Frank," Heddy told Holt, taking up the threads of a conversation that had begun before Lorelei entered the room. "If that handsome devil was within fifty miles of Laredo, I'd know it. He'd have been at my back door wantin' a piece of peach pie."

Out of the corner of her eye, Lorelei saw Holt smile, but barely, and bleakly. "If he shows up here," he told Heddy, "tell him I'll be back at John's place, outside San Antonio, in the next two weeks."

"You think he's dead?" Heddy asked.

Holt stiffened, and Lorelei wondered who Frank was, and what he meant to the man beside her. Not that she would have considered asking.

"No," Holt said, breaking a hot biscuit in half and slathering both sides with butter. "I do not."

"I wonder," Heddy mused, sounding worried. "If he's alive, he'd know you're in Texas. And if he knew that, you'd have heard from him by now. He'd want to help get Gabe out of jail."

From across the table, Melina caught Lorelei's eye.

Inwardly, Lorelei flinched. She tried not to think about her friend's man, and the fact that her own father had sentenced him to death.

"Most likely," Holt said evenly, "he's just lying low. Judge Fellows and that Bannings shyster railroaded Gabe. Maybe Frank figures they'd do the same to him."

The remark stung, as it was surely meant to do, and Lorelei flushed. Did Holt hold her responsible for her father's actions? Her hand trembled as she lifted her fork to her mouth. She was upset, but her appetite hadn't dwindled, and she was darned if she would let Mr. McKettrick drive her away from that table.

"Frank's probably in Reynosa," Melina put in.

Holt stopped eating. "What makes you say that?"

"He's got family there," Melina replied, and took a long drink from her glass of milk. "If he thinks the law is after him, that's where he'd go."

Lorelei had to look at Holt then, pride be damned. She was too curious about his reaction to this announcement to do anything else.

Holt was staring at Melina as though his life might depend on his ability to describe her every feature in exquisite detail. "Reynosa—that's where we're off to," he said slowly. "To buy cattle, I mean."

"Could be he knows we're headed that way, and he's waiting," Rafe surmised.

The Captain rose from the step, empty plate in hand, and came into the kitchen. He stood watching Holt, his expression solemn. "How far do you reckon Reynosa is from here?" he asked, very quietly.

Lorelei felt a strange tension stretch between the two men.

"Four or five days," Holt said, at some length. His gaze swung to Lorelei. "Three, without the wagon and the women."

Lorelei's throat closed, and her face heated. She couldn't have spoken for anything, not then.

"We need the wagon, Holt," Rafe put in. "You can't expect those wranglers to live on rattlesnake and jackrabbits. And the women have been keeping up just fine."

Holt was still glaring at Lorelei, and a muscle bunched in the hard line of his jaw. "I don't suppose you'd trust me," he said, very quietly, "to buy those damn cattle of yours without you standing at my elbow."

Lorelei straightened her backbone, stalled by dabbing at her mouth with her table napkin. "It is not a matter of trust, Mr. McKettrick," she said, just as quietly. "If I'm going to run a ranch, I need to know, firsthand, how to purchase the appropriate livestock."

"You think every rancher who buys a cow goes straight to the source, Miss Fellows?" Holt asked, in a falsely moderate tone that got under Lorelei's skin like a chigger.

"I have no idea how 'every rancher' conducts business," Lorelei replied. "I'm concerned with my *own* transactions."

Holt narrowed his eyes at her, and when she didn't shrink under his unfriendly regard, he pushed back his chair, stood up and strode right out the back door.

"Don't you want any pie?" Heddy called after him. Hastily, she got up from the rocking chair and thrust Pearl into Tillie's arms. "I'd better take him a slice of that dried apple," she fretted, grabbing for a plate and dishing up a generous serving. "He's some fond of dried apple pie."

*As if he'd starve without it,* Lorelei thought uncharitably.

She stood, with her food only half-finished, and scraped the leavings into the scrap pan. The silence in that kitchen seemed to hum, once Heddy had chased Holt into the dooryard with his blasted pie, and Lorelei would have sworn everyone was staring at her.

Her worst suspicions were confirmed when she finally worked up the courage to look and see.

Rafe regarded her thoughtfully.

Melina looked sympathetic.

John, the Captain and Tillie were staring at her, too.

"They're my cattle!" she burst out, on the verge of tears but too proud, by half, to shed them in front of a crowd.

"Yes, ma'am," said the Captain mildly. "They are. How about that poker game you promised me?"

"THAT WOMAN'S HEAD is made out of granite," Holt growled, as Heddy offered him a plate of her coveted apple pie.

Heddy chuckled. "But her heart isn't," she said.

After a few moments of hesitation, Holt took the plate, picked up the slice of pie and bit off a hunk. He didn't want to talk about Lorelei's heart, or any other part of her anatomy.

"What are you so scared of, Holt?" Heddy pressed. The crickets were putting up a racket, and a dog howled mournfully, somewhere nearby.

Holt chewed, swallowed and nearly choked. It wasn't Heddy's good pie sticking in his throat, though, and he knew it. "I'm not scared of anything," he growled.

"I'd allow as how that might have been true—up until the time you met Miss Lorelei, that is," Heddy said. She smoothed the back of her calico skirts and sat right down on the chopping block next to the woodpile. "She sure put a kink in your lariat, though, didn't she?"

Since he doubted that Heddy had ever read a book in her life, and therefore could not be held accountable for the metaphor, he didn't comment on it. "I wish she'd stayed in San Antonio. Better yet, I wish she'd married that crooked lawyer she was engaged to and gone to Timbuktu on her honeymoon. Instead, she sets fire to her wedding dress in front of God and everybody, and my life goes straight to hell faster than a log on a greased flume!"

Heddy made a creditable attempt not to smile and failed completely. Even in the twilight, he could see her eyes twinkling. "She burned her wedding dress?" His old friend gave a hoot of celebratory laughter. "What I wouldn't have given to see that!"

"Better you than me," Holt grumbled, and took another bite of pie.

"You're scared she'll get hurt out there on the trail, aren't you?"

He remembered the night he'd pulled all those leeches off her, and felt a little better. "No," he said.

"Not as long as you've got a breath in you, anyhow?" Heddy prompted.

"I've got a friend in jail in San Antonio, set to hang in less than a month," Holt ranted, as if she hadn't spoken. "John's going to lose his ranch if I don't help him rebuild his herd, and even then he's got Templeton to deal with. I can't find Frank Corrales. Rafe's down here, risking his scalp to help, when he ought to be on the Triple M with his wife and child. I've got a bunch of bunglers, drunks and petty thieves for cowhands, and *that woman* wants to handpick every single head of beef she buys!"

Heddy sat calmly on the chopping block, still grinning. Her big, work-reddened hands rested serenely on her broad thighs. "I've knowed you to handle a heck of a lot worse," she said. "How 'bout that time those renegade Comanches jumped you and Gabe outside of Crystal City? Killed your horses, if I remember correct, and the two of you barely got out of there with your hides still on. Walked across near forty miles of desert in the bargain. If I'd heard that story from anybody but you, I'd have figured it for a tall tale, but it was you that told me, Holt. And you weren't scared, neither. Just mad as hops over them dead horses."

Holt looked away, pretended an interest in the chicken coop. The pie had gone sour on his tongue, so he gave the rest of it to Sorrowful. "That was different," he said.

"Why? Cause it was you that might have been scalped, skinned or God knows what else, and not Lorelei?"

Holt was still holding the pie plate, and he would have liked to send it sailing across the yard, in pure frustration, but he knew Heddy prized her dishes, so he refrained. "She's got no idea what those savages can do to a woman," he said, miserably and after a long silence. "Do you know where we found that baby in there, Heddy?"

"Tillie told me," Heddy said. "It's a shame about those folks, murdered like that, but it happens all the time, Holt, and you know it. Them settlers know what they're riskin' when they stake out a claim in the middle of Comanche country."

"Do they?" Holt mused, and handed the plate over to Heddy for safekeeping. He rubbed his chin with one hand. "There were two little girls, Heddy. Their mother shot them, and then herself—"

"Let it go, Holt," Heddy told him, in a tone as close to gentle as he'd ever heard her use. "The boy's alive. That's what matters now. And you can't keep Lorelei back from whatever she means to do. How to live her life, that's her choice to make."

He didn't say anything. Didn't trust himself to sound sensible.

"Why'd you let her come along in the first place," Heddy asked, hoisting herself to her feet with a loud sigh, "if you were so all-fired worried about her?"

"She wanted those damn cattle. She's got some hare-brained idea about starting up a ranch on a little patch of ground she managed to get hold of, up by San Antonio. She would have followed us, on her own, and gotten herself killed, one way or another."

"So if you leave her here, you figure she won't stay put?"

"I *know* she won't."

"Then I guess you'd better stop fussin' over it and get on with your business," Heddy advised. "Like you just told me, you've got plenty to do without tryin' to hogtie Lorelei and get her to see things your way." With that, she headed for the house, the plate in one hand, Sorrowful galloping after her, probably hoping for more pie.

He stayed outside a while, and when he'd cooled off enough to go back into the kitchen, he found Rafe, the Captain and Lorelei playing poker at the table. John looked on, sipping his evening cup of coffee.

Standing behind Lorelei, Holt saw that she'd drawn a lousy hand. Moreover, she didn't seem to realize it was lousy, for she pushed three nickels into the pot and said brightly, "I'll see your five cents and raise you ten."

Smiling to himself, Holt caught Rafe's eye and folded his arms. As far as his face was concerned, he gave nothing away.

"See you ten and raise you another nickel," the Captain said. He kept his cards close to his chest.

Rafe threw his in. "Too rich for my blood," he said, still watching Holt.

As much to spite his brother as anything, Holt drew back a chair across from Lorelei and said, "Deal me in on the next hand."

Lorelei's cards were fanned, and covered the lower half of her face, but he still saw her cheeks go pink. She didn't look at him, though he suspected it cost her an effort to avoid it. After squirming a little—he wasn't sure if it was the cards or the fact that he meant to join the game—Lorelei tossed in a quarter. What the hell was she doing? Those cards she was holding weren't for shit.

The Captain considered long and hard, ruminating, rearranging his hand, then ruminating some more. Finally, he thrust out a gusty sigh and folded.

"Bluff!" Lorelei cried joyously, and scooped up the pot.

"Not so fast," the Captain said politely. "In this outfit it's customary to show your cards, Miss Lorelei."

She laid out a pitiful mix, each from a different suit, and not so much as a pair of deuces among them. Her eyes shone with defiant triumph when she met Holt's gaze across the table.

"Damnation," said the Captain.

"Go ahead and take your money," Rafe urged Lorelei, but he was looking at Holt, and his expression was anything but brotherly.

"You deal," the Captain said, shoving the deck over to Holt.

Holt picked up the cards and bent the ends back with the thumb and forefinger of his right hand. When he let them go, they snaked into his other palm, neat as could be.

Lorelei's eyes widened, then narrowed.

"Name your poison, Miss Fellows," he said.

She blinked. "Poison?"

Holt flipped the cards back the other way, caught them as deftly as he always did.

"Five card stud," Rafe said, planting himself beside Lorelei.

Holt slapped the deck down in front of the Captain. "Cut," he said.

"HE CHEATS," Lorelei complained, in a whisper, two hours later, as she struggled into her nightgown in the bedroom upstairs.

Melina, who had been reading an outdated newspaper by the light of a lantern, looked up, obviously confused. Tillie and the baby were already asleep. "Who?"

"Holt McKettrick, of course," Lorelei sputtered.

"I guess you lost," Melina observed, smiling a little.

"Lost? I was robbed."

Melina chuckled.

"It's not funny," Lorelei said, flinging back the covers on her bed. "The man is a sharp. Have you ever seen the way he shuffles? I swear he was dealing those cards from the bottom of the deck."

"Not Holt," Melina said, with quiet certainty.

"Why *not* Holt?" Lorelei demanded.

"He likes to win too much. Cheating would take the fun out of it."

Lorelei flopped down on the bed and wrenched the covers up to her chin, even though it was a hot night and she'd probably kick them off again before she managed to go to sleep.

"He *enjoyed* taking my money."

"And you wouldn't have enjoyed taking his?"

Lorelei sat up. If Tillie and the baby hadn't been sleeping in the next bed, she might have flung her pillow at Melina. "Whose side are you on, anyhow?"

"When it comes to you and Holt, I'm not sure," Melina answered sagely. "I kind of like watching the two of you go at it."

Lorelei muttered an exclamation.

"That's the way it is with Gabe and me," Melina said, very softly. "It's the way we make love when we can't be alone together."

Lorelei sat up, gulped and lay down again. "That's ridiculous," she said, but suddenly she wanted to cry, and it wasn't just because she felt so sorry for Melina.

"You're in love with Holt McKettrick," Melina told her, folding the newspaper and turning down the wick in the lantern until the light guttered and died.

"I am *not* in love with that man!"

She'd been in love with Michael. She'd *tried* to love Creighton, to please her father. Michael had never once made her angry. Neither had Creighton—until their wedding day. She'd been in a fine temper then, yes she had, and if there might have been a sense of relief mixed in, well, that had no bearing on anything.

"Good night," Melina said cheerfully. There were rustling sounds as she got into bed beside Tillie and the baby.

"I am not in love!" Lorelei repeated.

Melina sighed, a settling-in kind of sound. "Whatever you say, Lorelei," she replied sweetly.

"I loved Michael," Lorelei insisted.

Melina yawned. "You told me all about him on the trail," she said. "How sweet he was. How gentle. Nothing like Holt McKettrick, I'd say."

"Of course he was nothing like Holt McKettrick! Michael was sweet-tempered, and he never *once* raised his voice to me."

"You never said he was strong."

"He didn't have to be."

"I guess he never needed to be brave, either."

"He would have been brave, if the situation called for it," Lorelei argued.

"I think you liked him because he let you have your way and never talked back. That's what *I* think, Lorelei Fellows."

Tillie stirred, sat up. "If you two are going to scrap like a pair of cats," she grumbled, "do it someplace else. I've got to get up and make breakfast before dawn."

"Well!" Lorelei said.

Melina giggled and was soon asleep, snoring softly.

Lorelei wasn't so fortunate. She lay staring up at the ceiling for a long time, watching the shadows and wondering if Michael could have beaten her at five card stud.

# CHAPTER 31

NOT MUCH WAS STIRRING in Laredo just after dawn when the party gathered at the edge of town, ready to head out. Tillie and the baby stayed behind, with Heddy, but to Holt's consternation, Lorelei and Melina were present and accounted for, and they looked a sight more alert than the ragtag crop of cowpunchers he and Rafe had hired the day before. Hell, even the dog looked more alert than they did.

They hadn't traveled five miles when the Captain spotted a rider coming up fast from behind, and spurred his way to the front of the dust-raising throng to tell Holt. He and Rafe immediately turned their horses around, circling back to see who it was.

R. S. Beauregard drew back on the reins of the spavined nag he was riding, and his grin was as wide as some of the ravines back home in Arizona. "You owe me twenty-five hundred dollars, Mr. McKettrick," he told Holt, when he and Rafe came up alongside.

Holt waited, keeping his face straight, but a wild surge of hope sprang up inside him just the same.

Beauregard pulled a folded piece of paper from inside the pocket of his ratty waistcoat and held it out. "This is a wire from Judge Benjamin T. Hawkins, up in Austin. He's ordered a new trial for your friend Navarro."

Holt's heart thudded against his breastbone as he read the telegram, then passed it to Rafe. "You wouldn't be so foolish as to try and trick me, now would you, R.S.?"

The lawyer's eyes were bloodshot, and he still needed a haircut and a shave, but he looked sober enough. He tipped his dusty bowler and bowed slightly. "I assure you that I would not. And because our association is so new, I will overlook the fact that you just impugned my honor."

"That's generous of you," Holt allowed. He didn't fully trust R. S. Beauregard, but he liked him well enough.

"I'll set out for San Antonio by stagecoach—as soon as I receive my fee," Beauregard said smoothly. "Our original agreement, of course, was that I would travel north with your outfit upon your return from Mexico, but as an officer of the court, I feel I ought to be on hand to look after Mr. Navarro's rights until Judge Hawkins gets there."

"You ever heard of this Hawkins yahoo, Holt?" Rafe inquired, handing back the telegram.

"Yes," Holt said, studying R.S. for any sign of perfidy. "He's a federal judge, all right."

R.S. smiled benignly and stood in his stirrups a moment, stretching his legs. "Right about now," he boasted, "Judge Fellows ought to be getting word that an appeal has been granted. I don't imagine he'll like it much."

For the first time, Holt smiled back. "I don't imagine he will. When's this trial supposed to start?"

"Soon as Hawkins gets to San Antonio—maybe a week or ten days." R.S. cleared his throat. "About my twenty-five hundred dollars…"

Holt gave him the telegram. "You acquainted with Heddy Flett?"

R.S. nodded. "We've met," he allowed.

"Show her that wire, and she'll pay you what you're owed," Holt told him. The Appaloosa danced and nickered, eager to catch up with the rest of the outfit. "When I get back to San Antonio, I'd better find you hard at work on Gabe's case."

R.S. doffed his hat, tucked the telegram inside the sweat-stained crown, and bowed again. "Your confidence in me—such as it is—is well placed. I will see you in San Antone."

"You surely will," Holt replied. Then, with a nod of farewell, he reined Traveler around and gave the animal his head. Rafe kept pace on his gelding.

"You trust him?" Rafe asked.

"Right now," Holt answered, "I don't have a choice."

LORELEI, RUMMY FROM lack of sleep, half expected the whole Comanche nation to be waiting around the first bend in the trail. When there was no sign of them, she let herself wonder who it was Rafe and Holt had ridden back to meet. Curiosity woke her up like a splash of cold well water against her face.

Only minutes had passed when they returned, Holt passing within a dozen feet of her and Seesaw and never so much as glancing in her direction.

Lorelei told herself she ought to be glad to go unnoticed, given that she was fairly sure Holt had seen her tuck the parcel containing Mary Davis's bolt of gingham under the wagon seat before they left Heddy's that morning. He was bound to plague her about it, strict as he was about what he considered superfluous cargo. For all that, she felt snubbed, as surely as if she'd just been expelled from the Ladies' Benevolence Society all over again.

"You look a little down in the mouth," Rafe said, startling her. Thinking about Holt, she hadn't heard his horse draw up beside Seesaw.

She hoped the shadow cast by the brim of her hat would hide her expression. "I'm fine, Rafe," she replied pleasantly.

He resettled his hat. "You're not much of a liar," he said, with a companionable grin. "Guess that's one of the reasons I like you."

Lorelei's smile was genuine, if a bit wobbly. "Thank you," she said. "I think."

He laughed. His gelding strained at the bit, wanting to run on ahead, and Rafe controlled the animal with barely perceptible motions of one hand. "I guess I should have warned you against playing poker with my brother," he said. "He's an old hand at it."

"It was my lesson to learn," Lorelei replied, "and I've learned it."

"I thought maybe you'd want a chance to win your money back."

Lorelei shook her head. "I might be gullible, but I'm not *that* foolish," she said.

"So you mean to cut your losses and run?" Rafe asked easily.

"Cut my losses, yes," Lorelei said. "Run? Never."

Rafe smiled. "That's something I can't even imagine. You running away, I mean."

They rode in companionable silence for a while, and Lorelei wondered why it was so easy to be around Rafe and so difficult to be around Holt. If consulted on the matter, Melina would surely have said it was love. Lorelei had no intention of consulting her.

Holt was demanding, opinionated, unreasonable and reckless. He seemed to think the whole world was a trail ride, and he was in command. She couldn't love a man like that.

Could she?

THEY TRAVELED OVER hard terrain all that day. The heat was brutal; the glare of the sun, relentless. More than once, Lorelei thought with yearning of the shade trees back home on her ranch, of the soft featherbeds and savory meals at Heddy's place. She watched the horizon for Indians, and stayed out of Holt's way as much as possible.

Not a word passed between them, though her eyes tracked him until it seemed his image was burned like a brand on the inside of her forehead.

At sunset, they stopped to make camp alongside a lonely spring. There were no trees, and Lorelei felt exposed. If the Comanches came, there would be no place to take shelter.

To keep busy, and thus occupy her worried mind, she helped John Cavanagh build the campfire and put the inevitable beans on to boil. As usual, they'd been soaking in water all day. Heddy had sent along a batch of biscuits, and because John and the Captain had laid in supplies in Laredo, there were canned vegetables and fruit to complement the meal.

Lorelei was seated on a rock, eating her supper, when Holt appeared, crouching beside her. His manner was easy, but she sensed a certain tension in him, too. He hadn't wanted to approach her, she concluded, but for some reason, he'd done it anyway.

"How are you holding up, Lorelei?" he asked, very quietly.

She looked into his face, against her better judgment, and felt the same quivery jolt she always did. "I'm all right," she said carefully. Holt was easier to deal with, she'd learned, when he was giving orders or issuing some challenge. She knew how to handle his temper, but when he was kind, or pretending to be, she was at a loss. She set her fork down on her tin plate, her supper half-finished. "When will we be in Mexico?"

He gestured toward the south. "See those low hills in the distance? We'll cross them in the morning. Be in Reynosa by noon or so, if we don't run into any trouble."

"And once we're there?"

He turned his hat in his hands, pondering it. "We'll leave the wagon in town and ride out to a ranch I know of. Buy the cattle we need." He paused, drew a deep breath, then thrust it out audibly. His gaze came reluctantly to her face. "The trip back will make this part look easy, Lorelei. It's only right to tell you this—we're bound to tangle with the Comanches."

Lorelei shivered involuntarily, and she knew he'd seen it. "I've been expecting them right along," she admitted.

"They're keeping an eye on us," Holt said, still watching her intently. "Right now, we don't offer much sport, and they're probably still a little spooked because we passed the night at that mission. Once we've got the cattle, though, they'll want a share—and they'll come after it."

If Lorelei had been talking to anybody but Holt McKettrick, she would have put both hands over her face and wept for sheer terror and exhaustion, but her pride straightened her spine and made her jut out her chin. Her throat had gone dry as a dead man's bones in a desert, though, and anything she tried to say would have come out as a humiliating croak.

"If you're scared," Holt said, with a gentleness that was very nearly her undoing, "that just shows you've got good sense."

Lorelei swallowed. "Are you?" she asked, in a ragged whisper. "Scared, I mean?"

One side of his mouth quirked upward in that trademark grin. "I'm the trail boss," he said simply. "I can't afford to be scared."

"I don't see how you can *help* it," she admitted.

"It's a matter of riding herd over my thoughts," he said. "Some of them stray into some bad places, but I just drive them back onto the trail. When this is over, maybe I'll sweat a little, but right now I have to keep my mind on the work at hand. Trouble is a certainty, but when it sneaks up on a man, he's got nobody to blame but himself."

"I've never met anybody like you," she said. It wasn't a compliment, precisely, but it wasn't an insult, either. It was a pure statement of fact.

He grinned again, inclined his head toward Rafe, who was hunkered on the ground, playing cards with the Captain and some of the cowboys. "Haven't you?" he challenged.

Lorelei studied Rafe, then turned her attention back to Holt. "I think he's much nicer than you are," she said frankly. "More reasonable, too."

He laughed. "That's because you've never crossed him," he said, rising gracefully to his feet again. "If you ever meet up with his wife, Emmeline, you might ask *her* how 'reasonable' he is."

Lorelei looked up at Holt. She'd never meet Emmeline or any of the other McKettricks, most likely. Never set eyes on Holt's daughter, Lizzie, or the Triple M. Knowing that filled her with an inexplicable sadness.

"Once you've got the cattle and helped your friend Mr. Navarro, what will you do?" she asked. Her cheeks flamed the minute the words were out of her mouth, but she'd said them on purpose, and for some reason she needed to know the answer. She braced herself for the expected response—*mind your own business*.

He surprised her, as he so often did. "Go home to the Triple M," he said. "I miss my daughter, and I miss the land." He grinned again. "Hell, I even miss my brothers and the old man."

"I envy you that," Lorelei said. Maybe it was fatigue that was loosening her tongue. Maybe it was fear. Some need to connect with another human being, if only for a few moments. "I don't miss anybody, except Raul and Angelina, and they're probably better off without me around."

Holt frowned. He'd been about to put his hat back on, but now he hooked a finger in the crown and gave it a distracted spin. "What about the judge? I mean, I know hard words have passed between you, but—well—he *is* your father."

"He was William's father," Lorelei said wistfully. "Never mine."

"William?"

"My brother," Lorelei replied, figuring she was in so deep now, she might as well drown herself. "He was killed in a riding accident when he was nine. My father never got over that. Never got over wishing it was me that died, if somebody had to, instead of his only son."

Holt shook his head, as if he couldn't credit such a thing, though whether it was the judge's feelings he was rejecting, or Lorelei's perception of them, she couldn't tell. "If that's true, Lorelei," he said gravely, and at some length, "then I'm sorry for you, and even sorrier for him."

Lorelei's throat went tight. There it was again, that dangerous kindness. Dear God, she was helpless against it. "You've never wished Lizzie'd turned out to be a boy?" she asked. If he got mad, it would be a relief, because she'd have cause to fight back. She didn't like talking about her father; it made her feel desperate, lost and alone. Somehow, she'd never won his love, though God knew, she'd tried.

He set his jaw. "Never," he said. Then, without any warning, he held out a hand to her. "Walk with me a little while?"

She surprised herself by setting aside her plate and letting him help her to her feet. Her appetite was gone, but fear made her restless, despite her fatigue, and she told herself some exercise might help.

"What happened to your mother?" he asked, when they'd started a wide circle around the camp. A few people glanced their way, most notably Rafe and the Captain, but no one else seemed to be paying them much mind.

Lorelei wondered why she didn't bristle at the question. Maybe she was too tired, and too scared. She knew now that she should have stayed behind in Laredo with Heddy, if only because, that way, Melina would have stayed, too. But since it was too late, and since it was Holt she was talking to, she decided to keep that admission to herself. "She died when I was very young."

Holt scanned the horizon, though it was barely visible, in the gathering twilight. "So did mine," he said quietly. "I wish I remembered her."

The backs of their hands touched as they walked.

Quickly, Lorelei folded her arms, so it wouldn't happen again. "I'm sorry," she said, and she meant it. She knew how hard it was to grow up without a mother, what a hole it left. As a child, she'd ached when dusk came and the women of the neighborhood called their broods in to supper. Angelina had tried her best to fill the gaps during those difficult years, but it hadn't been the same.

All of a sudden, Holt stopped and turned to face her. The question he asked was so direct that it almost took her breath away. "Do you want kids, Lorelei?"

For a moment, she felt as bereft as she had on those long ago nights, standing in the yard in front of her father's house, listening to the voices of other children's mothers. How she'd longed to hear someone call *her* name.

"I think it's too late," she said, and nearly choked on the words.

"Too late?" Holt echoed, plainly surprised.

She looked away, looked back by force of will. "When I set fire to my wedding dress in the square that day," she told him, trying for a smile and failing, "it was an ending. I'll probably never get another chance."

His expression went from disbelief to a certain unnerving speculation. "You don't really believe that—do you? You're still young, Lorelei. Some man's bound to want you for a wife."

She felt a flash of temper, but it died quickly, doused by the discouragement that threatened to swamp her. "Yes," she said forthrightly, "I *do* believe it. Most women are married by the time they're twenty, and I'll be thirty come December. As for 'some man' doing me the grand favor of *wanting* me—"

"Damn it," Holt broke in tersely, "there you go, twisting what I say—" He'd been carrying his hat; now, in a restrained fit of irritation, he slapped it against his right thigh once, then plopped it back on his head. "What if it was a business deal?" he asked.

Lorelei's mouth fell open, and indignation surged through her, closely followed by curiosity. "A *business deal?* Oh, I will thank you to explain *that* question, Mr. McKettrick!"

He must have set his back teeth, because his jawline hardened visibly. "I wouldn't mind having a wife and more kids," he said, after a few moments of agitated silence. She'd have sworn he was working up his nerve, but this was Holt. He had a *surplus* of nerve. "Lizzie's almost thirteen. Before I know it, she'll be all grown-up, getting married or going away to school. It makes me lonesome just to think about that."

Lorelei was amazed. Holt McKettrick, admitting to a human weakness? "I'm sure there are a lot of women who would like to marry you," she said, reeling a little.

"I want a woman with some spirit," he replied. "Some gumption."

Lorelei felt as though she were caught in a current, being swept downstream at a breathtaking pace. And there was a huge waterfall just around the next bend. "That woman you left at the altar," she blurted, hugging herself against a nonexistent chill. "Wasn't she *spirited* enough for you?"

He glared at her, perhaps surprised that she knew. "No," he ground out. "As a matter of fact, she wasn't. And I didn't 'leave her at the altar.' I told her I'd go ahead and marry her, even though I'd still have to come here to Texas, one way or the other, and she refused."

Lorelei put her fingertips to her temples. "Of course she refused," she whispered. "She knew you didn't love her."

"That's the thing," Holt said, calmer now, looking deeply into Lorelei's eyes. She felt as though she had a harp inside her, and he was plucking at the strings. "About love, I mean. I loved Lizzie's mother—I know that now—but the realization was a bit slow catching up to me."

"Mr. McKettrick," Lorelei began, with exaggerated patience, "where *is* this conversation headed?"

His answer practically knocked her back on her heels. "I want a wife," he said. "You need a husband. Maybe we ought to team up."

"'Team up'?" Lorelei was incensed—or was it exhilaration she was feeling? "Like a pair of mules pulling the same wagon?"

He grinned. "That's not a very romantic way to put it."

Lorelei folded her arms, partly to form a barrier and partly to keep her heart from flying right out of her chest and perching beside his. "How would *you* put it?"

"Like I said, it would be a business arrangement in the beginning—"

"And you think that's romantic?"

"I think parts of it would be."

Lorelei blushed. She might be a spinster, and a virgin to boot, but she had a pretty good idea what those "parts" would be. "You," she said, "are a scoundrel. Are you—are you suggesting…?"

"That we'd be good together?" He had the decency to lower his voice, at least, but that didn't make the proposal any less outrageous. "Yes. Especially in bed."

That did it. Lorelei drew back her hand, ready to slap him silly.

He caught hold of her wrist, rubbed at the pulse there

with the pad of his thumb. "You're not afraid, are you?" he taunted.

"No!" she spat. Everything inside her was churning like debris caught up in a twister. She couldn't think straight.

"I think you are."

"Well, guess what, Mr. Trail Boss—you're wrong!"

"Am I?"

She wrenched free of his grasp and immediately wished she hadn't been so rash. She moved to fidget with her skirts before realizing she was wearing trousers instead. "It's pretty obvious what *you* would gain from such an arrangement," she sputtered. "The benefit to me, on the other hand, is more of a mystery!"

He touched her nose with the tip of one index finger, and even that slight touch sent fire roaring through her. "You'd have a husband. A home. Children."

"A *hateful* husband," Lorelei pointed out. "A home I've never seen and might well despise—" But the children. Oh, the children. There was a prospect she couldn't argue against. Suddenly, she wanted them so desperately that they might already have existed. She could almost see their faces, hear her own voice calling their names from the front porch of some distant ranch house....

"I'm not hateful," Holt said, with damnable confidence and despite mountains of evidence to the contrary. "The Triple M is one of the biggest ranches in the Arizona Territory, and I have a fine house. You'd like it, Lorelei, and you'd like me—at least part of the time. I'd be on the range all day, and at night—well, I think we'd get along just fine."

"You are insufferable!"

He shrugged. "Maybe so, but you know I'm right."

"I know nothing of the sort!"

He smiled. "I could prove it. Tomorrow night, in Reynosa."

Lorelei opened her mouth, then closed it again. "Can you possibly have the effrontery to suggest…?"

"That we spend the night together? That's exactly what I'm suggesting."

If the idea hadn't appealed to her so much, Lorelei wouldn't have been so furious. "Why, you—you *rooster!*"

Holt laughed. "Better a rooster than a chicken," he taunted.

"If you think you can goad me into immoral behavior—"

"Would you rather go back to that pissant place of yours and play at being a rancher?" Holt challenged. "You and I both know it's just a game, a way to spite your father."

She gave him her back, started to walk away, back to the heart of camp, where there were people. Where she would be safe from Holt McKettrick's audacious brand of persuasion, if not from Comanches. But he stopped her with one more challenge.

"We'll be spending tomorrow night at an inn in Reynosa," he said. "If you want to live your life, instead of just *pretending* to live it, leave your door unlatched."

Lorelei didn't turn to face him. She was too afraid of what he might see in her eyes if she did. "Good *night,* Mr. McKettrick," she said.

He laughed again. "Good night, Lorelei," he replied smoothly. "Not that you'll sleep very much."

HOLT HAD BARELY closed his eyes when dawn crept over the eastern horizon and teased him awake. The things he'd said to Lorelei—what the *hell* was he thinking?—had doubled back on him like a herd of frightened longhorns turning from the edge of a canyon.

He crawled out of his bedroll, rubbed the back of his neck and reached for his hat. Rafe snored on the ground beside him, but John was already up, with coffee brewing over the campfire.

Lorelei crawled out from under the wagon, sent a poisonous glance his way and headed for the bushes.

The sight of her cheered Holt, though the truth of it was, if he could have taken back the challenge he'd issued the night before, he would have done it.

He glanced down at his brother. If he told Rafe about the deal he'd offered Lorelei, his brother would either laugh out loud or punch him in the mouth, one of the two. Since he didn't need the aggravation, Holt decided to keep it to himself.

Lorelei had returned to camp by the time Holt got to the coffeepot. She looked fitful, and a bit frazzled, and he felt a stab of guilt. She'd been thinking about his rash proposal, the same as he had—probably for the better part of the night.

She came to a stop, like a coyote at the dim edges of a campfire's light, and gazed with naked yearning, not at him but at the coffee.

Some of Holt's guilt receded. He took a languid sip from his mug, let his eyes smile at her over the rim.

She blushed. Took a step forward, halted again.

John, watching from the other side of the fire, where he was mixing batter for what he called pancakes, flung a sour look in Holt's direction, reached for a cup and filled it with coffee. He carried the mug to Lorelei, extended it to her.

Her hands shook slightly, Holt noticed, as she reached out for it.

The guilt came back.

Holt shoved a hand through his hair. Wished he could walk over there and tell her he was sorry for baiting her the way he had, but the truth was that he'd meant what he'd said, so he couldn't rightly take it back. He'd wanted Lorelei Fellows from the moment he saw her burning that wedding dress back in San Antonio, but it had taken a while to face the fact.

Did he love her?

No, he decided. Probably not.

On the other hand, he'd believed the same thing about Olivia, Lizzie's mother. And he'd found out, too late, that he was wrong.

The problem was, he reckoned, that he didn't have an adequate definition for love. He got it confused with passion, and a host of other emotions.

He thought of his father, and Angus's second wife, Concepcion. Their alliance had begun as a partnership; after Rafe, Jeb and Kade's mother, Georgia, had died, Angus was left with three boys to raise. Concepcion, a widow herself, had stepped in, and at some point their common goal had turned into the best kind of love—the sort that endured.

Then there was Rafe and Emmeline. They'd done battle from the beginning. Now, they had a happy home and a child together.

Same with Kade and Mandy. What started out as warfare became an unbreakable bond.

Jeb—and Chloe. She'd come after Jeb with a buggy-whip, called him all manner of worthless and borne him a beautiful child. Once a rascal, Jeb was now the most devoted of husbands.

Holt sighed. For a while, he'd believed he loved Chloe, loved her fire and her intelligence and her go-to-hell attitude. But he'd known, even in the grip of the quiet passion he'd felt, that she could never care for any man but Jeb, and he'd been prepared to get himself out of the way, leave the Triple M for good, if that was what it took. If it hadn't been for Jeb, he'd have pursued Chloe, used all his powers of persuasion to win her. They'd be long-married by now, and Lizzie would no longer be an only child.

Back then, Angus had said the feelings would pass, and he'd been right. Holt thought of Chloe as a sister now, and that was the way it should be.

Here, today, watching Lorelei drinking that coffee, he knew this was entirely different. If she'd loved one of his brothers, nothing in the world would have driven him away. He'd have fought, tooth and nail, foul or fair, any way he had to, for any length of time. And if she'd married Rafe or Kade or Jeb, he wouldn't have interfered— but he would have bided his time. Waited as long as need be.

The implications of this scared him in a way the whole Comanche nation couldn't have done. What the hell did it mean?

Rafe startled him with a nudge, nearly causing Holt to spill his coffee. "Better pull your tongue back in your head," Rafe advised, "before you step on it."

Holt felt heat gather in his neck and rush into his face. Rafe was his brother and one of his closest friends, but right then he could cheerfully have knocked his brother's teeth down his throat. He whirled on Rafe, one hand bunched into a fist.

Rafe chuckled and pretended to leap back.

"Damn you, Rafe," Holt bit out.

His brother was undaunted. As usual. "Why don't you

sweet talk her a little, instead of always trying to get her mad?"

Holt relaxed, even smiled. "I like the way she looks when she's furious," he said. "Which is most of the time."

"I felt that way about Emmeline in the beginning," Rafe remarked, slurping his coffee and squinting a little in the smoke from the campfire. "Still do, sometimes. But life's a lot easier when I just accept that she's the boss and do as she tells me."

Holt lost his sense of humor right then. "No woman is going to give me orders," he vowed. And he was dead serious.

Rafe shook his head. "You poor fool," he lamented, and gave Holt a sympathetic slap on the back.

# CHAPTER 32

LORELEI HAD NEVER seen so many bawling, whirling, dust-raising cattle in her life. There must have been a thousand of them, churning about within the walls of a canyon on the Rancho Soledad, some spotted, some plain, and *all* bad-tempered.

"I don't want to buy any of the ones with horns," she said resolutely, sitting up straight in her saddle. "Merciful heavens, some of them must measure six feet across!"

Holt, beside her on his fitful gelding, grinned through the shifting swell of dirt billowing up around the whole party. "You won't have much of a herd," he told her. "They *all* have horns."

Lorelei blushed, and not only because she'd just betrayed her ignorance of livestock. Holt's proposition, made the night before, had taken her over like a fever, with all the attendant aches and tensions. "Oh," she said.

Holt watched her, resting a forearm on the saddlehorn. "Rivera wants ten dollars a head," he told her. "I think it's robbery, and I told him so, but in this case, he's holding all the cards."

Mentally, Lorelei counted her money. "I want two

hundred head," she decided, and then felt the sickening backlash of her pronouncement, like a punch in the stomach.

"Your place isn't big enough to run that many cattle," he said reasonably. "They need a lot of grass."

Lorelei tried to look more confident, and more knowledgeable, than she felt. "How many are you taking?"

"Five hundred," Holt answered matter-of-factly. "The Cavanagh spread amounts to almost twenty-five hundred acres." He grinned again; evidently, he'd guessed by her expression that arithmetic wasn't her subject. "You have about a hundred, give or take," he told her. "That means you can run maybe fifty head."

"How do you know how many acres I have?" Lorelei asked, raising a little dust of her own. Seesaw was getting impatient, like the gelding. Tired of standing still.

Holt's grin didn't falter, which only made it more irritating. "John's had his eye on that patch of ground ever since I met him," he said. His gaze glided over her, easy and smooth. "It makes sense to find out everything you can about what you want. You're more likely to get it that way."

Lorelei's cheeks burned. She knew he wasn't talking about land or cattle then, and she was both infuriated and intrigued. "Nobody gets everything they want, Mr. McKettrick," she said tightly, and rode past him to join Rafe and the Captain at the base of the canyon. She thought she heard Holt laugh, but she couldn't tell over the bawling of all those poor beasts.

An hour later, when the deal had been made and she'd parted with a considerable portion of her personal funds, it was time to head back to Reynosa.

Holt traveled at the front, like the head of some conquering army, with Rafe on his left and the Captain on his right. Kahill and another cowboy rode point, keeping the animals funneled into forward motion, with other riders behind them, on both sides, riding swing at the widest part of the herd. Still others took the flank position, bringing up the rear.

And even farther back, with a bandana over her mouth, lest she choke on the blinding dust, Lorelei and the least competent of the cowboy contingent served as drag riders. It was their job to chase any strays back into the herd.

Reynosa was only five miles from the Rancho Soledad, and they were the longest, loudest, dirtiest five miles Lorelei had ever traveled. The thought of driving those animals all the way to San Antonio, on the lookout for Comanches at every turn in the road, seemed almost impossible.

At last, the town came into view and, at Holt's instructions, the wranglers contained the herd in a grassy clearing next to a stream. This took "some doing," as John Cavanagh put it when he rode out on one of the wagon horses to look the animals over. The cowboys darted back and forth on their deft ponies, whistling and shouting at every stray, and finally the critters settled down to graze and quench their thirst.

Lorelei felt light-headed, as if she might topple out of the saddle at any moment, and clung to Seesaw with both legs and both hands. Rafe caught her by surprise when he rode up from behind, reining in next to her and the mule.

"Holt says you ought to go to the inn and get some rest," he said, and pointed one gloved hand. "That's it, over there."

Too weary, dirty and overwhelmed even to speak, Lorelei found the place with her eyes. It was a white adobe structure with a sloping red tile roof, surrounded by low walls. She just sat there, for a long moment, staring at it, riding herd on her thoughts, picking up the strays. She yearned for a hot bath and a soft bed and a meal that didn't include pinto beans, but she wouldn't let herself think beyond those things.

"You all right?" Rafe prodded, when she didn't move.

"Fine," she lied, and tapped at Seesaw's heaving sides with the heels of her inappropriate shoes. He took a few tentative steps toward the inn, then brayed and broke into a bone-jostling trot.

Lorelei used the last of her endurance merely to stay in the saddle.

As soon as the herd was secure, Holt set out for the Corrales place, two miles west of town. He'd asked directions at Soledad and would have preferred to make the trip alone, but the Captain insisted on riding along. He'd been Frank's commander in the Rangers, and that entitled him to go by his own reckoning and, though grudgingly, by Holt's.

The farm consisted of a crumbling mud hut, a couple of skinny milk cows and a vegetable patch stripped to stubble. An old man in a sombrero, flour-sack shirt, worn trousers and sandals came out to greet them as they rode up. He was unarmed, but he didn't look very hospitable.

Holt and the Captain reined in at a distance of a dozen yards or so and took off their hats to show they were respectful.

"What do you want?" the old man demanded in rapid-fire Spanish, and spat to let them know he didn't think two white men on good horses were necessarily a promising sign.

Replying slowly, because he hadn't had much call to speak Spanish in some time, Holt introduced himself, then the Captain, and asked for Frank.

The ancient Mexican's leathery face cracked into a smile wide enough and white enough to dazzle the eye. "You are friends of Francisco?" he asked, tossing in an English word or two.

Holt nodded. "Is he here?"

Frank's father looked back at the hut, and two yellow chickens waddled over the threshold. His gaze swung to Holt's face again, narrowed. The smile was gone. *"Sí,"* he said.

Holt and the Captain exchanged glances and dismounted simultaneously. Holt started for the hut, his strides long. The old man tried to grab his arm as he passed, but Holt shook him off.

At the doorway, he stopped, letting his eyes adjust to the dim interior. He made out a fireplace, a table and, finally, in the far corner, a narrow cot. Frank Corrales lay there, still as death.

"Frank?" The name came out of Holt's throat sounding rusty.

"Shit," muttered the familiar voice, as ragged and raw as Holt's own had been. "Am I out of my head from the pain, or is that Holt Cavanagh?"

Holt gripped the wooden frame, weak with relief. "It's me, all right," he said, and stepped inside when he figured he could trust himself to let go of the doorway. "What are you doing, laying around on your ass, you lazy Mexican?"

Frank laughed and tried to sit up. "Just resting up for the next fight, you sorry white man," he answered. He was soaked with sweat and his black hair was matted, but he was alive. Sweet Jesus, he was *alive,* and just then, that was all that mattered. "Christ, I thought you'd never get here. How's Gabe? Did they hang him yet?"

Holt crouched beside the cot, laid a hand on Frank's arm. Behind him, the Captain shooed away the chickens and came inside, his boot heels clunking on the packed-dirt floor.

"Gabe's still in jail, up in San Antonio," Holt said quietly. "What happened to you?"

Frank's fevered gaze strayed past Holt to the Captain. He executed an awkward salute before replying, "The bastards dragged me behind a horse. Must have traveled a mile or better before I managed to get to my knife and cut the rope."

"Who did it?" the Captain asked, and even though he spoke quietly, his tone was deadly.

"Templeton's bunch," Frank said. "Gabe and me, we were out hunting, and we'd just made camp for the night when they jumped us—took us by surprise. I reckon they thought they killed me, or they'd have come back when they realized I'd cut myself loose."

The Captain took his flask from the pocket of his shirt, unscrewed the lid and held it out to Frank.

Frank accepted the whiskey and drank deeply. Took a minute or so to settle back into himself after the jolt to his system. "Some Rangers found me, alongside the trail, and hauled my beat-up, dried-out carcass to Laredo. I wrote you that message, Holt, and hired a rider to carry it to you. I'm glad to see he got through—up until you showed up in the doorway just now, I wondered."

"How'd you get here to Reynosa?" the Captain asked.

"My old papa out there, he heard what happened

and came to get me. You ever ride that far in a donkey cart?"

The Captain chuckled, but it was a gravelly sound. Holt knew he wanted to find Templeton and the rest and rip their gizzards out, just like he did. "If that didn't kill you, Corrales, I reckon nothing would."

Frank laughed and took another draught of the whiskey. "I don't suppose you've got an extra horse," he ventured. "I love *mi padre,* but I'll go *loco* if I have to stay here with him and the chickens."

"I didn't come all this way to leave you behind," Holt said gruffly. "You got any broken bones?"

"A few cracked ribs," Frank admitted. "I'd mend a lot faster on the back of a horse, though. Help me to my feet, will you, Holt?"

Holt stood, feeling uncertain. It wouldn't surprise him if his old friend had a few internal injuries to go along with those cracked ribs, and he didn't want to make matters worse. "You sure?"

"Yes, dammit," Frank said, struggling to get up on his own.

Holt stepped in, draped Frank's arm around his neck and hoisted.

Frank gritted his teeth and groaned, but he was upright, anyway.

His pa had slipped inside the hut at some point, and he looked mighty worried. Holt didn't blame him for that.

"All right," Frank gasped. "Let's see if I can do this without hanging off of you."

Reluctantly, Holt withdrew, but he stayed within grabbing distance, and so, he noticed out of the corner of his eye, did the Captain.

Frank teetered, then swayed, but he finally found his

balance. "Damn," he breathed. "It's going to be good not to piss in a jug anymore."

Up until that moment, the air in that gloomy little hut had been thick with tension. Now Holt laughed, and so did the Captain, and even old Frank, Sr., cracked a smile.

"What about your pa?" the Captain asked. "He want to go with us?"

Frank put the question to his father, in Spanish.

The old man shook his head. Said something about looking after his chickens. There was a look of sorrow in his eyes, along with a glint of pride.

"*Adios, papacito,*" Frank said. He gestured toward a bedroll and some saddlebags in the corner. "That's my gear. I'd be obliged if you'd carry it a ways for me, Cap'n."

This time, it was the Captain who saluted. He gathered Frank's things, and the old man produced a battered rosary, which he pressed into his son's palm. Seeing that made Holt's throat tighten; he wondered how his own pa was faring, up there on the Triple M.

They made their slow way out to the horses, Holt and the Captain walking on either side of their friend. Frank's pa had led the animals to the water trough, and they'd drunk their fill.

"Best you ride behind me, Frank," the Captain said, gathering the reins. "That gelding of Holt's thinks he's still a stallion, and he comes unwrapped once in a while."

"Any horse Holt can ride," Frank said, "*I* can ride—sir."

"You're going to have to choose between your pride and your ribs," Holt put in, meeting Frank's gaze and holding steady. "If I were you, I'd favor the ribs, and prove up on the pride later."

Frank grinned, still a little wobbly on his feet. "Because I'm so damn glad you finally got here," he said magnanimously, "I'm going to let you have this one."

The Captain swung up into the saddle, slipped his left foot out of the stirrup and held out a hand to Frank. Holt helped him mount up, waited till Frank was situated, with a good grip around the Captain's middle.

*"Vaya con Dios,"* Frank's father said, looking up at his son.

Frank nodded, but he didn't speak. Maybe he couldn't, just then.

They set off at a walk, and Frank didn't look back, but Holt noticed he was clasping that old rosary in one hand. "My *papacito*'s donkey moves faster than this," Frank complained. "At this rate, Gabe'll be dead and buried before we get back to San Antonio."

Neither Holt nor the Captain applied the heels of his boots.

"Holt hired a lawyer," the Captain said, as they ambled along. "Gabe's getting a new trial."

Holt was thoughtful. "You mentioned John Cavanagh in your letter. How'd you know he was in trouble?"

"I heard Templeton's bunch talking about it, while they were trussing me up like a Christmas goose," Frank answered.

"What was their beef with you and Gabe?" the Captain wanted to know.

"They killed those settlers so Templeton could have their land. They needed somebody to blame, and Gabe probably seemed a likely choice since he'd had a run-in with the dead folks maybe a week before we got jumped. The rancher sold him a wind-broke horse, and when he went back to make it right, some heated words got swapped. Gabe, being Gabe, helped himself to a different horse, leaving the bad one behind, and the homesteader, he went to town and filed a complaint. Said Gabe was a horse thief."

"Damn fool Indian," the Captain muttered.

"I'd say it was the rancher who was the fool," Frank replied. "He made it mighty convenient for Templeton's men to cut him and the wife up and call it Gabe's handiwork."

Holt frowned. "According to the court records, when the marshal and his men rode out there and found the bodies, they found Gabe's knife, too."

"Wasn't Gabe's knife," Frank said. He was still sweating, but with every step the Captain's horse took, he seemed to sit a little taller, and he was sucking in fresh air like he'd been starved for it. "I've got it in my saddlebags. That's what I used to cut the rope when those murdering bastards were dragging me through the sagebrush."

Holt had been riding ahead. Now, he drew back on the reins, fell in alongside the Captain and Frank. "It's a pretty unusual blade, Frank," he said. "I remember when Gabe got it. He had it made special."

Frank looked impatient, which meant he wasn't as banged up as he looked. It was usual for Frank to be testy, especially when he thought somebody was challenging his word. "Get it out and look at it, if you don't believe me."

"Hell," Holt rasped, "I didn't say that."

"It's on the left side," Frank pressed. "Wrapped in a bandana. Get it out, Holt, and then tell me it isn't Gabe's knife."

Holt sighed. "If you say it's Gabe's, you ornery cuss, then it's Gabe's."

Frank smiled, but he was supporting his rib cage with one arm now, and clasping the front of the Captain's shirt with the other. "How've you been faring, up there in the Arizona Territory?" he asked, with the geniality of a man who has just won an argument. "You got a wife yet?"

"No," Holt said, but he couldn't help thinking of Lorelei, back at the inn. Most likely, she'd had herself a bath by now, and maybe even put on a dress. He knew she had one stashed in that too-heavy pack of hers. It made his groin hurt, just to imagine the ordinary things she might be doing. "No wife."

"He's got a woman, though," the Captain said, and spared Holt a half grin. "Pretty thing. She's got a gift for poker."

Frank gave a hoot of delight at that, though Holt wasn't sure whether it was her being pretty that pleased him so much or her affinity for poker. "What's her name?" Frank demanded.

"Lorelei," the Captain drawled, when Holt set his jaw and said nothing.

Frank's grin broadened. "Fancy," he said.

"Oh, Lorelei's fancy, all right," the Captain allowed, as if Lorelei was any of his damn business. "Whenever the two of them get within six feet of each other, the sky splits open and the rest of us have to dodge the blue lightning."

"With all due respect, Captain," Holt said evenly, "that's more bullshit than the herd left behind between the *rancho* and Reynosa."

Frank threw back his head and gave another hoot of laughter. "She's got you riled," he told Holt, when he'd settled down again. "That's a bad sign, *amigo*. A very bad sign."

Holt stood in the stirrups, and not because he needed to stretch his legs. "If your ribs weren't cracked already, Frank," he said, "I believe I'd drag you through the sagebrush a ways myself."

Frank just smiled.

"He wants her," the Captain said.

Holt scowled. "I've heard about enough out of you two," he said.

"You haven't heard the half of it," said the Captain, and his mustache twitched. "Has he, Frank?"

LORELEI TOOK ONE BATH, then had the water emptied out and the tub filled again, so she could take a second. After that, she put on a white cotton dress, which Melina had borrowed from the mistress of the inn, and sat alone in the inn's small garden, combing the tangles out of her freshly washed hair. She was winding it into a single thick plait when Melina appeared with a bowl of fruit, and sat down beside her on the stone bench.

"It's lovely here, isn't it?" Melina said, with a little sigh. "If it wasn't for Gabe, I think I'd stay."

Lorelei helped herself to a fig. The sweetness of it made her close her eyes and nearly swoon. "Don't say anything about leaving," she said dreamily. "I'm pretending we won't have to drive those blasted cattle straight through Indian country and deal with Mr. Templeton when we get there."

Melina laughed softly. "I didn't think you ever pretended anything, Lorelei," she said, "for all you claim you've been play-acting all your life."

Lorelei opened her eyes, because all of a sudden Holt's image had taken shape in her mind. "Well," she said, taking another bite of the fig, "I do. When I'm riding that cussed mule, I pretend I'm in a fancy surrey instead, wearing a ruffled dress and carrying a parasol. When I have to sleep on the ground, I make believe I'm at home, in my own bed." Tears gathered in her throat, thick and unexpected. Her comfortable life in San Antonio was over for good, and even though she wouldn't have gone back to it for anything, that didn't stop her from mourning the good parts.

Clean, crisp sheets.

A wardrobe full of pretty clothes.

More books than she could read in a thousand years.

Melina took her free hand, squeezed it.

Lorelei swallowed hard, and blinked. "I wish I knew if Raul and Angelina were all right," she said, very quietly.

Melina let go of her hand. "What about your father?" she asked gently. "Do you think about him?"

Lorelei nodded. "Yes," she said.

"He probably misses you."

"No," Lorelei said, and she was as sure of that as anything in the world. She knew the judge. She'd stepped over the line, and as far as he was concerned, she was as dead as William. The difference was, he wouldn't grieve for her. "If I ever have a daughter," she told Melina, listening to the distant bellowing of Holt McKettrick's cattle, "I'm going to love her as much as any son."

Melina didn't answer, maybe because she knew Lorelei hadn't intended to say what she had. She'd been thinking out loud, that was all.

Lorelei finished the fig and took another one. She was wildly hungry, now that she'd washed off at least two pounds of trail dirt. Once she'd appeased her stomach, she meant to shut herself in her room, strip to her camisole and bloomers and stretch out on her bed. She would

sleep and sleep, and sleep some more, until it was time
to saddle Seesaw and start back to San Antonio.

Unless…

Melina peered at her. "What's the matter, Lorelei?"

Lorelei blinked, sitting up very straight, the fig forgotten in her hand. Holt *wouldn't* actually come to her room
that night. He'd been tormenting her, that was all.

But suppose, when everyone else was asleep, he *did*
knock at her door, and the moon was high and the inn
was quiet?

Well, she decided, he'd find the door latched against
him, that's what.

Yes, she meant to lock it.

She almost certainly did.

FRANK AND THE CAPTAIN were downstairs, playing
poker with two *federales* and a *vaquero*. John had turned
in hours ago, directly after supper, and Rafe was where
Holt figured *he* should be—out with the herd.

Feeling downright conspicuous lurking in the upstairs
corridor, like a skulker, Holt glanced in one direction,
then the other. Nobody in sight.

Lorelei hadn't come down to supper with the rest of
them. Thinking she was sick, he'd approached Melina
and asked after her.

Melina had smiled, in that way women had when they
wanted to let a man know they were smarter than he was,
and said Lorelei was just fine.

Holt reached for the door handle, drew his hand back
as quickly as if the thing had suddenly turned molten.

It would be locked.

He ought to walk away, while he could still lay claim
to his pride. Just walk away.

He muttered a curse. Hooked his thumbs under his

belt and pondered his situation. He'd had a bath before supper, down the street, in back of one of the saloons. He'd had himself barbered, too, and he was wearing his last set of clean clothes.

Frank and the Captain had given him no end of grief about it, downstairs. Frank had gone so far as to sniff the air when he passed, and ask if Holt was wearing cologne.

He reached for the knob again and brushed it with his fingertips.

It didn't make sense to waste a bath, a haircut and a shave. That would be a poor use of time and money.

He swallowed, closed his hand around the knob and turned it.

His heart shot up into his throat and got stuck there. He heard it pounding in his ears, and for a moment he thought he would never draw another breath. He'd just turn up his toes and die, right there in the hallway, outside Lorelei's room.

He gave the door a push.

It opened.

Glory be and God help him, it opened.

"Holt?" It was Lorelei's voice, soft as a spring breeze and a little on the shaky side. "Is that you?"

He'd been struck dumb. He tried his damnedest to say something, but not a word came out. He could just make her out in the darkness, sitting up in bed, peering at him.

"Come in," she said, very quietly, "before I lose my courage."

He stepped over the threshold, closed the door behind him, lowered the latch.

"Suppose there's a child?" he managed, after standing there, still as a statue, for what seemed like ten minutes.

It wasn't in him to go back, but he couldn't seem to move forward, either.

Thin moonlight played on her perfect features. He thought she smiled a little, but that was probably wishful thinking, or his nerves.

"There won't be," she said, and she sounded sure.

"I won't hurt you," he heard himself say.

"You'd better not," she replied, watching him.

He approached the bed. Started to unbutton his shirt. At least he'd had the good sense to leave his gun-belt down the hall, in his own room. Nothing romantic about a Colt .45.

He sat down on the edge of the mattress to pull off his boots, and she made room for him, a heartening thing given all the hard words that had passed between them. "Have you ever done this before?" he asked.

"No," she said.

He closed his eyes, dealing with her answer. On the one hand, he was relieved. On the other—well—she'd been engaged twice, and she was nearly thirty. He'd considered the possibility that she had already been introduced to the experience and was just being coy. Now, he knew different. There would be pain, no matter how gentle he was, and that might scare her off for good.

"If you want me to leave," he said, "now's the time to say so."

She touched his back, tentatively, and he felt the heat of her hand right through his clean shirt. "And have you call me a coward? Not a chance, Holt McKettrick."

He turned to look at her. "I wouldn't do that, Lorelei. I swear I wouldn't."

"I believe you," she said, and stroked his hair. "You smell good."

He relaxed a little, even smiled. "So do you," he said.

Then he stood and shrugged out of his shirt, hanging it on the bedpost.

Lorelei's eyes widened, shining with moonlight. She was wearing a white flannel gown, buttoned clear to her chin.

"Take that off," he said. "Let me look at you."

She hesitated, then wriggled out of the nightgown.

Holt stared at her, stricken. She might have been made of alabaster except that she looked warm, and supple to the touch of a man's hands.

He unfastened his belt, then his trousers.

She squeezed her eyes shut, then opened them again. Wide. One hand went to her mouth.

"Still want to go through with this, Lorelei?" he asked, suppressing a smile.

"I don't see how it's anatomically possible," she said.

He laughed. "Trust me," he told her. "It is."

She sat up to take a closer look. "Tarnation," she whispered.

He pressed her gently back onto the pillows and lay down beside her. Cupped one of her full, warm breasts in his hand.

She shivered. "Mercy," she said.

"Nope," he answered, and bent to tease her nipple with the tip of his tongue.

She gasped, and her body arched. He would have lifted his head, but she stopped him, plunging both hands into his hair, holding him close.

He took his time, sliding a hand down over her quivering belly, to the nest of moist silk between her legs.

"Holt," she said. That was all, just that one word, but it held a whole dictionary's worth of meaning.

He burrowed through, teased her with a plucking motion of his fingers.

She let out a strangled groan.

"Stop?" he asked, making his way over satin terrain to her other breast.

She shook her head violently.

"More," she pleaded. "Please—more."

# CHAPTER 33

LORELEI CLUNG DESPERATELY to her reason, but her hold was slippery, especially when Holt kissed his way down to where his fingers played. When he took her into his mouth—boldly, brazenly *took* her—her response was involuntary, and at the same time powerful. It thrust through her like some furious and deafening wind, driving out her breath, made the whole of her body throb with a single thrumming pulse.

She turned her head into the pillow to stifle the primitive cries rushing up from that place where he feasted. She wasn't asking for quarter; she knew he would not grant it anyway. With every sound she uttered, he was more relentless, more demanding.

She began to plead, in small, ragged gasps—for what, she did not know. Her flesh was on fire, her skin moist with perspiration. Her spine arched, in a spasm of instinctive surrender, and still he would not let her go. He drove her harder, faster—draped her trembling legs over his shoulders and cupped his hands under her, raising her high off the bed.

She quivered, on the precipice of some terrible joy,

and he paused just long enough to flick at her with the tip of his tongue.

She came apart in that moment, like a star exploding in the distant heavens, hurling fire in every direction. That would be the end of it, she thought, in the grip of ferocious bliss—she would dissolve now into shimmering particles, like so much dust, and finally vanish.

Except that he caught her again, and drove her far beyond the first cataclysmic release, straight into the heart of an even greater one. In that place, there was no sound and no silence, no thought or image—only the blaze that burned away everything but her essence.

She was still buckling in the midst of the tumult when he lowered her to the mattress and entered her in one powerful motion of his hips.

The pain was a mere twinge in a maelstrom of sensation.

Her brain reeled as he delved to her core, withdrew and delved again. She clung to him fiercely, rose to meet him, compelled by some ancient, she-wolf part of herself. What was she striving for, with all the forces of her being? It couldn't happen again—it couldn't….

But it did.

They collided at the top of some invisible arch, and something seized inside of Lorelei, and then seized again. In those moments, she died and was reborn, fragmented and then came together again, a new creature, forever changed.

Holt's powerful frame stiffened; she felt the strain ripple through him, felt it under her hands and against her skin and most especially inside her. She raised herself to him, a tiny motion made at the limits of her strength, and he gave in at last, gave himself to her, all the heat and the wildness, all that he was or ever would be.

The descent began—physically, it was no more than a few inches, but to Lorelei, it seemed that only that feather-stuffed mattress kept her from falling and falling, forever and ever, through some endless inner sky.

They lay entangled, neither one speaking. Lorelei had lost the capacity for language; her mind was too vast for thought, and her body had dissipated to such an extent that she was a part of everything, and a part of nothing at all.

Gradually, though, she began to funnel back inside her own flesh, becoming aware of her toes first, then, oddly, her elbows. It was as if, one by one, she *remembered* the scattered parts of herself back into being. And she began to weep.

Holt raised his head from the curve of her neck, cupped her chin in his hand, whispered her name.

She cried harder.

"Did I hurt you?"

She shook her head.

"Then why are you crying?"

"Because—because I'm never go-going to be the same!"

"Lorelei, if there's a child—"

"It's not th-that! B-before, I *didn't know*—"

He frowned. "Didn't know what?"

"That it could be like that!" Lorelei sobbed. "I've m-missed so much—"

Holt kissed her, very lightly. Kissed her mouth, and kissed away her tears. When he looked into her eyes again, he was smiling. "So, I can conclude that you're crying because I didn't make love to you sooner?"

She felt a flash of glorious rage, singing in the very marrow of her bones. "Why, you *arrogant*—"

He laughed, kissed her again. "Or maybe it's because

you think it would have been like that with any other man besides me."

Her eyes widened, and if it weren't for the weight of his body half-covering hers, she might have battered him with her fists. "Of all the—"

He caught her wrists in his hands, pressed them with gentle force into the pillows. "Settle down," he said, still grinning. "It's never been anywhere near that good for me, either."

"Is that supposed to make me feel better?"

He ducked his head, still holding her wrists, and nuzzled his way to one of her nipples. "No," he said. "*This* is."

SHE WAS ALONE in the bed where she had either found the lost parts of herself or made the most spectacular mistake of her life. She felt Holt's absence even before she opened her eyes.

She should have been exhausted, given that she'd spent most of the night bucking under Holt McKettrick like a horse that wouldn't take the saddle, but she felt strangely exultant instead. As if she'd been trapped inside herself all her life, and he'd set her free—though not by wooing, not by cajoling or persuading. Oh, no. He had *driven* her out of her hiding place, and there was no going back.

Somewhere in the dooryard, a rooster crowed.

Lorelei sat up, biting her lower lip. *What now?* she asked herself. Would anything be different, between her and Holt, outside this room? Would they still be uneasy allies? Sworn enemies?

He hadn't said he loved her.

She certainly felt something—but was it love? It was peculiar, but before last night, she would have said she knew precisely what she thought about everything from shoe-blacking to sailing ships. Love? Why she'd have recognized it instantly. She'd loved Michael Chandler.

Hadn't she?

A light rap sounded at her door, and Lorelei scooted up against the headboard of the bed and wrenched the covers to her chin. "Who's there?"

"It's John Cavanagh, Miss Lorelei," came the shy response. "The rest of us, we're saddled up and ready to ride. Holt says you'd better come along, if you don't want to get left behind."

Lorelei flung back the covers and shot out of bed, snatching up her trousers and shirt. "Why didn't someone call me sooner?" she fretted, hopping awkwardly about as she struggled into her clothes. *Like Holt McKettrick, for instance!*

"I can't say, Miss Lorelei," John answered, through the door. "All I know is, Holt's got the bit in his teeth this morning. You hurry yourself up now. I'll stall him as long as I can."

Crimson-faced, Lorelei sat down on the edge of the mattress—where she'd behaved like a wanton fool the night before—and yanked on her shoes. She'd have blisters by the end of the day, but she couldn't take the time to put on stockings. "Thank you," she said ungraciously, and stuffed her hair up inside her hat. She'd braid it properly once she was on Seesaw, plodding along behind that dirty, noisy herd.

Within five minutes, she was downstairs. Rafe had saddled her mule, and he gave her a sympathetic glance as she rushed toward him, her bundled belongings bumping pitifully against her side.

"Guess you missed breakfast," he said, once she'd mounted.

Missing breakfast wasn't the half of it. She hadn't had

a chance to use the outhouse, or brush her teeth. And if John Cavanagh hadn't lit a fire under her, she'd still be up there in that featherbed, mooning like a befuddled schoolgirl. "I'll be fine," she said.

Rafe tied her pack in place, behind the saddle. "Melina's got some food for you, wrapped up in a dish towel," he said. Then he tugged at the brim of his hat, turned and walked toward his own horse.

Holt, meanwhile, was riding back and forth on that big Appaloosa of his at the front of the gathering, like Santa Ana about to overrun the Alamo. In that moment, Lorelei, born and raised a Texan, liked him just about as much as she liked the Mexican general.

Holt assigned riders to their positions, and the cowboys rode off to take their places—point, swing, flank and, of course, drag. Lorelei fully expected to bring up the rear again, as she had the day before, coming back from Reynosa. Well, let him do his worst. She'd swallow an *acre* of dirt before she'd let him know how she felt.

Two by two, the wranglers left, but Lorelei's name wasn't called. She sat there on Seesaw, her backbone stiff with pride, and waited. John was nearby with the wagon, and Melina sat beside him on the seat, but they might as well have been in Kansas City. That was how alone Lorelei felt.

To her surprise, Holt rode over to her, swept off his hat and regarded her with sun-narrowed eyes. "I'm glad you could join us, Miss Fellows," he said cordially.

Lorelei didn't dare speak. She'd make a blithering fool of herself if she did, so she just sat there, on that stupid mule, wishing she'd cuddled up with a rattlesnake before letting Holt McKettrick into her bed.

"Holt," John called, maybe out of mercy, "we'd best get that herd moving."

Holt straightened, made a show of putting on his hat. Taking his time, as much for her benefit as Mr. Cavanagh's. "Stay with the wagon," he said mildly. "John'll pull up at the first sign of Indians. If that happens, he'll give you a rifle. Get under the buckboard and shoot if you have to."

Lorelei wanted to cry, and not just because she was afraid of Comanches. Holt McKettrick had made love to her for most of the night, explored every inch of her person and turned her inside out, and now he was acting as if they were barely acquainted. She was damned if she'd let him think it bothered her.

"Holt," John repeated, more forcefully this time. "Stop devilin' that girl and take charge of this herd!"

Holt turned easily in the saddle and saluted Mr. Cavanagh. "Yes, sir," he said good-naturedly, and rode away.

Lorelei didn't move until the wagon started rolling. Then she prodded Seesaw to catch up, being careful to ride on Melina's side.

Her friend's brown eyes were luminous with understanding. Clasping the edge of the seat with one hand, Melina leaned out to offer Lorelei the food Rafe had mentioned.

Lorelei was starved, but she also feared she'd gag if she tried to swallow so much as a bite. She took the cloth-wrapped offering more because she was afraid Melina would tumble out of the wagon trying to give it to her than because she wanted it.

"Thanks," she managed.

"Eat, Lorelei," Melina urged, raising her voice to be heard over the cattle. "It's going to be a real long day."

Glumly, Lorelei nodded. The moment she uncovered the buttered bread and fresh goat cheese, a layer of dust settled on it. "I guess we'll be following the herd," she said, making a face and then taking a gritty bite. Even as she said the words, Holt and Rafe galloped ahead, side by side, to lead the way. The Captain and another man, slightly bent in the saddle, kept pace, one to the far right, one to the left.

John drove the wagon in behind them, and Lorelei looked back over one shoulder to see the point riders traveling about a hundred yards back. The herd was a bellowing sprawl of hide and horns, seeming to go on forever and raising plenty of dust.

"Won't we slow them down?" she asked Melina, wiping off her cheese with the sleeve of her shirt. "Riding at the front like this?"

"You want to be in back?" Melina retorted. "Where the Comanches could pick us off and nobody'd even know we were gone?"

Lorelei hadn't thought of that; she'd been too busy hating Holt McKettrick for using her and then casting her aside like an old boot. She shook her head and forced herself to finish off the food, trail dust and all. As unpalatable as it was, she needed the sustenance.

Half an hour later, she worked up the nerve to start another conversation. "Why didn't you wake me up this morning?" she asked Melina. John might have heard the question, but he gave no sign of it. Just looked straight ahead and kept the team moving, the reins resting easily in his gloved hands. The dog, riding in the back with the supplies, perked his ears up, as though he found the topic to be of interest.

"I figured Holt would have done that," Melina said, after mulling things over for a while.

Lorelei wilted inside. So everyone knew she'd squandered her virtue last night. Maybe they'd even heard her carrying on while Holt pleasured her. She could avoid most of them now, but when they stopped to make camp, she'd have to face at least some of those cowboys. She'd see the reflection of a fallen woman in their eyes.

She wished she could just topple off that mule and let the herd trample her, but she was either too brave or too cowardly—no telling which—to do that. So she just rode, miserable, ashamed and furious, all of a piece.

She took off her hat, let her hair tumble to her waist and reached back with both hands to gather and plait it. Melina handed over a little strip of rawhide to serve as a tie, but she didn't say anything.

She'd been partially right, Melina had, Lorelei conceded, about how things would turn out between Holt and herself, but at least Melina wasn't gloating. At the moment, Lorelei had to be content with small favors.

The sun was brutal, and even with the brim of her hat shading her face, Lorelei felt her nose and cheeks burning. Her milky skin had always been a secret vanity with her; now, even that was in jeopardy.

The herd traveled with excruciating slowness, and it was long past noon when Holt sent Rafe and the Captain back to ride on either side of the wagon.

"These horses are goin' to give out if we don't let 'em rest pretty soon," John called to Rafe.

"There's a stream up ahead," Rafe shouted back. "Maybe two miles from here. Holt says we'll have an hour, and then get moving again. Keep going until dark."

John nodded, adjusted his sweat-banded hat.

Melina shifted uncomfortably on the seat, and even Sorrowful began to prowl back and forth among the crates and rifles and bags of beans in the back of the wagon.

Lorelei yearned to stop, to feel solid ground under her feet and drink all the water she could hold. At the same time, she dreaded it.

The two miles Rafe had mentioned felt like twenty, but finally the stream came into view, a shimmering ribbon of cool, sparkling blue snaking through acres of dry, sparse grass. Lorelei kept riding until John finally hauled back on the reins and yelled, "Whoa!" to the team.

John helped Melina down, as soon as he'd set the brake lever and walked around behind the wagon, and his motions were so solicitous that Lorelei was worried. What if Melina's baby was coming? Maybe it was time— Lorelei didn't know—and maybe it was too early.

She dismounted, approached her friend, who was pressing both hands into the small of her back.

"Melina," she whispered. "Are you—is it—?"

Melina laughed and patted her arm. "No, Lorelei. I'm just tired, that's all. I got spoiled, sleeping in that feather-bed at Heddy's, and back there at Reynosa, too."

The word *bed* snapped Lorelei right back inside herself. Her cheeks pulsed, and she knew it wasn't just from the sunburn.

Melina looked at her curiously, took her by the arm, and led her to one side. "What's the matter with you, Lorelei? You're not coming down with something, are you?"

Lorelei peered at her friend. "Coming down with…?" She paused. Shifted from one foot to the other. "What?"

"When Holt came in from the herd this morning, he said you were probably late because you felt puny or something. That's when he sent Mr. Cavanagh to fetch you."

Lorelei felt a little better. Her heart, riding behind her navel all morning, rose to its proper place. "Holt spent the night with the cattle?" she asked carefully.

"Sure," Melina said. She frowned. "Where did you think he was?"

As tired as she was, with her shoes pinching and dust clodded in her hair and imbedded in every pore, Lorelei wanted to jump for joy. Not that she would have done anything so undignified, that is. Not in broad daylight, anyway.

"I didn't know," she lied.

Sorrowful leaped over the tailgate of the wagon, found a rock to do his business against and trotted over to nudge at Lorelei's thigh with his big head. She laughed, bent to pick up a stick and threw it for him.

He dashed after it.

"You ladies come and have some of this cold chicken from last night's supper," John said. "No tellin' how long it will be till we stop again."

The herd was blessedly quiet, lining the stream banks to drink, grazing on what grass they could find, but they'd brought legions of flies with them, and they buzzed around the horses and people, looking for something to bite.

Lorelei nodded to John to let him know she'd heard, and walked downstream a ways, away from the herd, to visit the bushes and then wash her hands. Fortunately, she had left the brush and was crouching beside the water when Holt approached, leading his horse.

He'd taken care not to let the company know he'd spent the night in her bed, she knew that now, but she was still irked by the way he'd treated her when they were leaving Reynosa.

"You feeling all right?" he asked, when she didn't

speak first. Hell would have frozen over before that happened, and maybe he knew it.

"I'm feeling just *grand,* Mr. McKettrick," Lorelei said, getting to her feet and starting past him. She'd splashed her face and swallowed about a gallon of water by that time. Now, she wanted some of that chicken John had mentioned, before the flies got to it.

Holt reached out and caught hold of her arm, and his touch brought back a rush of memories. Oddly, they didn't come from her head, where memories usually resided, but from the secret folds and curves of her body. "There's no call to be snippish," he said.

"Maybe not from your point of view," she replied, trying in vain to pull away.

He had the nerve to glare at her. "What's the matter with you?"

"Nothing," Lorelei snapped. "I give my virtue to a new man every night, and it doesn't bother me in the slightest when, the very next morning, he acts as if he's never met me before!"

Holt slammed his hat against one thigh. "Dammit, Lorelei, what would you have me do? Hand you a rose in front of the whole outfit? Quote poetry, maybe?"

She opened her mouth. Closed it again.

He wouldn't let her off the hook. "Well?" he demanded.

She folded her arms, rocked back on her heels. "You wanted to give me a rose and quote poetry?"

Color surged up his neck and flared beneath his new beard. "It was a figure of speech!"

"Holt!" It was Rafe, galloping toward them on his dusty horse. "There's a signal fire to the east—might be Comanches."

Holt swore, took a startled Lorelei by the waist and

literally flung her up onto Traveler's back. He was behind her and reining the gelding toward the rest of the party before Lorelei caught her breath.

As soon as they reached the wagon, he threw her off again, with such haste that she landed on her backside in the grass. Sorrowful wandered over and licked her face.

Melina helped her to her feet, and Mr. Cavanagh thrust a rifle into her hands.

"Get under that wagon!" he ordered.

Breathless, Lorelei scrambled to obey. Melina followed, and Sorrowful belly-crawled to join them. Lorelei waited for an arrow to thud into the dirt, inches from her nose.

Nothing happened.

Lorelei's hands began to sweat where she gripped the rifle. She watched Mr. Cavanagh's boots go by as he paced beside the wagon, swearing a colorful oath every once in a while.

"Do you see them?" Lorelei finally found the nerve to ask.

"No!" Mr. Cavanagh barked.

"Shouldn't you be under the wagon, with us? It wouldn't do at all if you got shot."

"Hush up, Miss Lorelei," he said. "I am tryin' to think."

Lorelei, for her part, was trying *not* to think.

"It's the cattle," Melina whispered. "They want the cattle, just like Holt said they would."

"Well, maybe if he just gives them a few—"

Melina looked surprised by this suggestion. "He won't."

"That seems unreasonable."

"He didn't travel all the way to Reynosa so he could give away the herd, Lorelei!"

Lorelei sniffed. "You needn't be so brusque about it."

"Give them some of yours, then," Melina challenged.

"I will," Lorelei decided. "They can have several. By the time they cook them, and eat and dance around the fire the way they do, we'll be safe and sound in Laredo." With that, she started to crawl out from under the wagon, bent on going right out there and presenting her proposal to the first Indian she happened to encounter.

Melina grabbed her shirt and pulled her back with surprising strength. "If you try that again, I swear I'll scalp you myself!" she hissed, wide-eyed. "You let the men handle this!"

"Shut up down there," Mr. Cavanagh ordered. The wagon shifted and creaked, and Lorelei figured he'd climbed into the box to get a better look at whatever was going on. She wished she could see, too.

Lorelei held her tongue as long as she could. Then she called, "Excuse me, Mr. Cavanagh, but do you see any savages?"

"I see a bunch of cowboys cinching in the herd," he replied, none too graciously.

"Maybe you shouldn't stand up there, like a lightning rod in a rainstorm," Lorelei suggested.

The wagon shimmied as Mr. Cavanagh jumped to the ground. His boots appeared, and then his face. He was bending from the waist, and he looked unfriendly.

"Miss Lorelei," he said evenly, "if those Indians do show up, I'd just as soon fight as answer any more of your infernal questions!"

Lorelei blushed.

He straightened again, mercifully, and Lorelei heard riders. She got her rifle ready.

The next face she saw was Holt's. He crouched in Mr. Cavanagh's former place, grinning. "You can come out now," he said.

"You might have announced yourself," Lorelei said. "I almost shot you."

"What happened to the Indians?" Melina asked. She crawled out from under the wagon, and somebody helped her up.

"They kept their distance," Holt told Melina, but he was still looking at Lorelei. "Maybe we've got a few ghosts riding with us yet." He extended a hand. "Are you coming out of there?"

Even the dog was gone.

Lorelei ignored Holt's hand and crawled back into the sunlight.

"If they want cattle—the Indians, I mean—you may give them some of mine." She got to her feet, brushing off her trousers and avoiding Holt's gaze.

He was too close, and she could feel him watching her. He stood. "I won't give them a damn thing," he said. "Except a bullet."

Lorelei felt exasperated. "Not even to buy safe passage?"

"Comanches don't make deals like that," he told her. "And if they do, they don't keep them."

"One too many broken treaties, I guess," Lorelei said. Now that her terror was ebbing, she felt irritable. "It's no wonder they don't trust us."

"Hellfire and spit," Holt muttered. "I didn't break any damn treaties." He strode away, still talking, slapping at his thigh with his hat. "All I'm trying to do is get these cattle back to San Antonio—"

"Now he's going to be even harder to live with than usual," Rafe said, with humorous resignation. He was standing right beside Lorelei, and he'd almost startled her out of her skin, popping up out of nowhere like that. She was glad she'd left the rifle under the wagon, because it might have gone off.

"What about the Indians?" Lorelei asked. "Aren't they coming?"

"You make it sound like you're giving a party and they're invited," Rafe observed, grinning. He stooped, retrieved her rifle and handed it to her. "They're not real sociable, as a rule."

Lorelei laid the rifle carefully in the back of the wagon.

"Better unload that first," Rafe said. "Otherwise, John might hit a bump in the trail and find himself missing an ear."

Lorelei sighed. "There are so many things to remember, I can't keep track of them all," she fretted.

Rafe took care of the rifle, dropped the bullets into the pocket of his leather vest. "You ever think of settling down somewhere besides Texas?" he ventured. "Say, the Arizona Territory?"

Puzzled, Lorelei studied his face. He didn't look as if he were teasing. "Do you have Indians there?"

"Apaches," Rafe admitted. "But they mostly leave us alone, up north. Cause more trouble around Tucson."

"Why would I travel all the way to the Arizona Territory?" Lorelei asked. "I have my ranch."

Rafe sighed, let his gaze follow his brother, now mounted on that fancy Appaloosa again, getting ready to spout more orders. She hadn't even had a piece of chicken yet.

Rafe's meaning finally hit her.

She put the back of one hand to her mouth. She'd thought her secret was safe after all. Now, she knew it wasn't. "Did he tell you about last night?" Her voice was very small.

"He didn't have to tell me," Rafe said, and reached out to squeeze her shoulder. "I know that look, when it's Holt wearing it."

"I'm such a fool," Lorelei whispered, unable to meet Rafe's gaze.

Rafe lifted off her hat and planted a brotherly kiss on top of her head. "Be careful," he said. And then he replaced her hat and walked away.

Before Lorelei could move at all, he was back on his horse, riding off to join Holt.

*You ever thought of settling down anywhere besides Texas? Say the Arizona Territory?*

*He didn't have to tell me. I know that look…*

*Be careful.*

Just a few words, but Lorelei knew she'd be the rest of the day sorting them through.

Mr. Cavanagh helped Melina carefully up into the wagon box, then opened the tailgate for the dog.

Lorelei caught Seesaw's reins, tossed them up over his neck and put her foot in the stirrup. The saddle seemed even higher off the ground and harder than before, and there was a wide stream ahead, waiting to be crossed. If she didn't drown doing that, well, there were still the Comanches.

She straightened her spine, drew a deep breath and kicked Seesaw into motion. Did she ever think of moving to the Arizona Territory? Land sakes, she had all she could do to survive Texas.

# CHAPTER
## 34

AFTER TWO DAYS of hard travel, they'd reached the outskirts of Laredo, unscathed. By Holt's reckoning, that was a miracle; the Comanches had made themselves visible, always at a distance, but for some reason he couldn't fathom, they had yet to make a move. Instead of easing his mind, this made him skittish, on a gut level, where words and thoughts didn't reach.

They were waiting, those Indians. Watching. And they wanted him to know it.

Right outside of town, Holt paid a local rancher for grazing and precious water, and kept the herd corralled as best he could. On the evening of September ninth, when Lorelei and Melina were safely housed in town with Heddy, Tillie and the baby, he rounded up John, Rafe, the Captain and Frank Corrales for some serious palavering. Mac Kahill had done his best to get in on the meeting, but Holt didn't want any wild cards. The cowboy had done his work ably, served as a ramrod with that sorry bunch of new wranglers Holt and Rafe had virtually scraped up off various saloon floors, but Holt still didn't trust the man enough to make him privy to his plans.

"These cattle, here," John said, when they'd all hunkered down in a circle, like Comanche warriors at a
powwow, "they may end up with the Cavanagh brand
on them, Holt, but they're really yours. Bought and paid
for."

Holt was having a devil of a time keeping his mind
on business. It had been that way since Reynosa, when
Lorelei had let him into her bed, and even though he
couldn't bring himself to regret what they'd shared, he
*did* regret his timing. The middle of a cattle drive was
no place for sparking, and he would have known that if
he'd been thinking with his head instead of his groin.
He'd mostly stayed clear of her ever since, trying to get
some perspective, but the damage was done.

"You sound like a man about to propose something,"
he told his foster father. It was too hot for a fire, so they
were gathered around a flat rock, by the light of a kerosene lantern. After the chin-wagging, there would be a
poker game, if Frank and the Captain had their way.

Even that made Holt think of Lorelei. She didn't know
a damn thing about five card stud, but what she lacked
in skill, she made up for in reckless audacity. He smiled,
and wondered what she was doing right then—reading
a book? Sitting down at Heddy's table for supper?

Taking a bath?

*Oh, God. Don't think about Lorelei naked, her skin
slick with water and soap....*

"I won't feel right about this until I know you're
going to recover every nickel you put into those cattle,
and the land, too," John said. The dog huddled close
beside him, and he stroked the critter's long yellow back
as he spoke. "I say we make an agreement and sign
papers so it's legal. I even have a name for the outfit—
The McKettrick Cattle Company."

"I like that," Holt allowed, with a slight grin. "But the ranch is still yours, John. You built it, you fought for it. You did the sweating and the bleeding."

"I meant to leave it to you anyway," John insisted, "because I know you'll take care of Tillie if anything happens to me."

Holt met the old man's gaze, glittering in the flickery light of that kerosene lantern. "You planning on dying right away?" he asked, with a lightness he didn't feel. Holt had been born independent, and he knew he could make it on his own, but there were two pillars supporting his concept of the man he wanted to become—Angus McKettrick and John Cavanagh. If either of them fell, he'd go on from there, having no other choice, but the idea of it shook him to his boot soles.

"It could happen any time," John said, quietlike.

"That's so," Holt admitted, surprised at the way his throat tightened. "But the same goes for the rest of us. Nobody here can swear he'll wake up tomorrow morning and saddle his horse."

"Just the same," John insisted, in a way that let Holt know he'd made up his mind, "I want the papers drawn up. That way, if some Comanche puts an arrow through my chest, I'll rest easy, knowin' two things…Templeton won't be running his fancy red cattle on my land, and Tillie will be all right."

"You'd best agree, Holt," the Captain said, leaning back on his elbows in the grass, booted feet crossed at the ankles. "I don't reckon John's going to pull his teeth out of this subject until you do."

"All right," Holt said, looking at John, remembering when he was a scared, defiant kid, with a chip on his shoulder. John had taken him in, straightened him out. Taught him to work and keep his word, and a thousand other things that went into the making of a man. "But I can't run that spread from Arizona, and I mean to go back there with Rafe, as soon as Gabe's free and Templeton's been dealt with." He shifted his gaze, took in Frank and the Captain. "I'll need partners, besides the old man, here. You two willing to help run this 'McKettrick Cattle Company' for a share in the profits?"

The Captain thrust himself upright, to a sitting position. "You mean that, Holt? Hell, I don't have a nickel to throw into the pot, and I'm getting on in years myself."

"You've got gumption, you're good with a gun and you know how to handle men like Isaac Templeton. That's good enough for me." Holt turned to Frank, who looked thoughtful. "What about you, Corrales? Will you throw in with us?"

"I think I'd rather have me a look at the Arizona Territory," he said. "You need any hands up there?"

"Always," Rafe threw in, before Holt could answer.

"What about Gabe?" the Captain asked. "You figure he'd want to stay around San Antonio? Provided, of course, that he doesn't end up with a noose around his neck."

Holt glanced toward Laredo, though this time he wasn't thinking about Lorelei. It was Melina who filled his mind, and that baby she was carrying. "I couldn't say," he said. "We'll have to ask him, soon as we get back. And he isn't going to hang, Cap'n. If I know one thing for sure, it's that."

The Captain smiled slightly, and gave an almost imperceptible nod of approval.

"I reckon Navarro will want to make a home for himself and his woman," John reflected, still petting the dog. "If he doesn't, I mean to tear off a strip of his hide."

Frank chuckled. "Gabe with a wife and a kid. Now, there's a picture."

Holt rubbed the back of his neck, felt a stirring in the pit of his stomach. It usually meant he should be on the lookout for trouble, that feeling, but now that Lorelei had to be taken into account, nothing was that cut-and-dried. "We'll have the papers drawn up soon as we get back to San Antonio," he said. "In the meantime, we've got a lot of miles still to cover, and a Comanche for every one of them." He reached for a stick he'd selected earlier, for the purpose, and sketched a map in the dirt. Everybody leaned in to peer at it. "I figure this is the easiest route, back the way we came." He scratched it out, drew another. A few pairs of eyes widened. "Not much water and damn little grass, but it's open country most of the way. Only a few places where the Indians might jump us, and Rafe and I can scout those out ahead of time."

Frank frowned. "*Jesu Cristo,* Holt," he muttered. "That's tough ground. Nothing but rocks, briars and snakes. Those cattle will be nothing but guts and bones by the time we get through there—*if* those Comanche devils let us pass, which they're not likely to do."

"They'll be expecting us to go the other way," Rafe mused.

"It doesn't matter what they expect," Holt said moderately. "All they have to do is watch us, like they've been doing ever since we set out on this trip. With a wagon, two women and over five hundred head of cattle, we'd be hard to miss, on any account. But I figure this is the best trail—it's more dangerous, but it's faster. We could cross it in three days, with a little luck."

Rafe frowned. "You can plan on *damn* little of that," he said.

"You have a better idea?" Holt asked mildly. Rafe

might be younger than he was, but he had experience driving cattle, having grown up on the Triple M, and while he wasn't book-smart, like their brother Kade, he was practical to the bone.

Rafe considered the question carefully, then sighed. "Nope," he said. Then he grinned. "I'd sure like to keep this hair on my head, though. Emmeline likes to run her fingers through it."

Holt chuckled, though he felt a tightening inside. If he didn't bring Rafe back to his Emmeline, safe and sound, he reckoned he'd never get over it. Never be able to face her *or* the old man, waiting up there in Arizona, hoping for word from Texas and probably trying to divine his and Rafe's whereabouts on some map.

"Everybody's in, then?" Holt asked. "If any one of you wants to stay right here in Laredo and call it good, there'll be no hard feelings on my part."

"In," said the Captain, pulling a deck of cards from his vest pocket.

"In," voted John, solemn as St. Peter overseeing the last judgment.

"Nothing better to do," Frank put in, with a wicked grin. He was still favoring those sore ribs of his, but other than that, he seemed fitter with every passing day. He wasn't cut out to do his recuperating on a cot in his pa's house, counting how many chickens pecked their way across the threshold.

That left Rafe. "Laredo's a fine town," he said affably, "but it's not the Triple M and it hasn't got Emmeline. Sooner we get these bawling critters up the trail to San Antonio, the better."

Holt stood, rubbed out the dirt-map with the sole of his right boot. "It's decided, then," he said. He nodded to the Captain, already shuffling his deck. "Don't be keeping these boys up half the night playing poker," he finished. "We're moving at dawn."

"What about you?" Rafe asked, following along as Holt started for his horse, still saddled and grazing under an oak tree nearby. "You planning to get a good night's sleep?"

"Unfortunately," Holt replied, noting his brother's grin and tolerating it. He hadn't told Rafe about that round with Lorelei, in the inn at Reynosa, but Rafe knew, just the same. "Yes. I'll be back here in my bedroll before that game winds down."

Rafe watched as Holt gathered the reins and mounted. The grin was gone. "Lorelei's a good woman," he said. "If you trifle with her, Holt, I will not take kindly to it. You hear me?"

Holt set his jaw. Tugged at the brim of his hat. "With both ears," he said, and urged the Appaloosa toward the scattering of lights up ahead.

"I TOOK ME A SHINE to John Cavanagh," Heddy confided, in a loud whisper, "and that's a fact. I'm wonderin' if he'd have me. Tillie says he don't have a wife."

Lorelei, seated beside Heddy on the back step, was grateful for the darkness, because it hid the expression on her face. Behind them, in the kitchen, Tillie and Melina were busy washing up the supper dishes. "It seems a little sudden," she ventured carefully. Mr. Cavanagh had never given any indication that he *wanted* a helpmate, as far as she'd noticed, and she didn't want Heddy to get her feelings hurt.

"When a body gets to be my age," Heddy answered, "'sudden' don't cipher up. John likes my cookin', and he knows I'd be good to his girl. I reckon if he comes back here, I'll just ask him, straight out."

Lorelei couldn't help thinking of Holt. He'd never mentioned marriage, and she wasn't sure she'd be amenable if he did, but watching Melina's belly grow, day by day, she had to wonder what she'd do if *she* was in the family way. The idea stirred a certain warmth in the tenderest regions of her heart, but it also scared her half to death. Suppose she was like her mother, and went mad from having a baby?

Holt had made no secret of his intentions—once he'd gotten Mr. Cavanagh's ranch on solid footing and cleared Gabe Navarro's name, he meant to go back to Arizona, home to his daughter and the Triple M. "Be careful, Heddy," she said gently. "Men are contrary creatures."

Heddy laughed. "That's one of the things I like best about 'em," she said, just as a rider came into the dooryard.

Holt. Even without the showy Appaloosa, or the waning moonlight, Lorelei would have known him by the quickening in her chest and the clench in the pit of her stomach.

He swung down from the saddle, in that easy way he had, and left the horse to drink at Heddy's trough. He took off his hat as he walked toward the two women, his teeth flashing in a trail-weary grin.

"Heddy," he said. "Miss Lorelei."

Heddy smiled and hoisted herself up off the step, smoothing her apron with large, rough hands. "Evenin', Holt," she answered. "Where's Mr. Cavanagh? I want a word with him."

"He's in camp," Holt said. "We're getting an early start in the morning."

Lorelei felt Heddy's disappointment as if it were her own. "I reckon I'll just have to go out there, then," Heddy decided. "You mind hitchin' up my horse and buggy for me, Holt?"

"I'll do it," he agreed, but he was looking at Lorelei.

She squirmed a little but didn't rise off the step. She liked being outside, under the stars. And anyway, Holt was there. Right or wrong, smart or foolish, she needed to be close to him, if only for a little while.

"Don't you go without me," Heddy told him. "I'm goin' in to put on my Sunday dress and get my shawl."

"I'll wait," Holt promised, still watching Lorelei. He stood at a distance of about a dozen feet and didn't show any signs of coming closer, which Lorelei supposed was a good thing, given past experience.

Lorelei didn't speak. She was afraid she might say something stupid if she did, or even burst into silly tears. Where this man was concerned, her emotions were a hopeless tangle; she was furious one moment and full of yearning the next, and there was no telling which one would come to prominence if she opened her mouth too soon.

"Anybody come forward to claim that baby?" Holt asked, when the silence stretched too thin for his liking.

Lorelei shook her head. "According to Heddy, the marshal says we might as well keep him. He'll send word to San Antonio if someone steps forward."

Holt sighed. "The trip we're about to take is too rough, and too dangerous, for a kid. Especially one that's still in diapers."

"Tillie won't leave him behind," Lorelei said, though she was sure Holt already knew that. It was just his way of worrying.

"No," Holt agreed, with another sigh, this one gustier than the first. He looked weary for the first time since

Lorelei had known him, and she felt a pang, tallying up the weight of the burdens he usually carried so easily on those broad shoulders of his.

She wanted to reassure him somehow, rise from that step and put her arms around him, tell him everything would be all right, but she wasn't so bold in Heddy's backyard as she had been in that room in the inn at Reynosa. Anyway, how could she assure him of such a thing? Fate had yet to confide in her. "You'll be shut of me in a few days," she said, because that was all she had to offer.

He cocked his head to one side, turning his hat slowly in his gloved hands. "Is that so?" he asked.

Again, Lorelei was glad of the darkness, because she blushed. "What happened between us," she began awkwardly, "well, it didn't make you beholden, if that's what you're thinking. I knew what I was doing."

"With all due respect, Miss Lorelei," Holt drawled, and in the dim light pouring out of the kitchen, she could see that his eyes were twinkling and one side of his mouth was quirked up, "that's about as far from what I was thinking as Texas is from Paris, France."

Her heart tripped over a few beats, regained its balance with a flailing tremor. "What *were* you thinking, then?" she managed. He was going to say he had cattle on his mind, of course. Gabe Navarro, probably. And Comanches.

She'd been a fool to ask such a question.

"That I'd like to buy your land and your share of those cattle out there," he said, with a nod in a southerly direction.

Lorelei tensed reflexively; it was as if he'd drawn back his hand and slapped her. Her eyes stung and watered, and it was a moment before she could catch her breath. *"What?"*

"You've proven your point, Lorelei. You broke away from your father and acquitted yourself on the trail as well as anybody I've ever seen. Now, it's time to be reasonable. With what I'm willing to pay you, you can start over in some other place. Maybe buy yourself a rooming house like Heddy has here." No mention of the marriage he'd proposed; no doubt, he'd changed his mind.

"What makes you think I *want* to 'start over in some other place'?" she demanded in a furious rush, but inside, she already knew the answer. She was a fallen woman now, tainted goods. If she was pregnant, everyone in San Antonio would know it soon enough, and they'd make her life a misery, brand the child as illegitimate. If she moved to San Francisco or Denver or Boston, she could pretend she was a widow, and open a respectable business.

It wasn't her land or her cattle Holt wanted. He was buying *his own* way out. Whether Lorelei was carrying his child or not, he'd be able to ride away with his conscience clear when he'd finished his business in Texas. He'd dallied with her, taken the most precious thing she had, and when he was gone, back on the Triple M, he'd probably never give her a second thought. Never wonder if he had another child somewhere, besides Lizzie.

"What's going through your head right now?" he countered, watching her quizzically.

Heddy chose that moment to return. "Where's that buggy?" she demanded. "I'm ready to go out there and get me a husband!"

Holt's mouth dropped open and, blessedly, Lorelei was able to forget her own quandary for a few moments.

"Heddy means to marry Mr. Cavanagh," she said.

"Get that buggy hitched," Heddy commanded.

Holt started to speak, stopped himself. He'd made a half gesture with his hat; now, he put it on his head. "Yes, ma'am," he said, and headed for the barn.

"Heddy," Lorelei pleaded, while they waited, taking both the woman's hands in her own, "what if Mr. Cavanagh says no?"

"He won't, 'less he's a damn fool," Heddy replied, bristling a little.

"What about your rooming house? All your things? Will you just walk away and leave everything you've worked so hard to build?"

"Don't amount to a hill of beans if you're lonesome," Heddy told her. "I'd as soon set a match to the place as live in it one more day, once Tillie and that baby are gone."

Lorelei thought of the featherbeds, and the pretty dishes. The hooked rugs and the lace curtains. Nobody knew her in Laredo. No one would point at her, if her belly started to swell, and say she'd made a fool of herself with Holt McKettrick.

She could start over right here.

The thought filled her with sweet sorrow. She almost made Heddy an offer on the spot, but there was still the matter of Mr. Cavanagh's accepting or refusing the other woman's proposal of marriage.

"Will you be back tonight? After you've talked to Mr. Cavanagh, I mean?"

Heddy beamed. "Maybe," she said, full of coarse confidence. "I reckon that depends on how things go when I put my question to him."

Lorelei kissed Heddy's cheek. "Good luck," she said, and blinked back tears of sadness and admiration.

Holt drove the buggy out of the barn and jumped to

the ground. Heddy trekked over, climbed aboard, and took up the reins.

"Took you long enough," she told Holt, and drove away.

Holt stared after her, baffled.

"Do you think he'll say yes?" Lorelei asked. "Mr. Cavanagh, I mean?"

"Hell," Holt growled, resettling his hat and watching the buggy disappear into the darkness, "I don't know."

"You wouldn't try to head out tomorrow, without Tillie and Melina and Pearl and me, would you?"

Holt turned back to Lorelei, and though his face was in shadow, she saw exasperation in every line of his body. "I might, if I didn't think you'd follow and get yourselves killed by Comanches."

She smiled, enjoying his discomfiture. All the while, her heart mourned. Her dreams were dying, dreams she hadn't even known she had until Holt McKettrick offered to pay her off like a discarded mistress.

"John will come by with the wagon first thing," he said, when she didn't respond to his gibe. "Be ready."

Lorelei ducked her head, because all of a sudden, there were tears in her eyes, and she'd die if he saw them.

He took a step toward her.

Lorelei froze, waiting.

But then he turned away, took Traveler's reins and mounted up. "Good night," he said. And then he was gone.

Lorelei stood on that very spot until she couldn't hear his horse's hooves on the road anymore. Then she went inside, expecting Melina and Tillie to be there, either giggling over Heddy's impulsive decision, or waiting, wide-eyed, for an explanation from Lorelei.

But the kitchen was empty.

Lorelei sagged into one of the chairs, folded her arms on the tabletop and laid her head on them. Heddy's clock ticked loudly on the wall. The house settled noisily on its foundations, as if to sleep. A piece of wood collapsed in the stove, with a whoosh of invisible sparks.

*I should get up,* Lorelei thought groggily. *Get myself to bed.*

But she didn't move. She simply didn't have the will to lift her head, let alone climb the stairs, exchange her calico dress for a nightgown and all the rest.

THE NEXT THING she knew, someone was shaking her awake.

She started, looked up blearily. Heddy stood over her, rimmed in the first pinkish light of a new day.

"Better get a move on, Miss Lorelei," she said, grinning from ear to ear. "My man'll be here with that wagon before you know it."

Lorelei sat bolt upright, blinking. "You mean he said yes?"

Heddy's grin stretched even wider. "Soon as we get to San Antone," she said, "we'll make it legal."

"Drink this," Tillie said, appearing from behind Heddy's girth with a cup of steaming coffee in one hand. "You done slept too long to get breakfast, but Melina's packing up your things right now. She said to let you sleep as long as you could, so I did." She paused for a breath. "Pearl and me, we're ready to go."

"You put a couple of pieces of bread together, with some bacon between," Heddy told Tillie. "Can't have Miss Lorelei fall off her mule from hunger."

"Yes'm," Tillie said. Dandling Pearl on her hip, she crossed to the stove to do as she was bidden.

"You're just going to leave?" Lorelei marveled,

getting out of her chair to make a hasty trip to the out-house. "What about your animals? What about your chickens?"

"Gave 'em to the neighbors," Heddy said dismis-sively. "Pack of trouble, anyhow. Now hurry up with you. Nobody in this outfit is in any mood to wait while you dawdle."

Lorelei rushed out. She was washing her hands and face at the pump when John Cavanagh drove in with the wagon. His grin was as broad as Heddy's, but it faded when he took in Lorelei's calico dress. Sorrowful barked a happy greeting from behind the box.

"You plannin' to ride twelve hours on a mule in that getup?" John asked.

"If I could have two minutes to change—"

Mr. Cavanagh shook his head. "Herd's already moving. We got to catch up as it is." He got down from the wagon box, marched into the barn and came out leading Seesaw and carrying his saddle and bridle over one shoulder.

Lorelei listened, her heart thundering, and heard the distant complaints of all those cattle. Felt the faint tremor of their passing in the ground, through the soles of her shoes. John threw the saddle into the wagon and tied Seesaw to one side, humming cheerfully under his breath.

Heddy, Melina and Tillie marched out of the house, possessions bundled. Tillie handed Lorelei the bacon and bread, then hoisted Pearl into the back of the wagon, scrambling up after him. John solicitously helped Heddy up into the box, then Melina.

"You comin' or not?" Heddy called, looking back at Lorelei, but not sparing a glance for her fine house, with all its simple treasures.

Lorelei hurried behind the wagon, handed her breakfast up to Tillie to hold, and climbed in with her and the baby and the bags of beans. John released the brake lever, and the buckboard shot forward so suddenly that Lorelei would have fallen on her face if Tillie hadn't taken a strong grip on her arm.

She rode with her legs dangling over the lowered tailgate, holding on tightly with one hand and eating her breakfast with the other.

*Goodbye, Laredo,* she thought, with mixed emotions, as they rattled and jolted down the main street of town, still mostly empty at that early hour. The windows of the shops and businesses were pinkish-purple, reflecting the first light of the morning. They passed a church, and the attendant cemetery, and then they were in open country.

Dust roiled as John drove straight through the center of the herd. Lorelei drew her legs back, lest she be gouged by one of those long-horned cattle, and Tillie helped her snap the tailgate into place.

After that, she rummaged through her pack for trousers and a shirt, and wriggled into the pants as inconspicuously as she could. The cowboys were too busy to look at her, but she wasn't about to take off her dress and put on the shirt, so she contented herself with the odd mixture of garments she was already wearing.

"Heddy's going to be my mama," Tillie told her, when they reached the front of the herd, and there was a lull in the noise. "Soon as they come across a preacher."

Lorelei reached out to take the baby for a while. He pulled at her hair, with a chubby little hand, and cheered her up immeasurably. "Does that make you happy?" she asked, unsure of Tillie's feelings on the matter of her father's sudden and imminent remarriage.

Tillie's smile was sudden, and brilliant as a flash of sunlight on clear water. "Yes'm," she said. "Now I can get a husband of my own. Give Pearl a daddy. I reckon I'd marry up with Holt, if he wasn't my brother. Sort of. Anyhow, he's sweet on you."

Lorelei nearly swallowed her tongue. Pearl planted a sticky kiss on her cheek and chortled, and she hugged him close. "Tillie Cavanagh," she teased, carefully avoiding the subject of Holt, sweet on her or otherwise. "I didn't know you wanted a husband!"

"'Course I do," Tillie answered. "I'd like a black man, but I ain't seen many of them lately. I heard once that there's some in Austin. I might go up there and find me one."

Lorelei laughed. "You've been with Heddy too long," she said.

Tillie looked puzzled at that. Her gaze shifted to Pearl's blond head, and she frowned. "You don't reckon it'll matter if I get him a daddy that ain't the same color, do you?"

Lorelei's heart ached. She put an arm around Tillie's shoulders and hugged her. "No," she said. "No, I don't."

"Heddy says folks will give me trouble about it," Tillie confided.

Lorelei thought it was unlikely that Tillie would ever travel to Austin or anywhere else to find a husband. Mr. Cavanagh probably wouldn't allow it. But she saw no reason to throw cold water on the young woman's hopes, fragile as they were. Since leaving her father's house, she'd learned that, sometimes, hope was all a person had to keep them going.

"I think you'll be very, very happy," she said gently, praying it was true.

At noon, they stopped at a deserted homestead, the herd streaming past on both sides, to draw up water from the well so the horses could drink. Lorelei used the time to saddle Seesaw, and climbed onto his back to ride astraddle, her calico skirts drawn up to reveal her trousered legs, her hat offering scant protection against the relentless sun. Soon, they were moving again, everyone gnawing on hardtack and jerky as they made their way to the front of the herd.

Rafe, riding with Holt, reined his horse around and galloped back to keep Lorelei company a while, and she was poignantly grateful for his company. She couldn't see any sign of Indians, but she knew they were close by, watching, because the little hairs on her nape stood up.

"Tell me about the Triple M," Lorelei said presently, like a child asking for a bedtime story.

Rafe gave her a sidelong look. "Maybe you'll see it yourself, one day," he said.

"That's not very likely," Lorelei answered. "Start at the very beginning."

Rafe chuckled, but there was a certain sadness in the sound. "Once upon a time," he began, "a real mean hombre named Angus McKettrick said goodbye to Texas and headed north...."

# CHAPTER 35

THEY WERE LESS than a day out of San Antonio when the attack finally came, and it was almost a relief to Holt. Waiting for that first skin-peeling shriek had his nerves jangling and his belly clenched, and he was ready for the fight. What he *wasn't* ready for was Rafe taking the first arrow, straight through his left arm.

The two of them had ridden ahead of the herd, to scout a rocky area for Comanches, and they found them, all right. The bastards had left their ponies out of sight somewhere, crouching behind boulders, and now that Rafe was hit, they came screaming from their hidey-holes, shrill enough to split a man's eardrums. Knife blades glinted in the dusty heat.

Rafe sprang off his horse, arrow and all, and his .45 was already spitting smoke and bullets before he hit the ground. Holt stayed right with him; they dove for cover and kept shooting. The panicked geldings took off on a dead run for the party traveling behind them, and Holt spared a breath to pray they'd make it.

An Indian leaped up onto the rock in front of them, blade raised, face contorted with the kind of reckless rage Comanches were noted for. Rafe put a bullet through his stomach while Holt reloaded his pistol. A slight sound behind him made him whirl and fire twice. Two dead braves fell on top of them, one with the top of his head gone, the other shot through the heart.

Rafe gritted his teeth from the pain as he shook free of the bodies, but he didn't favor his wounded arm. He didn't seem aware of it.

War cries ripped the air, underlaid by the thunder of approaching hooves and the hiss and ping of rifle shells. Holt would welcome any help he could get, but he hoped to hell the whole crew wasn't riding to the rescue, leaving the herd unprotected. There were bound to be more Comanches closing in from the rear, and *they* would be on horseback, ready to drive off as many cattle as they could.

Weaving through all that ruckus, Holt was sure he heard the braying of a mule.

He hoped that didn't mean what he thought it did.

The Indians were out in the open now, coming at him and Rafe from every direction. They fought back, each one covering the other while they reloaded, and reloaded again.

A shotgun boomed, and one of the braves flew backward off a high rock, arms outspread. After that, it rained bullets. The battle seemed to go on forever, but it probably lasted about fifteen minutes. At the end of the fury, a peculiar, reverberating silence fell.

Rafe slid down the rock, sat with his back to it, sweating and gasping for breath. He was feeling that arrow now, that was for damn sure.

Holt risked raising his head for a look and saw dead Indians everywhere. John, the Captain and Frank were there, on horseback, surveying the carnage, rifles ready for any fresh trouble that might happen to crop up.

And with them, riding that damnable mule of hers, was Lorelei.

Holt felt a surge of horror, and something else he couldn't identify, so powerful that it made him feel light-headed.

"Rafe's hit," he told the men, but he was looking at Lorelei. He couldn't take his eyes off her, for fear she'd topple forward with an arrow in her back.

Whoops and more gunfire sounded in the distance; he'd been right, for all the good it did him. The Comanches were helping themselves to the herd, and the wranglers were fighting back.

"Get back there and lend them cowboys a hand," John told the Captain and Frank. They hesitated, took a last look around, and rode out.

Lorelei jumped down off that mule and ran past Holt to drop to her knees next to Rafe. She dabbed at his wound with a wadded up bandana and asked the bone-stupidest question Holt had ever heard.

"Does it hurt?"

Pale as death and bleeding like a speared hog, Rafe chuckled. "Indeed it does, Miss Lorelei," he said. "Indeed it does."

Holt got Lorelei by the arm and hurled her back. While she was still regaining her balance, he yanked off his belt and wrapped it around Rafe's upper arm for a tourniquet. Rafe gasped when he pulled it tight.

John loomed over them both, handed Rafe a flask. "You better take a good dose of that," he said.

Rafe nodded and unscrewed the lid with his teeth while Holt assessed the damage. The flint arrowhead and a good four inches of the shaft were sticking out the back of Rafe's shirtsleeve. There was no telling how badly he was hurt, but one thing was for sure. The next couple of minutes were going to be worse than the initial injury.

"Least it isn't my gun arm," Rafe said, and downed some more whiskey.

"I'm sorry about this, Rafe," Holt told him, and he wasn't just talking about what he had to do next. It was his fault that Rafe was hurt.

"Just do it," Rafe ground out. "And do it quick."

Holt snapped the arrowhead off, then wrenched the shaft out with his other hand. Rafe didn't make a sound, but Lorelei let out a scream shrill enough to wake two or three dead Comanches. Blood spurted from Rafe's wound, and Holt gave the tourniquet another hard tug to stanch it.

Rafe finally passed out.

Neither Holt nor John spoke as they hoisted Rafe to his feet. He stumbled between them, his head rolling on his shoulders, and came to enough to stand. With help from both men, he managed to gain the saddle of John's mount, the spotted pony Melina usually rode.

John put a foot in the stirrup and swung up behind him, reaching around Rafe's slumped frame to grab the reins.

Holt turned on Lorelei then, and her eyes widened in her dusty, tear-streaked face when he stalked toward her.

"Get on that goddamned mule!" he told her, through his teeth.

She backed away from him, her eyes bigger still, but there was a tilt to her chin that said she wouldn't give much more ground. "Will Rafe be all right?" she whispered.

Holt stopped, bent to snatch his hat from the ground.

Rafe's was a few feet away, so he got that, too. Handed it to Lorelei. *"Get on the mule,"* he repeated.

She obeyed, which was a wonder in and of itself, and clung to the saddle horn with both hands while he mounted behind her. "Why are you so angry?" she inquired, as he reached around her to take the reins and steer the animal back toward the herd. The gunfire on the other side of the herd had died down by then; he hoped that meant the Comanches were on the run, but it could just as well be that the wranglers were all dead or wounded.

He gave Seesaw the heels of his boots, wishing he'd worn spurs. "It's bad enough that my brother took an arrow," he said, letting the words grind past her right ear. "You could have been killed out here, or taken captive, which would have been a whole lot worse."

He felt her shiver against his chest. "I know you said to stay with the wagon if the Indians came," she said, keeping her face forward and dragging each word up out of some deep part of herself, "but when we heard the shots, knowing you and Rafe were out here—well—I couldn't bring myself to hide." Her spine straightened, but she still didn't look back at him, which was a good thing, because he wouldn't have wanted her to see his face right then. "I had to *do* something, Holt. Even if it was wrong."

He hoped she didn't sense the softening in him. He was trail boss, and he couldn't afford to show weakness. Up until that moment, he hadn't realized he knew *how* to let down his guard, especially in the wake of a life-and-death fight like the one he'd just been through.

"When I give an order," he rasped, as furious with himself as he was with Lorelei, "I expect it to be obeyed. Is that understood?"

She didn't answer.

The herd was up ahead, and a quick count showed that all the wranglers were still intact. The wagon bristled with arrows, though, and there was no sign of the other women, or the dog.

Holt's belly clenched up again.

"Lorelei," he prompted, in a growl.

She turned her head, searched his face. "I don't work for you, Holt McKettrick," she said. She sounded tough, but her lower lip wobbled.

He might have laughed out loud if his brother hadn't been shot.

"While you're traveling with this herd, you *will* do as I say," he told her. The softness was gone; he felt hard from the center of his soul.

He quickened the mule's pace again and felt as though he'd just tossed back a double-shot of rotgut whiskey, the relief was so intense, when the other side of the supply wagon came in sight. Rafe was lying on the ground, with a saddle for a pillow, while Heddy and Tillie knelt on either side of him. Tillie stood a little distance away, Pearl in her arms, the dog panting at her side.

"Thank God," Lorelei whispered, on a long breath. "They're all right."

Holt rode up to the little gathering beside the wagon, hooked an arm around Lorelei's waist and removed her none too gently from the mule's back. She stumbled slightly before getting her footing, and glared up at him in humiliated fury.

"We'll see if the same can be said of the herd," he said, and reined Seesaw around. Off to his left, some thousand yards distant, he saw the Captain headed in on horseback, leading Holt's gelding and Rafe's, one on either side. It was another weight off his mind, but he kept reviewing everything that could have happened to Lorelei, riding into the middle of a fight like that, so he didn't feel one whit better.

It turned out his count was wrong. One of the wranglers had taken a header from his horse when the second contingent of Comanches came after the herd, and had broken his left leg. John and a couple of the other men were loading him up in the wagon.

Holt heard his pa's voice in the back of his mind. *God looks after fools, drunks and cowboys, boy,* Angus had said one day when the two of them were rounding up strays on the Triple M. *One time or another, I've been all three, so I'm obliged to Him for the favor.*

Holt spotted Frank and trotted the mule over to him. There were half a dozen dead Indians scattered on the ground; the others had gotten away. It was hard to tell how many there had been from the tracks, since the herd had churned up plenty of ground in all the excitement.

Kahill joined them before Holt could answer Frank's immediate, "Your brother going to make it?"

Kahill tugged at his dusty hat brim and gave a cocky grin. "Good to see you're still in the saddle, Boss," he drawled. "Hope your being on that mule doesn't mean your horse got killed."

"Traveler is fine," Holt said, and shifted his gaze to Frank. "Rafe's in for a hard time. I mean to go back and make sure the bleeding's stopped, and get him to that pint-sized doctor in San Antonio first thing."

Frank nodded, resting on the pommel of his saddle and watching Kahill with narrowed eyes. He was breathing hard, and his shirt was drenched with sweat.

"You hurt, Frank?" Holt asked.

Frank shook his head. Grinned. "No more than I was before this whole thing started," he said.

Holt turned back to Kahill. "They get any of the herd?"

Kahill shook his head. "Not so much as a hind-hoof," he said. "Might be they'll come back and make another try, though. They'll have blood in their eyes, those Comanches, after losing so many braves." He looked around, taking in the scattered bodies. "We gonna take the time to bury them, Boss?"

"As far as I'm concerned," Holt said, checking the position of the sun, "the buzzards can have them. We'll be lucky to make John's place before nightfall. Let's get this herd moving."

"You're not worried those red devils will come after us again?" Kahill pressed, though he straightened in the saddle and took a firmer grip on his reins. He didn't look as if he had an opinion on the prospect, one way or the other, but the fact that he'd asked showed a sensible concern.

"If I thought worrying would get us anywhere," Holt retorted, "I might take it up." Kahill rode off to get the wranglers back to their positions and prod the milling cattle into motion, and Holt turned his full attention to Frank. "That kid with the broken leg. He's got a rough ride ahead of him, like Rafe. John'll keep an eye on them, but he has the wagon to drive, and a peck of women to boot, so I'd appreciate it if you'd stick close by, in case there's more trouble."

Frank nodded, watching Holt closely. "You all right, *amigo?*" he asked quietly.

Holt met his gaze. "I'm not real sure," he said. There wasn't much Frank didn't know about him, so he saw no point in embroidering the truth. "When that arrow hit Rafe—"

Frank rode near enough to slap him on the shoulder.

"Better change horses, Boss," he said. "Your woman will be wanting her mule back."

Holt laughed, and it felt good. "If I wring her neck one of these days," he said, "will you testify that I was with you the whole time?"

Frank's eyes twinkled. "Swear it on a stack of Bibles," he said.

HOLT RODE OVER to the wagon and looked inside at Rafe and the young cowboy with the broken leg. Lorelei wanted to tell him to get off her mule, but she didn't figure she was in any position to issue such a challenge, so she bit her lower lip and held her tongue.

He spoke to the wounded men, Rafe first, and then the wrangler, but his voice was low, and strain though she did, Lorelei didn't catch a word of the conversation.

Even when the Captain brought the Appaloosa to him, and he moved from one animal to the other without setting foot on the ground, Holt didn't spare her so much as a glance. She waited until he'd ridden away to stomp over and get on Seesaw. One of the wranglers led Rafe's horse and the injured cowboy's, while John drove the wagon, Tillie and Pearl wedged between him and Heddy in the box. Melina reclaimed her pony, and soon joined Lorelei as the party moved forward in a storm of noise and dust.

"Bet Holt could have bitten a nail in two when he saw you in the middle of an Indian fight," Melina said.

Lorelei would have preferred not to discuss the subject, but there was a long ride ahead before they reached the Cavanagh ranch, and she knew Melina would keep plaguing her until she answered. "He was a little displeased," she admitted, rather stiffly. Her throat was parched with dust and fear, and her ears were filled, not with the complaints of several hundred thirsty, trail-weary cattle, but with the sound of guns going off and the furious screams of all those Indians. She wondered if she'd ever get that out of her head, or the image of Rafe with that arrow jutting out of his arm.

Another few inches to the right, and the wound might have been fatal.

And it could just as easily have been Holt who was hit, instead of Rafe.

Melina snorted, unaware of the upheaval inside Lorelei. "'A little displeased'? I've never seen a man look like that—white around the mouth, and like his skin had been pulled tight—and I've seen plenty. If he didn't have to worry about another Indian attack, and protecting all of us *and* the herd, he'd still be yelling at you."

"He did *not* yell at me." Lorelei straightened in the saddle. "He wouldn't dare."

Melina actually laughed. One would think, after they'd been set upon by Indians and Rafe and another man had been grievously injured, she would be in a more circumspect state of mind. "For a smart woman," she said, "you sure can be stupid sometimes."

Lorelei reddened. "Whose side are you on, anyway?" she sputtered. "I thought you were my friend!"

"I *am* your friend," Melina replied. "When you crawled out from under that wagon, jumped on Seesaw and rode after the men, I was so scared I almost died. I figured those Indians would get you for sure."

Lorelei looked sideways at Melina and saw a tear slip down her cheek.

And she said what she hadn't been able to say to Holt.

"I'm sorry."

Melina scrubbed at her face with the back of one

grubby hand. "Maybe you are, and maybe you're just saying that. Either way, I'm so mad I could snatch you bald-headed, and you'd better stay out of Heddy's way for a while, too, because she's likely to take a switch to you."

"Heddy would have done the same thing I did if it had been John out there, set upon by Comanches. So would you, if it had been Gabe—"

"But it was Holt," Melina pointed out, as Lorelei realized what she was saying and gulped back the rest of the sentence.

Lorelei kept her gaze turned forward, watching Holt. He was riding with Frank Corrales and the Captain now, and they all had their rifles out of the scabbards and ready to fire. As they reached the rocky place where the Indians had hidden, they readied themselves visibly for another fight, and they didn't even try to avoid the bodies in the trail.

In another few minutes, the wagon and side riders would pass, and then the herd. Lorelei closed her eyes against the images that aroused, but they only rose up bloodier and more vivid than before.

They traveled between the great rocks, the herd breaking into streams behind them, but there was no new attack, not then, and not when they came out into the open again. Lorelei drew back on Seesaw's reins, partly because she wanted to check on Rafe and the other man, and partly because she knew Melina would start up the earlier conversation again if she didn't.

Rafe's shirt was soaked with blood, but he'd raised himself partway up to sit with his back against the wagon box, his good hand supporting his wounded arm. The cowboy wasn't faring as well; he grimaced at every bump, and his narrow, too-youthful face was pale behind the obligatory coating of trail dirt. Tillie had made a bed for the baby in an old tool crate, and she knelt next to the other wrangler, pushing Sorrowful away when he tried to lick the man's hand.

Heddy turned in the wagon seat and skewered Lorelei with a look that said she'd have a few things to say, herself, when the opportunity presented itself.

Lorelei pulled her hat brim down over her eyes and concentrated on Rafe. "I suppose you're furious with me, too," she called, over the din, "just like everybody else."

He grinned. "No, Miss Lorelei," he shouted back. "I think you're brave to the point of stupidity, but I kind of like that in a person."

Lorelei laughed, something she'd never thought she'd do again after all that had happened that day. "You'll have a spectacular story to tell once you get back to the Triple M," she replied, and instantly felt sad, because when Rafe went back to the Arizona Territory and the family ranch, Holt would go, too.

She ought to be relieved by that knowledge, but she wasn't.

"I think you'd tell it better," Rafe said, jolting her out of her sudden introspection. "I can just see Emmeline and Mandy and Chloe all hovering around you, with their ears bent to hear the tale."

Emmeline, Mandy and Chloe. The McKettrick wives. Without even knowing the women, Lorelei envied them out of all proportion to reason and good sense. They had husbands, a home, children of their very own.

They belonged.

Lorelei swallowed hard. "I'd better get back to Melina," she said, when she thought the words wouldn't come out of her throat riding on a sob.

"Wait," Rafe said, trying to sit up even straighter and wincing from the pain.

Lorelei waited, though she wanted to bolt. Whatever Rafe was about to say, she suddenly didn't want to hear it.

"Holt was scared today," he told her. "He'll never admit it, but between me getting shot and you showing up on that mule, with the bullets and arrows flying every which way—well, it was just about more than he could take."

Lorelei bit her lower lip.

"I haven't known you all that long, Miss Lorelei," Rafe went on, "but in the time we've been acquainted, I've never seen you give up on anything you wanted. Don't start with Holt."

She pretended she hadn't heard that last part, over all the uproar of the wagon, the horses and a few hundred cattle, and went to rejoin Melina.

It was full dark, with just a slice of moon to provide light, when John Cavanagh gave a ringing shout of delight and slowed the wagon. Lorelei knew, with a lifting of her tired, battered heart, that the rangeland spread out before them was his own.

The stream up ahead, glittering darkly, was the same one that ran past her property. She was almost home, and she'd brought fifty head of cattle with her.

Her jubilation faded a little when she remembered that she might not be staying. It all depended on whether or not she'd conceived a child with Holt—she'd know soon enough, since her monthly, always regular as a Swiss clock, was due in another few days. If it didn't come, she'd sell her ranch to the newly formed McKettrick Cattle Company, buy Heddy's rooming house and find a way to get back to Laredo.

Was Laredo far enough away?

The cattle surged past the wagon on all sides, drawn to the stream, fairly trampling each other in their desperate thirst. They would have grass aplenty now, and they could rest. This was a considerable consolation to Lorelei.

When they'd all passed, Lorelei got down from Seesaw just to feel the ground under her feet. Holt wheeled his gelding around and rode back to the wagon.

"Can you make it to town tonight, Rafe, or should I fetch the doctor out here?"

"I reckon I could travel a ways," Lorelei heard Rafe say, "but I'm not sure about this cowpuncher, here. I think he's had about all he can take."

"I'll get the doc, then," Holt answered. Then, for good or for ill, he noticed Lorelei, standing nearby, watching the herd lining the bank of the stream. "Well, Miss Fellows," he added. "That's your land on the other side, isn't it? I'll have the men drive your cattle across when they've had their fill of water, but you'd probably better spend the night here."

Lorelei was too tired to argue the point, though the truth was, she wanted to sleep under her own roof, rustic as the accommodations were. "Whatever you say, Mr. McKettrick," she said, looking up at him. His shoulders blocked out a good bit of the starry Texas sky.

She thought she saw his jaw tighten, but she couldn't be sure, for the shadows. If he meant to say anything, Melina interrupted before he formed the words.

"I want to go to town with you," she told Holt. "So I can see Gabe."

He shifted in the saddle. "Tomorrow will be soon enough, Melina," he said carefully. "I'll take you in first thing."

Melina laid a small hand on Holt's boot. "I need to know he's all right."

"Frank and I will look in on him," Holt answered.

"I might be asleep when you get back from town," Melina protested.

"If you are," Holt promised, "I'll wake you. I've got to go now, Melina. Fetch the doc."

Melina started to speak, stopped herself and nodded.

"You go on," John Cavanagh said, when Holt hesitated. "Heddy and me, we'll look after the rest of the outfit till you get back."

Holt nodded, glanced in Lorelei's direction and rode off.

With the wranglers guarding the herd, the task of getting Rafe and the cowboy into the Cavanagh house fell to John and the Captain. Lorelei, Heddy and Melina went in ahead, to make a place for them. Tillie followed, carrying the baby, who was already sound asleep on her shoulder.

They settled the wrangler on the horsehair sofa, since it was too short for Rafe. He took his rest on a pallet on the floor, and seemed glad of it.

"Good to be out of that wagon," he murmured, when Lorelei crouched beside him with a ladle of water from the pump over the kitchen sink.

"Drink this," she urged, holding the back of his head so he could manage a few sips.

Within moments, he was asleep. It was probably a welcome respite, after traveling so many miles over a winding, bumpy trail.

Tillie took the baby upstairs, the dog at her heels, and didn't come down again.

John and the Captain busied themselves outside,

putting the team and wagon up for the night, and Heddy had gone straight to the kitchen, just as if she'd lived in that house all her life.

Lorelei approached warily, because she hoped there might be tea brewing and she needed some. Melina followed.

Heddy was stuffing kindling into the cookstove, her motions quick, confident and a little angry.

"I could drink a barrel of coffee and eat a whole buffalo," the older woman said, without turning around. "Melina, kindly see what's in that big cupboard over there that we can cook up. Lorelei, you sit yourself down at that table so I can chew you out proper."

Lorelei pulled back a chair and sank into it, resigned.

Melina bustled over to the cupboard and pulled open the doors, revealing jars of preserves—green beans, corn, stew meat, something that looked like chicken.

Heddy finished building the fire and reached for the coffeepot, marching to the sink to pump water with furious motions of her right arm.

Lorelei braced herself. Too tired to fight back, she was basically at Heddy's mercy.

When the pot was filled, and coffee had been measured in, Heddy turned to regard Lorelei, her hands resting on her ample hips, her face stormy as a tornado sky. "That was just plain foolhardy, what you did today," she said, glowering. "I never seen the like of it, in all my born days."

Lorelei wanted to lower her head, but her pride wouldn't let her do it.

"Did you do any thinkin' before you lit out on that consarned mule to save Holt McKettrick from them Comanches?" Heddy demanded.

"No, ma'am," Lorelei said. And it was true. She hadn't thought—not even as far as "saving" Holt. She'd known only one thing—that she had to be there, whatever happened.

"I don't suppose it occurred to you that with you underfoot, he had one more thing to worry about? He had a fight on his hands, with Rafe down and all that shootin' goin' on, and on top of all that, he had to protect *you!*"

This time, Lorelei did lower her head.

Heddy put a hand under her chin and made her look up at her. To Lorelei's amazement, the woman was smiling.

"Damnation," she said, "I'd have done the same thing, if I was your age and my man was in trouble!"

Lorelei stared at her, too confounded to speak.

Heddy patted her cheek. "You'd make Holt a fine wife," she finished. "Let's hope he has the horse sense to know that."

Lorelei flushed. Opened her mouth. Closed it again.

Heddy turned and went back to the stove. Melina, carefully avoiding Lorelei's gaze, had lined the worktable with jars of Tillie's canned food.

"I'll make us some slum-gooey," Heddy decided.

Lorelei found her voice again, maybe because the subject seemed a safe one. "Slum-gooey? What's that?"

"Mixture of whatever comes to hand," Heddy replied jovially, rummaging in another cupboard until she found a huge cast-iron kettle. "I'm going to need a lot more grub than this, Melina," she went on. "Them cowpokes ain't eaten all day, and one hell of a day it's been!"

Lorelei got to her feet, moving like a sleepwalker, and helped Melina carry jars to Heddy, who was busily screwing off the lids and dumping all manner of things into the kettle to heat.

The cowboys came inside in relays, gobbling up the slum-gooey and swilling down coffee. Lorelei thought she did well not to fall face-first into her plate.

# CHAPTER 36

IT WAS AFTER DAWN when Holt and Dr. Elias Brown rode out of San Antonio, the doc bumping along on a fat pony, with his medical bag tied to the horn of his saddle. Holt was in a glum mood—Elias had been occupied tending a gunshot wound when Holt had reached his house, and could not leave his patient until the injured man was past the crisis point. He'd gone to the jailhouse next, Holt had, and spent the rest of the night trying to haul Gabe out of a mental tar pit. Nothing would cheer him. Not the news that they'd found Frank in Reynosa, banged up but on the mend, and brought him back as far as John's place. Not the several visits Gabe had had from R. S. Beauregard during Holt's absence, and the assurance of a second trial. Not even the knowledge that Melina had come through the long journey unscathed.

Holt's spirits sank even lower when he and the doc topped the rise above Lorelei's place and saw what was left of her house—cinders, charred wood and scorched earth. Trees, still standing, but burned to grim and twisted skeletons.

The doc let out a low whistle of exclamation, surveying the blackened tangle of timbers where the cabin had been. The fire had traveled clear to the creek bank.

Holt nudged the Appaloosa hard with the heels of his boots, plunging down the hillside to dismount in the dooryard. The dirt around the remains of the house was pocked with the hoofprints of at least a dozen horses, proving what he'd already guessed—that this blaze had not been the result of a stray spark or a lightning bolt. It had been deliberately set. Chances were, if he rode the boundaries, he would see where the raiders had taken steps to contain it, keep it from moving onto Templeton's land.

Doc bounced down from the road to join him, sweeping off his hat and running a forearm across his broad, sweating brow. "Indians?" he asked, looking around at the wreckage with a grim expression. That was the first thing everybody thought when they came across this kind of destruction, and not without reason. Older, wiser Comanches had accepted the fact of the white man's encroachment, but there were still bands of renegades, fighting on in the face of defeat. Nobody knew that better than Holt did.

He shook his head in belated reply to the doctor's one-word question. "Not unless they've taken to shoeing their horses," he said. The ruin of the place galled him plenty, but it was the thought that Lorelei could have been there when it happened that fairly stopped his heart and trapped his breath in his throat. She'd have been in the middle of it, too, if she hadn't insisted on going on the cattle drive despite his objections.

"Doesn't look like there's much of anything we can do here," Elias observed. "Best we get on to Cavanagh's, so I can see to your brother Rafe and that cowboy with the broken leg."

Holt nodded, wondering how he was going to tell Lorelei that the house she'd pinned so many of her hopes on was gone. Wishing he could protect her, somehow, some way, from the harsh reality. At the same time, knowing it couldn't be done.

They crossed the wide stream in silence, and rode hard when they reached the other side.

Lorelei met them at John's gate, clad in a calico dress and pacing anxiously. "Thank God you're finally here," she blurted, with a note of contention in her voice, as though they'd dallied along the way, maybe to pick field daisies or just admire the countryside.

Holt was down off his horse before he thought about dismounting. "Rafe?" he demanded. "Is Rafe all right?"

Something gentled in Lorelei. Her fiery gaze cooled, and the small muscles in her face relaxed. "Rafe's fine," she said, shifting her gaze to the doc and wringing her hands as she went on. "It's Melina. She's been in hard labor since sunrise. Heddy says the baby should have been here by now, given the state Melina's in. She thinks there's something wrong."

Elias didn't wait to hear more. He rode up to the house at a good clip, untied his medical bag, sprang down from the saddle and hurried inside.

Holt swung one leg over Traveler's neck and slid to the ground, facing Lorelei. It was time to tell her about the raid on her ranch, and he searched for the words. There seemed to be a scant supply.

She searched his face. "What is it?" she asked, very softly, and without using much breath.

"Your place," he said. "It's been burned."

He saw her throat work as she swallowed, and wished to God, once again, that he could have spared her this.

For all the times they'd locked horns, for all the times he'd deliberately baited her, just to watch her get mad, delivering such news was among the most difficult things he'd ever had to do. And that was saying something.

She put her hands to her ears, lowered them again. "I thought I heard you say—"

"Somebody put a torch to the house, Lorelei," Holt reiterated miserably. It felt a lot like pulling that arrow shaft out of Rafe's arm, saying the hard but necessary truth. As with Rafe, he wanted to take the pain on himself, but he could only share it. "Burned away most of the grass, too."

Tears glimmered in her eyes. "No," she whispered.

Holt took her by the shoulders, as gently as he could. He was afraid she'd crumple to the ground if he didn't hold her upright. "There were plenty of tracks—I reckon when I follow them, they'll lead straight to Isaac Templeton's front door."

She put a hand to her mouth, and a sob escaped her throat, so ragged and so raw that it gouged at Holt's well-guarded heart with the impact of a lance. "Isaac Templeton's front door," she said, when she'd recovered enough to speak, "or my father's?"

He longed to pull her close and hold her, but the stiffening in her spine and the way she twisted out of his grip put paid to the idea before he could follow through on it. "Lorelei," he said, anguished.

She turned her back, walked toward the house with quick steps, one hand pressed to her mouth.

Holt had no use for Judge Alexander Fellows after the way he'd railroaded Gabe, but he found it hard to believe the man—any man—would visit that kind of vengeance on his own daughter. Watching Lorelei disappear into the house, he pulled Lizzie's ribbon from his vest pocket and smoothed it between his thumb and forefingers, like a talisman.

THE MOMENT she stepped back over the threshold of John Cavanagh's house and another of Melina's agonized shrieks met her ears, Lorelei set aside all that Holt had just told her. She would simply have to deal with it later.

Melina lay on a cot in the kitchen, where she'd been since just before the sun rose, her back arched, her face contorted and slick with sweat. Dr. Brown had already examined her; now, he was washing up in a basin of hot water, provided by an anxious and harried Heddy.

The doctor looked Lorelei over briefly as he accepted the towel Heddy had ready for him and dried his hands. "We're about to get down to serious business in here, Miss Fellows," he said evenly, his face calm. "If you're fixing to swoon or carry on or some such, I would appreciate your leaving. If you've a mind to be of help, on the other hand, then get yourself some fresh water and scrub every bare inch of flesh with that lye soap there. Heddy, you fill some kettles and set them on to boil, then find me some clean cloth. Sheets will serve, if you've got them, but they won't be good for much when we're done."

Lorelei hesitated only a moment—she'd never seen a baby born, by easy means or difficult ones—and she *did* feel a bit light-headed. Because Melina was her friend, and because she knew she wouldn't be able to live with herself if she failed either mother or baby, now of all times, she went over to the basin, threw its sudsy contents out the back door and poured fresh, scalding hot water into it from the teakettle Heddy kept simmering on the stove.

Heddy rushed up the back stairs, bent on fulfilling her own errand.

Lorelei hardly felt the shock of that hot water, plunging her hands into it the way she did.

"I'm scared, Lorelei," Melina confessed, gasping, visibly bracing herself for another of the ferocious contractions she'd been enduring for so many hours. "I want Gabe."

"You've got us," Lorelei said, kindly but firmly, drying her hands and face. "For right now, that's going to have to do."

Another pain seized Melina then; she bared her teeth, and her small hips rose high off the cot. Heddy had stripped her down earlier, put one of John's shirts on her to serve as a gown. The garment fell open as she screamed, revealing her belly, hard and round and knotted, burgeoning with the elemental struggle of a child breaking through the last barrier to life.

"Can't you do something?" Lorelei pleaded, in a whisper, as Dr. Brown supported the small of Melina's back with one hand and peered between her legs.

"Yes," the doctor said, with terse efficiency, "I can get this baby out, and the sooner, the better. Open my bag. You'll find a bottle of ether inside. Give me that first, then get out the carbolic acid and that small leather case. My scalpels are inside—pour the rest of the water from that teakettle over them, if there's any left, and for Jove's sake, be careful when you handle them. They're sharp."

Lorelei did as she was told, and then washed again.

Heddy returned with an old sheet, worn thin by time and use but clean.

"Tear it into strips," the Doc said. He'd doused his handkerchief in the ether Lorelei had taken from his bag, and the pungent scent of it filled that steamy kitchen.

Lorelei watched, almost paralyzed with fear, as he pressed it gently over Melina's nose and mouth.

"Hold this," he commanded, and Lorelei realized he was referring to the cloth and moved to obey.

Melina's feverish eyes rolled back in her head, then closed, and her body, tormented for so long, went limp.

Dr. Brown reached for one of the scalpels, fished from the boiling hot water with a pair of tongs, and grasped the handle. Lorelei looked on, wide-eyed, as he swabbed Melina's belly with carbolic acid, paused to take a deep breath, as if centering himself in that small, misshapen body of his, and then cut through Melina's distended flesh with one long, continuous stroke of the blade.

Blood spurted, and Lorelei swayed on her feet, stunned by the metallic smell, so strong that it reached her taste buds. She steadied herself by sheer force of will. Heddy was busy at the hazy edge of her vision, but Lorelei could not look away from the doctor and that hideous incision.

Melina groaned.

"Add another drop or two of that ether to the cloth," Dr. Brown barked, deepening the first incision with another deft motion of his scalpel.

Bile scalded the back of Lorelei's throat, and her knees turned to jelly, but she groped for the bottle. Her hand shook as she gripped it.

"Just a little, now," the doctor warned, without looking up. "Too much will kill her."

A cry of despairing terror rose up within Lorelei, but she choked it down, wrestled to hold it inside. Carefully squeezed a minimal amount of ether from the glass dropper onto the cloth covering Melina's face.

Doc suddenly gave a hoot of exultant laughter, both hands deep inside Melina's belly. "There's the little cuss now," he said jubilantly, and raised up a tiny, bloody human being, waving its arms and legs as if trying to climb the cord attaching it to Melina. "Got ourselves a strapping boy, here." With that, he hooked a finger inside the baby's mouth, then held him upside down by his ankles and gave the infant a light swat on the bottom.

Melina and Gabe's newborn son squalled with outraged effrontery.

"Glory be," Heddy breathed from somewhere in the shivering blur surrounding Melina, that cot, the baby and the doctor up to his elbows in blood.

Lorelei's knees buckled again. She stiffened them, again by an act of will, watching through a sheen of tears as the doctor laid the infant on Melina's chest, tied and cut the cord, and began suturing the wound shut. Heddy knelt on the opposite side of the cot from Dr. Brown, one big hand holding the squirming child so it wouldn't fall.

Melina stirred, moaned softly.

"More ether?" Lorelei whispered.

The doctor shook his head. "I'll be through here in a few minutes. She'll be hurting when she comes around, but my guess is, she won't mind it much when she gets a look at that baby boy."

Lorelei bit her lower lip, marveling at the infant, even though he didn't look all that prepossessing at the moment. He snuffled against Melina's bosom, all four limbs still moving, and made a soft, mewling sound. "A little laudanum, perhaps?" she ventured, thrummingly aware, in every fiber of her being, of that hip-to-hip incision, now being closed with catgut stitches and a huge needle.

"Laudanum might get into the milk," Dr. Brown said. "She's tough. She'll be under the weather for a few weeks, then good as new." He raised his eyes only when he'd tied off the last suture. "Don't just stand there," he grumbled. "One of you, wash that baby so he'll be presentable when his mama wakes up."

Heddy gathered up the child, crooning to him.

Dr. Brown nodded to Lorelei, and she set the ether-tinged cloth aside.

"You can go out back and tell the men this part's over," he said, with a slight smile.

Lorelei drew a deep breath, smoothed her hair and skirts, and headed for the outside door. Holt, Frank Corrales, the Captain and Mr. Cavanagh were all standing under the same oak tree, talking quietly, but the gestures of their hands and the set of their shoulders betrayed their worry.

She smiled, picked up her skirts, and descended the two steps to the ground. "Melina's had her baby," she announced, even as the bad news Holt had brought her earlier rushed back into her mind, demanding its due. "It's a boy."

Holt's worry-creased face came alive with a dazzling grin. "*That* ought to cheer Gabe up considerably," he said, slapping Frank on the back at the same time.

"Guess I'd better fetch Tillie in from the barn," Mr. Cavanagh said, grinning and rubbing the stubble of beard on his jaws. "She's been hidin' out there, with little Pearl, waitin' for Melina's travail to pass." They'd all been humoring Tillie with regards to the boy's name; in time, they'd persuade him to grant him a new and more suitable one.

The Captain flung down a cigarette he'd probably rolled himself and smashed it out with his boot. "Somebody ought to take the news to Rafe and that poor cowpoke," he said. "Like as not, they're thinkin' there's been another massacre." He sighed, and smiled sadly at Lorelei. "Might as well be me, I reckon," he finished.

As he passed her, he touched her arm. "Holt told me about your place," he said. "Right sorry."

Lorelei had been strong, because she'd had to be, for Melina and the baby, but now she stood utterly still, afraid if she moved, she'd fall into tiny, brittle pieces that tinkled as they struck the ground.

Holt approached only when the others were gone. She could tell he wanted to touch her, but he didn't. He kept his hands loose at his sides.

"You did a brave thing in there, Lorelei," he said quietly. She would always cherish those words, for here was a man who valued courage above just about everything else. When new trouble came, as it surely would, she could warm herself at the memory, like a winter traveler come upon a campfire.

A tear slipped down her cheek. "Don't you go being kind to me, Holt McKettrick," she whispered. "I won't be able to bear it if you do."

He crooked an eyebrow, and a hint of a grin curved his mouth. "You'd rather I was mean?"

She lifted her chin, sniffled inelegantly. Fixed her teary gaze on a point just over his left shoulder. "You'll be going back to town with the doctor, I guess. To tell Gabe he has a son." A shudder went through her. "I'd like to go with you. It's time I spoke with my father."

"All right," Holt said, but he sounded doubtful. "I don't suppose there's a grasshopper's chance in hell that you'd stay right here and let me handle this?"

"No," she replied, and made herself meet his eyes. She'd changed since the time—was it really such a short while ago?—when she'd marched out of Judge Fellows's house for good. She'd seen so much, learned so much. *Changed* so much. "I know you believe Mr. Templeton and his men burned my place, and you might be right. But if they did, it was at the judge's urging. I have to face my father, once and for all, and tell him that no matter what he does, he can't break me."

"Lorelei," Holt murmured. Then, in a stronger voice, he added, "You don't have to tell him or anybody else a damn thing. Let them see for themselves that you're somebody to be reckoned with."

She was startled. "You really think that?"

He chuckled, turning his hat in his hands. "You're damn right I do," he said. "You are Texas-tough, through and through, and I'm proud to know you."

Lorelei stared at him, speechless.

He lifted his right hand, ran the backs of his knuckles lightly along the length of her cheek.

"Do—do you still want to buy my land? The house is gone, I know, but the grass will grow back—"

He frowned. "What?"

"If Heddy's willing to sell," Lorelei said bravely, "I mean to buy her rooming house in Laredo. Set myself up in business."

Holt did not look pleased by this idea. No doubt, he was still thinking she and her father would reconcile, despite all that had happened, and she'd settle happily back into a spinster's life. That way, when he went back to Arizona, he could leave in good conscience, or at least telling himself he hadn't done too much harm. "Has it escaped your recollection," he said, "what the country between here and Laredo is like? How do you expect to get back there?"

"I'll ride the Wells Fargo stage," Lorelei said. "They have outriders, so it should be safe."

*"Safe?"* He slapped his hat against his thigh, then plopped it on his head.

"Perhaps it wouldn't be too far out of their way to stop by the Davis ranch, so I could give Mary her blue-and-white gingham."

"Oh, *hell* yes!" Holt snapped. "Wells Fargo delivers gingham to the middle of nowhere *all the time!*"

Lorelei felt better now that they were arguing, like usual. It would be easier, remembering moments like this one, when he went away. "It can't hurt to ask," she maintained.

Holt began to pace, the way Gabe might have done if he'd been there to wait out Melina's labor. "Lorelei, *will* you talk sense, for once in your life? You can't go back to Laredo and run some *rooming house,* and you sure as *hell* have no business risking your life for a bolt of cloth!"

"What would you suggest I do instead?"

He stopped his pacing. Stared at her. "Go back to San Antonio?" he asked hopelessly, because he already knew the answer.

"No," she said. "After I speak with my father, and say goodbye to Angelina and Raul, I'm going to put my offer to Heddy and make arrangements to leave for Laredo." She drew a deep breath, hoping he didn't hear the tremulousness in it. "Now, will you buy my land or not?"

"What if I say no?"

"Then I'll sell it to Mr. Templeton."

His eyes narrowed to slits, and he jerked the hat off his

head again and poked at her with it. "You wouldn't—after all he's done—"

"I would if I had no other choice," Lorelei answered, with a lot more certainty than she felt. The truth of it was, she hadn't even asked Heddy about buying the place in Laredo yet. There hadn't been time, between Rafe and the cowboy needing care, and then Melina having the baby.

"Fine!" Holt shouted. "I'll buy it, then! Name your price!"

She folded her arms. "Make me an offer."

He did.

She put out her hand. "Sold," she said.

Holt didn't take her up on the handshake. He pushed past her and stormed into the house, leaving her standing in the tall grass, wondering how she'd bear it when she didn't have him to fight with anymore.

TWO HOURS LATER, when Lorelei, Holt and Dr. Brown headed for town, Lorelei wore trousers and a shirt, borrowed from Tillie, and rode straight-backed on Seesaw. Her father would be scandalized when he saw her in that getup, with a mule for transportation, and that was fine with her.

For all that she'd tried to prepare herself, the sight of what had once been her ranch house nearly knocked the wind out of her. Gone, the cabin that had been her mother's childhood home, with all the earthly belongings she could rightfully claim inside.

Here, in this place, Lorelei had first planted her two feet and declared her independence. Now, there was nothing left but ash and charred wood; even the trees, old-timers with their roots going deep into the land, had been desecrated.

An unholy rage welled up within Lorelei as she took it all in, there on the bank of the creek, herself and her mule dripping water from the crossing.

Holt stayed close by.

"The trees," she whispered brokenly.

"They'll come back, Lorelei," he said gravely, and reached across, from his horse, to touch her arm. "Even now, the seeds are there, under the dirt, fixing to grow."

She turned to him. There were times when he amazed her, this complicated man. He'd fight the very devil himself, bare-handed, and laugh when he told the tale. The Comanche had never drawn breath who could make him break a sweat. And yet, in the face of this murderous destruction, he spoke of seeds, and the promise of life stirring under the soil.

"Holt McKettrick," she said, "if I live to be an old, old woman, I will never figure you out."

He grinned. "Waste of time trying," he said, taking Seesaw by the bridle strap and deftly steering both mule and woman forward—always forward. "When you get down to it, I'm not sure there's anything to make sense of, anyhow."

Her throat felt tight. There were so many things she wanted to say in that moment, but they wouldn't come together in her mind.

"Give that mule your heels, Miss Lorelei," he said, looking deep into her eyes. Into her very soul, it seemed. "We're burning daylight."

She laughed, but the sound came out tangled with a sob. She prodded Seesaw hard, and he took off for the hillside leading up to the road, a streak of jackass, gobbling up ground with his plain, sturdy legs.

Holt stayed with her easily, on that Appaloosa of his,

but he pretended it was a battle, keeping up with her and the doc on his squat, trotting pony.

She loved him for the effort. Loved him for the things he'd said about the trees coming back.

*Loved him.*

The realization of that was far more shattering than her father's betrayal could ever have been.

She couldn't love Holt McKettrick. She *wouldn't.* After that talk in Reynosa, when he'd suggested forming a "partnership," he'd never mentioned marriage again. He'd either been talking through his hat, or he'd changed his mind since then.

He'd leave, that was what he would do, provided he lived through the confrontation with Isaac Templeton that was bound to happen. He'd leave, when Gabe Navarro was free.

*He would leave and never come back.* That was the pure, brutal truth of the matter.

What would comfort her then? What seeds would stir beneath the ashes of her dreams, destined to grow tall and strong against the fierce Texas sky?

The answer made her press the palm of one hand hard to her middle. She was startled by a swift and terrible joy, a certainty too elemental to explain. *She was carrying Holt's child.* Her eyes widened, and her heart began to beat like the hooves of a wild horse, running free. Life would be hard from now on, but it would be wonderful, too.

"Lorelei?" Holt asked worriedly, from beside her. "You all right?"

"Sturdy as a Texas oak tree," she replied, and even though there were tears standing in her eyes, she smiled.

DR. BROWN tipped his hat to Holt and Lorelei at the outskirts of San Antonio. "Raul and Angelina will have a place with me as long as they want it, Miss Fellows," he said, in parting. "Holt, you keep that brother of yours off the trail for a while. I don't want that wound getting infected. Send for me if the boy has trouble with his leg, but the splint should hold."

Holt nodded and tugged at his hat brim. "Obliged, Doc," he said.

Lorelei watched Dr. Brown until he disappeared around a corner, headed for home, where, no doubt, other patients waited.

"I could go with you," Holt offered quietly. "To speak to your father, I mean."

"It's something I have to do alone," Lorelei replied, resigned. *There are a great many things I will have to do alone,* she thought.

Holt seemed to be in no hurry to head for the jailhouse and break the glad tidings to Gabe. "I'm going to ask you a favor, Lorelei," he said. "If you get through before I do, don't head back out to John's alone. Come over to the jail and wait for me. Will you do that?"

She nodded, tried to smile.

He rode close, touched her cheek and then headed off toward the center of town.

Lorelei reached her father's house a few minutes later. She tied Seesaw loosely to the picket fence out front, opened the gate and marched up the walk.

The judge took her by surprise by answering the door himself.

His gaze blazed with contempt as he took in her trousers, shirt and boots.

"So," he said. "You've come crawling back after all."

"I came to say goodbye, Father," Lorelei replied,

standing straight. In that moment, something died inside her—the delicate, unfounded hope that blood really was thicker than water. In this case, it wasn't. "You burned my house—or you got Mr. Templeton and his men to do it—thinking I'd give up. Well, you were wrong. I've sold it to Holt McKettrick."

The judge paled, then flushed. He smelled of rancid sweat and too much whiskey, and for the briefest flicker of time, Lorelei was a child again, despised for being female, for *not* being William. "God*damn* it," he snarled, looking as though he might go for her throat, strangle her right there on the front porch of his large, lonesome house. "You can't possibly know what you've done!"

"I know, all right," Lorelei said. As far as she was concerned, there was nothing more to say. She turned to walk away, from her father and from that house, for the last time, but he grasped her arm before she could take a step, whirled her around.

His face was gray with hatred and something else—fear, perhaps. "How did it *really* happen, Lorelei?" he rasped. "You laid yourself down with Holt McKettrick like a common slut, didn't you? You believed every lie he told you—"

Lorelei pulled free, her face hot with sorrow and indignation. All she could think about was getting away, but before she could make herself move, the judge gave a startled little cry and sank to his knees, one hand to his chest, his eyes round with pain and surprise. In the next instant, he fell forward, onto the plank floorboards of the porch.

Lorelei knelt, struggled with frantic hands to turn him over, but even then she knew it was too late. She didn't cry out. She didn't beat on his chest with her fists, though something deep inside raged to do just that. Instead, she leaned forward, letting her forehead rest against his, her tears wetting his face as well as her own.

She heard a team and wagon come to a quick and noisy stop in the street, but she didn't look up to see who was there. She knew it wasn't Holt, and that was all that mattered.

The front gate sprang open, creaking on its hinges. Rapid footsteps sounded on the stone walk. A meaty hand came to rest on her shoulder. "What's happened here?" asked a breathless voice. The accent told her who it was.

"Please fetch the undertaker, Mr. Templeton," Lorelei said, looking up at last. "My father is dead."

"You're a father," Holt told Gabe, through the bars. R. S. Beauregard was in the cell with him. Except for the sheaf of papers in the lawyer's hands, Holt would have worried that he'd gotten himself arrested. Most likely, the charge would be public drunkenness.

Gabe, who had been sitting on the edge of his cot, bolted to his feet, grasped the bars in both hands. "Melina—is she all right? The baby?"

"They're both fine," Holt said, and paused to clear his throat. All of a sudden, he was a mite choked up. "You've got a boy, Gabe."

The light in Gabe's dark eyes was something to see. He seemed to stand taller, and the jailhouse stoop in his shoulders vanished. "You're sure about Melina—"

"She had a rough time," Holt admitted. "But Doc Brown was with her. He saw her through, with some help from the womenfolk."

Gabe gave the bars an exultant wrench; Holt was surprised they didn't come loose from the mortar in the floor and ceiling.

"Congratulations are in order for more reasons than one," R.S. said, rising from his wooden chair and grinning. "Judge Fellows had himself a fine fit when he found out his verdict was on shaky ground, Holt. Far as I can tell, the case against Gabe here won't hold water."

Gabe's eyes glittered. "For God's sake, Holt," he breathed, "get me out of here."

"Some kind of ruckus going on down in the street," R.S. said thoughtfully, standing at the window.

Holt got a peculiar feeling in the pit of his stomach. "What?" he asked.

"How should I know?" R.S. countered reasonably. Then he called out to someone below. "Who's that in the back of that wagon?"

Holt didn't hear the answer, but R.S. did, and he let out a long, low whistle of exclamation before he turned to face Holt and Gabe.

"Judge Fellows," he said. "Damned if he isn't deader than a doornail."

# CHAPTER 37

LORELEI COULDN'T THINK coherently, couldn't get beyond the simple fact that her father was dead. Her mind seemed swamped, distracted, assaulted by a storm of contradictory emotions—anger and pity, sorrow and yet a certain distance, as if this event, in some curious way, had no true bearing on her life. A sense that while this was an ending, the death of many secret hopes, it was also a setting-free. It was an ending, but a beginning, as well.

Mr. Templeton, quietly solicitous, sent a passing boy for the undertaker, and sat with Lorelei on the step until the funeral wagon came. She watched numbly as her father's body was lifted, loaded into the back of that somber carriage like so much freight, taken away.

"Come with me, Lorelei," Mr. Templeton had said reasonably, when the sound of the hearse's wheels, rolling over the paving stones, finally faded away. He seemed so kind. How could he have been a party to the raid on her ranch?

But she'd shaken her head, refusing.

He'd left her, with the utmost reluctance, and she'd sat there on the step for a long time, her arms wrapped around her knees, mourning not the father she'd had, but the one she'd dreamed of having.

Presently, she rose, like a somnambulist, and wandered into the house, so familiar, and yet so curiously strange. It was cool inside those walls, full of midday shadows, and the only sound was the ponderous tick-tick-ticking of the long case clock in the entryway. Lorelei folded her arms, squeezed hard, as if to hold herself together.

She paused outside the closed doors of her father's study, then, possessed by some bold and direction-less compulsion, pushed them open, stepped over the threshold.

The scents of stale cigar smoke, whiskey and worn leather came at her in a wave, like ghosts. She took one hesitant step toward the desk, drawn to it by the same force that had propelled her into the room. There was something here that she wanted to find—*had* to find.

What was it?

She put her fingertips to her temples, willed the fog to clear.

Guided by some part of her mind that did not reason, she took the desk key from its hiding place beneath the judge's humidor. Smiled faintly. He'd thought no one knew where it was. She couldn't remember a time when she *hadn't* known.

Her fingers trembled as she opened the first drawer. Her knees felt wispy as feathers, and she sank into the big leather chair. The throne of authority, where she had never dared sit before. The seat she had approached so many times, with such trepidation, and such despairing hope.

There was her father's pistol, and the red leather box that held bullets. But it was the papers that drew her attention, and the reach of her hand. She took the documents out, unfolded them, one by one, read them with dazed eyes. At first, they made no sense. Property deeds. Loan documents. Letters. A ledger book.

*Stop,* warned a voice in her mind.

She ignored it. Opened the ledger to the first page.

A list of debts. A hundred dollars here, a thousand dollars there. And, in each case, the lender was the same. Isaac Templeton.

Lorelei's throat tightened as her mind slowly cleared. All of it—the house, everything, belonged to Mr. Templeton. Everything but the scrap of land and the small inheritance she'd claimed before she left home.

A sound in the open doorway made her look up, mildly startled.

Mr. Templeton stood on the threshold of her father's study, smiling ruefully, the way one might smile at an errant child, caught in an act of mischief.

"Lorelei," he said, shaking his head. "Lorelei."

Something woke up inside her; she felt a small, alarming leap of understanding. "You. You *owned* my father."

Templeton closed the doors carefully behind him. "Yes," he said, with a quiet, savage sort of indulgence. "If only you'd allowed me to buy that land. So many problems could have been avoided."

Lorelei's mouth went dry. "You burned my place," she murmured. "You—or your men—killed those ranchers, that poor man and his wife, and made sure Gabe Navarro was blamed."

"Speculation," Templeton drawled, but he smiled a wicked little smile.

She drew a deep breath, let it out slowly. "I can understand how you persuaded my father to pass a death

sentence on an innocent man. And Creighton is weak—
he would have done anything the judge asked. But how
did you sway the jury?"

Templeton sighed, pushed his waistcoat back to ease
his hands into his trouser pockets. Lorelei saw the gun
then, a pearl-handled pistol in a holster at his thick waist,
and her heart fluttered. "They all owe me," he said regretfully. "Sold their souls, willingly enough." He shook
his head again. Sighed. "I rather enjoyed killing that
rancher's wife. The way she struggled. It gave me a feeling I cannot describe. Power, perhaps. I fear I've devel-
oped a taste for it."

Lorelei shuddered. "Dear God."

He let his gaze slide over her, measuring. Anticipat-
ing. "Oh, Lorelei, it's a pity. Now, despondent over your
father's untimely death, and the loss of your ranch, and
probably a broken heart into the bargain, if what Mr.
Kahill tells me about you and McKettrick is true, you'll
have to shoot yourself."

"Mr. Kahill," Lorelei said, rousing from her befuddled state, increment by increment. "He spied for you,
then?"

"I have friends everywhere," Templeton replied,
and took a step toward her. "If 'friends' is the proper
term."

"Don't come any closer," she said. Her hand closed
over her father's pistol. Was it loaded? She didn't know.
Could she kill, if she had to, to stay alive? That, she *did*
know, and the answer was yes. "I don't want to shoot
you, Mr. Templeton, but I will if I have to."

Templeton smirked. "There are no bullets in that gun,
Lorelei," he said, almost regretfully. "You realize that,
don't you?"

Inwardly, Lorelei flinched. The judge would not have

kept a loaded pistol around, even in a locked drawer. For all his shortcomings, he'd been much too sensible to do that.

Outwardly, she was as cool as the creek that flowed by her ranch. "Maybe you're right," she said. "And maybe you're wrong. Do you really want to take the chance?"

The rancher rocked back on his heels, pretending to consider the possibility of his own demise, but his eyes were laughing at her. Deep down, he probably believed he was invulnerable. "Risk. It's a part of life, isn't it? The bullets are in that little leather box, you know, probably four inches from your fingers."

Lorelei felt a chill. Her father's pistol was a cold weight in her hand.

In that moment, she made a mistake. She looked down to grope for the box, and the bullets inside, and Templeton was on her that quickly. Despite his size, he moved with deadly grace, hooking an arm around her neck and cutting off her wind.

*My baby,* she thought. *Holt's baby.*

A noisy clattering sounded from the street, beyond the bay windows of the study, but she couldn't make sense of it.

With his free hand, Templeton pulled the pistol from her grasp, fumbled for the bullets, shoved two of them into the cylinder of the gun.

"I'll say I tried to stop you," Templeton fretted, breathing hard. "That will explain why your blood will be all over me. I tried to stop you. They'll believe me, Lorelei, because I own them all. Just like I owned your father."

He cocked the pistol; Lorelei felt the sound reverberate through her very bones. She struggled, like a drowning swimmer flailing for the surface, for air, but she was no match for Templeton's strength. She closed her eyes. The gun barrel pressed, cold and hard, at the hollow of her throat.

There was a crash as the study doors sprang open—then a flare of smoke and fire.

Lorelei fully expected to die, but it was Isaac Templeton who stiffened. Instinctively, she shifted away from the pistol, aware of his finger tightening against the trigger, and felt the discharge whisk past her neck. The roar of it was deafening.

"Lorelei!" It was Holt's voice, near as her breath, distant as the other side of the moon. He didn't round the desk, he vaulted right over it, gathered her in his arms. Held her fiercely. "Jesus, Lorelei, are you all right?"

"I—I'm not sure," she admitted, letting herself cling to Holt. "I think so, though."

He kissed the top of her head, held her even more tightly.

"Mr. Kahill," she said. "He worked for Mr. Templeton."

"Shhh," Holt breathed.

A great clamor rose in the street. People surged inside, streaming through the study doorway. Lorelei recognized Frank Corrales—the Captain—the constable.

*"Jesus,"* Frank gasped. "What happened here?"

"What the hell do you *think* happened, Frank?" Holt snapped.

"He was going to kill me," Lorelei told Holt, burying her face in his chest. Breathing in the scent that was his alone, drawing strength from it, moment by moment, heartbeat by heartbeat. "I found the ledger—my father had nothing left—it all belonged to Mr. Templeton. He had those poor people murdered, probably to get their land, and blamed Gabe."

"It's all right, Lorelei," Holt rasped. He cupped a hand behind her head, pressed her even closer.

"Do I still get my twenty-five hundred dollars?" asked a new voice.

Lorelei turned her head to look at the stranger, a man wearing rumpled clothes and a cheerful grin.

"R. S. Beauregard, ma'am," he said affably, as though they were meeting under the most cordial of circumstances. "I'm Gabe Navarro's lawyer. From what I've heard here, I'd say this is my client's last day in jail." He turned to the constable, who looked flummoxed, and broadened his grin. "You heard what the lady said, lawman. And you know it's true. Since you don't have Templeton to be scared of anymore, I reckon you might be willing to own up."

The constable stood over Templeton's body, and he looked as though he wanted to spit on it. "Get Judge Hawkins here as quick as you can," he said.

Lorelei looked up at Holt. "The others—Kahill, and the men who worked for Mr. Templeton—"

"We'll get them," Holt said. "Cap'n—Frank? Are you ready to ride?" His hold slackened, and Lorelei realized she was grasping his shirtfront in both hands. Reluctantly, she let go.

"Holt," she whispered. "No."

"Wait a minute," Mr. Beauregard interceded, belatedly troubled. "This is a matter for the constable and his men—"

"The hell it is," Holt said. The Captain and Frank looked on in silent, somber agreement. He turned to the constable. "You know what Judge Hawkins is going to do, once he hears the whole truth. If you've got a decent bone in your body, you'll turn Gabe loose, so he can ride with us."

"Holt, please," Lorelei whispered, but she knew she might as well have tossed the words into the wind. His course was set; there would be no turning him from it.

Just then, Angelina rushed in. Most likely, word of what had happened was spreading from one end of San Antonio to the other.

"Child," she said, her brown eyes gleaming with tears. "Oh, my poor child. Are you hurt?"

"Take care of her," Holt told Angelina tersely. "I'll be back as soon as I can."

"I have to go with you!" Lorelei cried, knowing all the while that it was hopeless, that he would not be swayed.

He pushed her gently into her father's chair, gripped the arms in his hands, and leaned over her. "Not this time, Lorelei," he told her gravely.

She began to tremble. She knew only too well what might happen if Holt and his friends went after Kahill and the others. She could already hear the gunfire in her head.

Holt moved away.

She rose out of her chair, grabbed at his arm. Missed.

Angelina, standing behind her now, eased her back into the chair.

The constable tossed a set of keys to Holt. They jangled ominously as he caught them.

"Tell Roy I said to let the Indian go," the constable said. "And have him send the undertaker back here."

Holt nodded, and they were gone—Holt, the Captain and Frank. The constable and Mr. Beauregard stayed with the body.

Lorelei was careful not to look at Mr. Templeton. He'd done so much harm, and he would have killed her if Holt hadn't come in when he did, but she was still sorry that he was dead.

"I think I have to throw up," she said.

Angelina nodded and provided a waste basket for the purpose.

WHEN HOLT unlocked the cell door, Gabe shot through it like a circus performer hurtling from the mouth of a cannon. "I'll explain on the way," Holt said.

"On the way where?" Gabe asked, cheerfully baffled, but plainly ready to do whatever needed to be done.

Nobody answered, and nobody slowed their steps.

There were three horses waiting in the street. Frank borrowed another, with a toss of a coin and a few hasty words to the rancher who owned it, and Gabe swung up onto the animal's back, Indian-style.

"Templeton's place?" the Captain asked, as the four of them rode out of town at top speed.

Holt shook his head. "John's," he said. "Kahill's there. When he hears what happened to his boss, he'll send somebody to Templeton's ranch for firepower. We'll be there to greet them."

The Captain nodded. "I reckon you're right about that."

Gabe bent low over his pony's neck, his wild Indian hair flying behind him. Whatever lay ahead, he was free, and he was glorying in that. Holt and the others played hell keeping up with him, even though they were all riding better horses. Every once in a while, Navarro threw back his head and let out a whoop, just because the wind was in his face and there were no bars, around his body, or his spirit.

An hour of hard travel brought them to the Cavanagh ranch.

The cattle grazed peacefully on the grassy range, their long journey over. Cowboys rode herd, easy duty, after the rigors of the trail.

The Captain turned to Holt. "How many men you figure we'll need, back at the house?"

"All we can get," Holt replied. "Leave five of them with the cattle, and tell them to be ready for anything."

Captain Jack nodded, and veered off to palaver with the cowpunchers.

Holt, Frank and Gabe kept going, Gabe still far in the lead. He had cause to hurry. His woman and his baby were waiting for him.

"Like the old days, *amigo,*" Frank said. "Gabe racing the wind, you and me a few lengths behind, getting our brains ready for a fight."

Holt nodded. He'd left a part of himself behind in San Antonio, with Lorelei. He hoped what remained would be equal to all that was ahead.

Gabe's borrowed horse stood in the front yard when they arrived, placidly nibbling grass, reins dangling.

"Seem a little quiet to you?" Frank asked thoughtfully.

The hairs on the back of Holt's neck were standing up like bristles on a boar. "Yeah," he said grimly. The place looked deserted, as if some great wind had blown through, carried everybody away.

They left the horses with Gabe's, drew their pistols as they went inside.

Silence.

"Rafe!" Holt called, from the foot of the stairs. His voice echoed through the familiar rooms.

No response.

Gabe appeared on the landing, pale under all that

jailhouse grime. Shook his head. "Nobody around," he said.

"Shit," Frank muttered. "You suppose we're too late?"

A faint whine reached Holt's ears. The dog? "Sorrowful?"

A yip.

Holt called again, raising his voice, barely catching the responding yelp. He followed the sound, Frank and Gabe right behind him.

Melina's cot was still in the kitchen, but empty.

The dog. Where was the dog? Holt whistled through his teeth.

Sorrowful began to bark, tentatively at first, then with rising excitement.

The noise rose through the floorboards, from the root cellar.

Holt dashed out the back way, rounded the house, and holstered his gun so he could use both hands to raise the cellar doors. The moment he'd laid them aside, Sorrowful leaped out at him, covered in cobwebs.

"Anybody down there?" Frank rasped. He didn't care much for holes in the ground. In the meantime, Holt bolted down the three rickety steps, into the dank gloom.

There was a squall, and as his eyes adjusted, Holt made out Melina, huddled in a corner, with a gag over her mouth. Her eyes were wide and frightened. Gabe pushed past him to release her.

Holt was almost afraid to look for the others. He made himself do it.

John, watching him with furious intensity. Heddy beside him. Both of them bound and gagged.

Frank rushed to turn them loose.

Rafe lay in the far corner, sprawled behind some dusty crates.

"They hit him in the head, Holt," John said hastily, the moment his mouth was uncovered. "He put up a hell of a fight, for a man with one arm in a sling."

Holt dropped to his knees beside his brother. Hesitated, then reached out to touch the base of Rafe's throat. There was a pulse.

Jesus, Mary and Joseph, *there was a pulse.*

"Rafe?" he repeated, almost strangling on the name.

Rafe stirred, opened one eye, then the other. A grin lifted the corner of his mouth. "You sure took your sweet time getting here," he said.

It was the second time that day that Holt had felt the whole world grind to a sudden stop—the first had been when he went to the Fellows' house, after learning that the judge was dead, looking for Lorelei, and found her with Templeton, the barrel of a gun pressed to her throat, cocked and ready to fire.

Now, here was Rafe, spread out on the cellar floor, with a goose-egg the size of a spittoon sprouting on the side of his head.

Holt doubled over, his arms clasped across his middle.

"Kahill took Tillie and Pearl," Heddy blurted, like somebody just coming to the surface after a long time under water.

John was already scrambling up the cellar steps.

Holt got to his feet, hauling Rafe with him.

"Somebody saddle my horse," Rafe said, blinking when they stepped into the sunlight.

"The hell," Holt bit out. "You're staying here with Melina and Heddy and the baby."

Rafe swayed on his feet, put both hands to his head.

Holt steered him toward Heddy, who was rallying fast. "Look after my lunkhead of a brother," he said. "If he tries to come after us, hit him with whatever's handy."

Heddy nodded soberly.

Gabe stood in the grass, holding his infant son, while Melina leaned against his side. Frank took her arm, led her gently into the house. Rafe followed under his own power, staggering a little.

Holt wanted to ride, but he waited, watching Gabe. Envying him a little.

"My boy. He's something, isn't he?" Gabe marveled hoarsely. Then, without waiting for an answer, he carried the child inside. Returned a moment later, with his arms empty and his eyes full.

At that instant, John burst out of the barn, mounted on Melina's spotted pony, just as the Captain arrived with seven of the wranglers.

Holt and Frank ran for their horses.

# CHAPTER 38

SEESAW WAS STILL tethered to the front fence. Lorelei waited until the undertaker arrived, with two assistants, causing enough of a stir to distract Angelina, and made a run for it.

Angelina was quicker than Lorelei expected, and dashed into the street, shouting for her to come back.

She gave Seesaw her heels and headed for the Templeton ranch.

The ride was long, but the mule never slowed, never stumbled, the whole rough way. Lorelei listened for gunshots with her whole being as she rounded the last bend, praying she wasn't too late. There had been two deaths already that day, her father's and Mr. Templeton's. She was determined that there would be no more.

Oaks and maples lined the driveway leading up to Templeton's fine, rustic house. Lorelei thought of her own trees, burned to specters, and felt a surge of rage.

A rider came up alongside her, from behind, and she was wrenched off Seesaw's back and onto the other mount before she could react. Mac Kahill smiled down at her.

"Welcome to the Templeton ranch, Miss Fellows," he said cordially.

Lorelei squirmed, but it was no use. Both her arms were pinned.

Kahill laughed. "Life," he said, "is full of sweet surprises."

She found her voice. "Let me go!"

He spurred his horse toward the house. "Not a chance of that," he told her. He dumped her to the ground, a few feet from the porch steps, and dismounted before she could get up, grabbing her hard by the arm. He paused, listening. "Hear that?" he asked mildly.

Lorelei held her breath. Riders.

"They're on their way, boys," Kahill called out, and a dozen men appeared, streaming out of the house, rifles ready. "Get ready for a shindig."

"Holt," Lorelei whispered.

"Hope you won't miss him too much," Kahill said, and flung her toward the steps.

"This ain't no time for sparkin'," one of the men remarked, leering, as Kahill grabbed the back of Lorelei's shirt and propelled her inside, through an entryway, and up a grand set of stairs.

At the top, he took both her hands, bound them together with his bandana, and pushed her to the floor with such force that she struck her head against something. Stars swam in front of her eyes, and darkness rose up around her, gulped her down whole.

She awakened, maybe seconds later, maybe minutes, dazed and sick to her stomach. Gunfire erupted outside, and she sat up, her heart in her throat.

Tillie raced past her, running down the stairs. "My pa is out there!" she screamed. "Don't nobody hurt my pa!"

Lorelei blinked, sure she must be hallucinating. "Tillie!" she screamed, in abject horror. "No!"

Tillie disappeared through the front door.

Another volley of gunfire, followed by a howl of enraged grief, rising above the other sounds.

"Your woman is in there, McKettrick!" It was Kahill's voice, taunting. Full of frenzied hatred. "The kid, too!"

Desperate, Lorelei finally wriggled free of the bond on her wrists. She got to her feet, collapsed, and got up again.

Bullets shattered the windows and thudded into the floor of the entry hall.

"Have it your way, Mr. Boss Man!" Kahill shouted. Lorelei watched, stricken, as he stepped over the threshold, overturned the fancy lamps on the long bureau just inside the door, and tossed a lighted match into the spilled kerosene.

The blaze caught on the fancy Oriental rug and raced toward the walls.

*Pearl,* she thought, suddenly and with a clarity that slammed into her middle like a sledgehammer. She tried to orient herself, hurried along the upstairs corridor, flinging open doors. So many doors.

Smoke billowed up from downstairs, and the gunfire went on, deafening, ceaseless. It sounded as if two armies were clashing outside, and Tillie had gone straight into the melee, but Lorelei couldn't think about that now. Couldn't think of the cry of sorrowing fury she'd heard a moment afterwards. She had to find Pearl.

The baby was in the last bedroom, sitting on a blanket on the floor, his face crumpled with silent sobs. Lorelei snatched him up, burst out into the corridor again, choking on smoke, looked wildly around for a rear stairway, but there was none.

There was only one way out.

By the time she reached the landing, the smoke was dense, and flames were leaping everywhere. A wall of heat met her as she tried to descend the stairs, bent low, gripping Pearl in both arms. The roar of the fire was thunderous, but beyond it lay a world of sudden and peculiar silence.

It was over, she thought.

She and Pearl were going to die, together, in a burning house.

But she had reckoned without Holt McKettrick.

Through the shifting smoke, she saw, or thought she saw, that big Appaloosa of his come right through the front door. Holt bent low over the animal's neck, spurred him up the broad stairs, and leaned down to grab her around the waist. Holding Pearl as tightly as she could, Lorelei felt herself hoisted onto Holt's horse. Brave as she was, she squeezed her eyes shut as they fairly flew down the burning steps; if that animal hadn't already been named, she thought, with frantic detachment, he ought to be called Pegasus.

Instinctively, she bent low as they bolted through the doorway, over the porch, into the fresh air and sunlight.

There were bodies on the grass, but Frank and the Captain and Gabe Navarro were still standing upright. Then she saw Tillie, shot through the chest. John was kneeling on the ground, rocking her in his arms, tears streaming down his face.

"No," Lorelei croaked, her throat parched from the smoke and the fear, holding Pearl even more tightly. *"No."*

Holt leaned to set Lorelei on the ground, and she swayed on her feet, stricken with grief. He dismounted, touched her shoulder, just briefly, as he passed, knelt next to Tillie, facing Mr. Cavanagh. "She's gone," he said quietly.

Tillie's eyes stared sightlessly at the sky.

John let out a long, plaintive wail of grief and protest.

Lorelei put a hand to her mouth, to stifle a sob, and the Captain took Pearl from her arms.

Mr. Cavanagh clung to Tillie.

"We've got to take her home now, John," Holt said.

A long time passed. Then John nodded, very slowly, and allowed Holt to lift Tillie's body off the ground.

Lorelei remembered little of the sad, seemingly endless trip back to the Cavanagh place. She rode Seesaw, and Holt carried Tillie on the Appaloosa, as gently as if she were a sleeping child. The Captain brought Pearl, and Gabe stayed close to John.

It was all there was to do, for any of them. Keep riding. Keep breathing. Keep groping from one heartbeat to the next.

*One week later*

HOLT CROUCHED BESIDE Tillie's grave, marked with the simple wooden cross John had carved himself, and tied Lizzie's blue ribbon around one of the bars. He'd done everything he came to Texas to do—gotten Gabe out of jail, found Frank Corrales, put the Cavanagh ranch back on its feet, but at what cost?

He rubbed his eyes with a thumb and forefinger. "I'm sorry, Tillie," he said, grinding out the words.

"It's not your fault, Holt," Rafe said, from somewhere behind him. Holt hadn't heard his brother approach.

Holt picked his hat up off the ground, put it on, and stood. He wasn't ready to face Rafe just yet, Rafe or anybody else. "You ready to ride for home?" he asked. John was grieving, but he'd be all right, with Heddy to love him through the rough spots. Gabe and Melina were properly married, and already making plans to build a cabin on the site of Lorelei's ranch house.

He didn't let his thoughts stray beyond that burned cabin, to the woman herself.

"I'm ready," Rafe allowed, "and Frank's saddled up, too. I reckon the question is, are *you* ready?"

At last, Holt turned. Rafe was watching him, arms folded, eyes wise. Seeing half again too much.

"I've done all the damage I could," Holt said, with a slight shrug and an attempt at a grin, which fell flat.

"You're just going to go off and leave Lorelei?"

Holt took his hat off again, turned it in his hands. Lorelei was inside the house, with Heddy and Melina, doing the kinds of things women did after a death. Cooking. Crying. Talking quietly. "You heard her. She means to buy Heddy's place in Laredo and go into the room-and-board business."

"You could talk her out of that, and you know it."

Holt sighed. "I wouldn't be doing her any favors." He gestured in that direction, with his hat. "She needs a different kind of man. One who won't get her shot at."

Rafe shook his head. "Seems to me, you need to make a choice, here. Ride out, leave a good woman behind, like you did once before, and regret it for the rest of your days. Or have the plain grit to claim what you want and take your chances, just like the rest of us."

Frank came out of the barn, leading their three

horses, saddled and ready for the long trip ahead. Holt pretended an interest in the event. The goodbyes had all been said—except the one to Lorelei. There would be no looking back.

Lorelei was going to be fine. Gabe and the Captain would get her safely to Laredo, since she was hell-bent on going, and taking little Pearl, now called John Henry, by general consensus, along with her. She had a backbone, Lorelei did, and one of the best minds Holt had ever run across. She'd make her way in the world. Probably marry a good man who wouldn't drag her off on trail drives through Comanche country.

"Say something, Holt," Rafe prodded gruffly. "Better yet, *do* something."

"It's best for her if I just go."

"I know you think that, but she might be of another opinion. For God's sake, at least ask her."

Frank drew up with the horses. Holt stared toward the house for a few moments, then looked back at Tillie's grave. "Mount up," he said. "We're burning daylight."

Rafe scowled, snatched Chief's reins from Frank's hands, and swung up into the saddle. Frank hesitated, then got on his own horse, a bay gelding bought in town. The two of them waited a moment or two, then rode off.

Holt put his foot in the stirrup, gripped the saddle horn in one hand. *Ride away,* he thought, and hoisted himself onto Traveler's back. Lorelei had renamed the gelding Pegasus—said he could fly.

Holt smiled a little as he reined the eager horse toward the road.

Rafe's words unraveled in his mind. *Seems to me, you need to make a choice, here. Ride out, leave a good*

*woman behind, like you did once before and regret it
for the rest of your days...*

He looked back, saw Lorelei standing on John and
Heddy's front porch, her head high, watching him.

He moved to raise a hand, the only farewell he figured he could manage, then let it drop back to his side.
She didn't move, didn't call out. She merely looked at
him, and from that distance he couldn't make out her
expression.

His throat tightened. Frank and Rafe were probably
halfway to Arizona by then, and still he sat there, in the
saddle, unable to go in one direction, or the other.

The least he could do was say goodbye.

He rode back.

Lorelei didn't move, just stood there, gripping the rail
of the porch, the wind playing softly in the loose tendrils
of dark hair around her face and neck.

"Think you could love a trail boss?" he heard himself
ask. Nobody was more surprised by that question than
he was.

Her mouth wobbled, and her eyes brimmed with tears.
"Yes," she said.

Holt got down off the horse, approached her, stood
just shy of the flower bed, one of the many things Tillie
had left behind to mark her passing. He looked up at her.
"It'll be a hard ride, up to Arizona," he warned quietly.

She broke loose with a shaky smile. "I'm used to that,"
she said. "Do you love me, Holt McKettrick?"

He grinned. "Yes, ma'am," he said. "I believe I do."

She felt her way along the railing, as though she wasn't
sure she could stand without holding on, then suddenly
flew down the steps and hurled herself into his arms.

He laughed out loud, spun her around in a circle of
swirling calico skirts, and then kissed her soundly. It

was an ordinary kiss, and yet it made something shift inside Holt, a healing, painful shift, like the setting of a broken bone.

"It won't be easy, being my wife," he said, when he figured he could speak without making a fool of himself.

"I'm not looking for 'easy,'" she replied, very softly.

"Good thing," he told her.

Rafe and Frank were back, looking on with stupid grins on their faces. Heddy and John appeared on the porch, along with Gabe, Melina and their baby boy. The Captain was there, too, holding little John Henry like he was born to play nursemaid.

Lorelei pulled free of Holt, held her arms out for John Henry. The Captain handed him over, with smiling reluctance.

"I'll get your things," Heddy told Lorelei, but she was looking straight at Holt. "Got them ready, just in case this hardheaded galoot came to his senses."

"I'll saddle up the mule," Gabe said, and made for the barn.

It happened that fast. One minute, Holt was set to ride out for the Triple M with Rafe and Frank his only companions. The next, he was taking on a woman and a child, and he knew it was for good.

Lorelei linked her arm through his, still holding John Henry. "You're an impossible man, Holt McKettrick," she said, "but God help me, I do love you with my whole heart and soul. If you'll stand by me, then I'll stand by you."

He kissed her again. "It's a deal," he said.

# EPILOGUE ⌒

*The Triple M Ranch, September 30, 1888*

ANGUS MCKETTRICK was a big man, gray of hair and broad of shoulder. He stood in the dooryard of his ranch house, beaming as the weary riders crossed the creek.

His gaze rested calmly on each of his sons, when they came dripping ashore, then swung to Lorelei, on her mule, with little John Henry perched on the saddle, safe in the curve of her arm.

"Shall I send for a preacher?" he asked, and Lorelei's heart warmed at the welcome she saw twinkling in his eyes.

Holt laughed and swung down off the Appaloosa's back. "We're already married, old man," he said. "Lorelei, this is your father-in-law. Pa, my wife."

Angus slapped his thigh with his hat, his craggy face splitting into a triumphant grin. "Best news yet," he said. "And who's the boy?"

"This is John Henry," Lorelei replied, as Angus approached. He reached up, and the child went to him willingly.

"John Henry McKettrick," Holt added.

Angus gave his son a speculative glance, though most of his attention was reserved for the baby.

"He lost his family in a Comanche attack," Holt said.

Angus held the boy a little more tightly. "He's got a new one, now," he said. He nodded a greeting to Frank, and Holt made another introduction.

Rafe shifted in the saddle. "Emmeline around?" he asked, casting a glance back at the fine house on the other side of the creek.

"She's in town, with all the rest of the women, Lizzie included," Angus said, eyeing the sling Rafe wore. "What happened to your arm?"

"Long story," Rafe said. "You reckon they'll be back soon? The women, I mean?"

Angus smiled. "Soon enough," he answered. He smiled up at Lorelei. "Come on in, Mrs. McKettrick," he said. "Time you made yourself at home."

Holt looked up at her. "Mrs. McKettrick," he repeated, grinning. "I like the sound of that."

She smiled, allowed him to help her down off Seesaw's back. "So do I," she answered.

An hour later, two buckboards rolled up outside the house, full of women and babies.

Lorelei recognized Lizzie instantly. She was a pretty child, with dark hair and her father's eyes, and when she saw Holt, she leaped out of the wagon and hit the ground running.

Holt laughed aloud, swept her up in his arms and spun her around.

"What did you bring me?" she demanded, when he put her down.

"A mother," he answered. "And a baby brother, too. Lizzie, this is Lorelei."

Lorelei braced herself as the girl's gaze darted from her to the baby and back again, sizing her up.

A breathless moment passed.

"Do you love my papa?" Lizzie demanded.

"Yes," Lorelei said.

"Then you'll do."

Lizzie moved in closer, to look at the child. "What's his name?"

"John Henry," Lorelei answered quietly. "He can't hear, Lizzie. I mean to send back East for some books, so I can learn sign language, and teach it to him. Maybe you'd like to learn, too."

Lizzie's eyes were luminous. "Oh, yes," she said. "May I hold him?"

Lorelei nodded, handed John Henry carefully to his sister.

"I reckon I ought to teach him to ride and shoot, too, when the time comes," Lizzie said.

Lorelei glanced at Holt, saw him grin. There was pride in his eyes, as he looked at his children.

John Henry gurgled and tugged at one of Lizzie's dark curls, and the bond was forged.

The other McKettrick women clustered around, all of them holding babies. There was Concepcion, with Holt's little sister, Katie, in her arms. There was Rafe's Emmeline, fussing over his injured arm. Kade's Mandy. Jeb's Chloe.

Lorelei's head spun.

When the others headed for the house, chattering, Holt took Lorelei's hand, held her back.

"Walk with me," he said.

They started toward the creek, sparkling in the late-afternoon sunlight. Lorelei took a deep breath. "There's something I need to tell you, Holt."

He looked down into her face. "I know," he replied

quietly. "I've seen you watching me, when you thought I wouldn't notice."

Lorelei smiled, laid a hand on her abdomen. She'd kept the secret long enough, waiting to be sure, though she'd wanted to tell him a thousand times, on the long journey up from Texas. "I'm going to have a baby. In June, I think."

His eyes glistened. He swallowed visibly, looked away, looked back. "That's good," he said hoarsely. Their fingers were intertwined; he lifted her hand to his lips, brushed a kiss across her knuckles. "That's very good."

Lorelei glanced toward the house, where the family was gathered. Soon, Kade and Jeb, the other brothers, would ride in from the range. "I'm going to be a while, getting them all straight in my mind," she confessed.

Holt touched his mouth to hers. "You've got a lifetime," he said.

*  *  *  *  *

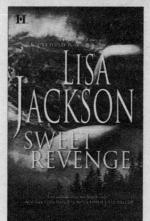

# REQUEST YOUR
# FREE BOOKS!

## 2 FREE NOVELS
## FROM THE ROMANCE COLLECTION
## PLUS 2 FREE GIFTS!

**YES!** Please send me 2 FREE novels from the Romance Collection and my 2 FREE gifts (gifts are worth about $10). After receiving them, if I don't wish to receive any more books, I can return the shipping statement marked "cancel." If I don't cancel, I will receive 4 brand-new novels every month and be billed just $5.74 per book in the U.S. or $6.24 per book in Canada. That's a saving of at least 28% off the cover price. It's quite a bargain! Shipping and handling is just 50¢ per book.* I understand that accepting the 2 free books and gifts places me under no obligation to buy anything. I can always return a shipment and cancel at any time. Even if I never buy another book, the two free books and gifts are mine to keep forever.

194/394 MDN E7NZ

| Name | (PLEASE PRINT) | |
|------|----------------|---|
| Address | | Apt. # |
| City | State/Prov. | Zip/Postal Code |

Signature (if under 18, a parent or guardian must sign)

### Mail to The Reader Service:
**IN U.S.A.:** P.O. Box 1867, Buffalo, NY 14240-1867
**IN CANADA:** P.O. Box 609, Fort Erie, Ontario L2A 5X3

Not valid for current subscribers to the Romance Collection
or the Romance/Suspense Collection.

**Want to try two free books from another line?**
**Call 1-800-873-8635 or visit www.morefreebooks.com.**

\* Terms and prices subject to change without notice. Prices do not include applicable taxes. N.Y. residents add applicable sales tax. Canadian residents will be charged applicable provincial taxes and GST. Offer not valid in Quebec. This offer is limited to one order per household. All orders subject to approval. Credit or debit balances in a customer's account(s) may be offset by any other outstanding balance owed by or to the customer. Please allow 4 to 6 weeks for delivery. Offer available while quantities last.

**Your Privacy:** Harlequin Books is committed to protecting your privacy. Our Privacy Policy is available online at www.eHarlequin.com or upon request from the Reader Service. From time to time we make our lists of customers available to reputable third parties who may have a product or service of interest to you. If you would prefer we not share your name and address, please check here. ☐

**Help us get it right**—We strive for accurate, respectful and relevant communications. To clarify or modify your communication preferences, visit us at www.ReaderService.com/consumerschoice.

MROM10R

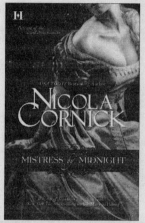

# LINDA LAEL MILLER

| | | | | |
|---|---|---|---|---|
| 77502 | THE CHRISTMAS BRIDES | ___ $7.99 U.S. | ___ $9.99 CAN. |
| 77446 | McKETTRICKS OF TEXAS: AUSTIN | ___ $7.99 U.S. | ___ $9.99 CAN. |
| 77441 | McKETTRICKS OF TEXAS: GARRETT | ___ $7.99 U.S. | ___ $9.99 CAN. |
| 77436 | McKETTRICKS OF TEXAS: TATE | ___ $7.99 U.S. | ___ $9.99 CAN. |
| 77364 | MONTANA CREEDS: TYLER | ___ $7.99 U.S. | ___ $7.99 CAN. |
| 77358 | MONTANA CREEDS: DYLAN | ___ $7.99 U.S. | ___ $7.99 CAN. |
| 77561 | MONTANA CREEDS: LOGAN | ___ $7.99 U.S. | ___ $9.99 CAN. |
| 77388 | THE BRIDEGROOM | ___ $7.99 U.S. | ___ $8.99 CAN. |
| 77330 | THE RUSTLER | ___ $7.99 U.S. | ___ $7.99 CAN. |
| 77296 | A WANTED MAN | ___ $7.99 U.S. | ___ $7.99 CAN. |
| 77198 | THE MAN FROM STONE CREEK | ___ $7.99 U.S. | ___ $9.50 CAN. |
| 77256 | DEADLY DECEPTIONS | ___ $7.99 U.S. | ___ $9.50 CAN. |
| 77200 | DEADLY GAMBLE | ___ $7.99 U.S. | ___ $9.50 CAN. |
| 77194 | McKETTRICK'S HEART | ___ $7.99 U.S. | ___ $9.50 CAN. |
| 77563 | McKETTRICK'S PRIDE | ___ $7.99 U.S. | ___ $9.99 CAN. |
| 77562 | McKETTRICK'S LUCK | ___ $7.99 U.S. | ___ $9.99 CAN. |

*(limited quantities available)*

| | |
|---|---|
| TOTAL AMOUNT | $ _____ |
| POSTAGE & HANDLING | $ _____ |
| ($1.00 FOR 1 BOOK, 50¢ for each additional) | |
| APPLICABLE TAXES* | $ _____ |
| TOTAL PAYABLE | $ _____ |

*(check or money order—please do not send cash)*

To order, complete this form and send it, along with a check or money order for the total above, payable to HQN Books, to: **In the U.S.:** 3010 Walden Avenue, P.O. Box 9077, Buffalo, NY 14269-9077; **In Canada:** P.O. Box 636, Fort Erie, Ontario, L2A 5X3.

Name: _____
Address: _____ City: _____
State/Prov.: _____ Zip/Postal Code: _____
Account Number (if applicable): _____
075 CSAS

*New York residents remit applicable sales taxes.
*Canadian residents remit applicable GST and provincial taxes.

# HQN™

## We *are* romance™

**www.HQNBooks.com**

PHLLM1210BL

Also available from

# LINDA LAEL MILLER

and HQN Books

**The Stone Creek series**
*The Man from Stone Creek*
*A Wanted Man*
*The Rustler*
*The Bridegroom*

**The Mojo Sheepshanks series**
*Deadly Gamble*
*Deadly Deceptions*

**The Montana Creeds series**
*Logan*
*Dylan*
*Tyler*
*A Creed Country Christmas*

**The McKettricks series**
*McKettrick's Luck*
*McKettrick's Pride*
*McKettrick's Heart*
*A McKettrick Christmas*

**The McKettricks of Texas**
*McKettricks of Texas: Tate*
*McKettricks of Texas: Garrett*
*McKettricks of Texas: Austin*